REBELWING

REBELWING

ANDREA TANG

RAZORBILL

RAZORBILL

An imprint of Penguin Random House LLC, New York

First published in the United States of America by Razorbill,
an imprint of Penguin Random House LLC, 2020

Copyright © 2020 by Andrea Tang

Visit us online at penguinrandomhouse.com

LIBRARY OF CONGRESS CATALOGING-IN-PUBLICATION DATA
Names: Tang, Andrea, author.
Title: Rebelwing / Andrea Tang.
Description: New York : Razorbill, 2020. | Audience: Ages 12+ |
Summary: At New Columbia Preparatory Academy in a near-future Washington, D.C.,
black market smuggler Prudence Wu and friends Anabel, Alex, and Cat become key players
in a conflict with the United Continental Confederacy.
Identifiers: LCCN 2019035601 | ISBN 9781984835093 (hardcover) | ISBN 9781984835116 (ebook)
Subjects: CYAC: Smuggling—Fiction. | Dragons—Fiction. | Revolutions—Fiction. | Preparatory
schools—Fiction. | Schools—Fiction. | Science fiction.
Classification: LCC PZ7.1.T3757 Reb 2020 | DDC [Fic]—dc23
LC record available at https://lccn.loc.gov/2019035601

Printed in the United States of America

1 3 5 7 9 10 8 6 4 2

Design by Jessica Jenkins.

Text set in Caslon.

For my first mama, who taught me to
love stories, and my second mama, who
encouraged me to keep telling them.

REBELWING

THE DROP ——————————— 1

The whole mess was a long time coming, but the drama really began when the long, sleek snout of a plasma gun interrupted Pru's breakfast.

"Good morning," said Alex, black-eyed gaze intent over the shiny chrome barrel he'd aimed at Pru's head. "We need to talk, please."

"Ah hawt finif muh foo!" protested Pru.

Her interrogator blinked. "Pardon?"

Pru swallowed her mouthful of cha siu bao, and said, "I haven't finished my food. My mama taught me not to talk with my mouth full."

Alex sighed. "Fair point." He adjusted the setting on the plasma gun with a flick of his thumb, as the weapon lowered. Like everything else he did, it was an annoyingly graceful motion. Figured that someone like Alex could make even borderline death threats look pretty. "All right, finish your pork bun and coffee. But after that, I have, like, an entire midterm essay's worth of questions for you."

"Abo wuh?" demanded Pru.

"Please finish chewing first too," said Alex.

With relish, Pru obeyed, catching errant sesame toppings with her tongue as soft bao dough gave way. The bun's cha siu filling had been marinated to perfection. "About what?" she repeated, when she was done.

Alex cast her an incredulous look that would have been hilarious if Pru hadn't still been sort of scared of the plasma gun. "What else? The dragon."

"You sure it wasn't a war wyvern?"

"Pru."

"I'm just saying, it looked an awful lot like—"

"It was a dragon, you shameless smuggler."

Pru licked crumbs from her fingers in mildly offended silence.

Wordlessly, Alex passed her a handful of napkins.

"Thanks," said Pru grudgingly.

He ignored her. The hand that hadn't passed her the napkins was twirling the plasma gun in a casual, alarming display of dexterity. "I mean it, Pru. What happened to the dragon?"

With a sigh, Pru took the napkins, and began dabbing at the cha siu bao crumbs scattered across the pleats of her uniform skirt. That was, she thought, an excellent question.

If Pru really stretched her imagination—because her imagination was pretty damn flexible—she could probably argue that the real root of her current trouble was procrastination. The first wyvern sightings, a shadow of metallic wings kissing the city walls amidst the lazy summer haze, had been easy enough for the Barricade Coalition government to write off as the hysterical ramblings of inexperienced sentinels. Since the end of the Partition Wars, the Coalition's Incorporated neighbors had made a passive-aggressive little hobby of testing all sorts of military wares in plain view of Barricader sentinels. If every ugly metal thing bearing Incorporated logos seen within five kilometers of Barricade walls was a real bona fide war wyvern, the peace treaty would have gone up in plasma fire years ago.

"We should make Masterson's drop now," Anabel had said during the first week of school. "Getting into Incorporated territory will be a lot harder if schools issue a lockdown."

"Please, they won't go into lockdown this early in the semester over one misidentified hunk of Incorporated metal," scoffed Pru. "Can't we put our side hustle on hiatus for a couple days? Summer break's been over for, like, five seconds, and I somehow already have a research paper and three exams to cram for."

Naturally, the second wyvern sighting hit the news five hours later. Barely twenty minutes after the first headline blared to life on Pru's phone, Headmaster Goldschmidt announced a campus-wide lockdown on New Columbia Prep, effective immediately.

"Well," said Anabel. "Now you have a research paper, three exams, and an anal-retentive Headmaster to defy, if we want to get paid."

Pru did want to get paid. Getting paid was how she afforded little luxuries like the textbooks she needed to pass the exams. Pru was luckier than most of the other scholarship kids—Mama made all right money, just not bougie private school money—but that also meant less generous bursaries, which meant finding creative ways to stretch her pennies. So Pru had pulled two all-nighters, half-assed the paper, and let Anabel book a private study in the school library to cover their illicit exit from campus, which, of course, was where the first seeds of disaster were planted. Therefore, Pru's thesis statement: dawdling was the source of all evil. She'd been a prep schooler for going on four years now. She'd hung a midterm paper or two on fouler bullshit than that.

But dawdle she had, and the Pru of that fateful day paid the price. Already jittering on her third thermos of coffee, her fingers twirling the holo-drive cylinder in an anxious, chrome-bright staccato across her thigh, Pru was unreasonably scared of being spotted through the one-way study window. Which was, Pru realized on several levels, ridiculous. Even if it were a double-way window—which, she reminded herself sternly, it *wasn't*—plenty of students kept cylinders for legitimate purposes. You needed them to store notes and textbooks, unless you were one of those weird pretentious kids hunched beneath enormous knapsacks who insisted on hardback, paper-bound everything. God bless and keep the lifespan of their spinal cords.

Pru sometimes took paper-bound smuggling jobs too, but those made considerably riskier drop-offs, even if the money was better. Really, if you wanted to buy black market media in Incorporated territory, a cylinder holo-drive was your cleanest bet for evading police brigades. Holo-drives were small, easily concealable, and, most importantly, well-primed for remote content deletion. Still, Pru wouldn't begrudge a paying customer some old-school sense of bookish romanticism.

Tap-tap-tap, went the holo-drive, insistent and illicit beneath the smooth metal desk, concealed under the standard-issue pleats of Pru's posh uniform skirt. Minutes slowed to a crawl. The thrum of Pru's heart inside her ears crescendoed. She felt ridiculous.

Cylinder smuggling is easy. You've done this, like, fifteen million times, and never once been caught, not even during lockdowns, Pru informed her brain. Grim experience had taught her that applying logic to the caffeine-hyped fog inside her head was a lost cause, but what else could you do? *Quit being such a big baby.*

Shan't, retorted her brain, which, in fairness, Pru had run pretty ragged with the latest crop of poorly solved problem sets and hastily scrawled bullshit essays. She cast a bleak, accusatory look at her depleted thermos, trying in vain to un-jitter-fy her fingers. Coffee: the cursed elixir of sleep-deprived, overachieving prep schoolers everywhere. The productivity potion that giveth and taketh away.

Where the hell was Anabel? Three years of running a book smuggling ring right under the shadow of New Columbia's walls—lockdowns, public safety mech patrols, and all—taught you a lot, but what it drilled in hardest was strategy. Anabel and Pru had theirs down to an art form:

One. When making a drop-off during a campus lockdown, book your alibi in advance. New Columbia Prep's faculty loved its stereotypes, and so far as Headmaster Goldschmidt was concerned, the anxious little grade grubbers who reserved three hours of library time five days early couldn't possibly be using that time to smuggle black market media into Incorporated territory like common delinquents.

Two. Put in face time during your first hour in the library, and no one would bother checking to see if you ever returned from your "bathroom break" during the second.

Three. Don't be fucking late to that first hour.

Like an answer to her prayers, or an eavesdropper on her inner monologue, came the telltale *whoosh* of sliding chrome.

Pru practically exploded toward the door. "Park! About damn time you showed up for the job, I was just about to—"

She paused. The boy at the door wasn't Anabel Park. He was probably another student, judging from his uniform—either a student or some terrible, sleep-deprivation-induced fever dream—but not a student Pru had seen around campus before. At the very least, she'd have remembered the knife-edge silhouette of those cheekbones.

So why did he seem so familiar?

"My name's not Park," said Cheekbones McFever Dream.

"Clearly not," said Pru faintly. She turned her chin up for a better look at him. Nonplussed, Cheekbones McFever Dream returned her scrutiny with dark eyes, deep-set beneath a wavy mop of equally dark hair. His white button-down, bright over olive skin, and schoolboy tie loosened at the collar made him look like a long-lost leading man from an old-fashioned film poster. Maybe he'd been summoned forth from the depths of history, newly arrived in their brave new world. Or maybe he'd escaped the pages of some teen romance comic Pru's mother was penning. That would explain both his alarming familiarity and distressing amounts of sex appeal. Maybe Pru could call Mama later and ask. *Say, Mama*, she imagined drawling, *funny thing, but you don't happen to be missing one brooding romantic lead disguised as a prep school kid, about my age, perhaps yea high? Why? Oh, no reason, just an anxiety-induced case of creepy déjà vu! Love you.*

"May I . . . help you?" asked the fever dream delicately.

"Sorry," mumbled Pru. "I'm waiting for Anabel Park. I thought you were her."

"I'm flattered." The full mouth twitched with amusement. "Though sorry to disappoint. Afraid I'm nowhere near as charming as the youngest and cleverest of the Park clan." He stuck his hands—

what Mama liked to call artist's hands, long-fingered and elegantly formed—into his trouser pockets. "I'm merely me."

"Who?" asked Pru. "I'm, like, eighty percent sure we haven't met."

"Alex," said the fever dream, then with an odd shift to his accent, "Alexandre Santiago, if you need to pull the school library records. Anabel Park and I are checking into this study, actually."

"No, you're not," said Pru. Indignation temporarily overruled self-consciousness. "Anabel and *I* are checking into this study. I'm supposed to"—hurriedly, she slid the holo-drive into her stocking—"meet her for a . . . a project here. The study should be booked in her name."

Alex's expression cleared. "That's the mix-up, then. She's also my project partner, for Modern Politics II. She booked our study too. If she's working with you for another class, she must have double-booked yours by mistake."

Irritation jabbed at Pru. "And you're so sure she double-booked me, and not you?"

Alex frowned. "That's not what I meant. You probably just have the wrong time slot."

"Look, my dude," said Pru, fishing out her phone, "Anabel told me two P.M., in study number five thirty-two, I've got it right here in the automated calendar. How do you know you're not the one who got the wrong time slot?"

"Fine," snapped Alex, producing his own phone, "we can check the official school records."

"Fine," agreed Pru, jamming a finger against her screen with more force than strictly necessary. The brightly colored library records burst into reproachful, three-dimensional life over her outstretched palm. "See here?" Triumphantly, she swiped a finger through the hologram to pull up the study bookings. "It should say right here, 'Anabel Park' and 'Prudence Wu.'"

"Maybe it *should*," said Alex amiably enough. The hologram colors gleamed in the dark mirror of his eyes. "But you might want to look again."

Pru, against her better judgment, looked. And groaned.

Anabel Park and Alexandre Santiago, read the entry for Study No. 532, West Library, 2:00 P.M.

"Clerical error, maybe," offered Alex with a shrug.

Murder, thought Pru with hysterical, malevolent cheer. *I'm going to murder Anabel. What's a little homicide between friends?*

"You'd have to ask Anabel," said Alex. "But do me a solid, would you, and give her a chance to finish her share of the Modern Politics presentation first."

"Did I say the homicide thing aloud?" Pru probably didn't need another coffee, but she definitely wanted one now. Maybe with something stronger mixed in.

"Look," said Alex, who was evidently inclined to take pity on would-be murderers, "wait until Anabel arrives. Once she's here, you two can sort out your scheduling mix-up—"

"No, no." Pru flapped a hand. "Don't take time out of your study date on my behalf. The mix-up is my fault, anyway." Which was a blatant lie. Pru wasn't the one who'd double-booked their alibi like some overworked secretary. Then again, if Pru hadn't procrastinated on the damn drop-off in the first place, she wouldn't be stuck here playing chicken with this obnoxious, tight-assed pretty boy.

She grabbed her knapsack with a grimace. The metal cylinder

dug cold against her thigh beneath the stocking. There was no help for that. It wasn't like she could text Anabel to reschedule, when they'd already delayed the job this long. Besides, Pru had been smuggling longer than she'd been friends with Anabel. Even on lockdown hours, what was one solo drop-off in Incorporated territory? Cake.

Alex's sharp black gaze tracked the staccato efficiency of Pru's movements. "Wyverns got you nervous?"

"What, those flying mechanical boogeymen?" scoffed Pru. "Rumors, that's all. Some caffeine-deprived guard manning the Barricade gates probably just saw a flock of really big-ass birds or something, and freaked the fuck out."

"Birds," repeated Alex, utterly deadpan.

"Fine, maybe not birds," Pru allowed, with a roll of her eyes, "but don't tell me you really believe in this bullshit about a revival of the war wyverns. You'd think the Incorporated would have thought of better scare tactics since the Partition Wars, with the amount of money the Executive General throws at their Propagandist. I mean, airborne stealth mechs that shoot top-grade plasma fire and kill on sight? In peacetime? They're not *real*."

Even growing up on classroom holo-footage of the Partition Wars, it was hard to believe wyverns, all razor-edged wings and jaws crackling with plasma fire, had ever been real. Anyone could build weapons for a war, but the Incorporated had built monsters. Nothing about wyverns would ever look real to Pru.

Like a switch flipping, those big black eyes went flat and cold. "Partition War veterans might beg to differ with that take."

As if some fine-faced rich boy would know. "The war ended,

like, a decade ago. Our government's just paranoid out of habit. Any leftover mechanical monstrosities the Incorporated engineers have cooked up aren't going to leave their territory."

"Right," said Alex. His sarcasm sounded lighthearted, or should have, but something dangerous lingered in the tilt of that expressive mouth. "Because you've spent plenty of time on Incorporated land, I'm sure."

"Yeah," said Pru, emboldened despite the anxiety thrumming through her gut. "I'm a real secret revolutionary. By day, I'm a schoolgirl of modest origins here in the hallowed halls of New Columbia Prep, surviving on scholarship sufferance. By night, dorm curfew be damned, I breach our fine city walls to spread Barricader values of freedom and liberty through their sad little corporate empire."

An abrupt smile dimpled his cheek. "I don't doubt you do. Enjoy your insurgency."

"Enjoy my study," Pru shot back, unable to contain that last bit of pettiness as she pushed past him. At least Anabel's name was on the study booking, which meant Anabel would find a way to cover for them both if Headmaster Goldschmidt decided to check records of Pru's whereabouts. Fixing trouble was what Anabel did, even when she was the cause of it.

"I'll give our favorite double booker your regards," Alex called after Pru as she rounded the corner. She snorted. Fine-faced rich boy he might be, but at least he'd stoop to match her petty for petty.

Pettiness wouldn't sub in for a decent wingwoman on the other side of the wall, though. That, thought Pru grimly, was what sheer dumb luck was for. Fair enough. Not like she'd have gotten this far in the book smuggling business without it.

♦

Barricader's Daily: Op-Ed
by Emilia Rosenbaum
Staff Writer

With rumors of wyverns on New Columbia's walls and Head Representative Lamarque in a new round of diplomatic talks with the Executive General of the United Continental Confederacy Incorporated, seemingly frivolous matters like cross-border media regulation are easily forgotten. Yet media regulation is also the hallmark of Incorporated power. The moment that marked UCC Inc.'s transition from a mere war mech manufacturer to a mega-corporation with the power of a sovereign nation wasn't expansion from the former United States into Canada and Mexico, or even the infamous rise of arms dealer Harold Jellicoe's mechanized wyvern flocks. It was the moment the Executive General instituted censorship laws within Incorporated territory, and Incorporated citizens let him.

And frankly, interfering with those laws is a dangerous game for Barricaders. The so-called "book smuggling" business—the black market by which citizens of the Barricade Coalition sell banned media to our Incorporated neighbors—thrives for the moment, but it won't thrive for long if the Executive General is provoked to war. Remember: no one—neither Barricaders nor Incorporated—will have access to free media if wyverns raze our city walls.

♦

SHEER DUMB LUCK, AS it so turned out, was not on Pru's side today.

Getting her creds past the sentries actually proved itself the easy part. That was another thing you learned as a prep schooler: making the stupid neckties and button-downs and precious-looking pleats work to your advantage. "Internship, you say?" asked one of the guards over the intercom. Pru could imagine him up in his comms tower, squinting down at the holographic student ID and carefully forged gate pass she'd pulled up on her phone, which she offered alongside the widest, most dopily earnest schoolgirl smile she could muster.

"That's right," she said, and made herself preen a little, trying to channel her inner Anabel. "I'm one of the students from New Columbia Prep's Modern Politics II seminar. You know those Barricader reps negotiating diplomatic efforts with the United Continental Confederacy?" Spelling out the full name of the Incorporated always made you sound one of two things: pretentious and trying too hard, or earnest and painfully genuine. Pru, smoothing her uniform pleats and leaning into the stereotype, could make either work. She pitched her voice artificially low, but lost none of the self-importance: "Well, *I'm* one of the student interns staffing them. You know, in light of the wyvern rumors."

"I don't like it," muttered one of the guards. "Barricader government does what it got to, but giving kids a front row seat to this wyvern bullshit don't seem right. This ain't the Partition Wars anymore."

"Wyvern *bullshit* is right," retorted a second guard. "No one's seen new wyvern prototypes in, what, fifteen years? It's probably just the UCC Propagandist's office shooting some life-size hologram reels from the war into the sky to give us a good scare. And some idiot on late night shift fell for it. I say these little prep school interns deserve an education in human stupidity. The sooner they learn, the less disappointing they'll find adulthood."

"Stupidity! Son, let me tell you—"

"I'll probably just be fetching coffee for the reps or whatever," interrupted Pru, before the argument could escalate, "but someone has to do it, you know? Maybe I'll even get to meet Head Representative Lamarque."

The original Barricader guard snorted. "No wonder you got into New Columbia Prep. So eager to staff Lamarque's peace talks with a bunch of Incorporated assholes. You a sympathizer to the Incorporated government, kid, or just hoping to pad your résumé?"

"The United Continental Confederacy Incorporated isn't technically a government," Pru recited, in her very best social studies drone. "UCC Inc."—she pronounced it like "ink," with tongue-clicking emphasis on the K—"is a private mech manufacturing company that continental consumers, with the exception of the Barricade Coalition, opted into during the Partition Wars. My tutors say this demonstrated free market principles, but—"

"Oh, for crying out loud, Jameel, let the girl through before she prattles us all to death." The second guard's irritation felt palpable even through the digitized auto-tuning of the intercom. Ducking her head, Pru smirked. "Prudence Wu, correct? Modern Politics II intern, New Columbia Preparatory Academy?"

"Yes, that's me." Pru grinned, waving her holographic phone ID under the camera with calorie-burning enthusiasm. If she went more chipper than this, she might actually combust.

"Fine. Go on through, honey."

The great chrome gate of the barricade hummed and lifted. With one last cheery wave at the comms tower cameras, Pru ducked outside the city limits.

No matter how many drops she made, something about being on the other side of New Columbia's walls, and miles from the next nearest Barricade city, raised the gooseflesh on Pru's arms. Superficially, things didn't look all that different from a Barricade city. You still found the same cloud-kissing skyscrapers, the same full-paneled, holographic storefront displays, the same mechanized vehicular lanes. Even the swarm of people who occupied it all, ebbing and flowing around street corners and sidewalks, looked the same, at first glance.

The second glance, though, gave you pause. Wrought from hunched shoulders and darting, glassy eyes, the crowd seemed perpetually madding, a many-headed beast of thin-lined mouths and barely concealed plasma side-carries. No one ever made eye contact, but everyone always seemed to be looking at you.

One of Pru's social studies teachers back at New Columbia Prep had called Incorporated territory the new Wild West once. What else could you expect from petty executives who'd sooner slit each other's throats for a promotion from the Executive General than look after the citizens who staffed their mech factories? Anything could happen out there. Mr. Salisbury had meant it like a joke, but Pru found the quip decidedly less funny when dropping off black market media outside New Columbia limits, no Anabel around to watch her back.

Pru hugged her elbows, pretended very hard to have no regrets about any of her life choices, and strode forward. At least she had the right address. Dick Masterson, small-time businessman and big-time fan of lousy, UCC-censored action comics, was kind of a sleazeball, so far as customers went, but he always paid in full when sufficiently nagged. No funny business with coin transfers or perpetually open tabs. When Pru rounded the corner to Hummel Avenue, the familiar sandy-haired, waistcoated silhouette was already leaning up against a holographic 2-D video game display three times his height. Masterson—decked out in the self-consciously trendy, red-tinted spectacles—made a great show of checking the time on his phone. "Prudence!" he called, without looking up from the scrolling neon numbers. "How good of you to join us. Where's your hotter twin?"

Pru stuck an arm against the game display, and leaned right up into Masterson's space. You needed to establish your boundaries with these sorts of customers, otherwise they'd never quit pushing you around. "That joke was a bust the first time you made it, and it hasn't gotten funnier in the past six months, douchecanoe. Anabel's at school."

"School?" Masterson's pale eyes narrowed behind the crimson lenses. "How wholesome."

"Gross."

"I'm just saying, a pair of nice, docile-looking Barricader preppies like you in this kind of side hustle, well." Masterson whistled. "It's practically a gateway drug to shadier business, yeah? No one would ever suspect girls like you. Real quiet types, but quiet girls are always the ones who screw you in the end, eh? *School.* Please." He chuckled, jerking a thumb backward at the video game display. "You know they make these in 4-D now? Big old virtual reality chambers. We could swing by some time, you and me. Get some quality time in, just the two of us."

"I'm good, thanks."

"Aw, come on, the games got remade for the censorship stan-dards, but everyone knows they're based on the original comics! You know, the ones you been selling me for—ow, jeez!"

Pru lifted her foot from his. "Yeah, say that a little louder. You want to get us both arrested?"

Masterson's mocking chuckle cracked through the air, whiplike. "You Barricader kids with your high horses and your stereotypes. Enforcement brigades don't patrol this close to your precious capital city of New Columbia, not with sweet Saint Gabriel Lamarque already in a flutter over these so-called 'wyvern sightings.'" He clutched at his chest, batting his beady eyes behind those ridiculous tinted spectacles. "After all, the last thing anyone wants is another war."

Pru flung her hands out, exasperated. "God, first that pretty boy in the library, now you. Is there anyone not obsessed with these stupid wyvern rumors?"

"Aren't you?"

"I'll tell you what I'm obsessed with, I'm obsessed with making this drop-off with enough time to hoof it back to school before bio lab. Don't forget my bonus pay. Headmaster Goldschmidt called a campus lockdown thanks to your wyverns, so you owe me another fifteen percent for all the extra school rules I'm breaking."

"They're not *my* wyverns," protested Masterson. "I look old or rich enough to be a mech manufacturer to you?"

"You look fresh as a daisy, Dick," deadpanned Pru, eyeing the crow's feet half-obscured behind his fancy lenses. Masterson had always dressed younger than he looked. "But still rich enough for my fifteen percent."

"Yeah, yeah. Anyone tell you you drive a hard bargain?"

"Only every black market book buyer." One eye on the street side, the other on Masterson, Pru slid the holo-drive into his waiting palm. "You know my account number."

Masterson clicked his thumb on the short side of the cylinder. A 3-D display sprang forth in a burst of light, Masterson's chosen comics displayed in lurid technicolor on the slickly animated bookshelf. With a low whistle, he ran his fingers through the options, thumbing through virtual pages to the illustrations inside.

"All good?" Pru demanded impatiently. Her caffeine-addled fingers were still twitching. "Because you need to shut that shit off before a patrol rounds the corner."

"Yeah, yeah." Masterson batted a distracted hand at her. "Remote content deletion still available?"

"So long as you've got a working phone. Just open the cylinder app and thumb in our usual code, and the whole shelf goes kaput."

"I'm impressed. You never disappoint, kiddo."

"Thanks. I'd say it's a pleasure doing business, but, well." Pru shrugged. "Mama raised me honest."

"Funny definition of 'honest' your mama's got."

"Hey, she's an author, remember? Enemy numero uno of the UCC Inc. state. 'Honest' means something different in the Barricade cities than it does out here in censorship central." Pru jerked her chin at the drive, now hidden neatly in one of Masterson's waistcoat pockets. "Never forget that our democratic love of free speech and artistic expression birthed your little black market entertainment economy. You're welcome."

Masterson grinned. "Fair enough. I'll miss those comics."

"You canceling your subscription?"

"Oh boy, this is about to get awkward, isn't it?" Masterson scratched the back of his neck, actually looking sheepish. "For what it's worth, you were a good business partner, kiddo. Sorry it had to end this way."

Over Masterson's head, red and blue lights—the signature of UCC enforcement patrols—flashed across Pru's sight line. Her blood froze. Violently, she swore, backpedaling into concrete. The hairs on her arms practically stood on end. "You *snitched* on me?"

Masterson made a great show of yawning. "Guilty as charged. Nothing personal. The Incorporated is as the Incorporated does, and cracking down on black market sales of censored media is all the rage this month. Never bid against the police brigades, sweetheart."

With a low snarl, Pru shoved Masterson aside, and glanced wildly down the alleys of Hummel Avenue for an escape route, an alibi, anything. The dead-eyed windows of half-grown construction projects stared back at her, useless and accusatory, abandoned by Incorporated architects who'd cast them aside to develop bigger, better, shinier buildings. Just like a book smuggler whose wares had outworn her worth. That ominous red-and-blue glow drew closer, but Pru's limbs, like a rusted-out cyborg's, had locked at all the joints. Fear-frozen.

Do something! she thought furiously at her brain.

Shit, shit, shit! replied her brain helpfully.

Then she saw it: the sliding door of an abandoned pachinko parlor, hanging slightly ajar, right across the street from that stupid game display. Pru launched herself off the concrete and through the entrance, just as a siren's scream pierced the air. Scooting down the pachinko parlor's darkened corridor, she careened past the creepily cartoonish slot machines, garish colors still low-lit with the final gasp of their battery reserves. Booted footsteps beat a clockwork rhythm outside. Someone shouted an order, muffled by the parlor walls. Pru's heart pounded against her sternum. Where the hell was the back door to this dump?

A plexiglass elevator winked at her between two dusty, dark-ened gaming ads, one of them in Spanish. Great, the parlor must be a prewar relic, if it still boasted banned-language posters. Incorporated management was like that: shuttering what they considered obsolete to chase innovation, like children abandon-ing last year's toys. Still, book smugglers on the lam couldn't be choosers. Head tucked, Pru pelted toward the door, jammed her finger blindly against one of the buttons, and nearly wept with relief when the plexiglass whooshed aside to admit her. It was a stupid idea, climbing into an untested elevator in an abandoned building, maybe even suicidal, but falling down a mystery elevator shaft was still better than falling into the hands of Incorporated police brigades. The UCC's Executive General had no qualms about disappearing his own citizens for breaking one too many censorship regulations; Pru didn't really want to think about what would happen to a book smuggler. Diplomatic immunity probably didn't apply when half your gate pass docs were forgeries.

The door slid shut. For a moment, nothing happened. Pru breathed out once, carefully, the way prep school therapists taught all their twitchy, anxiety-prone students. Her heartbeat pumped away in her ears, slowing just a little.

Then the floor dropped. Pru's stomach nearly catapulted through her throat. An expletive died on the roof of her mouth. It was one thing knowing, intellectually, how chancy the lifts in old buildings could get. It was another learning firsthand how roller-coaster quick they hurtled toward ground zero.

The lift kept dropping.

Spine curled into the corner, Pru watched the building floors rattle upward, the darkened elevator shaft sparking against the enforced plexiglass. Faster, and faster, and faster, she fell through the endless black, her fingers clutching the rusty rail. *Well*, some part of her thought, grim toned. At least no one would chase her down this particular direction. Small comfort. Anabel always said Pru needed to see the brighter side of things, and considering how many ways Pru could blame her current predicament on Anabel, honoring Anabel's wishes now seemed apropos.

Somewhere above Pru's head, a roar echoed through the dark.

No, thought Pru, growing dizzy with the certain onset of hysterics, not a *roar*. That couldn't be right. It must be the cables clattering against the elevator shaft. But still, the roar went on, distinctly animalistic, vibrating over the scream of the falling elevator.

Which was slowing. Pru blinked, wondering if she'd well and truly lost her mind at last. But no, she was right. The lift was still falling, but its descent had slowed to a steady pace, less a roller-coaster screaming toward gravity's deadly embrace, more a vertical subway train trundling gradually into its station.

At last, the lift ground to a halt entirely.

Pru rose from her crouch, blinking, eyes trying in vain to adjust to the dark. She had all of five seconds to wonder just how far underground she'd fallen.

Then something wide, flexible, and metallic—like steel-forged goddamn bat wings, Pru thought nonsensically—pried the plexiglass doors open with a clang. Yelling, Pru curled herself back into the corner, elbows covering her head. "What the fuck!"

The thing attached to the wings clambered through the newfound entrance. Pru took the sight of it in by pieces: the clinking, arrow-headed tail, the wingspan, the reptilian neckline and sheer, chrome-scaled body. It had eyes, too, in a shade of blue so pale it might as well be silver, bright enough to make you flinch.

A wyvern. But Pru had studied the grainy holograms of Incorporated wyverns from old war footage: their jerky robotic movements, dead eyes gleaming above death-dealing metal jaws. They didn't move like this, all curious, animalistic grace. And they never looked at anything the way these eyes fixed now on Pru, full of fire and furious intelligence.

When Pru was a girl, she'd loved every story her mother ever penned—the visual novels, the wireless dramas, even the nostalgically schmaltzy, made-for-home-cinema film specials. But her favorites had been Mama's plain-text fairytales. Mama said stories too big and strange for grown-ups belonged, always, to kids. Stories needed human hearts to rest inside, and kids' hearts, according to Mama, made the surest, strongest homes.

The earliest stories she'd ever entrusted to Pru had dragons in them.

The wild, chrome-winged thing forcing its way into the lift now was a machine. Logically speaking, it had to be—a very large cyborg, perhaps, or very small piece of hovercraft—but something manmade, nonetheless, a machine gone mad and strange. In all the ways that should have been most obvious, it looked very like a wyvern. Yet Pru, shielding her eyes from the thing's searing, silver gaze, could only think: *That's no Incorporated war machine. That's a motherfucking dragon.*

The thing approached, until it had Pru backed into a corner of the lift. Above her head, she heard the cables creak dangerously under their combined weight. She squeezed her eyes shut. A metal-cool *snout*, for lack of a better word, bumped her forehead.

It was about the last thing she noticed, before she heard the snap of the final cable. The elevator floor plummeted. A horrible crash rang through her ears. And then, Pru's world winked into oblivion.

BROADCAST REVOLUTION ———————— 2

Pru thudded into consciousness with a bang of her knee against a desk leg. "Shit! Ow!"

"Jesus Christ, Wu, did you space the hell out, or what?"

Pru stirred again at the sound of her name, and immediately wished she hadn't. The speaker's words, tap-dancing unpleasantly across her eardrums, cleaved straight through her skull, along with the piecemeal memories of the past two hours. Had it only been two hours since the beginning of this whole disastrous drop-off? She cracked an eyelid at the phone still clutched in her hand. *4:30 P.M.* Well, close enough.

"Are we still on lockdown?" she asked the cushion of her arms. Blinking her other eye open, she sat up. The bare bones furnishings of a West Library private study blinked back at her. "Is my alibi blown?"

"One, yes. Two, no, because I covered your ass by saying you were in the bathroom during lockdown room checks. I didn't expect you to make it back to campus on your own without getting caught, and I definitely didn't expect to walk in on you snoozing. What have you been doing?"

"What does it look like? Having some weird-ass dreams." Pru

scowled at the other chair's occupant. Sprawled between its arm-rests was the prettiest girl at New Columbia Prep, and the only other Asian kid in Pru's grade, which was probably how Pru had wound up friends with someone like Anabel Park at all. Some middle-class author's kid might not share much common ground with the youngest granddaughter to the late Brigadier General Cornelius Park, but at least they both recognized the importance of a buddy who'd loan you her spare pair of collapsible tin chopsticks at lunch-time. Pru, who spent weekend visits home buying cheap-ass knock-off pairs from the bodega under Mama's apartment, kept splintering hers on half-frozen dumplings. Anabel, who grew up with a nose for discretion, teased about a lot of things, but never that. It pretty much solidified their friendship.

Also, there was the whole illegal media smuggling thing.

"Dreams?" Anabel's perfectly lined eyes curved up at the edges. "About what, exams? This might be news to you, Pru-Wu, but this is New Columbia Prep. We've all had that one."

"No," said Pru. "Dragons."

"You mean wyverns."

"No," repeated Pru, feeling oddly insistent. "Dragons."

"Dragons."

"I think."

Anabel's expression shuttered for a moment, eyes narrowing just a fraction. Then she laughed. "Look, I don't say this to a lot of people who aren't me, but you gotta sleep more, girl." She sobered. "About that. I wanted to apologize."

"For what?"

Anabel's gaze flicked nervously past Pru's shoulder, before meeting

Pru's again. "You know, the whole drop-off deal. My fault for double-booking five thirty-two—that'll teach me to overschedule myself for the week, huh?" She leaned in slightly, and lowered her voice. "Seriously, though, what possessed you to go out into Incorporated territory alone to make the drop?"

Pru shrugged. "It wasn't a big deal. The guards at the walls swallowed the whole wide-eyed preppie act, hook, line, and sinker. 'Oh no, sir, please let me through, I'm just a lowly intern here on Head Representative Lamarque's diplomatic detail, and I really need an A in Modern Politics II to keep my scholarship—'"

"Pru!" said Anabel, aghast.

"What? Like we haven't pulled that act before."

"Yeah, but as a pair, you know? You're not even enrolled in Modern Politics II. What possessed you to go out there without anyone to watch your back? Masterson might have bitched and moaned about not getting his goods in time, but he would have paid up, eventually, lockdown bonus and all."

Red and blue siren screams flickered across Pru's mind. "You mean before or after he sicced Incorporated police enforcers on my ass?"

Anabel's jaw locked. "That's not funny."

"Wasn't funny to me either," said Pru. "I've skipped, like, half my phys ed electives since August. My cardio is way too shitty to go on the lam from the UCC without fair warning."

"He really sold you out?"

"Apparently, crackdowns on black market media are all the rage this week, and they've got the bribes to show for it. More luck, me."

"Jesus." Anabel sucked on her teeth. Her fingers clenched and unclenched the pleats of her uniform skirt. "I could straight up murder Dick Masterson. How are you napping in the library, and not stuck in some Incorporated gulag right now?"

"Oh my god, you watch way too many old wartime soaps. UCC wouldn't have stuck me in a gulag; they'd have put me in a crummy jail cell with some small-time pot dealers, and caused a nice diplomatic incident by calling up the nearest Barricader rep to yell about my violation of decency protocols or something." Probably. At best.

"Then why aren't breaking news headlines full of clickbait about the Head Representative bailing you out of Incorporated custody?"

Pru shrugged. "Run pretty fast, after all. Last phys ed core class must have stuck."

"Pru."

"Look, I don't remember exactly, okay?" Pru scrubbed her nails across the back of her head, mussing her ponytail. Irritation, anxious and ugly, itched beneath her skin. "It's not a big deal. Police brigades gave chase. I ran. Found some sketchy pachinko parlor where I hid out for a bit, and then . . ."

And then what? The blank space yawned inside Pru's head, curled around that unsettling dream of reptilian eyes, like two burning silver coins in its metal skull. "I don't know," she barreled on. If words tripped off your tongue fast enough, all slurred together like they didn't mean anything, you could almost convince yourself that nothing you talked about bothered you. "I guess evasive tactics took over my muscle memory. Anyway, what does it matter? I found my way back before our allotted time in the study was up, didn't I?"

Anabel's head canted sideways. She didn't look skeptical so much as strangely calculating. "How'd you get past the Barricade sentinels?"

The metallic wink of scales flashed across Pru's mind. She tucked her chin, pulling a face. She wasn't crazy. She'd had too much coffee, escaped the long arm of Incorporated law, and given herself some truly weird stress dreams in the aftermath. It wasn't anything to worry about.

"I think I must have stowed away on one of the transport mechs between UCC and Barricader territory," she said slowly. It would explain why she'd have dreamed about flying. "There are more than usual, what with all the suits from both sides of the Barricades running back and forth to yell at each other about this wyvern bullshit. And we've hopped free rides on the transport mechs before, yeah?"

Anabel canted her head. That calculating expression still sat on her face, like Pru was a black market book buyer whose tab didn't add up. "Why are you saying all this to me like it's a question?"

Pru shrugged, carefully blasé. Her heartbeat thrummed in her ears. "I told you, I don't remember exactly how everything happened. I think I might have passed out. Don't freak out," she added, seeing the way Anabel's mouth pursed. "Essay deadlines in European Lit have been kicking my ass. You know I haven't been eating or sleeping enough. I've been living on all-nighters, dude."

"And dreaming about wyverns, apparently."

"Dragons," corrected Pru again, before she could stop herself, and winced. Like she needed more help sounding totally nuts.

Anabel leaned forward and asked, without any inflection at all, "How many uppers did you stick in your coffee this morning?"

Pru's head jerked up. "You think I forgot how I got back into the city because I was too *hyped*?"

Anabel's answering gaze was opaque, coolly measured in that way that was probably taught to all of Cornelius Park's descendants at birth. "It wouldn't be weird, for you to take uppers. Dumb as hell, on a day you're waltzing off into Incorporated territory. But not weird. I mean, Jules O'Brien from my fourth period can't do multivariable calc without at least one upper mixed into his soda."

"Holy hell, Park!" snapped Pru. "Let's unpack everything you've said for, like, half a second, okay? One, the last time I boosted my coffee with uppers, I thought I was having a heart attack at the ripe old age of seventeen, and almost failed a pop quiz in Pre-Partition History III. No thanks. And two, it's not like I was exactly planning to make the drop-off by myself. I'd have taken a wingman—or, you know, *wingwoman*—if she hadn't double-booked our smuggling job for some cagey study date with that tight-assed pretty boy."

"Wow, okay, aggressive. Point taken, apologies reiterated." Anabel's mouth twitched, like it was trying to contain a grin. "Wait, pretty boy? Tight-ass? You don't mean Alex, do you?"

Pru flung her arms out, gesturing in exasperation at the clean white walls enclosing the study. "Yeah, the jerk who kicked me out when I came here to meet you about the drop-off. Where'd he go, anyway? I assumed you booked this space to get your Modern Politics II flirt on."

"No, I booked this space to work on a perfectly respectable Modern Politics II *project*, which will determine, like, a third of my grade. Lucky I landed the partner I did, am I right?" Her eyes narrowed at the blank expression sitting on Pru's face. "Wait. You do know who Alex is, don't you?"

"Uh." Pru searched her—apparently faulty, *thanks a lot, brain*—memory. "He said his surname was Santos, Santana, something?"

"Oh my god." Disbelieving glee lit up Anabel's entire face. "You really don't know!"

"You sound way too excited about this."

"Pru," exclaimed Anabel. "Santiago was his mother's maiden name. He uses it on the school records to avoid trading on his dad's family as best he can, but he's not really fooling anyone. His proper name is Alexandre Santiago *Lamarque*."

Pru blinked. "Shit."

"Yes."

"You mean."

"Yup."

"Lamarque, as in Head Representative Gabriel Lamarque of the Barricade Coalition." No wonder pretty boy had seemed so familiar. He wasn't one of Mama's brooding romantic leads after all. He was something far worse.

"Alex is his nephew, yeah," confirmed Anabel, who looked a bit like a cat who'd caught a particularly delectable canary. "Kind of see the family resemblance in hindsight, right? They've totally got the same ass—uh, arms."

Pru wasn't fully paying attention, trapped as she was inside her own one-girl horror show. "Lamarque, as in the family that pretty much single-handedly won independence for Barricaders during the Partition Wars."

"Yup."

"*Those* Lamarques. The political royalty of the Northern Front. The ones who beat back Incorporated war mechs from the walls of New Columbia. Who beat back *actual* wyverns."

"Indeed," agreed Anabel cheerfully.

"Lamarque University was on the top-choice matriculation list I gave to my university admissions counselor. I cross-registered for a history elective there once. I got an A-minus!"

"You should tell Alex. I'm sure he'd be impressed."

"Shit." Pru groaned and buried her head in her hands. "I was so *rude* to him."

Anabel patted her shoulder in a motherly sort of way. "If it's any comfort, he probably found it refreshing that you were a jerk to him instead of, like, proposing marriage or something."

"What the hell were you doing, planning a school project with a *Lamarque?*"

"Passing Modern Politics II with flying colors, hopefully. Oh, don't give me that look," Anabel added. "Alex and I are friends. My parents know his uncle from some boring-as-death Northerners' socialite network. Poor guy needed to partner with *somebody* in class, and it might as well be someone who won't sit starstruck the whole time."

"You've never mentioned him before!"

Anabel shrugged delicately. "You've never asked. Besides, it's not like he's around much. He takes most of his course requirements from home, with tutors and stuff. I think campus life makes him anxious or something."

"Yeah, welcome to the club," said Pru acidly. "So what's this big project you ditched our drop-off for anyway?"

A coy look entered Anabel's eyes. She blinked a few times, grin spreading. "Now, *that*," she said with relish, "I was hoping you'd ask. What are your plans tonight?"

"Studying. Sleeping. Stressing. I don't know, why?"

"Boring, boring, and boring. Come to the school auditorium with me instead, around seven P.M. or so."

Pru narrowed her eyes at Anabel, whose expression, as usual, gave absolutely nothing away. "Park. What are you planning?"

Anabel winked. "A Modern Politics II project that will put your little run-in with the police right out of your head."

"Park!"

"I swear you'll like it."

Pru pulled her chin in. "It's a school night, and I've already been almost arrested once today. I don't need more trouble."

"You won't be arrested," promised Anabel.

"But will there be more trouble?"

"Dude, you smuggle black market media!"

"Uh-huh, say that a little louder," hissed Pru. "Anabel. Is this going to be trouble?"

"Please, Pru-Wu." Anabel's grin widened. "It's for a *politics* class. What do you think?"

"Yeah, no." Pru shook her head. "Nope. Nuh-uh. Not going."

Anabel shrugged, crossing her long legs with an air of careful nonchalance. "Fine. Suit yourself."

"I mean it," insisted Pru.

Anabel smiled. "Okay. It's cool."

♦

THE NEW COLUMBIA PREPARATORY Academy's student auditorium was entirely too crowded for Pru's taste at seven P.M. on a school night.

"I shouldn't have come here," she muttered, for probably the fifth time.

"So you've said ten times in one hour," said Anabel absently. "Quit bitching. This is going to be fun."

Pru eyed her friend suspiciously. Ideal prep school stock had a ton of money, a ton of brains, or, in truly unfair cases like Anabel's, both. This particular cocktail of good fortune made Anabel fun—rendering her witty and generous and resourceful—but sometimes, Pru wanted to throttle her for the way she swanned through life, arch and giddy, with little care for whatever troubles she might drag lesser mortals into.

Anabel, as if sensing the anxious spike of resentment in Pru's gut, smiled a little softer, and tossed a loose arm around Pru's shoulders. "Hey, don't worry so much, eh? Watch the stage. I promise you'll like the performance."

"Performance?" Pru asked, but was drowned out by the sudden crescendo of applause from the audience, as the lights sank low.

A single spotlight bloomed to life at the stage's center, slowly illuminating its subject with an artist's tender, incremental precision. Here were a pair of shoulders pulled taut beneath soft cotton, here a jawline carved in sharp relief against the theater's shadows. The eyes, though, were what arrested Pru—dark as she remembered, but all the more striking for how soft they seemed now, looking out at their audience with improbably thoughtful care.

"I'm Alex," said Alexandre Santiago Lamarque. His mouth curved as he spoke over the answering screams of recognition from the audience. "Classmate and fortunate co-conspirator to the inimitable Anabel Park"—more shouts and whistles, from students who recognized another member of Barricader prep school royalty—"who, if she's not too busy running for Head Representative of the

Barricade Coalition by the time she's thirty-five, should really consider becoming a modern theater director, or at least a concertmaster."

"Oh no," said Pru faintly.

"Oh yes," said Anabel, gleeful.

"Those of you enrolled in Modern Politics II know all about our infamously high-maintenance midterm project—worth a third of the grade, naturally," continued Alex. Laughter from the audience, punctuated by a few exaggeratedly sympathetic groans, as he adopted the prim inflections of a stereotypical New Columbia Prep lecturer. "'Students must produce a work such as an essay, video, or performance project that comments upon the effects of Incorporated rule on the North American continent beyond the democratic sanctuary of the Barricade cities.'" The corner of his mouth tilted upward, as he bent at the waist with a gracefully self-deprecating little flourish. "Well. Ask and ye shall receive, New Columbia Prep." Looking up from the bow, his gaze shifted, almost imperceptibly, toward something at the back of the auditorium. The other corner of his mouth matched the first, tugging a smile into what should have been full bloom, except for its failure to reach his eyes. "And for those watching from beyond our walls, this goes out to you. Enjoy the show."

Pru twisted her head over her shoulder, looking for the source of the Lamarque boy's focus, but all she saw was the tangle of sweaty, school-uniformed bodies and the arch of the ceiling. Before she could make sense of that last sentence, a guitar riff blasted from the speakers. Alex lifted a mic from its stand, with the casual rock-star finesse of someone who probably hijacked prep school auditoriums on the regular, and began to sing.

"Holy shit," said Pru.

"I told you so," said Anabel, without so much as batting one of her perfectly painted eyelashes.

For a guy Anabel described as *anxious*, of all things, Alex sure did a bang-up job of hiding it. Pru recognized the first song—they all did—an old Partition War ditty from the Northern Front, crooned in flawless French into the mic, remixed with a heart-thrumming, rock-and-roll drumbeat. It should have come off cheesy and gimmicky, but his voice actually matched the vision he made, singing rich and low, tender with the bone-deep anger that always underlaid that song. Pru had to give props where props were due.

"Good lord," Pru shouted at Anabel over the amplified speakers, the delighted roar of the audience, "I swear to god you Northerners are so obnoxiously patriotic sometimes, you're practically Midlanders!"

"Perish the thought!" Anabel jabbed back merrily. "Just because the Midlands used to be the seat of the United States doesn't make you the center of the world."

"Hah! Like you Northerners could have mustered up the numbers to face down Incorporated armies without Midlander aid."

"As if you Midlands pansies could have held your own without a good Northern Front winter to terrorize those Incorporated hot-house flowers."

"You and your absurd love of the cold."

"What can I say? Most Northerners were Canadian before the Partition Wars. Even the Executive General's corporate armies blanch at the notion of camping out in our tundras."

When Alex moved into the second song, Pru sensed the way its first chords struck its audience, long before she heard the ripple of excitement through the crowd. He'd switched from his famous Northern family's native French to the language of the Southwest, the distant rebel territories still bucking under UCC rule. Spanish had been the first language forbidden by Incorporated censorship laws, but it rolled fluent from Alex's lips now, still a language of revolution, even here in the heart of the Barricade Coalition.

This, though, was no rebellious wartime ditty. Pru watched the way Alex leaned forward, mic cradled between his hands like a lover, and felt something intangible raise gooseflesh on her skin. She knew this song. It was an old radio staple that predated even the Partition Wars, a love song from another time and place, a minor-key ode to the space between two people. Even after Incorporated armies had broken most of the Mexican states down into the Southwest territories, the old Spanish ballad had trickled into underground nightclubs and secret radio streams, love and defiance twined like streetlights down a dark and dusky road.

Pru, dealing entertainment across censorship territories for going on two years now, recognized charisma when she saw it. Alex had that in spades, but this was something quieter, more tender: a genuine vulnerability that turned his music into a secret gifted to you alone—yes, *you*, singular member of this teeming audience—and nobody else. Even recognizing the illusion of intimacy for what it was, Pru felt the song's yearning ache slip beneath her skin, curling around her heart as the rest of the world fell away.

Pru shut her eyes and let Alex's music—foreign-tongued, longing and loving and furious—embrace her. Behind her eyelids, for one stupid, fanciful moment, she imagined chrome-scaled dragon wings, unfurled.

♦

New Columbia Preparatory Academy
Student Message Boards
Wednesday, 8:30 P.M.

READWEEKWEEDWEEK: yo, did anyone else catch that secret concert Alex Lamarque put on?? the school's most elusive yet popular sweetheart rears his pretty, brooding head, and how!

SANSMERCI: he & park hijacked the whole auditorium, like some guerrilla theater bullshit. admin's gonna be pissed. I hear park deliberately recorded & leaked the show past firewalls into inc. territory. better hope good old uncle gabriel can fix this one, 'cause UCC won't take that shit lying down.

VIKTORIAN: lol, u sure it was a concert? the way it's blowing up the forums, sounds more like they hired a stripper to give Headmaster Goldschmidt a lap dance like the senior class social VP did at school assembly 2 years ago.

SNOOZE_LOOZE: o man, I remember that! now THERE'S some shit that should have gone viral in UCC territory, haha. how do u like THAT for censorship, incorporated dickheads.

♦

PRU DIDN'T REALLY BREATHE easy again until she mumbled her excuses to Anabel and slipped up the auditorium stairs to its rooftop, above the press of an excitedly gathering afterparty, into the cool night air. Below Pru's feet, beneath nightfall's shadow, the sprawling buildings of the school's neatly manicured, ivy-covered campus looked like a fantasy novel. A gentle yellow glow spilled from the windows, like a kinder echo of the distant, watchful lights of the Barricade sentinels. Pru lifted her head skyward. Surrounded by so much artificial light, the stars were barely visible tonight, but she could still make them out, the faintest suggestion of a constellation. Resting her back against the auditorium's rooftop, Pru, ears still pulsing with a drumbeat's ghost, breathed and breathed.

Somewhere out on the city limits, a mechanical grumble crescendoed into a faint roar. Pru sighed. Vehicular lanes probably malfunctioning again. Automating everything did have its pitfalls.

"I didn't think anyone else knew about this spot," said someone behind her.

Pru twisted her head around as best she could. Standing at the opposite edge of the roof was Alex Lamarque, shirt sleeves cuffed, hands tucked in his trouser pockets. His face, bronze-cast in the half-light, had gone a bit red in the cheeks. Probably from spending the past hour belting into a mic. Pru tried to ignore the sudden, unwelcome pounding of her heart.

"Everyone needs a people-watching perch," she said.

One corner of his mouth tipped up, deepening a dimple. "Or a people-escaping perch."

"Hey, you said it, not me."

Alex, to Pru's great alarm, took a seat beside her. He smelled like subtle, expensive cologne, layered over stage lights and sweat. "Anabel seems to think you know a thing or two about escapes."

"Oh my god," groaned Pru. "For the last time, I'm not taking uppers."

"I don't think that's the kind of drug she meant."

Pru swiveled toward him. Up close like this, he seemed less like a fever dream and more like one of the countless good-looking, well-coiffed young men who populated prep school campuses throughout the Barricade cities. Something about Alex's rendition of Standard Preppy Hot threw Pru off, though. The sharp cut of his jawline below those soft dark eyes kept catching her gaze, an unexpected edge to his beauty.

"Dude," said Pru, "if I did drugs, I would fail all my exams. Anabel's great, but you guys are kind of a class apart, you know? I don't have a Gabriel Lamarque or some terrifying military Park cousin to bail me out if I take too many uppers, or flunk my classes, or stage illicit concerts full of banned music in the school auditorium. Was that seriously your Modern Politics II project? You couldn't just write some essays like the rest of us?"

"Essays preach. No one likes being preached at. But pretty much everyone likes hearing good music." His gaze, cast outward toward the city skyline, was so dark, the irises were indistinguishable from the pupils. "Isn't that why the Partition Wars were fought in the first place?"

"That's reductive as shit, and you know it," snapped Pru, before she could stop herself. "The Partition Wars were fought because back in the day, some warmongering asshole of a politician from the good old US of A got a load of the arms race hysteria taking over the world, and said, 'Hey, you know what's a good way to make a ton of money by screwing over the plebes? Cornering the continental market on weaponized mechs.' Supply and demand."

The Barricade walls, aglow with those familiar sentinel lights, swam bright in Pru's field of vision. She didn't dare look Alex's way, but she felt the steadiness of that quiet, black-eyed gaze boring into her. Why couldn't she seem to shut up? "That politician, the one who calls himself Executive General now? His private company was just that, once upon a time—private. It only gained power because North America chose to buy what they were selling. Don't you get it? Americans, Canadians, Mexicans, we *created* UCC Inc. The Incorporated didn't start banning books or languages or music until after we decided we just couldn't live without their mechs and guns, and by then, we were too far gone to give a shit about free thought or free speech or whatever your little concert was about."

Alex's answering laugh, quiet and sudden, startled her. Pru's shoulders went up, braced for mockery, but all she heard was mirth. "You know your history." He sounded delighted.

Pru scowled over the burn of her cheeks, which was quickly evolving into an alarming warmth in the pit of her belly. She wasn't used to delighting people, and she certainly wasn't used to delighting boys like Alex Lamarque. It left her feeling off-kilter. "Yeah, well. Some of us have scholarships to keep."

The Lamarque boy shrugged. "So you get it better than most, then."

"Get what?"

"All of this." Alex gestured broadly with one of those elegant performer's hands, the hands he'd inherited from men who'd built the Barricade Coalition. "The concert. The music. Why it matters."

A shiver ran down Pru's spine at the weight of his regard. "Not really," she said at last, trying to shrug it off, the same way she always shrugged off people's overblown expectations. "Unless by 'why it matters,' you mean getting some pain-in-the-ass midterm project done so you can save your GPA and get into university, and not, like, wind up working some horrifying dead-end UCC job on the other side of Barricade walls. Sometimes, good music can just be good music."

"Can it?" The gentle eyes snapped razorlike toward Pru. What was she supposed to make of a boy like this? Sharp and soft-spoken, he was a contradiction, like some Greek god's bastard kid, born half hurricane instead of half minotaur. "People on the other side of the Barricade walls might disagree. When's the last time an Incorporated citizen listened to a song that wasn't UCC-sponsored propaganda, or read a real novel, or spoke any language besides standard continental English?"

"C'est pas mon problème," snapped Pru.

The Lamarque boy blinked at her, comically surprised. "Tu parles français?"

"Oui."

"But you're—"

"Chinese?"

The side of his mouth quirked. "I was going to say American."

"You mean Midlander."

"Same difference." The smile broadened. "But I definitely meant 'American' in the old sense of the word."

"Hey, we're not all monolingual hicks, you supercilious Canadian," said Pru indignantly. "Plenty of New Columbia natives have some secret bilingualism or trilingualism the Partition Wars never quite stamped out, even back when we called it Washington, D.C. Dirty little immigrant inheritance, I guess."

"How's yours?"

"Hah! Borderline nonexistent. My venerable ancestors spoke Chinese, or so I'm told. My mama, the show-off, writes in English,

Chinese, French, *and* Spanish, but I don't have her brains, or enough hours in the day. Mama recommended prioritizing a continental language, and since, like, half the major Barricade cities are all on the Northern Front—or, excuse me, *Canada*—French it was." Pru shrugged. "Kind of wish I'd picked the Chinese now, to be honest." She jabbed a finger at herself. "Check out this face. If another Partition War breaks out, I could leave the rotting remnants of our old countries behind, and join up with the rest of the diaspora out in the Asian homeland."

"You think other continents are faring better than we are?" Alex's inky brows knit. "The Executive General's only getting more ambitious. Incorporated types have already started circling some of the South American and European governments, like sharks in bloody water. What's to say UCC expansion into Asia and Africa won't come next?"

"Bureaucracy, probably," suggested Pru, cheerfully nonchalant. "Lord, can you imagine all the paperwork it's gonna take to try and rule three or four continents instead of one? By the time all the right board members sign off, I'll be fluent in Chinese, living off those fancy soup dumplings in Neo-Shanghai, and probably, like, eighty years old and ready to kick the bucket anyway."

"You don't really mean that."

"Oh, maybe not," Pru allowed, with a magnanimous sigh. "Mama says learning Chinese is really hard." In the distance, Pru heard the grumblings of another mechanical roar. Traffic really was a beast tonight.

"And you wouldn't just leave North America behind to descend into some kind of horrible dystopia." His dimple flashed. "Because you'll always *be* American, you know. No matter what your face looks like." Dryly, he added, "Monolingual hick or not."

"Wow, preserve me from the charm of Lamarque men," said Pru, equally dry. Her gaze drifted toward the Barricade sentinel lights, the unseen shadow of the city walls. "You want some real talk? We already basically live in a grim dystopian present. I mean, come on. Three major nations reduced to a handful of walled cities defending democracy's last gasp, while dick-ass corporate authoritarians piss all over the rest of the continent? Check, and check. And honestly? It's not torture. Mostly, it's pretty tolerable. Boring as death, but tolerable."

Alex's jaw tensed. "It's easy to say that when you're protected by Barricade walls. You really think life in UCC territory is *tolerable*? Their citizens can't even watch a telenovela without facing Incorporated police charges."

"Sure they can," answered Pru easily, "if they buy the copies off a smuggler, and keep their mouths shut."

"So if they pay you off. You and Anabel."

Pru pursed her mouth around the expletive that nearly fell off her tongue. Smuggling media across the Barricades was pretty much an open secret, but something about the way he said it—so dismissive, like he'd already judged Pru and found her wanting—made her blood pound. "So Anabel told you about our side hustle, huh."

Alex leaned toward her, which, to Pru's embarrassment, kicked her pulse higher still. "Are you actually happy to be profiting off censorship and authoritarianism?"

"You do realize how weirdly ironic it is to shame someone poorer than you for politically difficult bookselling when your family surname came right out of a Victor Hugo novel, right?"

"Hey now, Jean Maximilien Lamarque wasn't just a few lines in a book—he was a real member of the French Parliament who served in the actual Napoleonic Wars and everything. Though whether he had Canadian descendants, I couldn't say," Alex added thoughtfully. "Also, you're dodging my question."

"Dude, don't start with me," snapped Pru, glad the night concealed the color rising in her face. "First, black markets are always going to be a thing. They existed before the Partition Wars, and they're going to exist well after, and if you think otherwise, you're naive as hell. Second, sorry if my side hustle offends your delicate bourgeois boy sensibilities, but some of us are hurting for cash, since the Office of Financial Aid, surprise of surprises, doesn't actually cover all the shit scholarship kids need. You think I'm using black market book money to, what, go rent a vacation home on the beaches of No Man's Land, like all you old monied Coalition families do when you need to make nice with Incorporated executives and talk about how pretty our newfound peace is? Think again, asshole. And third, if you really think invading a Barricaders' prep school auditorium to sing a few UCC-censored ditties is somehow *nobler* or *better* for those poor, downtrodden Incorporated citizens than the shit I smuggle, then you're no better than any other rich Barricader douchebag who wants to pat himself on the back for all his *charity work.* Hell, you're worse! Unless you hacked a firewall, it's not like the Incorporated could even hear your stupid performance—"

"They did."

Pru, pausing for air, practically swallowed it. "What?"

"We broadcast the songs," said Alex. "Anabel figured out how stream the whole performance on a couple propaganda channels in Incorporated territory." He didn't sound especially self-satisfied, or even all that excited about breaching diplomatic protocol on a school night. He sounded like a student answering a teacher's questions during lecture. "There's not much point to music that can't be heard."

"Have you lost your mind?" hissed Pru. Secondhand anxiety pounded a rapid-fire drumbeat through her already caffeine-abused nerves. "You *openly, knowingly broadcast censored media* onto UCC servers? A normal Barricader citizen could get sent to an international tribunal for that shit. You, you're a Lamarque! The Executive General's going to ask your uncle for your idiot head!"

"Which is exactly why I did it," said Alex, in tones of disturbing good cheer. "Famous names might not be good for much, but we're great for making a scene."

"What the hell do you need to make a scene for!"

The cheery expression shuttered as suddenly as it had bloomed. He gave her a smile, and with a pang, she remembered that face: it was the same awful look he'd leveled on the very back of the auditorium before the concert, a ghastly little grin that didn't touch his eyes.

The back of the auditorium. Of course. That was where Anabel would have set up a broadcast recording device. Pru swallowed. Alex's cold, spare smile hadn't been intended for anyone at New Columbia Prep, student or teacher. It had been intended for his real audience. For someone Incorporated.

"My uncle needed to create a distraction," said the Lamarque boy, his tone gone flat and businesslike. "So I obliged."

A third roar, far louder than the first two, drowned out anything else he might have said. As one, Pru and Alex swiveled toward the roof's edge. Pru's heart rattled beneath her bones. "Vehicular lane malfunction?" she suggested faintly.

Alex, jaw set and thin-eyed, shook his head. "That's no auto-vehicle." His gaze darted toward her. "Pru, listen—"

But she couldn't hear anything except the shriek of chrome sparking on bricks. A great, lumbering pair of wings rose over the edge of the roof. Pru blinked, taking the sight in piece by piece. Her brain felt like it was screaming. Scales. Wings. Chrome, or something like chrome, but flexible and delicate looking, winking continually in and out of sight, as if operating on a broken stealth modulator.

Eyes, silver and reptilian and blinding, burned through Pru's.

Then the scales were everywhere. Wings engulfed her. The auditorium roof fell away from Pru's feet.

3   JOY RIDE

For a dizzying moment that might have been five seconds or five minutes, all Pru saw was silver, and all she felt was an unsettling sense of buoyancy. If she still had a body—flesh and bones and blood constrained by gravity—she couldn't tell.

Then, piece by painstaking piece, her brain fell back under her control. Gradual awareness dawned on her, of a miniature city sprawled out below, brimming with lights and automated vehicle lanes and neoclassical buildings, walled off in the distance by—

"Oh," said Pru. She was flying above the rooftops of New Columbia.

No, not simply flying. Transformed. She was a creature of silver and chrome, cutting a silent and shielded swathe through the night sky's air. Her wings, wickedly and metallically scaled, fanned out around her, self-protective. Her body, once so anxiously breakable—found itself encased now in something stronger, brighter, namelessly powerful.

Pru threw her head back and laughed.

She could see everything, hear everything. Her eyes were no longer human eyes, but the lens of a movie camera, her ears picking up the sound of the streets like speakers on a 3-D streaming pad.

Within one moment, Pru took in the city as a bird's-eye postcard shot. Within the next, squinting, her eyes zoomed in on a young woman in athletic wear, jogging across Farragut Square. The gleam of passing headlights from the vehicular lane painted streaks of color across the runner's dark skin.

If Pru listened hard enough, she could hear the pulsing beats of the song blasting from the woman's detachable earbuds. It was some pop diva's club song, which Pru always forgot the lyrics to. All summer long, the single had swept trendy party joints, belting about booze and boys and uppers. The UCC had banned the song in Incorporated territory within the first week of its release. That week alone, Pru had dealt at least twenty cylinders of the offending diva's discography to nervous-eyed, shamefaced Incorporated customers.

She blinked, and found a pair of boys she vaguely recognized from school, one severely blond, the other with jet-black hair, whispering together on a park bench, heads bent together. "It's a school night," gasped the blond, "and your old man—"

"Doesn't need to know *what* exactly we're studying," said his darker-haired friend, laughing, as he planted a smacking kiss on the blond's jaw. "For all he knows, it's a *biology* exam—"

Face aflame, Pru hastily zoomed out of her schoolmates' rendezvous, and returned to winging her way listlessly above the city buildings. She blinked again. Something buried inside her mind sputtered, like a rusty exhaust pipe. She'd been here before, but she couldn't remember when, or how. Just that she'd borne these wings, suited up in these scales, and flown high over this city.

Blink. A plummeting elevator—

Blink. Silver eyes, blinding her through the dark—

Blink. Her brain racing and sputtering around fragments of memory, sensation, underlaid by a dragon's satisfied, mechanical roar—

Blink. Sinking deep inside a nest of scales, awareness sharpening, everything sharpening as gravity died, earth dropping away from her incongruously schoolgirl-looking lace-up shoes—

Blink. Sailing, half-awake, on wind currents, past oblivious Barricade sentries, invisible wings flapping over the wall, back into the city—

Blink. Human-footed again, no armor of scales, no silver wings, just herself, stumbling in a trance through the school library. Until her eyes, blurry, pause on a familiar number, engraved on a study door—

Abruptly, the world crashed into place around her.

"Ouch!" cried Pru. She rattled around inside her strange, scaly armor, turning over and over. The wings folded neatly around her as she rolled across grass, earthbound once more. When she scrambled to her feet—heavy, so damn *heavy*—the scales fell away like water, retracting from her human skin. Her vision returned to her, as her ears rang. A headache was slowly but surely pounding its way up through her skull.

Then she looked up, and was nearly blinded by a pair of silver eyes. Tilting a long, metallic snout at her was—

A dragon, her brain supplied, taunting. Violently, Pru shook her head. This did not improve the headache situation.

"You're one weird-ass robot," she told the winged, scaled thing that could not possibly be a goddamn fantasy dragon. At seventeen years old, she was at least a decade too old to believe in that nonsense.

This thing—this robot, or AI experiment, or whatever it was—had encased Pru in the softest and strongest brand of cybernetic armor she'd ever touched, spread its wings, and flown her across the city like a demented hovercraft.

There was more, though.

Pru recognized the thing's eyes. That blinding, silver burn. How could she have forgotten? Pru's gaze traveled over the painstakingly rendered body, swallowing the sight, bit by unbelievable bit. Whoever designed the totally-not-a-dragon had created a marvel of modern engineering. The scales both armored and streamlined the design, supple without compromising its strength. The wingspan boasted an almost translucent cast that definitely suggested a cloaking mechanism of some kind. Maybe a stealth modulator, like Pru had first guessed, or a network of reflective lenses, or some combination of both. The eyes, embedded bright inside the reptilian skull, tracked Pru's movements with such unsettling care, she half-believed the thing really might be sentient after all. As opposed to some overgrown robot gone rogue. Probably, the robot's engineer read even more fantasy novels than Pru had as a kid.

The wings lifted, stretching toward the sky. The motion revealed a telltale outline of detachable hatches concealed along the underbelly.

Pru had been inside the robot. No, not just inside—integrated within it, controlling the movements of the wings, the lenses of those scary silver eyes—at least on some level, piloting it.

Maybe that made it a mech, not just a robot. Pru had an Intro to Robotics teacher who'd stressed the difference before every single quiz, though given that Robotics I had wreaked havoc on Pru's GPA in her first semester, she didn't really trust herself to remember all the principles correctly. She was pretty sure she had this bit right, though—proper robots wandered about doing as they pleased; mechs were mobile suits designed for human pilots. The more advanced prototypes could sometimes move around on their own, but they functioned best with a driver in the seat.

Yes, Pru decided—still staring stupidly up at her great, chrome-winged monstrosity of a joy ride—she'd accidentally commandeered a mech. Not just any old mech, either, but some malfunctioning, dragon-shaped mobile suit that messed with your memories and let you observe the world in high definition, like a portable, 4-D virtual reality chamber. That could be a thing, sure.

Though that still didn't explain what kind of mech randomly rescued Barricader schoolgirls from plummeting to their deaths in Incorporated elevator shafts, or spirited them away from auditorium rooftops, or why, indeed, a mobile suit would be stretching its wings and staring at Pru with such bright, curious eyes, canting its head from side to side.

"What are you?" Pru whispered.

The mech, unsurprisingly, just kept staring at her.

Slowly, pulse vibrating inside her veins, Pru stretched a trembling hand toward the mech's snout. What would those cool, otherworldly scales feel like beneath her fingers? A machine's armor or a living animal's hide?

Pru didn't get to find out. With a mechanical growl, the mech flinched backward from her touch. Silver eyes glaring, it tossed its head, wings twitching.

"Wait!" cried Pru.

Too late. With a snap of those great silver wings, the mech took to the air, and in a dizzying blur of chrome, catapulted itself skyward. A moment later, it vanished from sight entirely.

Pru sat backward into the grass, hard. No trace of the mech remained. There one moment, then gone the next, like dreams you had on the waking edge of consciousness, nonsensical yet replete with that crazy, nameless brand of wonder, leaving only an ache inside your head or heart. The mech might never have existed at all.

Except, of course, for how Pru was getting grass stains on the ass of her uniform skirt, out here on this pseudo-suburban patch of god-only-knew-where. Wobbly-legged, she rose. A coffeehouse sat amidst some nondescript shopfronts a few meters away. Maybe someone inside had noticed a giant robot dragon trespassing on their lawn. Maybe they'd even brew Pru a decent cup of coffee, something hot and bitter, bracing and real. After the night she'd had, caffeine was nonnegotiable.

That was something else she'd have to contend with, Pru supposed, stumbling toward the coffeehouse. The sky was practically light again, which meant she'd never checked into dorm curfew, which meant she was definitely detention-bound whenever she found her way back to school. If she ever found her way back to school.

The coffeehouse door slid aside with a smooth, auto-tuned jingle. Immediately, Pru's nostrils inhaled the scent of—

"Cha siu bao?" she exclaimed in badly accented Chinese. She'd follow that warm, roast pork scent anywhere.

The hip young barista at the counter aimed a vaguely judgmental expression toward Pru. "Yes," said the barista, almost reluctantly, with a disdainful nod of a svelte, auburn-pompadoured head. Pru caught a flash of one shiny, cybernetic hand, the fingers' elegant gleam matching a pale, machine-made eye. Alongside its kohl-lined, hazel companion, it observed Pru from beneath long lashes. Cybernetic body parts weren't so unusual in this day and age, but Pru rarely encountered anyone who wore them with such intimidating grace.

Pru still had grass stains on the back of her skirt.

"Are you going to order or not?" asked the barista, stylishly mismatched eyes narrowing beneath the makeup. Pru's brain—taking in the hair, the slick-tailored suit, the metallic golden lipstick—fumbled briefly for a pronoun, then promptly abandoned this enterprise when her stomach growled. "Uh, how much for one of those cha siu buns?"

With a wordless purse of that gold-painted mouth, the barista shoved a menu—the old-fashioned, paper-print kind—in Pru's face.

Pru scowled, both at the barista's inexplicable rudeness and the inevitable "we're a trendy coffeehouse nyah nyah nyah" price inflation. Then she inhaled that roast pork scent again, and hastily fumbled for the coin transfer app on her phone. "I'll take a bun and a coffee, please."

Service, at least, was prompt, however unpleasant the coffeehouse's host. The rustic wooden tables were still empty this early in the morning, allowing Pru to stress-eat in relative peace. Biting into one of the cha siu buns, she groaned her delight. The treat tasted just like Mama's baking, the pork hot and savory inside the sesame-topped, perfectly soft golden bun. Really, Pru had to admit, you couldn't count any night a complete loss—cyber-dragon kidnappings aside—if it ended with fresh-baked pork buns and hot coffee in the wee hours of dawn.

Of course, right around then, Alex Lamarque just had to show up and point that plasma gun at Pru's head.

◆

The Eagle: Official News Feed of New Columbia Preparatory Academy
*"Third-Year Student Anabel Park Talks Partition War Legacies,
Famous Surnames, and Her Latest, Greatest Stunt"*
by Joseph Glazer

Brigadier General Cornelius Park had the sort of household name usually uttered in one breath with buzzwords like "conqueror," "maverick," and, of course, "partition." A controversial hero of the Partition Wars, Park is often credited with the bloody, revolutionary birth of our modern-day Barricade Coalition. A career strategist and soldier, Park's name first picked up notoriety by association with another famous name: Gabriel Lamarque. Most historians agree that the tide of the Partition Wars first turned when Park—on behalf of the young Lamarque, already a resistance leader in the making—masterminded a brutal series of military upsets over Incorporated forces in both the Midlands and Northern Front, with the aid of Gabriel's younger brother, Etienne Lamarque.

These days, nearly five years after his passing, the military mastermind has a new claim to fame: his notorious brood of clever, ambitious grandchildren. Tonight, the *Eagle* trades questions and answers with the Brigadier General's youngest, and perhaps cleverest, descendant—none other than New Columbia's own precocious prep schooler Anabel Park.

Let's cut to the chase. Is it true that you were responsible for illicitly streaming Alex Lamarque's guerilla concert from the New Columbia Prep auditorium on a UCC-owned propaganda channel?
[laughs] Wow, even student reporters don't beat around the bush, do you?

As in all things, New Columbia Prep students strive to be the best. Besides, we're grateful to your grandpa for carving out places on this continent where journalism can still exist!
Touché. You should know my answer to your first question, then. Yes, I organized the broadcast. But technically, I did not violate UCC law. Hacking firewalls and distributing illicit media is illegal, sure, but that's not what I did—I streamed Alex's performance live, on the wireless. If there happened to be a faulty firewall, which happened to leak the performance onto that unfortunately poorly secured Incorporated propaganda channel, well. That's not my fault. Diplomatic agreements between the UCC and the Barricade Coalition are for diplomats to manage, not schoolgirls.

Right. You were just cruising for an A on a school project.
In our defense, it was a final project for a class literally called "Modern Politics."

So you wanted to make a statement against UCC censorship?
Yes and no. I mean, politics are fundamentally about power. UCC Inc. rose to power on this very simple idea that the media we consume—music, books, news, whatever—shape our thoughts, which in turn shape our culture. When you get two distinct, opposing ideas of

what culture should be, you get the Partition Wars. Patriotism stopped being about standing by a country, and started being about standing by a tribe of people who believe the same things you do, which was why national governments ultimately failed. Now, the UCC hangs on to its power over the rest of the continent with this seamless blend of censorship and executive-sponsored propaganda—a kind of thought control, if you will.

Do you see this as a step toward filling your grandfather's shoes some day?

God, I hope not! My grandfather fought a literal war just to keep free thinking alive. I came up with an edgy idea for a school project to remind people what that war was about—so that, hopefully, they'll stop the next one from happening at all. Grandpa always said the most successful wars are the ones you end before they begin.

Why did you pick the songs you did? We noticed a good mix of languages in the set list!

The songs were mostly Alex's picks, actually—we wanted to showcase a lot of foreign-language music, since standard continental English is so strictly enforced as the only permissible language in Incorporated territory. Which is pretty dumb, considering how much of the continent's heritage is Spanish and French as well—and that's not even getting into smaller pockets of immigrant languages like Korean, which my grandfather spoke! Or Arabic, or Chinese, or whatever. The Lamarques are from the French bit of the Northern Front, so Alex grew up on their rebel songs, and his mum was Southwestern, so he has the Spanish know-how too. I think the whole thing came together really nicely.

What was it like working with Alex Lamarque? He's got a lovely voice, and great stage presence, but we'd never know it from how reclusive he usually is!

Yeah, Alex is careful with how he uses his platform, but he doesn't do anything by halves. I think we approached the project with a similar mindset. We both carry the weight of the war behind our family names, so he definitely understands that when we pull a risky stunt like this concert, it's bigger than just us, you know? Like, we get that we're basically branding this controversial performance as a "Park" thing, or a "Lamarque" thing, not just a "two kids named Alex and Anabel having a laugh" sort of thing. It's really important to be on the same wavelength with that stuff.

Okay, last question. How long before we can expect an illicit leak of this interview into Incorporated territory?

(laughs) Hey, if Incorporated citizens want a peek into the lives of Coalition prep schoolers, I'm pretty sure book smugglers have you covered on that front, no matter how much finger-wagging Emilia Rosenbaum does over at the Barricader's Daily. Sorry, Emilia! We don't control the will of the people!

♦

"THAT'S YOUR STORY?"

"That's the truth," snapped Pru. Getting a read on Alex was practically impossible. He'd listened to her spill her guts without interrupting once, not even at the bits about how the cyborg-dragon-*thing* rescued Pru from certain death in an elevator shaft, or about the temporary amnesia that ensued. He'd simply watched her with that inscrutably dark gaze, one ankle crossed over a knee as he leaned against the table. The plasma gun sat with disturbingly casual ease at his hip. What kind of prep schooler handled *plasma guns*, much less used them to interrogate near strangers in coffeehouses?

The same kind that performed illicitly streamed concerts from school auditoriums onto Incorporated propaganda channels to make reckless political statements, apparently.

"Hey!" Pru called over Alex's shoulder. "Barista guy—girl—um, barista person! Aren't you going to do anything about the crazy dude threatening your only customer with a plasma gun at point-blank?"

Slowly, the barista raised those mismatched eyes from the till, and turned the most disdainful expression yet on Pru. "No." A pause. "And it's barista girl, if you must. For the time being."

"For the time being?" asked Alex, brows lifted.

The barista shrugged their—evidently, her—shoulders. "I contain multitudes. Don't go dictating circumstances for my woman-hood, Alexandre."

"Wouldn't dream of it, Cat."

"You two know each other?" Pru demanded. Her voice jumped an octave on the last syllable.

"I'm pretty sure Cat would have called the authorities by now if we didn't," said Alex. The corner of his mouth rose ever so slightly. "Plasma gun and all."

"Nonsense," said Cat, sticking a tray of bagels into the bakery display. "I would have been perfectly pleased to call the authorities on my own mother, god rest her soul, if she made the sort of scene you did in this coffeehouse. The only reason I didn't see you arrested and turned over to the Barricaders' Courts is because you gave me at least an hour's notice that you planned to accost some schoolgirl around these premises. You did cut it rather close, Alexandre."

Alex shrugged. "Sorry."

"You knew I was going to be here?" Pru demanded. If her voice climbed any higher, she'd be squeaking out questions like a cartoon mouse.

"If it had been forty-five minutes, I would have had you both handcuffed," said Cat, sounding pleased at the thought.

"Your candor is noted," said Alex.

Cat rolled her eyes, jerked her head at Pru, and fired something off in Spanish, too quick and fluent for Pru to catch.

"It's not nice to threaten to shoot people in languages they can't understand," Alex told her.

Cat scowled. "She's a waste of your time and mine."

"She's a friend of Anabel's."

That, if possible, deepened Cat's scowl further still.

The coffeehouse door slammed open with a violent clang that cut off even the auto-tuned welcome jingle. Anabel Park strode through with a gait that made her school uniform look like some fantasy queen's robes, black hair impeccably glossy in its high ponytail, eyes furious. "Alex!" she thundered. Her gaze narrowed on the plasma gun at his hip. "What the hell do you think you're doing?"

Alex saluted Anabel with Pru's empty coffee cup by way of greeting. "Trying to pin down the whereabouts of a rogue, cybernetic dragon. You?"

"Finishing up press for your concert." Anabel blew wisps of dark hair off her forehead. "You know, convincing media outlets that we did something righteous and sexy in the name of Barricader values, but definitely not something that should actually land us in jail."

"You thought it would be fun," said Alex blithely.

"And I was not wrong," Anabel retorted in severe tones. "Music *is* fun. Damage control, less so. You owe me a favor, Lamarque. Stage managing isn't easy. Nor are public relations."

Alex tilted a stage-brilliant smile toward Anabel. "But you've made such an art form of both."

"Flattery doesn't count as my favor," Anabel informed him, but amusement crinkled the corners of her perfectly lined eyes. "I hope your uncle's satisfied. So far as I'm concerned, he owes me a favor too."

The brilliant smile winked out. "And he'll grant it, no doubt." Alex ran a palm over his face, eyes closed. "We needed to pull Incorporated focus elsewhere—anywhere—while we got Project Rebelwing back under control. Breaching their propaganda channels with an hour's worth of black market music got the job done. And hey." A hint of the dimple returned. "Meanwhile, Incorporated citizens hear what we have to say."

"For the price of a diplomatic incident," Anabel pointed out, unmoved.

"Good," said Alex grimly. "Because if it's diplomatic incidents we're concerned about, I think the *giant dragon mech* that escaped into Incorporated territory in the middle of a wyvern scare is probably due to cause a bigger one than a few rock songs. Arms races almost destroyed this continent once, remember? The distraction from the concert blowout buys us some time, but it'll run out eventually."

"At least the dragon turns invisible. It's got that advantage over a wyvern flock."

"When we're lucky. I don't like those chances. We need Rebelwing home and safely stabled, sooner rather than later."

Anabel folded her arms. "So you interrogate my friend at gunpoint?"

"I interrogated a thief who's committed grand theft auto on our best and only defense against a reportedly rebooted wyvern flock, yes."

"Hey!" cried Pru. "That's enough!" Twin pairs of snapping dark eyes whipped toward her, as if remembering Pru's presence for the first time. "First, I'm a book smuggler, not a thief, you unbelievable dick. I move media products between Barricader and Incorporated territory; I don't *mug* people. Second, it's not my fault I got sucked inside that crazy dragon mech monstrosity, okay? I didn't exactly ask for the Full Reptile Experience: Mobile Suit Edition. Third," she paused for air, "what in actual hell is going on?"

Anabel's shoulders slumped. "I should have told you everything from the beginning."

"No, you shouldn't," said Alex and Cat in unison.

Anabel directed a ferocious glare at Alex, but her gaze softened on the barista. "Cat," she said, her voice gentle, "none of this is your—"

An auburn eyebrow arched. "Business?"

"Fault."

The barista shrugged. "It is, rather. Both my business, and my fault."

"*What* is?" Pru practically shrieked.

"The dragon, of course," said Cat, in a tone devoid of emotional inflection. "Our wayward Rebelwing. That's what this pair of imbeciles is trying and failing to tell you about. The dragon mech you just joy-rode was the product of an old and foolish engineering dream."

"Uh-huh, sure. What kind of mech engineer would dream up a *dragon*?"

"The kind that knows a thing or nine about how wyverns are made," drawled Cat, "and worse, what they're made for." She shrugged. "I was born in the slums of an Incorporated wyvern factory, licensed to a self-styled engineer named Harold Jellicoe."

"*You?*" Pru stared at the barista who'd served her a tray of coffee and cha siu buns barely an hour ago. She tried to picture her building war machines for the UCC instead of selling overpriced snacks to Barricader schoolgirls. "You created the dragon? Project Rebelling, or whatever you called it?"

"Project Rebelwing. One of my earliest designs, with Alexandre's input, of course. He has been crucial to my work." Cat's pale, cybernetic eye flicked toward Pru. "I am only a barista on Monday, Wednesday, and Thursday mornings. Or did you think all the mechanical wonders of the Barricade Coalition—the vehicles, the high-speed rail between the cities, et cetera—simply sprang to life by magic?"

Pru swallowed, gazing around at the coffeehouse's three occupants. Cat, golden lips pulled thin, artificial hand clenched into a fist at her side. Alex, his expression opaque, inky brows curved over those soft, steady eyes, plasma gun still gleaming inches from his fingertips. And Anabel, hovering between them, pink-cheeked but immaculate, looking utterly miserable.

She'd been Pru's best friend.

"What are you guys, exactly?" asked Pru, very quietly.

Cat's chin lifted. "Engineering student at Lamarque U. Double concentration in contemporary cyborg modding and war mech programming."

"Part-time, fourth-year student at New Columbia Prep," said Alex.

Anabel wouldn't lift her eyes. "Pru, listen—"

"No, Anabel, go on," said Pru, words still dropping from her mouth in that odd, quiet voice that didn't feel fully her own. "What are you, really? Because I thought you were a schoolmate. A friend. Not someone who runs around behind my back, unleashing mechanical monsters on the continent."

"I'm not unleashing mechanical monsters on the continent."

"Wow," drawled Pru. "High bar, Park! I know you always aim to overachieve. Still, never thought you'd lie to me, making up some bullshit about Modern Politics II—"

"I never lied to you!" snapped Anabel, eyes lifting at last. "Every word I've said is true. I really do take the Modern Politics sequence at school, and so does Alex. You know Modern Politics II includes a work-study component. Some of our classmates do assistantships or fellowships with media companies or inter–Barricade City communications and transport departments. Me and Alex, we're enrolled with Cat in the same internship at Coalition headquarters."

"What the hell kind of internship? Robot Reptiles 101?"

"Of course not! We do projects for the benefit of the Barricade Coalition government. It's . . . look, government projects on our level are sensitive, okay? I wanted to read you in, Pru. I've been trying to convince Alex to recruit you for the internship all semester long. I thought maybe, if you guys just met face-to-face—"

Pru's stomach dropped to her toes. "The meeting at the library. You deliberately double-booked me, didn't you? It was never about the alibi. It was about this stupid government project, or whatever it is you're up to." She barked out an incredulous little laugh. "Holy shit. You Anabel Park'd me. I've seen you do it to customers on the other side of the Barricades, and I've seen you do it to bitchy classmates, but I never thought you'd do it to me."

"Don't be absurd," snapped Anabel. "We had a drop to make, and I wanted Alex to see what you were capable of. I was going to make proper introductions between the two of you, and I would have succeeded, if you hadn't hared off on your own just because I ran a couple minutes late. Two goals, one meeting. What's so wrong with that?"

"What's wrong with that?" Pru strode into her friend's space, heedless of the dangerous look in her eyes. "You handled me. Like I was some . . . some game piece, to be moved around at your convenience. Like I was too stupid to have a say in the grand plans of the illustrious Anabel Park."

"Don't be an asshole." Anabel's expression had taken on a cold, clinical cast that made the insides of Pru's skin twinge. She'd seen Anabel whip out that ice queen stare before. She'd just never been on its receiving end. "Pru, you skipped out on, like, ten classes in our first semester alone. Be honest—how likely were you to show up to a meeting about an *internship* opportunity, versus book smuggling work? At least for the second one, you'd feel obligated to turn up for the money."

Every inch of Pru went still. The coffeehouse had gone utterly silent. Before her, three faces blurred, as if viewed through a faulty camera lens. "Well," said Pru at last. Her voice felt like a splinter, lodged inside her too-tight throat. "Glad you're finally willing to admit how you really feel."

Without another word, she stood up, crossed the room, and shoved her way out the coffeehouse door, the auto-tuned welcome jingle a mocking echo in her ears.

IMPRINTED ———————————————— 4

Dramatic exits worked a lot better when you actually had some idea where you were going. Pru got about as far as the patch of grass where the mech—the dragon—had dumped her off. Pru stared dumbly at the ground for a moment. Then she sat down, grass-stained skirt and all, and, to her mortification, burst into tears.

Footsteps padded out to join her a few minutes later. "Hey," said Alex Lamarque, "mind if I sit for a minute?" He sounded more awkward than any Lamarque Pru had ever heard. Then again, Alex was the only Lamarque she'd ever met in person. It was probably easy not to sound awkward on pretaped news broadcasts, or old political documentaries.

She wiped at her nose with an elbow, wanting vaguely to die. "You'll get grass stains on your trousers," she informed him thickly, but scooted over to make room.

"My trousers have seen worse." Alex stretched out beside her, long legs crossed at the ankles. "Are you okay?"

"Fine, now that I'm not staring down the business end of a plasma gun." Pru scrubbed at her wet cheeks. "I just have something in my eye."

"I believe they're called tears."

"Shut up."

"Here." He produced a handkerchief from seemingly nowhere, a soft square of ivory starting to go a bit threadbare, but clearly well made.

Pru snorted. "My god, you really are a bourgeois boy." But she accepted it all the same, the linen still warm from his hands.

"I embrace some stereotypes." Even burying her face in the handkerchief, half-blinded, she could feel Alex's regard resting on her, heavy and inscrutable. What did you do, pinned under eyes like those? His was a gaze that melted the hearts of a rock concert audience one minute, then squinted through a pair of pistol sights the next. Pru shivered.

"I'm sorry about the plasma gun," Alex said at last. His weight shifted beside her. "I work for the military division of Barricade Coalition. That mobile suit, the dragon—Rebelwing—she went missing a couple weeks ago. Thanks to Cat's genius, Rebelwing's the closest the Coalition's army engineers have gotten to creating a mech that could take down wyvern flocks, but the dragon's behavior is still unpredictable. That makes her dangerous, in more ways than one. And when you just molded to those scales and wings, like you were made for them, I thought . . . well, I didn't know what to think. But I shouldn't have scared you like that."

Pru shrugged off his apology. "I figured you didn't actually want to kill me."

"Thanks."

"No, really," said Pru. "I noticed the setting on the pistol grip ticked to 'stun,' which, let me be clear, Captain Space Opera, would still have been very uncool. But, like, the no-kill setting is something, I guess. If I saw some girl flying a giant robot reptile over New Columbia, I'd probably have panicked and shot my own head off. How did you even figure out where I was going to land?"

"Tracked Rebelwing's coordinates. Not always reliable, with those stealth mechanisms, but Cat helped—turns out she programmed some emergency protocols for getting the dragon to land in certain locales. Like the field behind the coffeehouse where she happens to work." Alex hummed thoughtfully. "You know, I don't recall plasma gun settings getting covered in New Columbia Prep's core curriculum."

"They're not. Anabel—" Pru swallowed. "Anabel taught me how to eyeball pistol settings, when we first got into book smuggling. Don't see why she ever bothered, honestly."

"Teaching you plasma gun safety?"

"Book smuggling." Pru shrugged one shoulder. "Not like Anabel ever needed the money. I knew that. I figured she was just in it for the thrill, and because—" Pru bit her tongue before she could say, *because it was something stupid and fun we could do together.* "I get the need for a dumb thrill from time to time, for an anal-retentive overachiever like Anabel. But this fancy, hush-hush Coalition internship of hers? You'd think the Barricader government bigwigs would frown on interns who deal illegal anything."

"Not necessarily."

"No?" Pru snuck a glance at him. Alex's jaw had set, carving a sharp profile against the lightening sky. A photographer from a propagandist's office couldn't have set up a better inspo-shot.

"You break every rule, when your intent serves the right cause," said Alex.

"Yeah? And what's that?" asked Pru. "Screwing the UCC by any means necessary? Is that what you tell the university admissions counselors when they ask for your five-year plan?" Not that a kid named Lamarque would need help with admission to any university anywhere in the Barricade cities.

Alex smiled. Not the toothy, public grin he'd turned on his concert crowd, but a private curve of the mouth, small and searing. "Restoring democracy to the continent. Restoring the marketplace of ideas. Not just for Barricaders. For everyone."

"Wow," said Pru. "I just told my admissions counselor that I want to pass Honors Literature II and score a spot in a less boring elective next year."

"Sure," said Alex, "but shouldn't everyone on the continent be allowed those opportunities too? We call Incorporated citizens ignorant because they live on the wrong side of the Barricades, but ignorance is really just a different kind of fear."

"And you think you'll stamp out the terror of the Executive General's reign by, what, putting his citizens through their paces bullshitting Honors Lit essays?"

"I think letting them study uncensored literature at all is a start."

"That's so trite," said Pru. "Like ideally, yeah. No shit, jailing teens for reading edgy superhero comics is messed up. But why is that a Barricader problem? Why is that my problem? I'm just a dumb kid with a side hustle, trying to get through school. Completely useless to the Coalition, or whatever political crusade its interns have cooked up."

"Anabel thinks otherwise."

Pru didn't quite hide her flinch. "Anabel thinks I'm a greedy little charity case."

"No," said Alex quietly. "I really don't believe she does. She's got an eye for these things. You're quick on your feet, adaptable. Good at keeping your eyes on the prize."

"Smuggling skills."

Alex shrugged. "Transferrable smuggling skills. Coalition could use that."

Pru opened her mouth, then closed it again. She couldn't remember the last time anyone had told her she was useful for anything besides petty, cash-winning crime, which wasn't really something you could write about in a university admissions essay.

Silence drifted between them, and grew immediately awkward. *Say something*, she urged her brain. *Say literally anything.*

"You still haven't explained why the Barricade Coalition needs a giant robot dragon that sometimes turns invisible and kidnaps people for joy rides," said Pru.

"That's not for you to know," said a new voice. Pru started. She'd been so wrapped up in arguing with Alex, she hadn't even noticed Cat's approach. Now, the barista—barista-slash-engineering-student, apparently—hovered over Pru, mouth a disapproving golden slash. "You've ruined everything."

"Not necessarily," protested Alex.

Cat sniffed. "I am ninety percent certain."

"By what statistical formula, exactly?"

"Oh, I can't think what," drawled Cat. "But perhaps my expertise in matters of my own engineering design might allow me some confidence." Her gaze snapped toward Pru, the single cybernetic iris burning bright as the dragon's eye. "I built Rebelwing for Alexandre," she said bluntly. "She's perfect for him, not you."

"Um," said Pru, unsure whether she was supposed to be offended or relieved. "Cool? Like, don't take this the wrong way, but that joy ride left me kind of airsick. I'm totally good with seeing Puff the Mecha-Lizard returned to her rightful, uh, master—"

"No one cares," snapped Cat. "The dragon has imprinted on you."

Pru blinked. "Come again?"

"Imprinted," Cat repeated, biting off the syllables with unnecessary fervor. "Do you know, ideally, how a mech works?"

Pru's mind drifted guiltily back to her terrible robotics grades at school. "Probably not, no."

"A mech and its pilot must work as one," said Cat. "The organic and the inorganic. A symbiotic relationship between two uniquely complementary beings. The trouble is, most pilots are human beings, and human beings are rather inconveniently sentient."

"Um. Sorry?"

"A normal, mindless machine simply cannot respond as quickly and instinctually to a human brain's desires as a mech pilot requires in combat," continued Cat, ignoring Pru. "That is why Rebelwing is sentient too. A particular advantage over Incorporated wyverns."

"The dragon is *sentient*?" squawked Pru. Still, that explained a few things, like why this mech had seemed more like a living animal than a death-dealing wyvern, much less your average mobile suit. "So it's . . . you literally designed a super-advanced stealth suit that can fly, turn invisible, enhance human senses, and has a *will of its own*?"

"Precisely," said Cat, sounding pleased. "It's also equipped with a number of upgraded weapons technologies. My own design, of course."

"Awesome," said Pru faintly. She felt dizzy.

"The sentience allows the dragon to forge a unique bond with the human in the cockpit, but it's a particular process. Pilots are used to choosing their mechs. A sentient mech chooses its pilot, not the other way around. I suspected Rebelwing had imprinted on you when Alexandre called me about the rooftop incident. When you mentioned your memory loss in the elevator shaft, I knew for sure." At Pru's incredulous expression, Cat shrugged. "You cannot expect me to have been fully absorbed in donut displays for twenty minutes. I did overhear most of Alexandre's interrogation. The temporary blank space in your memory is a side effect from the imprinting process."

Pru massaged her temples. "If this . . . Rebelwing's so great, how did you lose her in the first place?"

"For the same reason prize stallions escape if you leave a stable door open," said Alex dryly. "I did tell you this would be the cost of sentience, Cat."

Cat sniffed. "We wanted to create a mech smart enough to imprint on your brain in the cockpit! She wasn't supposed to be smart enough to sneak out of a military compound, much less hop a Barricade wall!" Her glare snapped toward Pru. "And she wasn't supposed to imprint on anyone besides Alexandre."

Pru glared back as good as she got. "I didn't ask to bond with Robo Reptile, you know," she said, pushing clumsily back to her feet. Grass stalks scattered off her skirt.

"Where are you going?" demanded Cat.

"School," snapped Pru. "Robo Reptile is clearly a problem for the Coalition and its interns, not me. You keep your mech on a leash next time." Those last words left a bitter pang of guilt in Pru's mouth. Silver eyes blinked inside her head, as she remembered how it had felt to see the world through those eyes, really *see*, the whole city cast into sharp, cinematic definition.

"You can't go back to school," said Alex.

"Watch me."

He grabbed her elbow. "If Cat's right—and she'll be the first to say she's usually right—you can't just waltz back into a chunk of city overflowing with civilians. So long as Rebelwing thinks you're her rightful pilot, she'll never stop looking for you."

"Not until we reverse the imprinting process," said Cat.

Pru jerked herself out of Alex's grip, cheeks hot as she redirected her glare toward him. "And how the hell do we do that?"

Alex raked his fingers through his hair, curling the ends. For the first time, Pru noted faint purple shadows beneath his eyes. They'd all gone far too long without a wink of sleep. In a weird way, it really was a typical prep schooler's night. "We go someplace safe from prying eyes and try to force the dragon to follow. Cat can manage the . . . unimprinting process from there." He wouldn't meet her eyes. "You'll have your life back. If that's what you want."

"It is," said Pru instantly. She paused. "But where will we go?"

The Lamarque boy slipped a small, surprised smile her way. "To see my uncle, of course."

◆

*Barricading Beat: Your Number
One Source for Citizen Journalism!*
Posted by BRIGHTEYES006

As of Wednesday, 3:00 P.M., rumors have emerged of meetings between UCC Inc.'s Executive General and so-called "father of wyverns" Harold Jellicoe himself. In light of the disturbing reported sightings of winged mechs over New Columbia's walls, does this signify an escalation in the arms race—and a threat to Head Representative Lamarque's carefully negotiated peace with our Incorporated neighbors? Discuss in comments!!!

◆

THE UNDERGROUND METRO RIDE toward the residence of Gabriel Lamarque, square-jawed people's hero of the Partition Wars, and elected Head Representative of the Barricade Coalition, was decidedly awkward. The train, usually packed with New Columbia's miserable car-free commuters, ran crowd-free and smoothly this early in the morning. That left Pru and her three unlikely companions—Alex, Cat, and Anabel, who'd emerged from the coffeehouse narrow eyed and unspeaking—scattered across the train compartment. Alex and Cat bent together, muttering at each other in low, urgent Spanish. Which left Pru curled in one corner seat and Anabel tucked into another. Silence stretched thin between them like cheap butter.

"Can we talk?"

Pru jerked her head from the grimy side window. Anabel, rising from the opposite seat, hovered over her. One perfectly manicured hand rested on her hip, the other clutched a railing. Only the pallor of her knuckles gave away how uncomfortable she actually felt.

Pru closed her eyes. "Not sure what we have left to talk about."

"You could have called, you know," said Anabel. "Or texted me.

When you got to the study before I did, and ran into Alex. You didn't have to go tearing off into Incorporated territory by yourself like some kind of idiot adrenaline junkie."

"I had a drop to make."

"*We* had a drop to make," Anabel corrected icily. "You just decided to handle it alone, without so much as a word to me."

"Wow, really, you want to talk about withholding information? And by the way, you didn't seem to care much at the time. Too busy revving up an audience for your revolutionary rock show."

"I'm not your mother," snarled Anabel. "It's not my job to teach you common sense. I figured no harm, no foul; you came back unscathed, right? Until you started talking about dragons and memory gaps. I played it cool so you wouldn't flip out, but then I texted Cat and Alex—"

"Oh, good," said Pru, feeling brittler still. "More fun facts you share about me with your Coalition buddies. Without my knowledge. What a hoot!"

Anabel glared, once, then shut her eyes, breathing out slowly. "Okay. There's a lot I should have been straight about with you, right from the start. I meant that, when I said it back at the coffeehouse. I really am sorry. But Pru, can you put yourself in my shoes for, like, fifteen seconds? I signed about a hundred different nondisclosure agreements about this internship. I couldn't just spill my guts to whoever I wanted, whenever I wanted. And you were—"

Pru's mouth twisted. "—just a criminal?"

"Would you let me finish?" snapped Anabel. "I'm a criminal too, don't forget. The only difference between my crimes and yours are that I started smuggling on a Barricade Coalition permit."

That shut Pru up.

"When we met," said Anabel, "I had this half-baked idea about using the book smuggling trade to expose Incorporated citizens to the Barricader way of life. It's not cool that whole groups of people stuck living under the UCC's thumb can't read or listen to whatever they want, just because they lack the resources and connections to emigrate to a Barricade city, you know? Besides, people always crave stuff that's taboo. It was an opportunity for us. I pitched the idea to one of my cousins who works with Lamarque—under-the-table support for dealing free media in Incorporated territory. Quiet, cheap, easy way to undermine UCC authoritarianism. Jay agreed with the bare bones of my strategy, but I had no clue how to actually smuggle shit until I met you."

Understanding dawned on Pru. "Second semester of our first year. When we started running holo-drives past the Barricade sentinels together. You offered to play bodyguard and teach me self-defense in exchange for a cut of the pay. I always wondered why General Park's granddaughter wanted black market money. But it wasn't really about the money, was it? It never was."

Anabel bit her lip. "I couldn't share all my shady Coalition shit with you because that wasn't my call to make. But that doesn't mean you weren't my friend. I hope you still are."

Pru rolled Anabel's words around inside her head for a long moment. "Tell me something true. If I hadn't been a book smuggler—if I'd just been that other gawky Asian girl in your first-year class at prep school—would we be friends now?"

Anabel met Pru's gaze, unflinching, and swallowed hard. "Probably not. I'm not great at forming relationships that aren't about making other people . . . useful to me. I'd blame the way my family raised me, you know—Barricader values first, always—but I think maybe this is just who I am. But that doesn't mean you aren't important to me. I didn't know who you were back then. I do now."

And that was Anabel all over. It always had been. The General's granddaughter, the silver-tongued young strategist who built tools, or weapons, out of everything she could get her hands on. Her confession hung between them for a moment, an uncertain offering. Pru studied Anabel from beneath her lashes, the pinched look of Anabel's lipsticked mouth, the tight-fisted fingers on the metro railing. Anabel was being honest with Pru. That was a brand of vulnerability particular to Anabel, and one she didn't share with just anybody.

"Well, *jeez*." Pru heaved an extravagant sigh. "Now I just feel *bad*. You and Alex and your highbrow political loyalties."

The side of Anabel's mouth curled. "Formative from the cradle, I'm afraid."

"Yeah, okay, that's the thing." Pru felt her own mouth twist. "You want to know why I didn't text you about making that drop solo yesterday? I know I should have. I didn't think. But I'm pretty sure the reason I didn't think was because I didn't want to."

Anabel's eyebrows climbed, a silent question.

Embarrassment hunched Pru's shoulders inward. "I don't have a Cause with a capital *C*, like you or Alex do. That's not how I was raised. I don't have anything, really, to set me apart from the other kids at school—I'm not the best student, or the best athlete, or super rich, or anything like that. But I thought maybe I was smooth, at least smooth enough not to need General Park's youngest and cleverest babysitting me in a low-risk—"

"Mid-risk."

Pru resisted the urge to roll her eyes. "Fine, yeah, a mid-risk drop. Maybe going solo without telling you was dumb and reckless, but I worry about so much shit all the time. I wanted to prove that smuggling—conning authorities, sneaking around, eyeing up quick escapes—*wasn't* something I needed to worry about. I just wanted to be good enough at this one thing, on my own. That's all."

Anabel shook her head. "Needing people doesn't mean you're not *good* at something. Most book smugglers work in crews. There's a reason why university admissions reps are always blathering on about demonstrating teamwork skills." Her gaze softened toward the opposite end of the compartment where Alex and Cat bent their heads together, Spanish still rolling easy and low voiced between them. "I don't think people are really made to be alone, you know? Life's full of scary shit. We all need someone to watch our backs."

"Uh-huh," said Pru, very dryly, "which is Anabel Park for 'trick my best friend into enabling my secret sketchy Coalition business with nary a word.' Which is all fun and games, it turns out, until giant mech dragons start kidnapping people for midnight joy rides."

"Hey, in my defense, Cat and Alex's pet project was so not part of my original plan. How was I supposed to know you'd run off and imprint on the damn thing?"

"She imprinted on *me*!" cried Pru, indignant.

Anabel's mouth twitched, but her eyes went somber. "You're the reason I know how to forge gate passes and read a street corner better than Grandfather's military men. I should have just told you that I wanted Alex to see what you were capable of. I forget, sometimes, that not everyone in my life's a mark. For that, I really am sorry."

Pru leaned her head against the window. Genuine praise from Anabel Park, especially during a fight, was rare, and praise from literally anyone always left Pru feeling strangely vulnerable, half warm, half suspicious. "Alex said you wanted me for the Coalition too. That you told him I'd be useful to your . . . cause." Whatever that meant.

"Well, yeah. The skills you taught me aren't useless, Pru. You could help me keep tabs on what media content's selling hot, plot out different routes for crews to pass through UCC-controlled neighborhoods without alerting their police brigades, locate underground libraries and tunnel passages, that sort of thing."

"You are crap at navigating those tunnels without escort," Pru agreed.

"And screw you very much too, Wu."

Pru spread her fingers across the foggy glass, watching her prints appear and disappear. "Look, this is going to sound awkward, but I have to ask. After this whole, um, un-imprinting process is done. If, hypothetically, I never want anything to do with the Coalition or its sketchy secret internships again, are you and I still friends?"

Anabel, heaving a tremendous sigh, plopped into the seat beside Pru's. Their shoulders knocked together. "Coaltion, shmoalition. Internship or no, I'll still need someone to share sticky rice with at lunchtime."

Pru released a long, pent-up breath of air. Her stomach uncoiled itself. "Oh, I see. You're still finding ways to make me useful to you!"

"Hey, girl's gotta have priorities."

Pru snorted, knocking her shoulder against Anabel's slightly harder than necessary. "Glad you know what you want."

"But doing a Barricade Coalition internship together would be pretty sweet too. It would look great on your university applications!"

"Don't push your luck, asshole."

Anabel laughed. Almost against her will, Pru's mouth twitched in response. Their friendship wasn't exactly what it had been yesterday morning, before disastrously miscommunicated meetings and rogue robot lizards and secrets laid inelegantly bare between them. But they weren't broken, either. Pru could trust that much.

Marching toward something other than first-period calculus at eight A.M. on a Thursday morning felt weird and tawdry and a little daring, even for Pru. Marching toward the tourist-beloved home of the elected leader of the last free cities on the North American continent felt downright surreal.

Pru pictured filling out her truancy slip for Headmaster Goldschmidt's office. *REASON FOR ABSENCE: forgot to turn in problem sets because secret government-sponsored robot lizard kidnapped me off roof of school building; negotiations with the hero of the Partition Wars still pending.*

The Head Representative's Mansion sat on a well-cut lawn near the center of New Columbia proper. When Alex led their group straight past the manicured gardens and iron-wrought gates, Pru glanced his way in surprise. "I thought you made an appointment to see your, uh, uncle." Referring to Head Representative Gabriel Lamarque as anybody's uncle still felt weird to Pru, but admittedly, her barometer for weird was a little skewed at the moment. Sentient dragon mechs had a tendency to do that, it seemed.

"We did," said Alex.

"You might want to make a turn, then."

"The Head Representative will not be taking an off-the-books meeting with a band of miscreant teenagers at the *Mansion*," snapped Cat, twisting her head around to glare at them both. "We're going to—"

"Please don't say a secret underground bunker," said Pru. "My heart can't take the cliché."

"A *safehouse*," said Alex in bracing tones. "Here." He paused at a nondescript door, crammed among the newly built townhouses around the city corner, and whistled, a quick, minor-key succession of notes.

An intercom clicked on. "Eyes," instructed the auto-tuned voice.

Alex lifted his chin, unblinking, as the camera perched atop the door scanned one retina, then the other. Evidently satisfied, the door hummed, sliding aside in one smooth motion. "Thank you for cooperation," chirped the intercom.

What followed was a series of steps—not even an escalator, but actual stone steps. "Aha," whispered Pru, triumphant. "I knew it. A secret underground bunker!"

"Please stop talking," said Anabel.

The winding staircase ended in a door that Cat proceeded to kick open. "We have come to restore my dragon mech to Alexandre's imprinting coordinates," she announced tonelessly.

"Oh my god," said Anabel. With one hand, she hauled Cat backward by the elbow—bold move, by Pru's estimation, but one that Cat took with surprising calm. With the other hand, Anabel covered her eyes, fingers stretching to massage her temples.

As one, the occupants behind the kicked-open door looked up

from the conference table. Pru recognized the man at the center immediately, his blue eyes bright beneath a thick crown of well-coiffed hair. Gabriel Lamarque's face, still boyishly handsome even fifteen years after the heyday of the Partition Wars, represented different things to different people. A folk hero to some, a twinkling-eyed traitor to others, and everything in between, he was utterly jarring in the flesh, an airbrushed magazine cover made real.

"Why, if it isn't the young Cat herself!" called Head Representative Lamarque, in alarmingly jovial tones. Those famous eyes crinkled at the corners, giving his smile away before it fully formed. He nudged one of the other suits at the table with one elbow. "Don't look so scandalized, Hakeem. I did warn you that my nephew's friends have a habit of dramatic entrances."

The man he'd nudged, a lean whip of a man with skin as dark as his graying hair was pale, snorted. Pru knew this one: Hakeem Bishop, the Head Representative's Chief of Staff. He'd been a friend and contemporary to Anabel's grandfather. "Don't think I've forgotten your own misspent youth, Gabriel," drawled Bishop. "Teenagers are dramatic by definition."

"Yes, well, at least these teens report rogue mechs to the correct authorities. I'm quite certain the rules of responsible guardianship dictate that I'm supposed to ground Alexandre otherwise."

"You ought to ground him anyway, the way the press is going on about this secret rock show he threw after curfew at New Columbia Prep. The Park girl too!" he added, pitching his voice for the benefit of the man on Lamarque's opposite side.

The third man, visibly the youngest of the trio, offered a slow, enigmatic smile. "I find Anabel tends to do as she pleases, regardless of the family's input," he drawled, draping himself backward in his seat. The motion made the fine blue wool of his suit sigh over his shoulders. Pru, watching, half expected him to prop his feet up on the conference table. As his head lifted, a fancifully white-dyed streak of otherwise pitch-dark hair dipped over his eyes. He winked. "Well met, Cousin."

"Screw you too, Jay," returned Anabel cheerfully. "And for the record, our secret rock show did a fine job of distracting Barricader press and Incorporated authorities alike from our little runaway lizard problem, so you're quite frankly welcome."

"Ah, the lizard problem," mused her cousin—Jay, apparently. "And so we return to the matter of Cat and Alexandre's curious little creation." Pru tried not to fidget as he gave their ragtag band a vaguely unimpressed once-over. New Columbia Prep had boasted a Jay Park in one of those hokey notable alumni displays at the school library. He'd graduated shortly after the Partition Wars, and was one of the youngest advisors tapped to serve the Coalition government. Noticing Pru's stare, he flashed another white-toothed grin. Handsome too. Maybe that was some kind of secret law: you couldn't work for the Coalition government unless you were also infuriatingly hot.

Alex stepped forward, then, features schooled. "I take full responsibility for the events that have transpired for the past two days," he said, voice full and unwavering, like he was back on that auditorium stage again. "For what it's worth, Cat and I think it's a pretty simple fix. If Rebelwing has imprinted on Pru, she'll be able to summon her here, where we can go about deleting the imprint."

"So you told me in your message," said Gabriel Lamarque, chin in his hands. "I admire your sense of responsibility, Alexandre. But why so eager to delete the imprint?"

Alex's dark brows snapped into a *V*. "A mech can't imprint on two pilots."

"True enough," allowed his uncle, one side of his mouth curving upward, "but why bother redoing an imprint if Rebelwing has already chosen *one* perfectly serviceable pilot?"

"Serviceable!" Cat practically squawked, fair skin mottling.

"Relax, he's not really talking about me," muttered Pru.

"Oh, I'm sorry," said the Head Representative, tone innocuous. Very slowly, he lifted his head and looked at Pru, unwavering. Within a space of seconds, he'd gone from boyish, Cool Uncle Mode to the legendary hero of the Partition Wars. Pru took a step backward. "Were you not the young lady who received the imprint?"

"Well, sure," stammered Pru. She backed up farther still, and narrowly avoided planting a heel into Anabel's ankle. "But I'm not a real military pilot or anything. You can't mean to *keep* me imprinted. Like, that makes no sense at all, dude—uh, sir. I mean, Mr. Head Representative. Sir."

Still pinning her beneath those eyes, the quicksilver bloom of Lamarque's smile took Pru by surprise. She could see it now, what Anabel meant about the resemblance between Alex and his uncle. Blue-eyed Gabriel lacked the dusky undertones to Alex's complexion, and boasted a hint of silver at his temples that accompanied a couple extra decades, but their skin stretched over the same elegant bones, their resting expressions full of the same intensity of conviction. Looking a Lamarque directly in the eyes for too long felt a bit like staring straight at the sun: overwhelming, and kind of uncomfortable, but replete with a warmth that was hard not to crave.

"On the contrary," said the Head Representative, "I believe you may have an opportunity here. I'm told you're the book smuggler who partnered up with Miss Park here."

Pru shifted her weight from one foot to the other. "I didn't know she was working on behalf of Coalition business."

"Naturally not," said Hakeem Bishop. "Just committing normal, garden variety crime."

Pru felt her own lip curl. "Minus the government endorsement. Sure."

"Pru," said Anabel in a warning tone.

"I didn't come here to be insulted," snapped Pru. The abrupt anger in her gut overrode her anxiety. "Book smuggling's a crime in Incorporated territory, yeah, no shit. Either the Barricade Coalition is for it or against it. You can't endorse one kind of smuggler, then turn your nose up at the other, Mr. Bishop. Anabel's said it herself. She's as much a criminal as I am."

Anabel shrugged. "Not gonna lie, Pru's got a point. We wouldn't have pulled half the Coalition-approved media drop-offs without everything I learned from her."

Gabriel Lamarque's smile grew. "I see why you two are friends."

"The shared passion for illegal media dealing?" suggested Bishop.

"Why, the shared passion for free expression, Hakeem!"

Bishop's jaw ticked. "Passion is all very well, sir, but that doesn't alter the particular problem we currently face regarding Miss Wu. Or haven't you forgotten what's been trending on the news media cycles all night?"

Pru frowned. "Excuse me?"

Bishop hit a button on the conference table. The surrounding walls flickered into darkness, then, with a low hum, lit up with what Pru quickly recognized as news headlines. She frowned, squinting. "What's—" Then she read the headlines. "Shit. Shit. *Shit.*"

Scrawling before her eyes like technicolor doom were a series of gossip column titles. "Preppie Caught Crossing Borders!" read one, followed by "Book Smugglers among the Best and Brightest?" One even boasted a fuzzy motion capture—poor quality, and focused on the back of the subject's head rather than a recognizable face—but Pru could make out her own ponytail and school uniform, paused beneath a video game display in an Incorporated zone, Dick Masterson's red hair and tinted spectacles bright beside her.

Anabel hissed a low-throated expletive.

"If it makes you feel any better, Alexandre's little rock show did eat up most of the views and consumer attention," said Bishop, looking like he'd bitten into something sour. "No respectable news source has yet picked up on your extracurricular activities. And none of those prurient gossip rags or chit-chat forums seem to have identified you by name. Still, the physical descriptions and commonalities between varying eyewitness accounts didn't make your identity difficult for us to piece together. It will not be long before, shall we say, less benign entities do the same."

"Which is why," said Head Representative Lamarque, "it is fortunate that we have brainstormed a solution!"

"A solution," said Pru faintly, still staring at the scrolling tabloids.

"Indeed. Hakeem is right, that people will likely piece together your book smuggling activities at some point, in which case you'll find yourself at the center of a minor but exceedingly troublesome diplomatic incident, and slapped with a criminal record, not to mention probable expulsion from school."

Pru tried very hard not to throw up. "Great," she managed.

"It is fortunate, then," continued the Head Representative, "that records from New Columbia's Barricade sentinels currently indicate that you were, in fact, a student intern in my detail during my latest mech policy negotiations with our Incorporated neighbors, giving you a perfectly respectable reason for your presence in an otherwise unauthorized UCC zone." Blithely, he added, "Of course, anyone who double checks with the registrar at New Columbia Prep will discover that third-year student Prudence Wu isn't enrolled in Modern Politics II at all, and that your gate pass ID is an admirable forgery. Which will certainly compound your criminal record, I'm afraid."

"With due respect," said Pru, "I'd love to get to the 'solution' part of this conversation."

The smile flashed again, alarmingly white. "Modern Politics II has an add-drop enrollment period after midterm projects for half-credit internships, contingent on sponsorship by a valid work-study employer. The Head Representative's office would certainly qualify. I'd even throw in a legitimate gate pass ID to sweeten the pot."

Pru took a long minute to process the implications of the offer. Then she rounded on Anabel, a bit frantically. "Did you conspire with the Head Representative to trick me into joining your weird, terrifying government internship?"

"She did not," said Gabriel Lamarque, in placating tones. "Though I agree with Miss Park. You could serve the Barricade Coalition government quite well in your own way, if you chose to."

"Like helping with the book smuggling project!" said Anabel excitedly.

"Like test-piloting Project Rebelwing," said Head Representative Lamarque.

"What?" shrieked Pru, in unison with Anabel, Cat, and Alex.

Lamarque mugged a perturbed expression. "I don't see what the shock here is," he said mildly. "Miss Wu needs a cover story for her presence in Incorporated territory, and she certainly can't run about smuggling books anymore, not with the risk of increased scrutiny now that the tabloids have had their say. Meanwhile, we need a pilot."

"Uncle, with due respect," said Alex, thin lipped, "you *have* a pilot."

His uncle's gaze softened on him. "Perhaps. I have a young woman with a probable mech imprint. But if we were to delete it, I have no guarantee that the dragon would choose to imprint on . . ." For the first time, he hesitated.

"Me." Alex's voice was quiet. "You don't trust that Rebelwing would imprint on me."

"Of course she would!" snapped Cat. "That was the entire point of her design!"

"Was it?" One of Gabriel Lamarque's eyebrows climbed. "I seem to recall that when you first pitched the creation of a living metal dragon to me, you spoke of designing a sentient mech. A mech that chooses its own pilot instead of the other way around, so as to maximize compatibility and efficiency in the field, to outpace and outfight wyvern flocks. Weren't those your words?"

"Yes! And my mech would *choose Alexandre*. He's the ideal test pilot for a sentient mobile suit, well-trained, committed to the cause, there's no reason the mech *wouldn't*—"

"And would you stake the Barricade Coalition's future on that?"

"I—"

"Would you stake Alexandre's life?"

Cat fell silent, mouth twisting.

"I thought not." Lamarque didn't look triumphant. He looked sad. "Remember why you and Alex built her, Cat. Project Rebelwing was never just about a single prototype. If Rebelwing proves successful at bonding a pilot and performing in combat, she'll be the model for dozens of other sentient mobile suits. And that—well, that will be the Coalition's best guarantee of a secure future."

Pru cleared her throat. She regretted that, vaguely, when six pairs of eyes snapped toward hers. "Um, I'm sorry if this is a stupid question, but uh . . . why do you need a pilot so badly for this Rebelwing mech right now?" Her laugh, when she forced it out, sounded more like a croak, but years of smuggling experience in tight corners urged her to barrel on, heedless of her pounding heart. "I mean, sure, we're never going to be bosom buddies with UCC Inc., given the Partition Wars and that whole corporate fascism thing, but the future of the Barricade Coalition? Really?"

"Yup." Jay Park, surveying the others with heavy-lidded calm, leaned forward ever so slightly. "I'm afraid so. I mean, look at all this, Prudence." He gestured expansively at his own body, draped carelessly over its seat at the table. "You really think I'd be here in this great bothersome emergency meeting instead of out to brunch at that posh new fusion restaurant on the corner of H Street if anything less than liberty itself were under threat? I could be having filet mignon. I could be having bulgogi. I could be having filet mignon *and* bulgogi."

"Depressingly, he characterizes himself accurately," muttered Anabel.

"Sticks and stones, cousin." Behind those sleepy eyes, though, was a certain sharpness that belied Jay's happy-go-lucky tone. It darted about the room, as his gaze flicked from one face to the next. "Now, who wants to tell our charming young smuggler the fun part behind this avant-garde little mobile suit project? Or have we all had quite enough of wringing our hands over wyverns?"

"Jay!" snapped Hakeem Bishop.

"Not you, Bishop," continued Jay blithely, "I know wringing your hands over wyverns is your very favorite pastime, and wouldn't wish to deprive you of the small joys in life."

"Wyverns aren't real," Pru blurted out, all autopilot, before realizing how foolish that sounded while hanging out in a creepy basement chatting cybernetic dragons with her elected representatives. "I mean, not the way they were during the war," she backpedaled. "No one's confirmed a real sighting since—"

"Two nights ago, half past midnight," said Cat.

Hakeem Bishop pinched the bridge of his nose. "Yes, Cat, by all means, let us disclose sensitive government information to an underage felon."

"Have you ever seen a wyvern?" Cat demanded, ignoring the Chief of Staff. Her metallic eye bored bright into Pru, as she spat the words. "I'm not talking about the grainy holograms you see in old footage of the Partition Wars and Incorporated propaganda videos, where you can barely tell head from tail. I'm talking about standing in the shadow of a bona fide war mech's wingspan, at the mercy of a manufactured monster that blasted your family away into ash, and wouldn't hesitate to send you after them. Looking it straight in the eye, and feeling death on your heels. Because I have." Her mouth twisted. "I was just a snot-nosed little Southwestern toddler during the uprisings.

Then my family caught the wrong end of a riot, and I got packed off to the labor camps, to engineer the same things that killed them. Because make no mistake: wyverns are war machines. And war will always be the UCC's greatest source of profit."

"The Partition Wars are over."

"The Partition Wars are over," mimicked Cat, practically dripping disdain. "God, what do they teach you in that prep school of yours? If you don't think the Executive General will shell out a fortune to Incorporate the Barricade cities at the first sign of New Columbia's weakness, you don't deserve to pass your history exams. If Etienne and Julia were still alive, you'd never—"

"Cat." Gabriel Lamarque's voice, softer than Pru had ever heard it on a live broadcast, sliced across the room. "That's enough, please."

Cat tucked her chin, looking primed for a fight, before her gaze flickered toward Alex and Anabel. Whatever she saw in their faces must have changed her mind. With machinelike efficiency, she ducked her head and slammed out of the room fists clenched.

Anabel glanced around, expression open and vulnerable for a few seconds, before settling into something determined. Wordless, she jogged after Cat. Alex turned to follow, but his uncle's hand landed on his shoulder first. "Let Anabel see about Cat, Alexandre."

Alex looked ready to argue, but gave a curt nod instead.

"Who were Etienne and Julia?" Pru asked in a small voice, and regretted it instantly when Alex flinched, a full-bodied movement that shrank him away from the rest of the room's occupants, sharp jawline drawn tight.

"My parents," he said. He didn't offer anything more.

"Wyverns are a war profiteering business," said Hakeem Bishop.

"And the sightings on the Barricade walls are very much real. Cat is right about that much."

"Not just any wyverns," said Alex. "These were different."

Bishop sighed. "Alexandre—"

"I know what I saw," insisted Alex. He even talked like his uncle, soft-spoken, but with a conviction that somehow enveloped the entire room. "The design and flight patterns on the footage from the Barricade sentinels don't match up with the wyverns being deployed during the Partition Wars. These are more aggressive. Sharper. Smarter." His breath hitched, before he added, "This is Jellicoe's work."

Jellicoe. Pru shifted uneasily from one foot to the other. It was the same name Cat had mentioned back at the coffeehouse. The Incorporated engineer who'd put her to work in his wyvern factories.

"With the number of arms dealers vying for profits from the Executive General, we can't know that for certain."

Alex flashed a small, grim smile. "You got intel on a Jellicoe product demo, what, forty-eight hours before the first sightings? The timing all tracks."

"I won't ask how you mysteriously acquired intel you were never cleared for," said the Head Representative in dry tones, "but I'm going to assume her surname rhymes with 'lark.'"

That grim little smile gave way to an expression of pure innocence that would have done Anabel herself proud. "Are you denying its validity? Is Harold Jellicoe, prize arms dealer of the UCC, demo-ing a new product, or isn't he?"

"I knew all that time you spend around the press corps would come to no good end," said Gabriel Lamarque in slightly mournful tones. "Nonetheless, I agree that these wyverns are an evolved model, and I'm not pleased to see them nipping at Coalition territory. Nor am I exactly wild to be, for the moment, outnumbered. We only have one Rebelwing, after all. We need everything she has to give, and Rebelwing needs her pilot. Be glad she's picked one."

"This probably isn't a good time to mention that I've failed my mech piloting license exams, like, five times, right," said Pru desperately. "I'm telling you, Cat might have a stick up her ass, but she's right about one thing. Robo Reptile's made a mistake."

Alex rounded on her. "Do you know how long Rebelwing went missing?"

"How the hell should I know? Not my dragons, not my fantasy circus!"

"Three days," he continued, as if she hadn't spoken. "The moment wyverns were sighted over the city walls, our best weapon vanished. And we had no idea where to begin looking. Until a girl from New Columbia Prep got caught peddling black market books on the wrong side of the Barricades. That was you. Rebelwing—sentient, intelligent Rebelwing—emerged from hiding because she chose to save *you*."

Pru's mouth went dry. She'd thought he was angry, but anger—fiery and straightforward—didn't encompass the storm behind his expression. "What are you saying?"

His mouth curved. And just like that, the hurricane that was Alexandre Santiago Lamarque settled back into something boy-shaped and terribly young. "That maybe I was wrong." His gaze tracked sideways, a minute little flick of the face that hid his expression beneath his lashes. "Rebelwing doesn't need me. She needs you."

"That's absurd."

Alex's hands spread, his body language open and wry. "Very little about this situation isn't, but there's not much we can do about that right now, is there? Right now, we need you to bring your mech home."

Pru, still staring at him, swallowed her terror. Licked dry lips. "How?" she croaked.

Alex looked at his uncle. "Is the mech landing pad open?"

Gabriel Lamarque's handsome features split into a wide grin. "If I say so? Certainly."

He stood, buttoning his suit jacket, looking for all the world like he was preparing to make a speech at a gala, not escorting a would-be teenage felon to an exclusive military base. Hakeem Bishop and Jay Park rose to flank the Head Representative on either side. "Right this way."

Pru opened her mouth to say something, anything, and instead found herself falling in step behind them. She wasn't sure how these blue-blooded Coalition families managed to turn ordinary people into unwitting ducklings, but she would have gladly forked over the whole of her smuggling earnings to learn that trick.

"I don't know how to do it," Pru managed, as they trailed down a hallway, her and Alex and these three horribly important government men. She wished, more than anything, that Anabel were with them. She even kind of wished Cat were with them. Anything to put a buffer between herself and these Coalition suits. Hell, anything to put a buffer between herself and Alex, whose inscrutable black gaze hung with the weight of expectations she didn't understand. "Like, I have no idea how to summon the thing *deliberately*."

"Willpower," said Alex. "Piloting a war mech requires training and finesse, but getting a sentient machine to come when you call? You have to want it."

They emerged at what appeared to be a miniature stadium. It could have passed for a university sports arena, save the high metal walls. Pru whistled. "Holy crap. So this is where Coalition taxpayer money goes, huh?"

"Lucky for you, at the moment," muttered Bishop. Louder, he added, "Even without an active war on our hands, our military does, remarkably enough, require adequate training grounds for new war mech prototypes, Prudence."

Pru rolled her eyes, which only brought the morning-bright rays of sunlight into over-sharp focus. "So, what, I stand here, click my heels together, and wish really hard for Robo Reptile to appear, and then you'll let me go face the music at school for my no-good truant ways?" By her count, she'd have absences in all three of her morning classes by now, which meant at least three corresponding Saturday night detentions, unless her government representatives turned out to be in the habit of writing excuse notes on behalf of juvenile delinquents who accidentally bonded with sentient zillion-dollar war mechs.

"The heel clicking is optional," said Gabriel Lamarque.

Pru swallowed something she'd probably regret saying to the leader of the Barricade Coalition. "How will I know if it's working?" she asked instead.

"You'll get inside Rebelwing's head," said Alex. "You'll be able to catch sight of wherever she's gone, and call her back. You remember how the world looked inside the cockpit, right?"

Unbidden, New Columbia sprawled across her mind's eye again, panoramic high definition, like an interactive film ad. How could she forget? "Yeah."

"That's what it should look like. You'll know."

Pru shut her eyes and, feeling faintly ridiculous, wished as hard as she could. She needed a shower. She needed sleep. She needed to soothe the anxiety rollicking about in her gut. And she needed to quit replaying the moment she'd run into Alexandre Lamarque instead of Anabel in that godforsaken library study.

A few seconds later, she cracked open one eye. "It's not working."

"Are you focused on Project Rebelwing?" asked Bishop.

"Obviously," hissed Pru through grinding teeth.

"You look as though your head might explode," observed Jay Park. "Maybe you should—"

"Maybe everyone should shut up and let me concentrate!" Pru shut both eyes again, and tried to unclench her jaw.

"It's still not working," said Bishop. Even with her eyes closed, Pru could picture the downturned cast of his mouth. "Perhaps Cat was mistaken. Perhaps we all were. It's been a long night and longer morning. We ought to let the girl go home to her mother."

"Pru." Someone's hand landed on her shoulder, a bit stiffly placed, but long-fingered and warm. "What did it feel like, piloting her?" asked Alex.

Such a simple question, but how to answer it? How did you articulate the wingspan of your arms, the expanse of the city rendered sharp and strange, the freedom, holy crap, the *freedom* of it. Tears, ridiculously, pricked at the corners of her eyes. She felt so stupid—so tired, and confused, and overwhelmed by the past twenty-four hours of her life—but when Alex asked how piloting felt, all she wanted to do was cry for the joy of it.

Or maybe that was just the all-nighter's toll kicking in. It could go either way at this point, really.

Heels of her hands over streaming eyes, Pru saw it, then: the scrape of metal along concrete. She blinked, feet rooted, but some part of her mind sped along, coasting down—no, up, up the side of a building, twisting through sunlight, and landing—

She heard the shouts of the others, before she opened her eyes, but she already knew what she'd see. When she lifted her head, the dragon was still half-invisible, silver chrome creeping steadily over translucent edges as the mech uncloaked itself. Pru stumbled forward, pulse in her throat, waiting for the mech to flee, like before. To disappear. To reject her.

Her forehead met cool metal. Eyes slitted against that bright reptilian scrutiny, Pru's hands rose to cradle the shape of that carefully rendered snout, the slide of winking scales. Like magic. Like Mama's fairytales made real after all, even now at seventeen, on the grim brink of adulthood.

Then, for the second time in as many days, Pru fainted dead away.

♦

Idol Gaze: Celebrities & Lifestyle

"The New Political Cool: Meet the Fresh-Faced People's Heroes of the Barricade Coalition"
by Joseph Glazer

No, they're not film stars, though thanks to their work, the film industry continues to thrive—at least, legally speaking, behind Barricade walls. Nevertheless, veterans of the Partition Wars like Head Representative Gabriel Lamarque and his famously hand-picked cohort have achieved a level of mystique and allure more commonly ascribed to entertainers and Internet personalities than stodgy politico types. Popular think pieces have famously chalked up the newfound sexiness of Coalition leaders to their relative youth—Lamarque himself was barely twenty at the height of the Partition Wars, and retains a certain youthful swagger even now in his forties.

The sheer number of fresh-faced teens and twentysomethings that came of age—and made their careers—in the Partition Wars has undoubtedly created a new normal for politics and government. That said, not everyone thinks younger is better. Columnist Emilia Rosenbaum wrote in a fiery *Barricader's Daily* editorial last year, "The charismatically youthful appeal of the Lamarque branding has ensnared a generation of impressionable youths more entranced by the glitz and glamor of Gabriel Lamarque and his entourage than the actual grit of serious politics. The so-called 'new cool' of the Lamarque brand boasts an in-your-face style, but questionable substance. His government's youth-targeted internship program, for example, risks luring adolescents and twentysomethings into a complex world of dangerous intrigue that they are ill-equipped to handle."

Others, however, argue that the Head Representative's "new cool" brand of continental politics, buoyed by the ambitious wunderkinds throwing themselves behind his movement, is the very thing that's kept the Barricade Coalition standing in the face of the United Continental Confederacy's sheer corporate firepower. "The UCC has the numbers on their side," says Tamika Gonzales, a former Coalition intern, now a documentary filmmaker. "The folks pulling the strings at the top of the Incorporated ladder have more money, more guns, and more land. We were totally outgunned and outmanned during the Partition Wars. But we built a space for the Barricade cities off the people's desire for a place to come as you are—to exist free of shackles on speech, expression, or identity. And the people who fought for those cities, the ones running the Coalition now—people like Gabriel Lamarque—were pretty much kids when they first took a stand in the war, you know? Sometimes, I think we forget how young everyone was back then. How much we had to lose."

The Partition Wars may be over, but the fate of the Barricade Coalition remains as uncertain as any emergent power surrounded by hostile neighbors. Will Lamarque's new cool continue to see his young, democratic government through increasing political and military pressure to Incorporate? Only time—and the will of the next generation—can tell.

◆

"SO, NO MORE GRAND theft lizard incidents?" asked Anabel around a mouthful of Korean black bean noodles.

"Ha ha," said Pru. "No, whatever new sleep mode algorithm Cat foisted on her giant metal experiment seems to be working. No mechanical dragons interrupting bio lab or trying to break into the dorms to spirit me off. Rebelwing won't touch me, and I won't touch her."

"Until your mother agrees to sign the permission forms."

"Yeah, about that." Pru poked at the peanuts in her sticky rice with one metal chopstick. She hated peanuts. "I kinda sorta haven't told her yet."

Anabel leaned across the lunch table, pitching her voice low. "Well, when are you going to?"

"I don't know. It's not really the sort of conversation you have over the phone, you know?"

"You'll have to tell her some time. We're supposed to meet with Head Representative Lamarque after school today to deliver the paperwork."

"Yeah, I know." The peanuts, slowly but surely, were being ground to fine dust, which was probably making them even grosser. Pru tried not to stare too enviously at the noodles twirled around Anabel's chopsticks. "I kind of just, um, told Mama to meet me there."

"You did *what*?"

"Keep your voice down," hissed Pru. "What, you want the whole student body asking questions about what you really do for Modern Politics II?"

Anabel rolled her eyes, but her mouth still formed a nervous line. "Let me get this straight. You can't figure out how to tell your mother you scored a work-study internship with the Coalition government that she needs to sign off on. But you text her asking to meet at the *Head Representative's Mansion*, and everything is just A-OK?"

"I figured it would be easier to talk there, with Lamarque around to help explain things."

"You mean to razzle-dazzle her." Anabel's cat-eyed gaze looked something halfway between accusatory and amused. "You're counting on the Head Representative to work that old Lamarque family charm on her, so she won't yell at you for getting yourself mixed up in this mess in the first place."

"I said nothing of the sort!"

"Methinks the lady doth protest too much."

"It's barely been a week since they verified that I had an imprint for . . ." Instinctively, Pru's eyes darted once around the cafeteria, then back to Anabel. "For Rebelwing. It's a lot to process, okay? It's just, this whole thing seems a bit more believable if there's an actual adult human present to verify that it's all above-board. Security clearances and secret robot dragons and all." She took a reluctant bite of sticky rice, scrunching her mouth up around the mashed-up peanuts. "I don't know about you, but I think secret robot dragons are the sort of thing that demand adult supervision in order to seem, like, respectable."

"Especially if the supervision comes from Gabriel Lamarque."

"That too." Pru frowned. "Though to be honest, I don't think Mama was all that impressed with the name dropping. Said something about how they'd met before." Which, Pru had to admit, should have surprised her less than it did. Mama's fame as a writer had peaked during the Partition Wars. That a young, newly lauded author would cross paths with the great defender of free expression himself during those tense, bloody days was practically inevitable.

Mama had never so much as breathed Gabriel Lamarque's name before, though. Pru tried not to feel the sting of the secret, however thoughtless. It wasn't anything personal. Mama never liked talking about the Partition Wars, at least not in any serious way. Pru had given up asking those sorts of questions early in her childhood.

"Still." Anabel tapped the lacquered ends of her chopsticks against her lip. How she managed that trick without smearing her lipstick everywhere, she'd have to teach Pru some day. "You think he'll sway her? After all, he *is* our divided continent's noble defender of democracy." She grinned around the chopsticks. "Also, he's got those true-blue Lamarque eyes."

Unbidden, Pru thought of the *other* set of Lamarque eyes she'd encountered for the first time that week, dark and sharp set. How they looked late on a school night, crinkled with mirth and smiling at an audience screaming for Alexandre Santiago, the rock star schoolboy. How they'd looked the very next morning, hot with suspicion through the steady-handed sights of a plasma gun.

"Yeah," said Pru. She bit off another flavorless mouthful of dry peanut mash. "Maybe."

SCHEHERAZADE AND PROMETHEUS ——— 6

Being inside the Head Representative's Mansion was weird. Much like the Lamarques themselves, their official residence felt too self-consciously glamorous to be entirely real. The grand foyers and stern-eyed portraits would have suited a high-definition online magazine, or even an old-fashioned hardback coffee table book. Something with a highbrow continental history theme, photos of the Head Representative's portrait gallery displayed alongside some nice, heroic-looking war photography from an old Northern Front battle from the Partition Wars. That would do nicely for this place.

"I'm sorry Mama's running late," mumbled Pru for the third time.

Gabriel Lamarque, seated across from her at his great oak desk—oh god, they were literally sitting right *here*, in the Head Representative's *actual office*—stirred another cube of sugar into his tea with one hand, batting her apology aside with the other. "Please." Laugh lines crinkled the corners of his eyes. "If Sophie Wu's the same woman I knew twenty years ago, I'd be insulted at anything less than a fashionably late arrival."

"Thanks," said Pru. "For, like, doing all this, I mean. Sitting down with us in your office. Talking about the whole dragon thing. Letting me bring my mother."

"Of course. How could I refuse?" Lamarque's eyebrows climbed, waggling. "Or do you really believe all those tabloid stories about how I spirit the young people of the Barricade cities out from under their parents' noses to join my murky world of political gamesmanship?"

"You make yourself sound like some kind of revolutionary pied piper," said Pru, before she could think better of it. She clapped a hand over her mouth, but the Head Representative just laughed.

"No pied piping for me, not without the carefully reviewed permissions forms of a parent or guardian." He was still smiling, but something behind that clear-eyed grin shuttered, just for a moment. "I wouldn't wish my own adolescence—or your mother's, for that matter—on today's children. It's not a world anyone wants to return to. We do what we can to . . . well, you know."

"What, stave off dystopia?" suggested Pru, bolder now and only half joking.

Lamarque's grin went impish. A ghost of the boy he must have once been emerged between the curl of his mouth and the drawl on his tongue as he answered, "Something like that, I suppose. An increasingly difficult task, with more and more wyverns sighted on the walls of New Columbia."

Pru frowned. "Cat and Alex both mentioned a name. The guy supposedly responsible for this whole wyvern scare. J-something."

The Head Representative's expression clouded. "Jellicoe. Harold Jellicoe. Or, as tabloids love calling him, 'the father of wyverns.' Back in the heyday of his executive career, he revolutionized the way the UCC builds its war machines. It's how he became the Executive General's top arms dealer."

"The one doing some kind of product demo?" Pru swallowed, disinclined to dwell too long on what kind of product someone called the father of wyverns would be demo-ing. "The one Alex wasn't supposed to know about."

Gabriel Lamarque rubbed a hand over his nose. "Good memory. Yes, it's true that Jellicoe invented the original wyvern prototype, and equally true that Barricader intelligence has eyes on an upcoming exhibition of his new product line, but arms dealers are a dime a dozen in the UCC. We can't make assumptions, you understand."

"With respect, sir," said Pru, "that's just fancy language for 'yeah, we totally know it's this bitch, but our PR people are making us cover our asses.'"

A laugh startled out of him. "You really *are* Sophie's daughter, aren't you?"

"Guess I am." Pru scuffed a foot along the leg of her seat. "So you and Mama were war buddies back in the day, huh?"

"We were." Lamarque's expression remained clear, but he didn't offer up any further information. Hero of the Partition Wars he might be, but Pru kind of figured he had to have some politician-slickness to him too. It all seemed part and parcel with how Lamarque managed the things he knew against the things he had to do: the quiet, benign way he shuttered on some subjects while opening up like a sun over the clouds on others.

"Did you keep in touch at all, after?" Pru pressed, then bit her tongue. What a stupid question. Mama would have said something, surely.

"Not really, I'm afraid." He offered another smile, almost compulsive. "People do drift apart. My fault, probably."

The intercom on the oak desk buzzed. "Miss Sophie Wu to see you, sir."

"Send her in."

The sliding door to the Head Representative's office rumbled aside. The woman waiting at the entrance wasted no time sidling in. Her heels—poking out from a pair of pinstriped men's trousers—clicked languidly across the office. Dark eyes narrowed over a pursed scarlet mouth that looked redder still for the winks of silver threading her pitch-black chignon. "Prometheus," she drawled, husky voiced. "What a way to reunite, eh?"

Gabriel Lamarque rose to his feet, the very picture of charm as he buttoned his jacket. "No need to call me names, Sophie."

"You're my elected representative in a hard-won democracy, and I'll call you anything I like," said Sophie's mother, sounding unimpressed, and possibly bored.

"Mama!" squeaked Pru.

Lamarque waved it off. "It's all right."

"All right indeed," said Mama. She stopped just short of the Head Representative, looking him up and down. "Office life suits you, Prometheus. Wouldn't have guessed."

Opacity smoothed over his expression, making the man over in marble. He might have been a statue of some ancient historical figure, rather than the affably grinning flesh-and-blood creature who'd occupied the office moments before. "We all grow up at some point."

Mama's chin went up, vowels wide and mocking as she spoke. "And didn't you *just*."

Lamarque's clean-shaven, square-cut jaw tensed, a motion reminiscent of Alex in his more frustrated moments. The Head Representative glanced toward Pru. "Your daughter tells me you know the basics of the Coalition's work-study offer, but want some blanks filled in."

"Certainly, I do," said Mama cheerfully. "And lucky for you, I know just where to start, so I won't waste your time." Her feet shifted slightly, fists curling. Then, before anyone could utter another word, Pru's mother punched the leader of the Barricade Coalition clean across his celebrated jawline.

◆

Metafeed Books: War Week Special
"Spotlight on Sophie 'Scheherazade' Wu"
by Maxwell Vandermeer

This week, nearly two full decades ago, saw today's founding Barricaders and the Incorporated forces sign the formal peace treaty that finally declared an official end to the long and bloody Partition Wars. To celebrate this landmark anniversary, Metafeed Books sits down with artists who played a part in the war effort — from avant-garde documentarian Isobel Tanaka, to guerrilla theater actor turned alleged spy Aaron Eddington, whose family in peacetime went on to found the famous Eddington Heights Academy. However, a series on Partition War artists would be remiss not to kick things off with Sophie Wu — or, as she's better known in some circles, Scheherazade.

Is it true you got that nickname from an Incorporated Propagandist's office?

Depends on who's asking! Here, I'll rephrase your question for you: Did I get a nickname, of any kind, while working in an Incorporated Propagandist's office? To wit, did I ever work in the pocket of the enemy?

Did you?
(laughs) I love the folks at Metafeed. You don't scare from the tough questions!

Of course not! So, have it out, Scheherazade, did you cut your teeth on storytelling in the lion's den?
Hell of a way to put it. Sure, like most kids born in UCC-controlled territory, I had my run-ins with the Executive General's people. I was educated, spoke the right kind of English, and could manage a keyboard, so they stuck me in the Office of the Propagandist for a while there, which was fine and dandy until—

Gabriel Lamarque got his hands on you?
And the rest is history.

And that's it? Come on!
Look, it was pretty simple. I wanted to create wireless plays and visual novels and all those inconveniently freewheeling, imaginative things that UCC Inc. frowns on. So I fought for it.

And won.
Sure!

Or are you the brand of Barricader that isn't satisfied with the

Coalition as it stands? Would you spread Barricader values across the rest of the continent, if you could?

(laughs) A bit imperialistic, isn't that? Emilia Rosenbaum may be a sanctimonious little shit — and yes, you can quote me on that — but she's right about some things. The people who joined up with UCC Inc. had their reasons for Incorporating. Are some of them shitty reasons? Sure. But it's their own reason, their own choice. And at the end of the day, free choice is supposedly what we, the enlightened citizens of the venerable Head Representative Lamarque's government, are all about.

Sophie Wu's latest wireless drama series, *Hunting Down Dragons & Other Fairytales for the Age of Nostalgia*, drops this Friday. Subscribe right here at *Metafeed*, and don't forget to tune in next week for an exclusive interview with Aaron Eddington: actor, artist, educator, and spy!

◆

"WHAT'S GOING ON IN there?"

Alex dipped into view, interrupting Pru's half-hearted fantasy of merging with the elegant little couch outside the Head Representative's office. As it was, she'd sunk so low into the cushions, she probably looked like she was trying to hide between them. Not a bad idea, all things considered.

Instead, she glanced dolefully up into his eyes and said, "My mother just punched your uncle in the face."

Alex blinked several times at this proclamation. His silence lasted just long enough to highlight the indistinctly raised voices behind the office door. "Do you think it's an assassination attempt?" he asked.

"Your uncle hasn't called for a security detail yet." Someone behind the door snarled an expletive. Pru winced. "And he's plainly still alive, so if she's in murder mode, Mama's losing her touch. They kicked me out"—she paused to check her phone—"wow, almost fifteen minutes ago. Hell of a time to wait for a killing stroke."

"The Barricade Coalition is grateful for Mama Wu's mercy. What started the fight?"

"Me, presumably." Pru hesitated, remembering how Mama had sounded on the phone while Pru babbled about an internship opportunity with the Coalition government, and how good it would look on university applications, and wouldn't Mama like an opportunity to chat about her daughter's work-study with Head Representative Lamarque himself? An honor, such an honor.

Mama had gone quiet, then said in a funny voice, "Sure, kiddo. Why not? I'll talk to Gabriel. I'm glad he's extended the invitation."

"What," said Pru, laughing nervously, "like you're on a first-name basis with Gabriel Lamarque?"

"Last we met, we were." Mama hadn't offered anything beyond that. Then she'd turned up in the Head Representative's office three days later, walked right up to his fine oak desk, and sucker punched him. Pru probably would have found the whole thing funny, in an absurd sort of way, if she weren't so mortified.

Alex was frowning. "Your mum doesn't want you working with us?"

Pru felt her mouth curl involuntarily at *mum*, the Northern twang to his odd hybrid accent, weirdly charmed. "I don't know that *I* want me working with you. I'm not exactly an ace pilot, or the carefully groomed scion of an old revered Barricader family. Like, you do re-alize I'm way likelier to crash a zillion dollars' worth of ragey robot reptile into a skyscraper than to successfully defend North American democracy in the event of a second Partition War, right?"

Pru had survived most of her prep school career by avoiding ac-tivities she was likeliest to fail at. Test-piloting a living weapon was probably one of them. And being single-handedly responsible for the downfall of the Barricade Coalition would look a lot worse on her résumé than almost flunking Intro to Robotics.

It was the wrong thing to say. Alex's frown deepened, inscruta-bility layered into those inkwell eyes of his. Pru folded her arms and tucked her spine against the couch, bracing for anger or, worse, disappointment.

"Is Rebelwing's imprint really so terrible?" he asked instead. "You're not wrong to be afraid, but there's so much more to Rebelwing than fear. You should know that better than anyone. You've been in the cockpit. You've *flown*. I saw your expression when you called the mech to the landing pad, that morning in the safehouse."

"Yeah, well, then I fainted. But no," Pru allowed after a moment. She thought of the city, spiraling, cinematic. "It wasn't—it's not—terrible. The imprint, I mean."

Alex smiled. It was a shy, fleeting thing, not at all like his aggres-sively charismatic stage face, but more than enough to raise Pru's pulse, which offended her on principle. Alex was hot, but hot was easy to pull off, if you were rich and confident and cared about clothes and grooming. *Quit falling for that basic shit*, Pru ordered her pulse.

Ba-bum-ba-bum-ba-bum, replied her pulse, willfully rebellious.

The door slid open with a slam that nearly gave Pru a heart attack.

Out stalked Mama, Gabriel Lamarque on her heels. "Shove it up your pretty backside, Prometheus," Pru's mother said to the Head Representative of the Barricade Coalition, lipsticked mouth savoring all the consonants. "I'm not one of your fawning sycophants. I've given quite enough to your wars. I'll thank you not to snatch up my daughter too, if you please." To Pru, she snapped, "Come on, kiddo. We're leaving."

"Um," said Pru, glancing between the two furious adults and Alex's stricken expression. "Ma, this is probably a not-great time to tell you that I'll probably get kicked out of school for illegal book smuggling if I don't take the Head Representative's work-study offer, right?"

"Believe me, I tried that line of argument," said Gabriel Lamarque. Gingerly, he rubbed his jaw.

"Yeah, nice try, asshole," said Mama. "Public schools exist for a reason. New Columbia Prep's not the only decent university feeder in the Barricade cities."

"Mama!" cried Pru, unsure whether to be more scandalized by Mama swearing at the hero of the Partition Wars, or the cavalier dismissal of a school whose tuition had eaten up most of Mama's freelance money.

"Well, it's not," said Mama, her mouth a thin crimson line. "Nothing wrong with New Columbia High. Pru would do just fine there. Barricader prep schools don't have a monopoly on smart kids, just on smart rich kids."

The Head Representative sighed. "I'm not denying that, Sophie. But it's not wrong for children to—"

"I'm not talking about children, plural," said Mama bluntly. "I'm talking about *my* child. She's not a soldier, she's a student. And the

Partition Wars are over, Incorporated weapons demos and wyvern rumors be damned. I realize this may be a new concept for you, but no one's obligated to fight battles for your convenience these days."

"I want to pilot Rebelwing," Pru blurted out.

The entire room seemed to expand, then zoom in on Pru. "Not for anyone's convenience," she mumbled, hot-cheeked under the attention. "Except maybe mine."

Mama was right. Pru would probably do just fine at New Columbia High. Plenty of friends and neighbors, with equal smarts but modest means, had done more with less. If she transferred now, she could quit worrying about how big everyone around her seemed: bigger brains, bigger bank accounts, bigger ambitions. She could quit feeling small. For one taut moment, she was tempted.

Then she remembered how dragon wings felt. In Rebelwing's cockpit, she hadn't been small at all. "I don't want to leave New Columbia Prep, Mama, not when I've only got a year left before university." Pru swallowed. "And, you know, if the UCC really is developing new wyverns, I'd rather not see the city go up in a blaze of plasma fire before I even graduate. I have the mech's imprint. This will work." Sometimes, when you said things aloud, even if you didn't really have the confidence to back them up, you could fake certainty.

"Kid," Mama began, "this isn't something you just—"

"I think maybe we should talk alone," interrupted Pru. Her pulse drummed a steady rhythm inside her throat, but she met her mother's eyes. "You and me. Please."

Sophie Wu's fiery gaze softened, just a fraction, the shift in her face probably invisible to anyone who hadn't lived under her roof for seventeen years. She nodded once, sharp, and turned back into the Head Representative's office. Pru, biting back a curse, cast a desperate look at the Lamarque men, who were staring after Pru's mother with identically raised brows that would have been comical if the situation weren't such a shitshow.

Gabriel Lamarque smiled, or tried to. His facial muscles, usually so obedient to positivity, didn't seem inclined toward the expression just then. Again, he rubbed the spot on his jaw where Mama had socked him. "Take your time," he said. His voice, habitually rich and friendly, sounded thin, like he'd spread it beyond his means. "Maybe she'll listen to you. I'm afraid she's not in a mood for hearing much of anything from me."

Pru, chewing on the inside of her cheek, ducked past him into the office. The door shut behind her. Inside, Mama was sitting on top of Gabriel Lamarque's great oak desk, stilettos shucked and ankles crossed. A long white cigarette jutted from the corner of her mouth, which she lit with irritable efficiency. "So," she said around the plume of smoke, "we seem to find ourselves at an impasse, kid."

"You can't smoke in here," said Pru.

"Watch me."

"You also can't go about punching the leader of the last free cities of the continent in the face. God, I still can't believe you punched him in the face."

"It's a very pretty face, but surprisingly sturdy. It shall recover."

Pru buried her palms against her eyes. "I don't get it, Ma. I thought you'd be pleased about me making something of my education."

"Aw, kid." Her mother sighed explosively around the cigarette. "Yes. The Coalition—and Gabriel Lamarque—will make something of you, and your education, if you let them. But is that what you want? Really?"

"I don't know!" snapped Pru. "Why does everyone keep asking me that, like I have to know my whole life plan and career path at the age of seventeen? You guys are worse than the university admissions counselors back at school."

The corner of her mother's mouth curled. "Admissions counselors? My only child wounds me!" Sobering, she plucked the cigarette from her mouth, and said in a low voice, "Look, I get it, okay? This is probably my fault on some level. I should have told you about my history with Gabriel Lamarque, and the kind of person he is, a long time ago. I don't like talking about the Partition Wars."

"Did something happen between you two?" Pru pressed. "Please don't tell me the Head Representative of the Barricade Coalition is secretly a supervillain, or a scorned ex-lover of yours, or something equally horrifying." A terrible thought struck Pru. "Oh god, we're not secretly related, are we? Is this why you never told me who knocked you up during the war?"

"Well, he's not a supervillain," Mama conceded. She sounded like she thought she was being pretty magnanimous with that pronouncement. "Quite the opposite, really." She pulled a face, mouth twitching. "And no, he's not your secret bio dad, so you can quit worrying about whether you're being accidentally incestuous every time you make eyes at young Alexandre."

"Oh my god!" Pru was going to die. She was going to sink through the floor of the Head Representative's office and die, right here, right now. "See, this is the kind of talk that most family therapists would have a field day with. Where are you even getting that from?"

Mama snorted. "I may be over the hill, and one of those wretched career women who the *Barricader's Daily* columnists are forever ragging on for sending their kids to boarding school, but I'm still your mother. Give me some credit here. I know what you look like when you're sweet on someone." She batted long eyelashes. "You have my eyes."

"No one says 'sweet on' anymore," said Pru. She also didn't have Mama's eyes, but Pru didn't say that part aloud. Mama, with her wide brown eyes and timelessly neat bone structure, had been blessed with the sort of careless beauty that followed its mistress happily into middle age. Pru wasn't bad looking, not really, but some asshole's genes—probably her father's, all things considered—had bequeathed her limp hair that framed a bowling ball of a head, a forgettable face, and eyes that mostly made Pru look like she might doze off at any moment. Which, given her sleeping patterns lately, was probably kind of fitting.

"Whatever," said Mama. "I only wanted to give you your due diligence on Lamarque men. There's trouble that's worth the pair of cheekbones it comes with, and then there's trouble that's not. The Lamarques are the latter."

Pru, frowning, crossed her arms. "So he's not evil," she mused aloud, "and he's not some terrible floozy who got you pregnant and, like, abandoned you to the trials and tribulations of single motherhood. But something still went sour with Gabriel Lamarque during the war, didn't it?"

Mama took a long drag off the cigarette. "Sure. It was me. I soured." She tapped the ashes off the side of the Head Representative's desk. "Specifically, I soured on Prometheus. Nothing personal, mind you. We partnered together for a long time. Worked well together, everyone said."

"But?"

"But nothing. Prometheus and I just stopped seeing eye to eye at a certain point."

"How come you keep calling him that?"

"What, Prometheus?" Mama exhaled on another cloud of smoke. "Because he brings fire to the people. I expect that much will always be true about him. He brings warmth and light and more passion than is sensible for anybody. You ever wonder why the UCC's most infamous weapons of choice were wyverns—not bombs, not cyborg shock troops, but mechs literally, deliberately constructed in the shape of mythical predators?"

"I don't know, Mama," said Pru. "Melodrama? Boredom? The thwarted artistic dreams of a creepy weapons engineer who watched too many monster movies?"

"Fear," said Mama. "Because make no mistake, my girl, the Executive General wanted us scared. Too scared to think, and therefore biddable. Killing will win you a war, if you spend enough blood, but fear—real, mindless fear—will win you subjugation. When I was seventeen, practically the entire continent had already Incorporated. The Barricading movement was a joke. Revolution was barely a child's fantasy. Until Gabriel Lamarque showed up."

Mama blew smoke at the pale, elegantly arched ceiling. "You want to know how you turn the tide of a culture war? You give the people a paragon. Some symbol of hope and goodness, ready-made for a pedestal. And if you're smart, you find yourself a paragon who's a true believer, charismatic and pretty and just goddamn genuine enough to make you want to believe in his cause, the same way you believe in the man. Prometheus—Gabriel—was perfect."

"I'm sensing a 'but,'" said Pru.

"Oh, there isn't one, not really." Mama waved the cigarette like a stage prop before sticking it back in her mouth, smoke blooming in hazy shapes around the Head Representative's desk, which would smell of burning tobacco for days to come, Pru was pretty sure. "Prometheus is the real thing. He'll ask you to fight and die for him, and send you off to do it, and if you do lose life or limb or soul to his cause, he'll mourn your loss too. And the worst part is that he'll *really mean it*. Probably shed some real goddamn tears at your funeral and everything. Which, in my opinion, just makes this all harder on us than it really has to be."

"Isn't that a good thing, though?" Pru pressed. "Like, wouldn't you rather have a leader who believes in the same things you do than one who doesn't?"

"Aw, kid." Mama's smile around the cigarette was thin lipped. "Prometheus and I fought side by side about a million years ago. Back then, I sided with him willingly—hell, happily. He never coerced me to do anything I didn't want to do. I'll cop to all that." She exhaled smoke. "But whoever said that now, a million years later, he and I must still march through life in lockstep, like the sweet, stupid kids we were? Who says you have to believe the same things forever?"

Pru blinked. "You're an author. He's the Head Representative of the Barricade Coalition. How could you *not* believe in the same things?"

Mama blinked back. "Goodness. I'd forgotten how simple everything was, at seventeen."

"Don't condescend to me."

"I'm not," said Mama. "That's what I'm trying to tell you. Kid, I *was* seventeen, when I left my cushy desk job pushing propaganda for an Incorporated office. Seventeen, when I ran off to side with the Barricaders in a war I wasn't sure they could win. I know how it feels, to make those choices. I haven't been seventeen in a long time, but I do remember what it's like, to really believe in something, with all your heart." She pointed her cigarette at Pru. "My question, daughter mine, is this: Do you?"

Pru had no good answer to that. "I believe in finishing school where I started," she said at last. "And I believe in not getting myself thrown in jail for petty crime. And I . . . I believe that I'm supposed to fly Rebelwing. Or try, at least. If nothing else, work-study will be good for university admissions. Isn't my education worth a few hours in a cockpit?"

Silence hung between them for the space of another drag on Mama's cigarette, the darkness in her eyes unreadable. "You tell me, kiddo. If Incorporated wyverns breach the wall. If we see a second Partition War in our lifetime, and you're deployed to the front lines. Will your education still be worth it?"

Pru eyed the orange glow of the cigarette. She tried to imagine what Mama must have seen in those war-torn days before Pru's birth: monsters made of metal, calibrated for the kind of fear that made your own brain betray you.

Unbidden, she remembered Alex smiling in his rumpled schoolboy tie outside Cat's coffeehouse, how he'd talked about sharing *the marketplace of ideas*, the same dreamy way people in romance novels talked about *true love*, like the exchange of information and expression could armor you against anything. *Ignorance is really just a different kind of fear.*

"If my education's not worth fighting for," Pru said at last, "then what the hell else was the first war for?"

Mama met Pru's gaze with another thin-lipped curve of her mouth, not quite a grin. "Touché, daughter mine." Her eyes were bright with some unnamable emotion. "Very well, I'll sign the permission forms on two conditions. One," she ticked off her index finger, "you and Prometheus check in with me biweekly. I want progress reports on what you're up to. If this is going to be a work-study with parental sign-offs, it's also going to be a work-study with a reasonable level of parental supervision. Gabriel Lamarque so much as takes you on a field trip into a UCC zone without my say-so, and I'll take his balls. Clear?"

Pru's jaw twitched, half exasperation, half relief. In truth, she'd expected something like that. "Crystal. But what's the second condition?"

Mama was already sliding off the Head Representative's desk, smoothing out her trousers while the cigarette dangled from the corner of her mouth. "Oh," she said breezily, sashaying back toward the door, "you're grounded for your entire summer break for the whole book smuggling thing. You hurting for more money during the school year? Don't worry about my feelings—you *tell* me, understand? You don't want jail time for petty crime? Don't do petty crime."

"Don't do petty crime?" Pru echoed, incredulous. "You punched the Head Representative in the face!"

"Sure I did." Mama bent to retrieve her high heels, and tossed a grin over her shoulder, through the lingering haze of smoke. The smell of tobacco burned beneath Pru's nose. "I consider myself tough, but fair. Now let's go tell Prometheus and his pretty purple jaw that we've reached an agreement on this Modern Politics II bullshit."

COLLISION COURSE ————————————— 7

Modern Politics II, when you got down to it, was actually kind of a terrible class, even when you were only doing the watered-down, half-credit version designed for burnt-out overachievers who couldn't stomach the midterm project. The teacher looked ready to fall asleep next to the flickering 3-D smartboard, reading the contents of the slides off in a monotone. Pru had picked up on all his talking points the night before, just from doing the reading. Hell, she'd picked up *more*.

From her seat at the back of the lecture hall, Pru could see at least five kids texting under their desks. Two more looked busy writing up what were clearly assignments for other classes. Three in Pru's row were blatantly snoring, the light from the smartboard animations playing over their closed eyelids.

"Well, yeah," said Anabel, when Pru observed as much. "Everyone knows showing up to lecture for Modern Politics II after midterms is pretty much a formality. This bit of the course isn't really about discussions or essays. The entire point is the work-study. People are too busy kissing ass at their internships to treat it like a proper schoolroom class."

"Or staging illicit rock concerts in the auditorium."

"Or securing jobs for after university!"

"Or learning to pilot giant dragon mechs."

Anabel's mouth curved. "Or that," she admitted, low-voiced. "You ready for next period?"

"Does it matter?"

"Come on, don't be like that," chided Anabel. "Most kids doing community service for black market media smuggling would probably be stuck, like, picking up trash on the beach after one of those big gaudy No Man's Land parties, or cleaning public toilets or something—"

"Gross!"

"—so you could at least pretend to be passably excited about getting to *ride around in the cockpit of a sentient, state-of-the-art war mech* for yours."

"I'm not—" Not what? Pru hesitated. The notion of what she was really doing, sounded out in actual words, was batshit crazy if you lingered on it too long. "Why yes," she imagined explaining during a university admissions interview, "I'm test-piloting Project Rebelwing, a sentient mobile suit prototype literally shaped like a fairytale dragon, which also happens to be the Barricade Coalition's best line of defense against the cybernetic monsters cooked up by the fearmongering, arms-dealing megacorporation trying its level best to stamp out democracy!"

"A work-study internship for Modern Politics II" just sounded so much cleaner.

"I'm not ungrateful," Pru said, as they started down the hall toward the off-campus trains. "Alex asked me if the imprint was so bad, that day Mama signed off on all the paperwork. I told him it wasn't. And it's not. It's—"

Exhilarating. Terrifying.

"Scary, but kind of neat," said Pru.

"Oh, *Alex* asked." Anabel bumped her shoulder against Pru's.

"Why are you saying his name like that?"

"Like what?"

Pru rolled her eyes. "Never mind." She was halfway down the platform escalator when Anabel caught her elbow. "He talks about you, you know," said Anabel. "Alex, I mean."

This both was and wasn't a conversation Pru wanted to be having twenty minutes before she was due in a training yard with a giant metal dragon. Gently, she shrugged Anabel's fingers off her jacket sleeve. "Uh huh."

"I'm serious." Anabel's nose wrinkled, as she pitched her voice low, into an approximation of Alex's. "He's all, 'Pru said this, Pru said that, oh Anabel, why is she like this?' I told him if you're getting under his skin that badly, he should tell you, not me."

"I know I annoy Alex," said Pru, stepping onto the metro platform toward the Head Representative's Mansion. "Which is valid, since he annoys me too. You don't have to rub it in."

Following suit, Anabel exhaled, sharp and blustery, the way she did when something annoyed her. "Don't take this the wrong way, Pru-Wu, but you're maybe the second dumbest smart kid I know."

"Gee, thanks." A horrible possibility occurred to Pru. Glancing toward Anabel's pinched, narrow-eyed expression, Pru gathered all the Good Friend Wiles she had, and said, "Just because he and I don't get on doesn't mean you can't . . . like him." It even made a certain kind of sense, Anabel liking Alex. They were cut from the same cloth, both of them all sharp-boned elegance brimming with passion: young scions of old, important Barricader families that practically pissed liberty. Pru wondered why she hadn't considered the pairing before.

Anabel shot her a funny look. "Of course I can like him," she said. Then, like a stone sinking into the pit of Pru's belly: "And I do. I always have, ever since we were children."

Well. Like she'd told herself two seconds ago. That made sense. Pru twitched her shoulders, as if shrugging off a sudden, invisible weight, and pretended to be super interested in the train that came rumbling up to the platform. "Come on," she told Anabel, rough voiced, stepping through the sliding doors, "a giant mechanical dragon awaits us. Put on your excited face."

◆

Barricading Beat: Your Number One Source for Citizen Journalism!
Posted by 1amARQu3 FAN

An anonymous tip suggests that this year's round of No Man's Land parties — the infamous beachside extravaganzas for the glamorous and wealthy from both sides of the Barricades — will see a series of new product exhibitions by some of UCC Inc.'s most notorious entrepreneurs, sure to shock and awe! What are your predictions for the guest list, and what sort of mechanical marvels and monstrosities might appear on display? Discuss in comments!!!

◆

THE "TRAINING YARD," AS twinkling-eyed Gabriel Lamarque had called it, was a nice euphemism for the video game–worthy military base that greeted Pru at the address he'd assigned her. It made the mech landing pad where she'd first summoned Rebelwing look like Pru's childhood bedroom. She whistled long and low when the fine chrome door whooshed aside to admit her. "What is this, a space station?"

Chrome, the same bright silver as Rebelwing's scales, plated the floor as far as her eyes could see, rising into convex walls that swooped a graceful arc toward the distant blue of the sky, like the inside of a moon missing its top. Slicing razor-thin angles through its center was a series of balconies boasting three-dimensional camera displays trained on the great silver floor below. It was as if an overbudgeted space opera movie set had gone and had a baby with a modern art exhibit at some avant-garde museum.

A clear glass elevator descended through the balcony levels. Jay Park, resplendent in a dove gray waistcoat, emerged flanked on either side by Cat and Alex. Self-consciously, Pru smoothed the pleats of her secondhand uniform skirt.

"Let me open by making this clear," announced Anabel's cousin in mournful tones. "Supervising this work-study period is technically Hakeem's job. As Chief of Staff to the Head Representative, he's responsible for the care and handling of our military resources, not least of which includes Project Rebelwing. However, out of the goodness of my heart, I have volunteered—"

"Voluntold," said Cat, clipped and corrective. "He was voluntold."

"I have volunteered," Jay continued loudly, "to train you in the art of mowing down your enemies with a giant mechanical lizard. Should be good fun for us all, barring engine grease on my pocket squares."

"Us?" asked Pru. Her gaze darted between Cat's habitual scowl and the sideways set of Alex's enigmatic smile.

Jay's eyebrows lifted. "Us," he confirmed. "You. Alex. Cat."

"What do I need them here for?" Pru blurted out before she could stop herself.

Jay's eyebrows almost disappeared behind the snow white sweep of his bangs. "There's precious little point in learning to pilot a state-of-the-art war mech without a worthy opponent, Prudence. Rejoice, opponents don't get much worthier than young Alexandre here. Once you've mastered basic flight maneuvers, we'll try some sparring. You'll be facing off against Alex in your first combat assessment, which will take place precisely . . ." With casual finesse, he pulled a holographic calendar up on his phone, three-dimensional Coalition colors springing to dire, numerically alarming life. ". . . oh, six weeks from now."

"Six weeks!" yelled Pru. She'd gotten more time to study for calculus finals. She hated calculus.

"Harold Jellicoe's product demo is scheduled six weeks from now, according to the latest intel," said Alex in carefully neutral tones.

"So?"

"So we'll want Rebelwing saddled with a reasonably competent pilot by then," said Jay. "That's half the fun of an arms race, you know. Never being certain of the exact specs of your enemy's arsenal, and thus frantically building your own on limited time. Quite a bit like studying for midterms, as I recall."

"What the hell am I supposed to be doing in *six weeks*?"

"What else?" Jay gave one of those unconcerned shrugs that old monied Coalition boys clearly never grew out of, even late into their twenties. "Learn. You wouldn't want to fail Modern Politics II. Or die," he added thoughtfully.

"Until those six weeks are up, Hakeem Bishop has thoughtfully stationed me here to ensure that Rebelwing doesn't malfunction and kill you both," said Cat dryly, inspecting her knuckles. "Jay and Alexandre, unlike yourself, may be experienced war mech pilots, but neither are engineers."

Pru eyed Jay's fine suit, his fashionably dyed hair. "You're a war pilot too?"

"Darling," said Jay, batting his lashes and sounding uncannily like Anabel, "I'm a Park. You know what they say about Cornelius Park's grandchildren: we were born with war mech ignition keys in one hand, a plasma gun in the other, and a silver spoon in each and every one of our well-bred mouths. Now, let's get started, shall we? We'll begin with the basics. Let's see how well you fly a few laps around the field."

Pru pulled a face. She'd never liked piloting mechs of any kind— even the benign, old-fashioned transport mechs that ferried passengers between Barricade cities and Incorporated zones. She hadn't been lying to the Head Representative about the number of times she'd failed her licensing exams. By the time she finally scraped through the practical by the skin of her teeth after the requisite forty hours in a cockpit, she'd sworn up and down that she'd never willingly get behind the wheel of a mech again. That was what automated vehicles, metro passes, and ride share apps were for.

Still, she'd thought piloting Rebelwing might go better. The next hour of so-called "basics" proceeded to prove her thoroughly wrong.

Piloting a sentient mobile suit wasn't anything like piloting the clunky practice mechs Pru's grouchy licensing instructors had foisted on her. For one thing, you had no steering wheel, and for another, you had no terrified yet underpaid adult sitting next to you in a cockpit, ready to slam the well-worn emergency brake in case you started—completely by accident!—diving toward an automated vehicular lane. Pru supposed that on some base level, she ought to be grateful for that.

She was still pretty terrible at the whole exercise, though. The first time she'd flown as one with Rebelwing, she hadn't thought of the cockpit as a cockpit. She'd simply been a silver-winged thing above the city, unsure where she ended and the chrome-crafted flurry of scales began. But here, sitting in the center of this obscenely expensive training yard, trying to bend a state-of-the-art mobile suit to her own lackluster will, Pru was too aware of all the ways she didn't fit. The space of the cockpit felt either too small or too large no matter what she did. Its construction had been flexibly designed, crafted from millions of tiny metal scales that shifted and rippled and heaved under the mech's—and its pilot's—whims. As such, the size of the interior fluctuated, sometimes encasing you skin to skin, an embrace that turned the dragon more into an extension of the human body than a standalone mech; other times, the walls of the cockpit expanded, stretching outward from the pilot's seat.

Idly, Pru wondered if they'd all be better off if she invited one of the Coaltion's various backseat mech drivers to hang out here in the cockpit with her. Let someone else wield the responsibility of this great temperamental metal beast, while she sat here flexing an imprint that hadn't done much at all for her so far, unless you counted the headache slowly pulsing its way from her temples toward the front of her skull. The least they could have provided was a copilot who'd know what the hell they were doing.

Instead, they'd provided her with an earpiece full of pissed-off engineer.

"I do not understand!" Cat was practically yelling over the ear-piece's comms device. "You escaped Incorporated territory in that mech! You survived your joy ride over the rooftops of New Columbia with no preparation at all! What on earth is the matter with you now?"

Pru glared through the lenses of Rebelwing's eyes, trying in vain to pull up from that endless silver floor. This, incidentally, did nothing for her headache. "Gee, I don't know," she snapped. Spitefully, she twitched her fingers through the scale-walled cockpit until she found the wireless system, then jacked the volume up for emphasis. "Maybe the constant barrage of *people yelling in my ear!*"

She might never be used to this sensation. It wasn't like trying to pilot a transport mech, and it wasn't like taking the train, or even running around under her own power. It was all of those feelings, and none of them. Nothing could really prepare you for this sense of moving across air and land as something *more* than yourself, the cockpit of your mech built into the span of arms that were now wings, the windows of a vehicle reflected in high-definition camera angles through eyes that could scan the world around you at three hundred and sixty degrees.

And now, Pru couldn't figure out how to steer the damn thing. She had a better shot at scoring full rides to every university on the continent than she did of convincing Rebelwing to fly an entire lap. Hell, Pru would cry with gratitude if the mech so much as moved five feet in the correct direction. *Fly UP, you stupid lizard,* she tried to tell Rebelwing, thinking as hard as she could about the imprint on her brain.

But, like most things involving Pru's brain—schoolwork, anxiety levels, her attention span during that terrible Modern Politics II lecture—the mech seemed determined not to cooperate.

"I do not understand," Cat repeated. "You have the imprint. This should *work*."

"Well, it doesn't," said Pru mulishly.

"Just try," snapped a new voice. This one sounded nothing at all like Cat. Alex, Pru realized, stomach flipping. "For god's sake, Pru," he said, like he was one of their stupid prep school teachers, already disappointed before he even finished marking up one of Pru's more half-assed final exams.

"It's not that easy!" Pru massaged her temples, and tried to ignore the vaguely mortifying prick of tears behind her eyes. "I didn't train for this like you did—"

"You have the imprint," said Alex.

"Well, if you think you can do so much better, why don't you come here and get in the cockpit yourself!" Pru's mouth snapped shut. Silence in her earpiece.

"I would," said Alex, without any particular vehemence, voice cold and calm. "But I don't have the imprint."

The accusation sat unspoken in the crackling wireless space between them. Pru squeezed her eyes shut, jaw tight. Resentment churned like a miserable hurricane in her belly. "All right, Robo Reptile, you heard him, *move your damn tail*."

Too quickly, the ground exploded out from under her. With a shout, she tried to fling her arms out for balance, only to remember that they were wings now, wings slicing the howl of air as they fanned out before her. The world tilted, as Pru fought the mech for control of their melded bodies. "Slow down, slow down!"

Rebelwing was not interested in slowing down. Probably, she was mad that Pru had cursed her out so many times in the span of one hour, and was exacting her robot retribution.

"Pru!" Static in her ear. She couldn't tell who'd yelled her name. Maybe Alex, maybe Cat. Probably both of them at once, wondering why they'd ever entrusted this gazillion-dollar tantrum lizard into the hands of a mopey teenage felon.

"Slow it down!" yelled Alex-slash-Cat in her earpiece, only it came out sounding more like "Slow," a very noisy clatter, followed by a hiss, "it," clatter clatter, long buzz, oh, listen to that, a lovely high-pitched microphone shriek, "DOWN!"

"I'm trying, I'm trying!" Pru yelled back, which was kind of an impressive feat, considering how she was pretty much spinning ass over heels through airspace. The yelling only seemed to encourage Rebelwing, who—with a rebellious, mechanical hum—hurtled even faster across the field. Sunlight screamed through the lenses of its eyes, straight into Pru's.

"Slow down, slow down, slow down," she babbled through rattling teeth, thinking the orders as hard as she possibly could at the beast. Faith. She needed to have faith in this alleged neural connection she shared with the giant metal monstrosity currently trying its cheerful best to kill her. Easy enough. Faith.

The dragon roared, and began plummeting toward earth.

"No, no, no!" Chrome tiles zoomed in on Pru's eyeballs. All meditative thoughts of faith and oneness with machinery fled her brain. "Pull up, pull up, oh my god, pull up!"

Rebelwing flew faster.

The great silver field grew deadly against Pru's sight line. If someone was speaking into the earpiece, Pru couldn't tell. The voice had dissolved into an incomprehensible hum.

Pru shut her eyes. Her final, absurd thought was that it really was for *nothing*—meeting the Head Representative, getting Mama to sign off on the internship, all of it—since smashed-up corpses couldn't get thrown out of school or attend university anyway.

The dragon slowed.

Pru cracked open one mistrustful eye. She wasn't imagining it. Like that broken elevator in the Incorporated pachinko parlor weeks ago, the mech really was slowing her descent. At this rate, Pru would develop a crippling fear of heights before she got anywhere with the whole piloting thing.

With one final rattle of her gears, Rebelwing screeched to a halt just above the floor, then collapsed in a heap. Through the lenses of her eyes, Pru spotted the mech floating opposite them, a small, oblong transport aircraft. Leaning halfway out the mech's popped top was Alex Lamarque, earpiece still in, one hand raised high and clutching a remote emergency break. Wind breaking over the tops of those great chrome walls peeled his dark hair back from an uncharacteristically chalk-pale face. He looked pissed.

Pru flexed her fingers first, then her toes. When she found that both sets of joints still worked, she unbuckled herself from the manual restraints inside the dragon's cockpit. Grunting, she yanked on her arms until Rebelwing reluctantly freed her limbs from her metal body. Girl and dragon went from one to two. Pru ground one newly freed elbow against the top of the mech until one of the exits popped with a hiss. She pulled herself out of the opening, swearing under her breath as the metal edges caught along the pleats of her uniform skirt.

"What the hell was that?" yelled a voice in the distance, half drowned by the wind.

It took Pru three blinks to recognize Alex balanced astride the oblong mech opposite Rebelwing. Without the zoom-in features behind the dragon's eyes, he cut a distant shape on the peripheries of Pru's straining sight line. She gave her earpiece a good clap, flipping its mic function back on.

"—half-assed and suicidal!" Alex was yelling, his voice now magnified against Pru's eardrum. "If you weren't going to take this seriously, my uncle should have just let you get expelled from school and have done with it!"

"Yeah, I got it," Pru said loudly over the wireless, to cover the panicked thump of her heart. It was jarring, hearing Alex so openly angry, fury turned hot and kinetic, instead of cool and taciturn. "Thanks for saving my life, by the way. Sorry to have taken you out of your way."

"I wasn't going to let you *crash our best anti-wyvern weapon* to your death."

Pru's nails pinched her palms. "Good! I'm glad my death didn't inconvenience any of you!"

The figure in the distance made what looked like a suspiciously rude gesture. "You know that's not what I meant!"

"Whatever." Before Alex could retort, Pru yanked the earpiece from her head and tossed it back into the depths of the dragon's cockpit. She could still hear him shouting faintly in the distance. Ignoring him, she turned and slid down the dragon's back to the grass. She landed shaky-legged, heart still racing, took one unwieldy step, and nearly collided with a very bemused Jay Park.

Anabel's cousin glanced at Pru as though appraising an expensive automated car that might have a defunct motor or two. "Well," he said, crisp voweled, "that could have gone better, wouldn't you say?" The corners of his eyes crinkled. "Lucky thing I got to observe most of it from a distance, or it would have been two lives poor Alex would have to save this afternoon."

Well, screw you too, Male Knockoff Version of Anabel, thought Pru. Aloud she mumbled, "Hell of an understatement," and tried to shoulder her way past him.

His fingers caught her elbow. Pru bore it tense muscled. She was getting really sick of members of the Park family manhandling her when all she wanted was to storm off in a properly self-pitying huff. "Alex isn't trying to be unkind," said Jay. "No one in their right mind would expect a kid test-piloting a sentient mech for the first time to do a perfect job. He's just protective of—"

"Liberty. Democracy. Yeah, yeah, I've heard the speeches."

Jay shot her a funny look that reminded Pru uncomfortably of Anabel's more judgmental expressions. "Cat," he said. "Alex is protective of Cat. They've been through a lot together, you understand? We know this arrangement isn't easy on you, but it's not easy on them either. This," he dropped her elbow to gesture expansively at the dragon, "was their dream for a long time before you came into the picture."

Pru folded her hands behind her back, abruptly uncomfortable. Cat had been an Incorporated citizen once upon a time, she remembered. "How did it happen?" she asked Jay. "I mean, I got Cat's whole spiel about her old life back in the UCC. But how does a formerly Incorporated refugee cross paths with a Lamarque? Why would she and Alex . . ."

She trailed off at the sight of Jay's foxlike Park-bred smile. Slowly, he shook his head, thoughtful amusement written across his features. "That's not my story to give away. You really want to know, you go to the proper source."

Pru stared at him, aghast. "What the hell is that supposed to mean?"

"My word, how is it that all of my young cousin's friends are simultaneously so clever, yet so remarkably thick-headed?" Jay knocked his knuckles lightly against Rebelwing's chrome-scaled flank. "Alexandre tells me that Rebelwing sought you out herself. Found you. *Chose* you. Cat may not be overly fond of you—or, well, anyone—but I won't fault that girl's engineering skill. If the beast she specifically designed to imprint on Alexandre Lamarque imprinted instead on you, well." He gave a low whistle. "Our Rebelwing must have good reason."

"If you're trying to tell me that Alex and I have anything remotely in common, you're crazier than your cousin," said Pru flatly.

"Thick-headed, the lot of you," Jay repeated mournfully. His long dark eyes gleamed at her. "Have you considered that maybe, just maybe, you don't know everything there is to know about a boy you've interacted with for all of, what, four hours total? Anabel tells me you didn't even realize Alex was Gabriel Lamarque's nephew when you first met."

"I did so recognize him!" lied Pru, cheeks heating. "It just . . . wasn't immediate, okay? Not everyone follows the digital society pages on the holo-networks every hour of every day!"

"You might consider the society pages, for a start, at least," said Jay. "You could learn something valuable about the boy whose mech you're meant to pilot."

"Like what, his favorite color? His dating life?"

Anabel's cousin was already shaking his head, turning to walk across the field. "Six weeks until your first combat assessment, Prudence! Don't forget, if you can't fly, you can't spar!"

"His secret identity as a problematic yet charismatic vigilante?" yelled Pru. "His tormented history with his childhood music teacher?"

Hands in his trouser pockets, Jay tossed a wink over his shoulder. "All yours to discover, dear girl. Meanwhile, do try and convince Rebelwing not to kill you, or more importantly, everyone in your vicinity. Haven't you heard? Liberty itself is at stake."

With a frustrated huff, Pru rounded on the dragon. Alex's emergency remote brake had put Rebelwing back in sleep mode, the lights in the eyes dulled, like a faded memory. Feeling silly and helpless, Pru lifted her fingers to its dormant snout, as if stroking a live animal. "What's going on with you, girl?" she whispered. "You're the one who picked me. What am I missing here?" She swallowed a nonsensical lump in her throat. "Why . . . why am I not enough?"

The cool metal beneath her fingers remained silent, hiding the unknowable.

A FAMILY PORTRAIT ——————— 8

Pru hated few things more than she hated chronically awkward social encounters. It got under her skin, the tension pulled sharp by all the words tied up unspoken on people's tongues. Now, that knotted-up feeling infected her biweekly training sessions. Rebelwing would misbehave beneath the touch of Pru's mind while Cat made cutting remarks. Jay Park was no better, alternately sighing and yawning over her earpiece. He probably wished Pru and her dragon were a fusion restaurant or high-end speakeasy bar instead of the Coalition's dubious new protector of democracy.

Alex hadn't said so much as a word since that first lesson. He'd bowed out halfway through the second lesson with some flimsy excuse about a makeup exam in physics, and now, for the third, he'd vanished entirely. It made something itch angry beneath Pru's skin every time she thought about it.

She'd made the mistake of beginning to read more news. Just headline alerts at first, but now she couldn't seem to stop herself from thumbing over every piece of clickbait that so much as teased a mention of wyverns. Every op-ed on Incorporated weapons tech development and eyewitness account of winged shadows on sunny days dug further and further under her skin, until she wanted to crawl out of her own body. Like a scab that demanded to be picked at, more and more wyvern stories scrolled in bold, ominous text across the holographic displays on Pru's phone, and she couldn't quit making herself bleed.

War's coming, war's coming, taunted the anxious buzz growing inside her brain, *this Jellicoe guy is going to sell something terrible to the Executive General at his demo, and it's gonna be your fault the whole continent falls under a reign of corporate fascism, all because this one dumb mechanical lizard got stuck with a lug like you for its pilot instead of Amazing Alex.*

"None of you ever bother explaining it to me, you know," Pru complained loudly to the sky during Flying-Slash-Disaster Lesson Number Four, as she hauled herself out of Rebelwing's cockpit after her fourth not-quite-crash landing one afternoon. Her assignment had sounded as easy as ever: demonstrate basic steering principles by flying one clean lap, but Rebelwing clearly had other ideas. The final hour of training was winding down, and she'd barely made more progress than she had when she nearly ran Jay over in her first week. "It's all 'feel the connection with your mech, Pru,' and 'trust your imprint, Pru,' but neither you nor Cat tell me how that's supposed to translate to steering the godforsaken thing!"

Someone chuckled dryly on the other end of the earpiece. With a start, Pru recognized Hakeem Bishop's voice as he said, "A surprisingly useful point, Miss Wu."

Pru blinked. "Where's Jay?"

"Putting his feet up after calling in reinforcements," said Anabel's cousin, his voice tinny over the mic. He probably literally was putting his feet up, over on one of those fancy balcony railings. "Young Coalition interns who don't respond to my gentle mentorship—"

"Benign neglect, you mean," corrected Hakeem Bishop.

"*Gentle* mentorship," repeated Jay airily, "is not the best tack for all youths. Some of you need a bout of coaching from someone with a . . . shall we say, blunter style."

"What is this, good mech piloting coach, bad mech piloting coach?" demanded Pru, incredulous.

"This," said Bishop in droll tones, "is the kick Mr. Park here has been failing to deliver to your entitled little rear. Or have you forgotten that your first combat assessment is in six weeks?"

"Five now," called Jay merrily.

"You've made a good start by identifying what's wrong," continued Bishop. "Steering and obedience. Rebelwing's sentience means she's not biddable the way typical war mechs are, so typical war mech pilots can't train you in the most crucial aspect of piloting. Not even Jay Park."

"Oh, good," said Jay, sounding relieved. "Does that mean I can leave early for that restaurant reservation I made? Because the chef is—"

"No. What happened to the Lamarque boy? Isn't he supposed to be here too?"

"I scared him off," said Pru bitterly, ignoring the way her heart twisted at the mention of Alex. "With my atrocious flying skills. We're not talking right now."

"Well, scare him back," said Bishop. "Rebelwing is his responsibility too, which makes your atrocious flying skills his problem. And no, Jay, Alexandre's responsibilities do not absolve you of your own."

"Jay told me to learn more about Alex," said Pru, "like I'd be better at piloting sentient mechs if I were a more dedicated fangirl stalker or something."

Bishop emitted a noise that sounded suspiciously like laughter. "Maybe you would be."

Not this again. "I refuse to spend my hard-earned smuggling money on a society pages subscription."

"We'll leave the nature of your criminal earnings aside for the moment," said Bishop dryly. Was this how he'd spoken to Gabriel Lamarque, or even Mama, back in the days of the Partition Wars? Had he and Brigadier General Park co-wrangled young revolutionaries with that same cocktail of wryly delivered humor and relentless perfectionism? "Not all information is to be found in the most obvious places, Miss Wu, but sometimes the answer is right in front of you, and you have a far better eye than you seem to believe. Try using it for a change. You're dismissed."

◆

Barricader's Daily
"UCC Executive General Denies Wyvern Rumors"
by Enrique O'Malley

In light of recent diplomatic meetings with Head Representative Gabriel Lamarque, the office of United Continental Confederacy Incorporated's Executive General Roman Finlay has issued a strong denial of involvement in rumored wyvern sightings over the Barricade Coalition city of New Columbia. "No war mech deployments, wyvern class or otherwise, have been approved by the Executive General," said an

Incorporated spokesperson. "If these are real war mechs, they most certainly were not sanctioned by UCC leadership."

Two additional mechs said to resemble Incorporated war wyverns were spotted over the south side of New Columbia's walls this morning, bringing the total sightings in the past month to four.

♦

IN HER FIRST YEAR at New Columbia Prep, Pru's disastrous grades in Intro to Robotics had, like an alien disease in one of Mama's creepy sci-fi serials, somehow infected every other aspect of school life with pure, undiluted misery. Doing well in World Lit or Pre-Partition History or even calc classes didn't seem to matter to her brain, which had fixated entirely on her inability to program the simplest robots to behave themselves. She couldn't enjoy friends. She couldn't even enjoy books. All she could focus on was the panicked, sick sense of failure in her belly every time she walked into the robotics classroom, and the irrational certainty that her chances of getting into Stanford or McGill or Lamarque U were surely dead in the water now. Foolishly, at fifteen, she'd convinced herself nothing else could possibly feel that shitty.

Of course, it wasn't like fifteen-year-old Pru could have predicted this whole Puff the Sentient Mechanical Lizard situation. Being indirectly responsible for the death of democracy in North America was probably marginally worse than not getting into a top tier university. Hindsight only got bitchier with age, it seemed.

"You look like you want to die," Anabel observed during the pre-curfew study hall one night. They were crammed into her dorm room, perched together on one of the narrow beds, trying to puzzle their way through twentieth-century European history. Or, at least, Anabel—who'd appropriated a ton of old paperbound source material from the library—was. Pru was mostly sulking.

Opening one bleary, bloodshot eye, Pru shunted someone's gloomy predictions of World War II aside with a teddy-bear-socked foot. "I read the news," she said by way of explanation.

"What, more bitchy op-eds about book smuggling? I've told you, you can't—"

"Wyvern lookalikes," said Pru. "A couple more, spotted on the city walls this week." She swallowed the now familiar knot of cold anxiety. "I thought, hey, one time could be a fluke, but now . . . now maybe it's not, maybe they're real, maybe they're going to attack New Columbia and then attack all the other Barricade Coalition cities, and we'll all be Incorporated and die, and it's going to be all my fault because I can't get a mechanical lizard to fly *one clean lap* around your cousin's obstacle course."

Over the spine of *An Introduction to the Sino-Japanese War*, Anabel cut Pru a deeply judgmental look. Even in pajamas, Anabel looked like a centerfold in one of those old-fashioned paper fashion magazines. "That," she said, "assumes a truly impressive amount of self-importance. Actually, it assumes a lot of pretty improbable things. I counted at least three 'maybes' in that entire catastrophizing spiel, and there probably should have been more."

Pru pulled at a frayed thread on the ratty *Don Quixote* T-shirt she'd worn over her cotton pajama bottoms, and fought a sudden urge to cry. "I should have let Mama pull me out of school after all," she said thickly. "I can't do it, Anabel. Rebelwing might have imprinted on me, but every time I'm in the cockpit, it's like . . . you know that feeling when you cram really hard for an exam, but then you hit a problem set you just completely blank on, no matter how hard you rack your brain?"

What a stupid question. Anabel Park had never met a problem she couldn't solve in her entire life.

"Yes," said Anabel, startlingly blunt. When Pru looked at her, surprised, the Park girl shrugged, like failure was no big deal. "I don't know everything, Pru-Wu, I'm just very good at pretending. You've met Jay. It's one of the more underrated skills that runs in the Park blood, like revolutionary sentiment and grandiose speechmaking runs in the Lamarques'. Everyone screws up. If your enemy foils you at one angle, you try a different one. Basic tactics, really."

"Rebelwing's not my enemy, though," argued Pru.

"She kidnapped you off a rooftop and nearly ran Alex over; she fits the basic parameters for enmity right now. And you know what else is basic tactics? Know thy enemy."

"But I don't! That's the entire problem. I don't understand how Rebelwing thinks at all. She's . . . oh."

The epiphany hit her with the force of a mech with no emergency break. "Anabel. How was Rebelwing's imprinting function programmed?"

"You'd have to ask Cat for the finer details," said Anabel, sounding bemused, "but the general principle was programming Rebelwing with a personality matrix that would map onto a pilot of similar disposition. Why?"

"Bingo!" crowed Pru. The mattress creaked under her weight as she snatched up Anabel's manicured hands. "Alex and Cat wanted her to *choose Alex*. Her specs were primed to imprint on *Alex's* mind. Which means Rebelwing's personality matrix must have been programmed with some kind of . . . memory, or impression of him. Something that would predispose her to bond with him."

"Pru." Anabel sounded pained. "I'm glad you're having this breakthrough, but my French tips, if you please."

"Sorry!" Pru freed Anabel's fingers, heart pounding. "If I can just figure out what bits of Alex went into Rebelwing's programming, maybe I can figure out what Rebelwing wants from *me*."

"You could just ask Alex," said Anabel very carefully. Was Pru imagining things, or had the color deepened on her cheeks? "Or Cat."

"Yeah, right, admit to Robo Reptile's mom and dad that I couldn't figure this out myself? The last thing I need to give them is more proof that I'm useless. I just need some time in Rebelwing's cockpit, alone, so I can poke around her memory bank for a couple hours. Maybe there's an algorithm Alex co-created, or some holo-photos of him, or a vocal print. *Something*." Then she deflated. "I have no idea when I'm going to have the time to find it, though. Training's so tightly regimented and supervised, and it's not like I have a spare set of keys to the arena."

"Well, *you* don't." A smile stole across Anabel's face, as she reached into one of her pajama pockets. "But you forget whose cousin I am."

Pru stared at the gleaming silver key disc resting in the palm of Anabel's hand. "Why do I have the distinct impression that Jay did not just voluntarily hand over the keys to a multimillion-dollar training facility to his underage cousin?"

"Believe whatever you want to believe, Pru-Wu." Anabel dangled the key above Pru's nose. "All I know is that Jay very casually mentioned dropping a Hakeem Bishop–shaped anvil on your ass today. He may or may not have left a key behind in the foyer tray of the family manor when he went off to a whiskey tasting. A careless mistake."

Sometimes the answer is right in front of you indeed, thought Pru sourly, but she couldn't stop the grin from spreading all over her face. "I've got an open study hall period after lunch tomorrow," she mused. "Surely, no good prep schooler worth their salt could fault me for spending an extra hour on my Modern Politics II internship, right?"

♦

REBELWING'S MEMORY BANK GAVE Pru's dorm room a run for its money for sheer clutter. It contained an array of development code, command voiceovers, and a truly impressive amount of video footage, programmed into the same camera lenses through which Pru usually navigated in the cockpit. Jamming herself forward in the pilot's seat, she scrolled through the manual remote Jay had taught her how to use. Thumbing through the remote's touchpad sent a whirl of images across the field of Pru's vision. Most of it was unremarkable: recordings of Pru's disastrous flight logs for the past couple weeks, fuzzy recordings of someone—Cat, probably—delivering monotone vocal commands, sandwiched between a few screens full of scrolling code that presumably dictated Rebelwing's imprinting algorithms. None of it was remotely useful.

Pru, a few neck cricks and a faint headache away from thorough defeat, felt her eyes drift shut for a moment. She'd used Jay's manual remote to lock Rebelwing down in stealth mode, leaving them both invisible, and kept a practiced smuggler's ear out for intruders in the training pen, but the hour was running late, and Pru wasn't wild about explaining what she was doing on government property after designated flight hours to angry Coalition officers. "This was a stupid idea," she muttered at the mech. "I should just quit while I'm ahead and—"

Her seat lurched sideways. Pru yelled, grabbing its edges for balance. The camera lenses sputtered and flared, as the chrome-scaled walls of the cockpit bucked around her. "What the hell!"

Panic spooled in her belly. Why did she always let Anabel enable these terrible ideas? Rebelwing had clearly decided to bring Pru's worst fears to violent, physical life. The dragon was going to get her killed, or worse, caught in flagrante delicto by people who had every good reason to see her expelled from school. The imprint wasn't working because Pru had proven herself the screwup she was, and now Rebelwing was punishing her by trying to kettle-cook the taste of Worst Pilot Ever out from her own cockpit.

"This is a complete overreaction!" Pru yelled through chattering teeth at the mech's angrily vibrating walls. Somewhere, even amidst utter terror, lingered a sense of indignity over the sheer unfairness of the whole situation. "You are such an asshole lizard! You chose me, remember? I didn't ask for any of this! How dare you punish me for . . . for at least *trying*! Just let me *try*, goddammit!"

The vibrations stopped. Pru's short, sharp exhales echoed in her ears within the sudden cocoon of quiet. Slowly, she unclenched her fingers from the edges of the pilot's seat. "You chose me," she repeated. Her voice shook, as she braced unsteady hands along those chrome-scaled walls. Life—strange, cybernetic life, but life nonetheless—hummed beneath those scales. Waiting for Pru to prove herself. "We both want this," whispered Pru. "So help me understand what you need."

Another beat of silence. Knots tightened along the base of Pru's aching spine. *Breathe through the fear,* she told herself. *Just like a smuggling drop. You snuck out of school and everything. You got this. You—*

The twang of a guitar chord rang over the sound system, so loudly the vibration thrummed straight through Pru's bones. Swearing, she fumbled for the volume controls, but not before the rest of the song came pouring out of the speakers, the minor key melody wistful and familiar.

"Alexandre," called a man's voice. Even on the tinny recording, amusement was palpable, soaring over the music. "*Mon fils,* is that you?"

Pru's eyes flew open. *Mon fils.* My son.

Unfurling across the view screen in age-muted colors came a dark wood-paneled living room. The camera panned over stacks of books: Antoine de Saint-Exupéry's *Le Petit Prince* sat atop a collection of what looked to be Spanish-translated Madeleine L'Engle paperbacks, mixed into a heavily dog-eared collection of C.S. Lewis's complete Chronicles of Narnia in the original English. A few stuffed animals, the largest of them an enormous dragon-shaped plushie, were scattered among the novels. Pru stared for a moment at the toy dragon, its cartoonishly crinkled eyes smiling cheerfully at her from beneath its fuzzy, posable wings. A name tag clipped to the end of its tail read, in wayward childish letters, *A L E X.*

Seated at the center of the room like a queen upon her throne was a startlingly beautiful woman with shining dark ringlets, legs crossed on the leather sofa. Cradled behind the guitar in her arms, a boy of seven or eight plucked studiously at the strings, his features obscured beneath a wild mop of that same thick dark hair.

The woman's hands stilled the boy's small fingers, along with the music. She laughed. "Oh, your son is learning our love songs beautifully, *cariño*." She spoke with the faint Spanish accent common to born-and-bred Southwesterners. "He'll be illegally playing underground concert clubs in Old Guadalajara by the time he's thirteen, if he takes after you. And yes, you can quote me on your little family video. Don't think I didn't see you sneak your shiny new autocamcorder in, Etienne."

Etienne and Julia. Pru's belly twisted as she stared at the little boy tucked between Julia's arms. So these were Alex's long-dead parents after all.

"Me!" scoffed the speaker behind the camera—Etienne—in wounded tones. Warmth underlaid his voice as he drew closer to Alex and Julia. "I'm not the one who started Alexandre on piano lessons at four and guitar at six, Julia, much less the legendary songstress who used to play three secret shows for every Mexican music hall the UCC tried to shut down. Once a rebel, always a rebel."

"But always a musician, first." The woman raised a pair of terribly familiar eyes toward the camera, dark and fathomless and utterly penetrating. "Always an artist."

"What do you think, Alexandre?" Julia's Spanish accent rolled an extra flourish over the *R* in her son's decidedly French name. She set their guitar aside, and tucked his mop of dark curls under her chin, as he giggled. "Shall we raise you for art, like me, or for war, like your dramatic gringo of a papá here?"

"Dramatic gringo!" squawked Etienne from behind the camera, dramatically.

His wife's eyebrows climbed. "I've heard you fight with your brother. Dramatic gringo is generous."

"I love Gabriel," said Etienne, "but he's too trusting. Too easily satisfied." Something in his voice had shifted. "The assumption that we're safe behind our Barricades, that the UCC will leave us alone now that a ceasefire's been called and treaties have been signed, it's a mistake. Incorporated executives are too hungry to leave our cities safe forever. And besides"—the camera bobbed as Etienne took a seat beside Julia—"there's the rest of the continent to consider. There's the rest of the *world*. Not everyone has the privileges of those born behind Barricade Coalition walls."

"You want to move against Jellicoe."

"Jellicoe built the first wyverns, Julia," said Etienne, low and urgent. "It's what made him so valuable to the Executive General's military. He didn't get rid of his labor camps just because the war ended. All he cares about is his bottom line: revenue."

"*Cariño*—"

"There are children Alexandre's age working in those camps. We could put an end to it. To the camps, to Jellicoe, to his whole disgusting operation—"

"I agree."

"Just because my older brother is too distracted preserving the peace behind our walls to see beyond—what did you just say?"

"I said that I agree with you, you absurd, beautiful crusading man," repeated Julia patiently. The corner of her full mouth twitched. "Sophie Wu was right, you know. I married into madness when I married into your family."

"*Ma chérie*," said Etienne, with feeling, "I honestly cannot tell if you're insulting me or enabling me in this moment."

"Let's call me a multitasker," replied his wife dryly. To Alex, who'd been watching his parents with wide, curious dark eyes, she said, "Go, practice your piano scales, *mijo*. Your father and I will be busy for the next hour."

"Doing what?" asked Alex, the child's voice colored with more curiosity than suspicion.

"Planning something exceedingly stupid," said his mother cheerfully. Then, to her husband, "Shut off that camcorder, my love. We need to discuss strategy."

The footage paused, along with Pru's heart. She inhaled through her nose, once, twice, fingers twitching over Rebelwing's touchpad. Three more videos sat in the queue the dragon had loaded onto the view screen, waiting to be played. With shaky fingers, Pru tugged her phone from her pocket, and thumbed open the society pages' search engine. It didn't take her long to find what she was looking for: the obituaries of Etienne and Julia Santiago Lamarque. They'd died when Alex was twelve. Pru, when she wracked her brain, faintly recalled headlines and footage of the state funeral for the Head Representative's younger brother and his wife. A road accident involving a transport mech, supposedly. Tragic, but unremarkable, save the victims' famous surname.

None of the news outlets had said anything about a scheme against the Executive General's top arms dealer. The father of wyverns himself.

Pru stared at the somber, scrolling text of the obituaries. *Transport mech accident.*

"Bullshit," she whispered at her phone, and hit play.

The next video took a moment to boot up, before two shadowy figures jerked slowly into focus.

"—*calice de tabarnac!*" one of them hissed. "Gabriel, *je crois*—"

"Swearing in Québécois doesn't make your anger any likelier to sway me," said the opposite figure, in a voice that had graced news broadcasts since Pru's childhood. The Head Representative. Weariness hung heavy on the well-worn amusement in his tone. "Etienne. I cannot condone the things you've been doing behind my back. But you knew that already, didn't you?"

The speakers stood in the hallway, before a familiar couch. With a start, Pru recognized an evening-shaded rendition of the foyer where she'd once sat beside Alex, listening to Mama fight with Gabriel Lamarque. Now Gabriel—younger, the silver absent from his hair and his face unlined—bent toward a lean blond whip of a man, their shoulders knocking together.

"*Je sais*," spat Etienne, raking long pale fingers through his hair. He was built slighter than his handsome, soldierly older brother, like he'd been made for the ballet instead of the battlefield, his sun-golden head bright as a candle compared to Gabriel's brunet coif, but they had the same blue eyes, set over the same sharp, aristocratic bones. "*Tu pense que*—" With a frustrated snarl, Etienne switched abruptly to English. "I'm not an idiot."

"Your wife begs to differ," drawled the Head Representative. "As did Sophie, once upon a time."

"Sophie Wu stopped taking your calls a year and a half into your first term as Head Representative, so don't try to weaponize our old war buddies against me," snapped Etienne. His shoulders slumped at the momentary hurt that skittered across his brother's face. "Forgive me. That was a low blow. But this was as much Julia's idea as mine. She and I are united in this."

"Your unauthorized attacks on Harold Jellicoe's private compound, you mean? And how would that poll among the electorate, eh, my own brother and his wife committing treason?"

"Oh, I'm a traitor now, am I?" Etienne's voice dipped flat and cold. His eyes, narrowed on his brother, were twin chips of ocean-blue ice.

"Of course not! I'm not talking about what you are, I'm talking about what you look like to everyone else!"

Etienne's pale hair obscured his gaze, as he gave a slow shake of his head. Danger threaded every tension-pulled inch of his body language. "You've changed since the war. What did we fight for? I thought it was freedom from Incorporated tyranny, but you seem to think it was for the right to make pretty compromises with men like Jellicoe while children waste away in his camps, bare kilometers from the walls of your precious New Columbia."

"Alexandre," said Gabriel.

"Don't you dare use my son as—"

"No," said Gabriel Lamarque, in a different voice. "Your son is here."

Both sets of blue eyes flickered toward the camera. Etienne's squeezed shut, as his expression crumpled. "*Mon fils*. How long have you been standing there?"

"You told me I could play with the camcorder," said a small voice. "I'm sorry, Papa. I heard your voice, and Uncle Gabriel's, so I thought . . ." Hitched breath. "But I didn't know—"

"I'm not angry, Alexandre," said Etienne. His jaw set. "In fact, I'm glad you're here. You're getting older. It's important that you learn what's worth standing for." He rounded carefully on his brother. "So long as we live, Julia and I will continue sabotaging Jellicoe's compound. We will free as many children as we can, and destroy whatever wyvern prototypes we can find in the factories.

Arrest us now, if you'd like. But don't pretend you never had a choice, brother."

The video ended. Pru didn't have to wait long, this time, for the next one to start.

A flurry of motion exploded across the view screen. Pru swore, flinching from the white noise that flooded the sound system. As the camera righted itself, Julia Santiago's face fell into focus. A bruise was blooming over one dark eye, and her cheeks were streaked with soot, but the stark, understated beauty of Alex's mother was unmistakable. "Alexandre," she called. "Alex, *mijo*, I don't have much time, so I'm using the last of our reserve power to transmit this video. I—your father is dead." Grief crumpled her features as she spoke, but Julia persisted, steel under her voice. "We miscalculated. Jellicoe was ready for us. He sprang a self-destruct mechanism in one of the wyvern factories. Almost all the children working there were killed, except . . . except one. Badly hurt, but a survivor. A fighter, just like a little cat. I'm copying the child's coordinates to you and your uncle, so you know where—"

An explosion rocked the lens. Voices rose in alarm over the sound of plasma gunfire in the distance. "It's over." Julia's eyes closed. She tried to smile. "But save the little cat, Alex. If we can save even one child, it will all be worth—"

Another explosion. A final smile bloomed across Julia's features, even as tears leaked out from beneath her lids, carving long streaks through the soot on her face. "Don't forget to practice your scales every day, *mijo*. Guitar and piano both. Even when the world is falling apart, the music still matters, all right? Sometimes, that's when it matters most. And never doubt that I l—"

A final explosion shorted out the remainder of the video.

Pru pressed the heels of her hands against stinging eyes, thumbing angrily at the tears at their corners. Exhaling through the threat of a sob, she skipped to the next video in the queue. Second to last.

The picture took a moment to calibrate, shuddering in and out of focus. Someone blinked over the lens. "You're not Etienne," said the voice from behind the camera, young and suspicious. "Or Julia."

"No, I'm not." The answering voice had deepened since Pru last heard it on the recording, but there was no mistaking that mop of dark hair, or the great black eyes peering out from beneath its fringe. Barbed wire crisscrossed the fences behind him, beneath the half-light of a graying sky. "I'm Alex."

"Who's Alex?"

The boy—not the round-faced child he'd been, nor the svelte young man Pru knew now, but Alex at the dawn of his teens, all jutting bones and growing shoulders—swallowed, lifted his chin, and said, "Their son. What's your name?"

A pause tightened between boy and camera. Then, as if offering something breakable on outstretched fingers, "Your parents called me Cat." *The little cat.* The back of Pru's head thudded against the cockpit seat. Of course. That machine-made eye Cat wore. There would be a camera at its center, to allow its owner a full range of vision. The engineer's eyes recorded everything she saw. Literally. And that included Alex and his family, never truly off-camera, even in these quiet, stolen moments of a war-worn childhood. Pru studied the barbed wire in the footage, letting its implications settle into her mind.

"Cat," repeated Alex. "I'm going to get you out of here."

"You?" Even a few years younger, even trapped in an Incorporated labor camp, a familiar skepticism colored the way Cat spoke. It almost made Pru smile. "What are you, twelve?"

"Fourteen!"

"And you, a fourteen-year-old, are going to sneak me out of Harold Jellicoe's famously well-guarded labor camp."

Alex's jaw set, the subtle, stubborn twitch of that facial expression jarringly familiar on this younger, softer face. "I promised my parents I would."

"Are you here alone?"

Alex bit his lip.

"*Mierda*," swore Cat. "You are, aren't you? How did you make it past the sentinel mechs? Good god, does anyone even know you're here?"

"I'm good with mechs. And no, not right now," Alex admitted. His smile was too thin for someone three years younger than Pru was now. "But my uncle will, inside the hour. I figure that's about as long as I need to convince you to sneak out the back gate with me, before the next round of sentinels show up."

"Your uncle the Head Representative?"

"Uncle Gabriel won't just send a Coalition ops team to save some Incorporated kids under Jellicoe's thumb," said Alex bluntly. "He's . . . it's not like he doesn't want to, but it's his job to keep the peace, you know?"

"Then why the hell did you come here?"

"Because he'll send whatever it takes to save *me*."

A blink over the lens. "You're using yourself as bait? For someone you've never met?"

"We have too met. We met, like, ten minutes ago."

"You could die!"

"We both could, yeah," agreed Alex. He gave a mulish little shrug. "But Papa said once, when I was a kid—"

A snort. "You're still a kid."

"—that it's important to know what you stand for. And like I said." A strange, hungry expression flickered over Alex's face, painting vulnerable planes where he hadn't yet grown into those Lamarque cheekbones. "I made a promise." His hand extended between them. "Please. Will you come?"

The footage ended. Only one video clip remained. Pru took a breath, checked the manual remote to make sure Rebelwing was still locked in stealth mode. Then, swallowing, she hit play.

The camera lens jerked around a few times, before settling on an engineer's workshop. Gone were the barbed wire and muted hues of the Incorporated factory. In the background hung the flag of the Barricade Coalition: a white starburst against a navy blue field. Pinned beneath it was the seal of the city of New Columbia: swords crossed over a flame red poppy. Before the camera, a pair of hands—Cat's hands, gloved in worker's synthetics—poked and prodded at the deconstructed pieces of what looked like a hastily crafted robot. "Wrench."

Someone shuffled off-camera. A tiny silver wrench arced through the air, and landed in Cat's outstretched palm. Cat grunted her thanks, and returned to prying apart the robot. "I need to ask a favor of you. Wire."

"Favor, eh?" A ball of neatly rolled-up chrome-plated wire landed next. Alex ambled into view. He looked the same age he had in the previous recording: still a few years shy of his present-day self, all gangly limbs and soft features. "Sounds like a bigger deal than handing you discarded robot bits or an engineering kit."

The camera shuddered. "You say you're good with mechs. You were good enough to get past Jellicoe's sentinels. Well, I'm a good engineer. I built my own damn prosthetics after Jellicoe nearly killed me. I've studied cyborgs and robots and every kind of mech under the sun. I know how his wyverns work. And I know Jellicoe's not going to stop building them, not so long as they turn a profit."

"I know," said Alex softly. "Where are you going with this?"

Cat dropped the wrench and wire with an angry clang. "I want you to help me build something stronger than a wyvern. Something that could blow those disgusting machines to pieces and eat them alive."

"Like a dragon?"

"Take this seriously!" snapped Cat. "Also, aren't those the same thing as wyverns?

A smile fought the corners of Alex's mouth. "No, they're not. Not always. You don't read many fantasy novels, do you?"

"In UCC-controlled territory, practically choking on censorship regulations? Astonishingly not. I'm asking for your support in crushing Jellicoe, not creating some . . . pale copy of his monsters."

"That's not what a dragon would be." Pru could practically see the gears turning, lightning quick behind this younger Alex's gleaming dark eyes. "Not one we made. It would be better. It would be *ours*. Not all mechs have to be monsters."

"And what would differentiate our dragon from Jellicoe's wyverns, pray tell?"

Alex's smile grew in full at the word *our*. "Free will."

Cat sucked in a breath. "Sentience. You're talking about programming sentience into artificial intelligence."

"Yes."

"Engineers have been working on that for years."

"Yes."

"No one's succeeded."

"No one invented the lightbulb before Thomas Edison decided to, either. Think about it, Cat." Alex leaned over Cat's worktable, long hands twisting together. "Jellicoe could never build something that freely chose its companion pilots. No one Incorporated could. It would be too human. Too *kind*."

Cat said nothing. The camera was shuddering again, as she stripped her gloves.

"Come on, *mi gato*," whispered Alex, and he sounded like a gangly-limbed boy once again. Bright, painful hope colored his inflections. "You want to build something that will tear apart Jellicoe's monsters? This is the way. I'll help you. I promise. You know I keep my promises." Pru blinked, listening to this younger Alex's voice crack on the recording, and wondered exactly how many days or weeks or months had passed since his parents had died trying to save Cat, and kids like her. How many times he'd replayed his mother's final video message.

Cat's palm clamped down over Alex's wrist, the fist blunt and sturdy, starkly so against the lean elegance of his tapered musician fingers. Hers were the no-nonsense, labor camp–bred hands of an engineer, boasting calluses visible even on shaky video footage.

Pru, watching, waited for Alex to pull free from the girl's grip. He didn't.

Cat released a shuddering breath. "Okay," she said. "Let's build a goddamn dragon. Together."

The video shorted out.

"Enjoying the show?"

That voice hadn't come from the video footage, but Pru recognized the person speaking over her earpiece, his vowels cool and clipped. Swallowing hard, she thumbed at the remote, then unbent her knees so she could pop the roof of the dragon's cockpit.

Leaning over the translucent edges of the mech, still wearing an earpiece, all grown up and looking thoroughly displeased, was Alexandre Lamarque.

"How the hell did you get in here?" Pru blurted out. "We don't have a scheduled training session! And stealth mode is on!"

Alex's furiously furrowed eyebrows rose. "Stealth mode turns Rebelwing invisible. It does not, amazingly, turn her into a literal ghost." As he spoke, he gave Rebelwing's outer shell a couple solid knocks with his fist. Slowly, the layer of translucency receded from the mech's silvery hide. "As for why I'm here, I have a war piloting license, military ID that authorizes regular access to mech training facilities, and *keys*. Unlike you."

"Well, la-di-dah." Pru yanked Jay Park's keys out of her pocket. "Shows what you know, bourgeois boy."

The eyebrows dove back into a V. "Pickpocketing Jay Park's keys does not help your case."

"I didn't steal them," snapped Pru, weirdly hurt by the assumption. "Anabel gave them to me."

"Still doesn't mean you should be here."

"Why not? I'm trying to bond with Rebelwing!" protested Pru. "I've only got, like, four and a half weeks before the combat assessment." Like Alex Lamarque himself could forget. The excuse sounded so flimsy, even to her own ears, she wanted to curl up into a ball. How could she possibly make this worse? "I can't afford a bad mark on my transcript for this internship. Lamarque U is my top choice."

Ah. That was how.

Alex's eyebrows climbed so high, they practically disappeared into his hairline. "Breaking and entering charge on Coalition government property would definitely make your application stand out."

"Look." Pru folded her arms. "Current appearances notwithstanding, I'm not stupid. I know Rebelwing was primed to imprint on you, which means she had to have something of yours programmed into her own personality matrix. So I went digging through her memory banks, to figure out how to make her work with *me*." A beat of silence stretched between them, and then he asked, very quietly, "Do you really care?"

"Do I—Jesus, Alex, I live here too!" snapped Pru. "There won't be any universities left to reject my applications if Incorporated arms dealers storm the Barricade cities with an army of evil robot lizards. So before you give up and—and, I don't know, break Rebelwing down for scraps and start over again, I thought I'd try to figure out how to be the sort of pilot she needs." She ignored the odd, hindbrain-generated panic at the thought of the dragon torn asunder and mined for parts, the white-blue eyes going permanently dim. "You guys are the ones who keep telling me I need to treat this stuff seriously."

"So you rifled through my parents' recordings, and Cat's—"

"Because Rebelwing gave them to me!" Pru burst out, and clammed her mouth shut again. Why couldn't she ever keep decent control of her words around him? Alex's eyes were very dark, and very focused on her. She tried again, averting her own gaze.

"I was on the verge of giving up, you know. I was breaking school rules and government rules all on this harebrained hunch that maybe, just maybe, I could learn something useful. I went through the memory bank for an hour, maybe more. Nada. And then right when I was going to call it a day, declare myself a failure after all, Rebelwing threw a fit. When I finally got her to calm down, she'd . . . queued up that video footage. Like a peace offering or something. I don't know," she barreled on, one hand going up to tug out her earpiece, "it was clearly a mistake. I'm sorry if I saw things I shouldn't have. It won't happen ag—"

Long fingers closed around her wrist, keeping her earpiece in place. Alex leaned toward her, still wearing that crazy focused expression. "You don't know that it was a mistake."

Pru's jaw hinged open and shut. "Of course it was. I just trampled all over your personal shit, not to mention Cat's, and I don't even have anything useful to show for it."

The corners of Alex's eyes, bizarrely, crinkled. He looked more like his uncle this way, on the verge of wry laughter. "One. It's my personal shit. When I feel like it's been sufficiently trampled, I promise I'll let you know. Two. I'll reiterate in other words: how will you know that what you saw wasn't helpful until you give the piloting another try?"

"Oh, ha ha."

In reply, Alex ducked back out of the cockpit.

"Hey, I'm trying to apologize to you here! Come back so I can be properly contrite!"

His voice answered her over the earpiece, crackling slightly. "Oh, I'm coming back. But not alone. I've been working on a harebrained hunch of my own for your past couple work-study sessions. So long as we're both here at the training compound, we might as well test it out."

"What? I thought you were just playing hooky because you were mad at me!"

"Well, I was, a little," he admitted. Something clanged around, alarmingly loud, in the background of his mic. "So I decided to do something productive about it."

"This doesn't feel productive!"

"Strap yourself in and close the cockpit hatch. Also, don't forget the earpiece. You're going to want it, trust me."

"I don't trust you at all right now! What in hell is happening?"

She didn't have long to wait. She'd barely settled back into the cockpit seat, when a second mech landed with a rattling thump opposite the dragon. "What the actual hell!" yelped Pru.

"Meet Quixote," Alex said over the earpiece. "I've been piloting this little guy since I was thirteen. He was my very first mech, so he's a little old, but rides smoothly enough."

"Quixote"—which Pru definitely wouldn't have described as a little *anything*—looked like the sort of combat mech they used to make movies about, in the days when mobile suits were first bursting onto the scene of mainstream tech culture. It was a tall, humanoid contraption equipped with floppy but durable-looking metal limbs that would ensure a long-legged stride and long-armed reach. Painted in absurdly cheerful shades of primary red and blue, the mech couldn't have looked less dangerous next to Rebelwing.

So why were all of Pru's instincts screaming at her to run?

"You've given me an idea for a training exercise," said Alex, continuing in the same pleasantly informative tone. "Rebelwing was designed primarily as a mobile suit equipped for combat and stealth, not an ordinary transport mech. It's possible we've been going about bonding you to the imprint all wrong."

"Okay," said Pru warily, one eye still fixed through the dragon's eyes at this innocuously red-and-blue-limbed robot. "But what does that have to do with your pet *Man of La Mancha* robot?"

"Don Quixote the knight errant was created by Miguel de Cervantes a solid three centuries before Dale Wasserman penned the musical, thank you very much," said Alex, "and his namesake is here to put some pressure on you. Don't worry, I'm piloting him in sparring mode, not real time combat strike mode, so we won't go too hard on you. For now."

"What do you mean, sparring mode?" Pru's belly went cold. "I still have five weeks."

"Closer to four," corrected Alex in innocuous tones. "And as my mother used to say, practice makes perfect."

"That is such bullsh—"

Quixote jumped.

Jumped was a terrible word for it, actually. One second, Pru was side-eyeing those improbably gangly robot limbs, and the next, the robot had launched itself skyward, disappearing into the blue.

Flew, more than jumped, thought Pru. Or better yet, *ninja'd*. That was a verb, right?

She squinted through the dragon's eye lenses, looking for some sign of Quixote, when something torpedoed into the back of the dragon. "Holy shit!" The piece of Pru's brain that buzzed with the dragon's consciousness flared with surprise, then rage. The machine that encased her woke up all at once, wings flaring outward, as the dragon gave a great mechanical bellow, trying to fling the other mech off its back.

"So, what was your hot take on those videos?" Alex asked conversationally. His mech wrapped spindly arms around the dragon's throat.

"Screw you!" yelled Pru through rattling jaws as she fought her own panicking mech from its cockpit. *Calm down, calm down, calm down,* she thought furiously at the imprint, probably not very calmly at all.

"Interesting takeaway!" If Pru didn't know any better, she could swear Alex thought he was being funny. It figured that a guy as humorlessly no-chill as Alex would think trapping Pru in an impromptu robot brawl was funny.

"Well, now I know why Cat is so in love with you!" Pru shot back, which was probably a low blow, but she figured it was allowed when she could literally hear the cables inside the dragon's neck straining beneath Quixote's grip. If this was *sparring* mode, she really hoped she never saw real combat any time soon.

A derisive snort. "She's not!"

"Oh, really?" Pru didn't know who Alex thought he was kidding. *Mi gato,* he'd called her, *my Cat,* like anyone could help falling in love with him, hearing a boy like Alex beg you with outstretched hands to run away and build a better world. Pru slammed her own palms against the cockpit walls. *Fly,* she demanded.

Rebelwing kept thrashing, but to the dragon's credit, Pru did feel her take that infuriating squirming to the air. *Huh,* thought Pru. *Progress.* "The video footage in Robo Reptile's memory banks says otherwise!"

"That's hardly a *romance*. We were literal children!"

"Yeah?" Pru tried to concentrate on directing the dragon through the air, great chrome wings flapping, Quixote still clinging to its back like a deranged mech-riding hitchhiker. "Is that you talking, or Cat?"

"Cat, for sure," said Alex altogether too cheerfully. "The summer I turned sixteen, she declared that it would be . . . what was it she said again? Right." He adopted Cat's crisp and slightly clinical cadence: "'educational for a boy my age to know some girls preferred kissing other girls over kissing boys, thank you all the same.'"

The dragon flipped upside down midair. Pru gave a thoroughly undignified shriek.

"What? It's a perfectly reasonable preference, Pru." The earpiece crackled a few times, but Alex still sounded remarkably poised for someone hurtling skyward on the back of a pissed-off mechanical lizard. "Cat, as you'd imagine, was pretty matter-of-fact in the explanation."

"I wasn't screaming about *that*," howled Pru, hanging upside down in the cockpit, as the dragon spun through the sky. "I was screaming because we're going to die!"

"Well, aren't you going to do something about that?"

"You could quit strangling my mech!"

"Make me."

Pru emitted a despairing, furious snarl that probably made her sound more like a dragon herself than its terrified pilot. "Who taught you this adrenaline junkie bullshit, anyway? Your uncle?"

"My dad," corrected Alex, amusement hinting around the edges of his voice. "And it's called defensive mech piloting."

"Defensive!"

"Well," Alex allowed, thoughtful. "Defensive mech piloting with combat forms." He and his mech were still clinging to hers like some freaky-limbed howler monkey.

Pru ground her teeth together. She needed him *off.* The dragon's consciousness hummed agreement in the back of her head. "Yeah, well, guess it paid off when you . . . you know."

Shall we raise him for art or war? Julia had asked, a million years ago.

Pru closed her eyes. In the end, Julia's son had made his own choice. Which meant Pru could too.

"It's about wanting it enough," she reminded herself, repeating Alex's words. It was about wanting something for herself. No one's choice but her own.

Her eyes popped open.

Feint, Pru thought at the dragon, clenching a fist inside the expanse of its left wing. Miraculously, the mech actually responded to her wishes this time, jerking sideways. Over her earpiece, she heard Alex grunt, startled. Quixote's grip loosened slightly.

"You have questions," he observed, scrambling for purchase.

Pru wasn't having it. *Again,* she asked the dragon, which complied with a tiny swoop that left Quixote dangling off the dragon's tail. "Questions? I have fifth-period bio lab, which I'm going to be late for if I don't buck you off!"

"Interesting source of motivation," gasped Alex over the earpiece, clearly trying to climb over the dragon's spine. Outside, metal limbs screeched over the dragon's chrome-plated hull. Alex and Quixote were actually managing an impressive job of defying gravity, all things considered.

"I told you already, unlike you, I don't have a guaranteed slot at my top choice university," snapped Pru. She flexed her fingers, trying to get the dragon to flick its now Quixote-weighted tail. "I can't fail that class."

Quixote's long-taloned, red-and-blue fingers scrabbled along the ridges of the tail, which had begun to swoosh wildly back and forth. "I can't believe you're thinking about your bio grades right now," called Alex, shouting to be heard over the crash of gears inside his cockpit.

"Well, what do you want me to do, envision you as the Executive General of the UCC?" demanded Pru. She blew stray wisps of hair off her nose, momentarily forgetting her terror, but annoyed with him all over again. "Or Harry Jellybelly—"

"Harold Jellicoe." Was he *laughing*? Incredible. "And no, I don't. I'm coaching *you* through this, not me. If you're motivated by not wanting to fail fifth-period bio, then don't fail fifth-period bio."

"Gee, thanks."

"I'm amazed you managed to take that as an insult!"

"How was I supposed to take it?"

"As an observation that you and I are different people," yelled Alex as something clattered loudly near his earpiece. Quixote tried to jump again, to leap onto a more secure piece of the dragon, and nearly fell off entirely. "Rebelwing, whatever's stuck in her memory banks, still chose to imprint on *you*. Whatever she saw in you already exists. You don't have to fake something you're not!"

Pru gave the dragon another jerk, but Quixote and Alex clung stubbornly to the tail. "*You* yelled at me the first time I officially test-piloted the dragon."

"Because I thought you were going to get yourself killed! I didn't— oh, shit."

Quixote's weight disappeared off the end of the dragon's tail. The bottom dropped out of Pru's stomach. Static crackled violently in her earpiece. "Alex!"

She'd been concentrating so furiously on dislodging him, she hadn't given real thought to what happened to a wingless mech thrown midair several hundred feet off the ground. The dragon's eyes zoomed in on the red-and-blue figure dropping through the sky. "Alex!" Pru screamed again. He didn't answer.

As one, Pru and the dragon dove.

Part of her mind was screaming along with her vocal cords. The other part of her mind—the one that coasted on air currents with metal wings, and saw the world through high-definition reptilian eyes—made calculations, like she was working through a problem set on an exam with a ticking time limit.

She'd need to swoop *beneath* Quixote to catch the other mech in time before Quixote and Alex both went splat. Pru squinted through the dragon's eye lenses, hard enough to pinch her temples, trying to figure out the right angle. "Hey now," she murmured at the mech thrumming around her. "I know we haven't gotten on so well these past few days. But how fast can you—we—just . . . fall?"

In answer, Rebelwing dropped.

Later, Pru wouldn't be sure how to describe what happened in that moment. Just that she'd been utterly, eerily certain of herself and the span of her—no, *their*—body, the joint capacity of girl and dragon to catch the ridiculous boy windmilling toward gravity's deadly embrace. The world had sped and blurred around her. Color and light exploded on her field of vision through the eye lenses, the world screaming past the screen too fast for her brain to process.

And somehow, at the end of it all, she'd wound up perched on the far edge of the Coalition government's training field, Quixote dangling around Rebelwing's neck.

Pru's head pounded, a steady drumbeat inside her skull. But she and Rebelwing were earthbound, at least. Also, not dead. How nice.

Someone groaned, the sound shorting in and out over her earpiece. Pru sat up, a hair too quickly, which set her head pounding even harder. She ignored the pain. "Alex?" Her throat was raw, probably from all the screaming and terror. "Bourgeois boy, is that you?"

"Technically," rasped the voice on the other end of the wireless, "you and your mum would qualify as bourgeois too. You voluntarily attend a prep school, and your mum makes professional art for a living. How is that anything *but* bourgeois?"

Pru shut her eyes, and dropped her head back against the cockpit seat. "Really?" she said, without lifting her eyelids. "You choose to have this argument now?"

"I kept meaning to bring it up, but you always distract me with, like, more immediate and infuriating arguments." He sounded bizarrely pleased about this, which Pru could only chalk up to sheer adrenaline from the joy of not being smashed to a zillion pieces on his uncle's training field. "Now seemed as opportune a moment as any."

"Glad to hear that our near-death experience—which was completely your fault, by the way—hasn't rattled your charming personality." Pru unstrapped herself, flexing stiff joints and rubbing at the red imprints of the safety restraints on her skin. "Your friend Quixote really did a number on us."

"Us?"

"Me and Rebelwing."

"Ah, of course. The imprint." A smile snuck into his voice. "How's the bond?"

"Strengthened by terror and rage, so thanks for that. Are you insane? If I . . . if we hadn't caught you—"

"We'd have had ourselves a nice little safety parachute drill."

A beat passed between them. "Excuse me?"

"We were never in real danger," said Alex. "Think about it. Remember how mad your mum got at my uncle before she even agreed to sign the permissions forms for the work-study?" His voice softened, almost imperceptibly. "No one would actually let you—or me, or Cat and Anabel, or any of us—get hurt, not on Coalition time. I wouldn't remember to put Quixote in sparring mode, only to forget all the other fail-safes, like parachutes." Then, a bit more wryly, "Besides, I think I learned my lesson from the first time we officially let you ride the dragon around this field. Poor Jay nearly lost his head."

"Oh my god, you're never going to let that die, are you?" They'd never been in real danger. Pru didn't know whether she wanted to laugh, all giddy relief—or pry up the hatch on the dragon's cockpit, drag Alex out of Quixote, and shove him off their tangled mountain of mech limbs. See who'd bother catching him then.

"So, what did it for you?" Alex sounded genuinely curious. "You were just as much of a mess as usual at the beginning of the sparring—"

"Thanks!"

"—but you guys smoothed out almost completely by the time we wound up in free fall. How did you manage that? What changed?"

Pru paused on her automated retort, half-formed and sardonic on the tip of her tongue. With an effort, she swallowed. Unbidden, the footage from the dragon's memory bank replayed itself across her mind's eye. Alex learning music scales at his mother's knee. Alex listening to his father rail against his uncle's cowardice. That final, aborted plea from Alex's mother.

Alex at fourteen, breaking into Incorporated labor camps and dreaming of dragons.

"I don't know," Pru said at last. "Desperation? Sheer animal survival instinct? How did *you* do it?" The question flipped itself around far too easily, images of barbed wire still stuck on the backs of Pru's eyelids. "When you decided to save Cat." She shifted, feeling exposed and intrusive all at once, but still the words tripped out of her. "I mean, I'm sorry, but you were just a kid. How could you really know you'd get yourself out of there? How could you know you'd get *Cat* out of there?"

"I don't know," echoed Alex, dry voiced over the wireless. "Desperation? Sheer animal survival instinct? I had to do it," he added, after a beat. His tone shifted. "When Mama sent Cat's coordinates to Uncle Gabriel, Jay and Hakeem fought for three days."

"Over how to save her?"

"Over whether to save her at all." He spoke in the same clear, measured way he always did, but these words, dropping from Alex's mouth so slow and painstaking, laid him bare even so. Pru hugged her elbows and said nothing. "Jay was all for it. He grew up babysitting Anabel while their parents were on business in Seoul, you know, and whatever blue-blooded airs he performs in public, he can't bear the idea of leaving a little girl alone in a place like Jellicoe's camps, no matter where she comes from. But Hakeem didn't like the risk, the thought of destabilizing such a fragile peace for the sake of one kid. And my uncle . . . my uncle was in mourning. I didn't know whose side he'd take. So I decided for him."

"You were in mourning too," Pru pointed out, quietly aghast. "Alex, your *parents* had literally just died."

"I was, and yeah, they had," agreed Alex. "But if I hadn't made my choice, what would they have died for at all?"

"You were a kid!"

"So I've been told." The sound of a smile tugged at his voice, along with another emotion Pru wasn't sure how to identify. "But kids grow up."

Pru swallowed hard. Her fingers brushed over the scales of the cockpit, felt Rebelwing ripple in response across the imprint in her head. "I think it takes more than growing up, to pull off what you and Cat did," she told Alex. "I think it takes downright *audacity*."

A couple beats of quiet stretched out from Alex's end of the earpiece. For this one weird, fanciful moment, Pru imagined the two of them inhaling and exhaling in sync over the wireless.

"Maybe that's what we share," said Alex. "What Rebelwing looked for, when she chose to imprint. A certain audacity."

Pru flushed, embarrassed by this suggestion, and unsure why. "Bullshit," she said lightly. "I'll have you know that I haven't got a drop of audacity in my body. I'm a very well-behaved—"

"—book smuggling delinquent?" he finished dryly.

"Up yours."

He laughed. "What's audacity, if not dealing black market media to Incorporated citizens?" He had that quality in his voice again, the one that practically hypnotized the audience when he spoke and sang on stage. The one that almost tricked you into thinking that you, equipped with nothing but yourself, could magically knit this angry, broken-up continent into something warm and whole.

"What's audacity, if not the bullheaded way you pick fights, or stand your ground when you think I'm wrong?"

"I do not pick fights! And you are frequently wrong!"

"Uh-huh." He sounded thoroughly amused now. "What's audacity, if not sneaking out of school to break into government property like some kind of unhinged lone criminal, all to defend democracy and higher education from the clutches of the Incorporated?"

"Excuse you, I am not a lone criminal, I work with the youngest and cleverest of Parks, thank you very much."

"Anabel's not here."

"Nope, but you are." Pru, stretching out the remnants of whiplash in her neck, offered a thin-lipped smile to the insides of Rebelwing's cockpit. "Congratulations, Alexandre Santiago Lamarque. Consider yourself my latest accomplice."

♦

New Columbia Preparatory Academy
Student Message Boards
Friday, 2:00 P.M.

SOUR16: yo 5th period bio lab is the goddamn worst. it's like this school conspires to schedule the most boring-ass classes for the worst parts of the day.

READWEEKWEEDWEEK: lol those smartasses taking the modern politics seminars get off so easy!!! that sleepy-looking asian chick who's always following anabel park around came in like 10 min late for bio last week. the lab instructor didn't even care — just took one look at her late pass & told her to grab a beaker. lucky bitch, getting to slack!!!

SNOOZE_LOOZE_2: not to mention getting to ogle alex lamarque's ass.

READWEEKWEEDWEEK: dude that boy is fine as hell, but he's so taken.

SNOOZE_LOOZE_2: says who?

READWEEKWEEDWEEK: barricading beat, for one.

EFFINGCORPORATE: also, like 3 diff gossip rags, lol

SNOOZE_LOOZE_2: please, barricading f*cking beat? everyone knows those anonymous edgelords make shit up all the time. what kind of prep schooler are you? verify your news sources, bro.

SANSMERCI: doesn't matter anyway, lamarque junior's probably secretly betrothed to anabel park to secure a ruling dynasty for the barricade cities.

QUOTHWHAT24601: a really hot ruling dynasty. almost hot enough to make u wanna give up the democratic experiment & be a monarchist lol.

SANSMERCI: true, they'd have really pretty kids.

READWEEKWEEDWEEK: nah, that's all bullshit, he's totally banging her friend.

SOUR16: guys, I literally don't give a f*ck who park or lamarque or any of their friends are banging. this bio period is literal torture. can someone please just send me the answers to these stupid lab questions???

◆

AS A KID GROWING up in her mother's modest apartment, Pru had unironically loved the training montages they always showed off in hokey action films. Mama—who sometimes got work scripting those scenes—never quit making fun of Pru for it. Pru had defended her rights to her own schlocky taste with valiant dedication to movie nights featuring titles like *Phoenix Warrior 3: Reloaded!!!,* all three exclamation points splashed over the poster in flame-edged font. Halfway through her allotted six weeks of dragon piloting training, though, Pru was ready to delete her copy of every single stupid Phoenix Warrior movie in existence. Phoenix Warrior and his friends clearly had nothing on cybernetic dragons, or their crazy hard-ass handlers.

Also, real-life training montages were actually kind of terrible to live through, even within the confines of a dragon-shaped mobile suit.

"Repeat the exercise, please," drawled Jay Park over Pru's earpiece. He sounded like one of those hot but secretly sadistic wicked monarchs in fantasy video games. Infinitely unimpressed, but just amused enough by his jester's antics to keep her jumping through hoops.

Literal hoops. Pru ground her teeth, as she cast a mistrustful eye toward the crackling blue loops of force field energy that Jay had arranged for their training session. Pru's dragon-piloting skills had seen a noticeable uptick since her square-off against Quixote. By breaking into the training facilities to bond with Rebelwing and fight with Alex, she seemed to have passed some arbitrary test of worthiness.

Still, obstacle courses—giant, scary-ass force fields shaped like actual, flaming circus hoops—went way beyond the work-study call of duty, in Pru's opinion. She'd clipped a wing on one of them last week, and the crackling electrical backfire had sent Rebelwing into a tailspin she'd barely recovered from. There was agility under pressure, and then there was agility under the yoke of utter terror.

"Up," she muttered at the dragon, which pulled up just a hair too fast, and nearly slammed them into one of the force fields again. They got through the rest of the course fine, but Jay made Pru fly it a couple more times, "just to really get the agility maneuvers down." Likelier that he was just trolling her. At the very least, the whole ridiculous exercise ate up the rest of the work-study period, saving her from anything even more troublesome. "Nice work this afternoon!" Jay called cheerily over the earpiece. "Next week, if we talk the Head Representative around, maybe we can start on the plasma fire targeting!"

"*Plasma* fire?" squawked Pru.

"It'll be fun." Innocuously, he added, "If he's in a daring mood, we might even convince Alex to pilot Quixote and chase you around the training yard again—"

"Okay, thanks, got it!" Pru interrupted loudly, and tossed her earpiece aside. She wasted no time beating a hasty retreat back to the metro.

She found Anabel waiting on the platform when the train rolled back into the New Columbia Prep station. Just in time to deposit Pru—sweaty, grouchy, and probably nursing another round of whiplash—back at school for bio lab. Great.

"Don't look so cheerful," said Anabel, no doubt taking in Pru's stormy expression. She looked Pru up and down and tutted with a mixture of sympathy and judgment. "Let me guess. My cousin's putting you through your paces?"

"What tipped you off?"

"Oh, I one-upped him at a family dinner last weekend, or some such thing. Gotta keep ahead of the competition, you know?"

Pru groaned as she dragged herself onto the escalator. "I see. So I'm left in the crossfire."

Anabel popped up beside her with a casual shrug. "Pretty much."

"Wow, are all Parks this petty?"

"Sure, but I'm the pettiest of them all," said Anabel, lofty and unconcerned. "About that, I was going to ask a favor."

"You mean besides playing whipping boy to your vengeful cousin."

"Ew, mental image!"

Pru sighed. "What do you need?"

"For starters? To do something about your obvious crush on Alex."

Pru's heart clenched. Well, she'd seen that one coming, at least. "Look, I'm sorry, okay? Not that there was anything going on to begin with, but I'll step off your boyfriend—"

"My *what*?"

"Alex," Pru clarified, irritated. "You said you liked him. I'm not that big of an asshole."

"Oh my god," said Anabel, looking ready to burst. Her cheeks were very red. "Not like *that*! The boy is pretty, and I can appreciate a nice piece of art as much as anyone, but he's not my type."

"Then why are we standing in front of the metro escalator, becoming steadily later for bio lab?"

"Because," said Anabel, practically preening, "*you*, on the other hand, are very much *Alex's* type."

"Why, just because his pet dragon imprinted on me?" Pru demanded, strangely offended by these implications. "Rebelwing's specs are impressive, but last I checked, she didn't come with a built-in matchmaking app."

Anabel clicked her tongue. "The dragon's not the one who won't shut up about you. I told you, Alex has been insufferable since the moment he pulled that plasma gun on your pork bun."

"That . . . sounds like a truly terrible euphemism," said Pru. "Anyway, if this isn't a 'keep your hands off my man' favor, what kind of favor is it?"

"An 'I need backup on an unauthorized intelligence-gathering adventure in Incorporated territory' kind of favor." Carefully, Anabel lowered her voice. "I got a tip. It's about the wyverns, Pru."

That, Pru had to admit with a lurch in her gut, made way more sense than fighting over a boy. "So you're asking the biggest delinquent you know."

"You say 'delinquent'; I say 'seasoned risk-taker,'" said Anabel with a blithe wave of her hand. "My tip is about a retreat in No Man's Land this weekend—one of those socially stilted yet luxurious mixers for the rich and indulgent from both sides of the Barricades. Highly exclusive invites, limited to so-called 'influencers,' and always hyped up like hell, given the whole forbidden fruit nature of mixing company twenty years after a civil war. Supposedly meant to promote compromise and peaceful exchange across Barricader and Incorporated lines, actually just meant to scope out the enemy over cocktails on the beach. Maybe throw in some hate sex here and there."

"I know what No Man's Land is, thanks," said Pru, recalling footage of socialites in skimpy bathing suits lounging among sandy dunes with kegs of beer. "And I refuse to have hate sex on behalf of your weird spy mission, I don't care how unpatriotic that makes me."

"Relax, Pru-Wu, no one's asking you to have sex, hateful or otherwise, with anybody. Just to go on a date."

"A what?" squawked Pru.

"Keep your voice down! For Christ's sake, it's a beachside social, not a torture chamber. Alex and I both have invitations through family networks, but we need plus-ones. You can be his."

"Why?" Pru tried not to wail. Judging from Anabel's expression, she failed.

"Because," said Anabel patiently, "as part of *my* research duties for my Modern Politics II internship, I've been looking into Harold Jellicoe's much-discussed little product demo, and it's not taking place three weeks from now. It's taking place this weekend, at No Man's Land—or at least, a fun little preview is."

Pru stared. "The Executive General's top death-machine maker? He's demo-ing his wares at a beach party?"

"Do you know another Harold Jellicoe? Presumably, he picked the location and the earlier date to attract investment from Incorporated buyers, and to scare influential Barricader guests into voting for UCC-friendly politicians during our next elections. Alex and I need to get eyes on that tech, and we need plus-ones who won't slow us down, or worse, go whining to our families about what we're really up to."

"Then why not just go with each other?"

"A Lamarque and a Park alone together at a party like this get noticed. A Lamarque and a Park fooling around on a group date with other teenagers are just two more dumb rich kids looking for a good time with their fellow privileged socialites."

Pru crossed her arms. "Fine. If, theoretically speaking, I'm Alex's plus-one, then who's yours?"

"Oh," said Anabel. Her expression shifted just slightly, a twitch of the mouth someone who'd known her less well would have missed. "Cat."

"*Cat?*"

"You don't have to broadcast it for the entire metro, Pru-Wu."

Pru eyed the faint color rising on Anabel's cheekbones. "Wait a minute. Are you legitimately into Cat? For real?"

"She's the most talented weapons engineer we know, and a tremendous asset," said Anabel, cool voiced, but the blush didn't abate.

"That wasn't a no," Pru pointed out. Anabel had never really expressed a gender preference so far as her paramours went—there had been a lithe blonde girl in their first year at New Columbia Prep, a dimple-cheeked young man of North African extraction their second, and a few once-off dates in between—but they'd all been unilaterally beautiful, charming, and gregarious.

Cat, on the other hand, might actually be a serial killer. Pru could take that bet. She'd seen the way the engineer pried those robot guts apart on Rebelwing's recording footage.

"Please tell me," said Pru in pained tones, "that you're not orchestrating an elaborate espionage mission against UCC Inc.'s most dangerous arms dealer just to get a girl to go out with you."

"Don't insult me," said Anabel. "I'm orchestrating an elaborate espionage mission against UCC Inc.'s most dangerous arms dealer to defend our walls from future wyvern attacks, one-up Jay at family dinners, *and* get a girl to go out with me."

"No offense, but that sounds like literally the least romantic date of all time."

"Don't be a hater, Pru-Wu. Some girls are best wooed by wine and flowers." Anabel shrugged. "Others prefer bloody vengeance on war profiteers who exploit child labor. There's no wrong way to be a woman in love."

"Why Cat?" Pru blurted out before she could stop herself. "It's . . . like, she's good-looking enough, I guess, in this severely well-put-together way? But it's *Cat*."

Anabel tucked her chin in, corners of her mouth pulling upward.

The loftiness fell away, like a cape discarded, the girl caught coltish and bare beneath. "She's never anything other than exactly what she decides to be. It's like . . . when I watch her work on a piece of engineering, or talk to Alex, or hell, put on that ugly barista apron, she's always herself. No matter what, she always does precisely what she thinks she ought to." Anabel shook her head slowly, a sort of wonder lighting her gaze. "That girl, she was born under UCC Inc. rule, and she survived labor camps and disfigurement and displacement— everything that should have broken a person apart. Instead, she literally took those pieces of herself and . . . put them back together into the person she wanted to be. How *don't* you fall for that, once you've seen it for what it is?"

Pru cast a narrow, assessing gaze at Anabel, the affable queen bee, teenage pride of the Park clan, and everything their schoolmates had ever aspired to be. Pru took in the shy bend of Anabel's head, the pink in her cheeks, the slightly dopey lift of her mouth.

"Holy shit," said Pru, agog, "you really *are* besotted."

"I'm not *besotted*," protested Anabel, nose wrinkling. "That makes it sound so juvenile."

"Moon-eyed, then," said Pru, who was starting to enjoy this.

Anabel rolled her eyes extravagantly. "So, does your being an insufferable dick about my feelings mean you're in, or what?"

That sobered Pru a little. "This is dangerous," she said bluntly. "Like, all joking aside, you know that, right? A beach party is one thing, but this is a beach party with legit murderers in Armani suits on the guest list."

"It's a risk," admitted Anabel. "But you agreed to pilot Rebelwing for a reason, Pru. And I think we both know that it wasn't just to pad your university apps. No one goes to university in a continent overrun by Jellicoe's wyverns. We need to know what he's planning. We *need* this information."

The sudden steel under Anabel's voice reminded Pru, with a strange wrench in her gut, of Etienne Lamarque. The footage from the dragon's memory bank blared across the eye of Pru's mind: Etienne and Gabriel arguing in the darkened hallways of the Head Representative's Mansion about the future of the continent. The talk of art and war. The worth of one child. The look in Julia's eyes before she'd died.

Pru inhaled slowly, quelling the sudden weight inside her chest. "Fine." With grim determination, she began hauling Anabel toward the Academy's bio labs. "I have three exams I was going to spend this weekend studying for, but who cares? We can go risk life and limb for the liberty of the North American continent instead. If we don't end up spending the next thirty years as political prisoners, it'll make great conversation for university interviews."

"You see, Pru-Wu? I knew I could count on your priorities."

Pru opened her mouth to retort, but before she could think of a good one, her phone buzzed. Thumbing the screen awake, she read through the text from Alex: *Heard about Anabel's plan for No Man's Land.* A brief typing icon emerged, stopped, emerged again. *I hope you'll help. But you don't have to if you don't want to.*

Pru's mouth twitched, torn between scowling and smiling, as she typed back, *I don't know what you take me for, but I'm not about to leave you dateless and stranded at a party full of Incorporated sharks.*

A pause. *HJ always has an extra trick up his sleeve. There's more to this demo than attracting buyers.*

Like the trick that had killed Alex's parents. Pru bit her lip. *Like what?*

I don't know. Just be careful, ok? Please.

Pru's fingers hovered over the screen. She considered making a joke. She considered changing the subject: to Anabel and Cat's budding romance, to the upcoming combat assessment, to anything but the strange clench of dread in Pru's belly at the memory of Julia and Etienne Lamarque, young, in love, and doomed too soon at Jellicoe's hands.

Are YOU ok? Pru typed at last. Hurriedly, she hit send, before her traitor brain could start waffling over whether asking sounded too weird.

A read receipt popped up almost immediately. More typing. More pauses. More typing again. Pru's belly clenched once more, in a completely different way.

I'm asking Cat to bring a few of her gadgets, Alex texted at last. *In case we end up in some kind of fight-or-flight situation.*

Pru stared at that incredible nonanswer of a text. *Better hope we don't,* she typed back with trembling fingers. *Also, was that a pun?*

The next text came far quicker than the earlier ones: *You'll be fine.* Followed by: *Also, don't pun shame me.* Accompanying the message was a winking animated dragon. The cheery little cartoon face was, Pru had to admit, stupidly adorable.

She bit her lip against a smile of her own, despite herself. Maybe he was right: she'd be fine. Maybe they'd all be fine.

Anabel and Alex covered all four tickets to the No Man's Land weekend, which did a complicated series of things to Pru's feelings. "You
could probably write it off as a work-study expense and get the tickets
covered by Coalition money," Pru told Anabel.

The other girl waved her off gently, like Pru had just suggested writing off a food vendor's pack of fries as a work-study expense. "Sure,"
said Anabel, "but then we'd have to fill out, like, five million pages of
paperwork. Besides," her eyebrows climbed, "are you sure your mum
would sign off on a boozy beach weekend, good cause or no?"

At that, Pru shut her mouth. She'd made good on Mama's demands
for weekly check-ins on her progress with Rebelwing, but blowing
off homework for a weekend to help her friends spy on a bunch of
evil arms dealers at a ritzy shoreside getaway probably fell outside the
parentally approved parameters of acceptable internship activities.

"Thought so." Anabel shrugged, then in an aside, meticulously
off the cuff: "Don't sweat the money, Pru-Wu."

Pru knew, in a clinical sort of way, that Anabel, Alex, and most
of Pru's other school friends weren't scholarship kids. Moments like
these, though, the disparity between them still managed to sneak up

on Pru. She remembered what Alex had said that day on the training fields: *Your mother makes money from art, and you still attend prep school. You're bourgeois too.*

Fair enough, Pru conceded to the Alex in her head, jaw twitching. But there's "moderately successful author's daughter" bourgeois, and then there's "throw money at No Man's Land like it's pocket change" bourgeois. Completely different species, dude.

◆

THE REALITY OF WHAT she'd agreed to finally struck Pru hard between the eyes when the four of them arrived at the beachside rental. The cabin wasn't a cabin at all. It was really a small, upscale house, painted a shade of lily white that perfectly matched the tops of the waves cresting gently against the pale stretch of shoreline. The little house sat atop a series of artfully winding stilts, granting it a bird's-eye view of the beach. To get up to the front door, you hopped aboard an intricately carved, open-air lift—clearly designed by the same fanciful architect who dreamed up the stilts—where you swiped your key card for a winding journey skyward.

It was like a childhood treehouse fantasy crossed with a Coalition representative's summer home. Pru unhinged her jaw to say so: "This is—"

"—an excellent vantage point for observing Incorporated activity," finished Cat, with an approving little nod. It was maybe the happiest Pru had actually seen Cat look in real life.

"Um," Pru began, then caught the warning glance from Anabel. "Sure, buddy. Great spy tower. The best . . . avant-garde treehouse spy tower money can buy."

"Speaking of which," said Anabel, "are we all clear on the plan?"

"This itinerary says dinner's being catered at six P.M.," said Alex, staring intently at his phone. "We should probably drop our stuff off and head over." He talked as if mingling over fresh seafood and champagne was some sort of sting operation, which, given the entire reason they were all here, wasn't actually that far off the mark. Pru sighed.

"I've gotten us a table next to a bunch of Incorporated executives—either rivals or old business partners to Jellicoe," Anabel continued. "They'll probably recognize my face or Alex's from holo-tabloids. Either they'll think we're well-bred scions of our respectable political families, due to inherit Barricade Coalition leadership, or assume we're spoiled teen socialites trying to impress our attractive yet comparatively uncultured commoner dates with family money and party invites. No offense to present company, of course."

"None taken," said Pru dryly.

"Our job is to convince them of the latter." A gleam that spelled trouble had entered Anabel's artfully cat-lined eye. "We want to seem unthreatening, so no one will suspect us of being worth attention, and also vaguely gross, so no one will *want* to pay attention to us."

"So you're proposing—"

"Public displays of affection!" concluded Anabel proudly. "Don't look at me like that, Pru-Wu, I'm not telling you to make a porno. We just need to be disgustingly lovey-dovey enough at dinner to make our neighbors avert their eyes, so they'll keep ignoring us when we show up for the fireworks display on the beach at nine P.M."

"Makes sense," said Cat, with a curt little nod, but the side of her gold-painted mouth ticked up as—to Pru's amazement—she laid slightly possessive metal fingers over Anabel's elbow. "Like this?"

Anabel beamed. "Exactly like this. Very good, Cat. Pru and Alex, watch and learn."

Pru shook her head, coughing and ignoring the heat climbing up her neck, as she pointedly avoided making eye contact with Alex. "Fireworks display?"

"A euphemism for Jellicoe's demo," said Alex. How he could sound so grimly calm when Anabel was instructing them on how to fake hanky-panky for their stupid spy cover, Pru had no idea. "Incorporated arms dealers like to play coy with their toys—no one spells out 'weapons demo' in plain terms, but people invested in the industry have a way of knowing when and where it's happening. Makes it feel more exclusive. Half of salesmanship is theatricality. We'll have a few hours to kill between dinner and the demo, so let's spend it scoping out likely investors in whatever Jellicoe's selling."

They wound up under a breezy white canopy, seated at a circular table sporting several ornate place settings, which made Pru painfully self-conscious of her cheap flip-flops and short-sleeved chambray frock, despite the tide washing up on the beach just down the hill from their little shindig. Seats were well-spaced for testing romantic waters: far apart enough to allow elbow room, close enough for neighbors to hold hands in plain sight. Around them, men and women in bright, expensive colors milled about, passing between waitstaff in elegant black and white.

Pru breathed out slowly, trying to tame her nerves. It wasn't that she hadn't gone out with people before. She'd kissed a pretty red-headed boy from her calc tutorial group in second year once, behind a dumpster—super classy—and another schoolmate, less pretty but more drunkenly eager, during some school dance Anabel had dragged her to. But she'd never been on the sort of date where you ate fancy food served to you by fancy people, like you were auditioning for roles as the sort of wealthy, respectable adults who always knew which place setting utensils to use, and never ran into awkward silences between platters of shrimp cocktails.

Anabel and Cat seemed not to notice her discomfort, leaning into each other, an odd softness to Cat's mismatched eyes that Pru had previously only ever seen her bestow on Alex. Anabel, though—Anabel, Cat looked at with a gaze just shy of moonstruck.

One of the middle-aged suits at the neighboring table coughed loudly and looked away. Laughing into Cat's neck, Anabel smirked.

Neither of them had to fake a thing, Pru realized with a jolt. Cat was clearly every bit as into Anabel in all her conniving glory as Anabel was into the austere engineer. Watching the way the two of them spoke now, knees brushing, Anabel's hands lively and animated, a reluctant dimple deepening Cat's cheek as she listened, unwavering, Pru wondered how she'd ever figured either of these girls in love with Alex.

Probably, whispered her traitorous brain, because it was hard to imagine anyone *not* being in love with Alex. *Who's really moonstruck here, Pru?*

Oh, shut up, you malfunctioning piece of organic machinery, retorted Pru. She grabbed a fork and sliced into some asparagus with mutinous vigor, one eye fixed on Alex.

Catching her gaze, he leaned forward. Pru's heart rate did something alarming.

"Where do you suppose Jellicoe is?" he murmured into the shell of her ear.

Business as usual, thought Pru, unsure why that disappointed her. She jerked away from him. "Probably socializing with some other UCC guys, waiting to make a dramatic entrance."

A thoughtful crease bloomed between his brows. "Well, any idea how to go about socializing with the enemy?"

"Maybe start by not referring to them as the enemy," advised Pru, spearing a piece of salmon. "Peacetime cooperation, blah blah blah."

The crease deepened. "We came here for information."

"Information at a boozy beach party. You gotta ease into it a little. Watch people's body language. Wait for opportunities. Have a little fun with it, don't look so stiff."

"You'd know, huh?"

Now Pru was the one scowling. "Oh, would I?"

"You give good smuggler's advice. Watching people's body language. Waiting for opportunities." She couldn't read the look in his eyes, but it did strange things to her belly. "I knew you were smart."

"I just have common sense," said Pru, weirdly defensive. "There's a reason teen book smugglers are a dime a dozen. Haven't you read all those op-eds in the *Barricader's Daily* about the delinquency of our generation and our mercenary disregard for rules and institutions? Anyone can do what I do. I'm not—I know that whole imprint fiasco might have gotten some people's hopes up about me, but you don't have to treat me like I do something special."

He turned abruptly from her, like she'd struck him. "Why do you always do that?"

"Do what?"

"Put yourself down all the time." Why did Alex look *hurt*, of all things?

"I don't!" Did she? "I just think it's stupid to build anything or anyone up to be better than they really are!"

"See?" His jaw twitched. "There you go again."

"Whatever." Pru slouched. "Can we please stop talking about this and go back to eavesdropping on the evil arms dealers, like we're supposed to?"

"Please do," said Cat curtly. She disentangled herself from her loving staring contest with Anabel, looking only passingly regretful. "Meanwhile, I'm going to trawl the perimeter, see if I can get eyes on Jellicoe." One metal hand brushed Anabel's shoulder. "Be good, kids." She flicked an unimpressed cybernetic eye toward Pru and Alex, before strutting off through the crowd of other tables.

Anabel followed up Cat's glare of judgment with one of her own. "If this is your version of flirting, I have many, many notes, none of them positive. You're giving a *performance*. Remember: annoyingly smitten teen socialites. Less arguing, more PDA, please."

"Fine!" With jerky motions, Pru slid her seat around the circular table until her knee banged up against Alex's leg. "Better?"

"Ow," said Alex, discreetly rubbing his thigh.

"I said public displays of affection, not public brawling," hissed Anabel. "You're supposed to look like teenagers madly in lust, not angry middle-aged divorcés who want to kill each other."

"We don't want to kill each other," Alex protested.

"Speak for yourself," retorted Pru.

An aging, well-dressed woman seated beside the Incorporated suit from earlier turned at the heat in Pru's voice, cool amusement painted across her face. "Trouble in paradise, dear?" she asked, with a slight sneer, as she looked Anabel up and down. "I do hear that Cornelius Park's brood of grandchildren keep lively company, though I hadn't realized serious young Alexandre was quite such a ladies' man."

"He has many hidden depths," deadpanned Anabel without missing a beat. She rounded on Pru and Alex. "Get it together. This whole ruse is useless if you leave all the fake dating up to me and Cat."

"Nothing fake-looking about *your* dating," groused Pru under her breath.

"Because Cat's a good partner under pressure. So are both of you, usually. So stop whining and start flirting."

"How?" asked Alex, in a slightly strained voice. At the next table, the UCC woman tittered into her neighbor's ear, staring right at them.

Pru, whose fear of being forced to make more small talk with the minion of an evil corporate superpower did, in fact, outweigh her fear of seeming ridiculous in front of tight-assed pretty boys, slid a frantic hand over the back of Alex's neck, massaging one thumb gently along his nape. Alex emitted a soft little gasp, but instead of flinching away, aimed an assessing look at Pru. He dropped a casual hand to her thigh, gracefully affectionate, almost possessive.

"No HJ in sight." Cat had returned. Glancing toward Pru and Alex, she nodded with what looked, amazingly, like grudging approval. "Better," she said. "About time you two picked up some slack."

"I'm sure I don't know what you mean," babbled Pru. She craned her neck, trying to check the UCC woman for a reaction without being obvious about it. To her relief, the latter rolled her eyes in extravagant disdain, returning to the shrimp cocktails.

Pru waited for Alex's hand to leave her thigh. It didn't, calluses steady and rough against her bare skin. Maybe from handling musical instruments. Maybe from handling plasma guns. Probably from both.

"Oh, I'm sure you do," he drawled. His tone, dipped low and flirtatious, was pretty obviously an act, but it shot a completely inappropriate shiver through her. He still hadn't removed his hand. Did she want him to?

Oh, no no no. Don't go down that path, brain. You came here with a job. Focus. Who here's pulling purse strings on what the father of wyverns is selling?

The answer, to Pru's immense frustration, could have been anyone. Jellicoe's associates at the next table—including the prudish Incorporated couple—seemed more interested in discussing the quality of the tuna tartare than weapons markets.

"The shrimp leaves a bit to be desired, but this must be a fresh catch, much better than last year's ceviche!"

"Now, the champagne on the other hand—"

"Adequate. Even that reclusive Lamarque boy had a glass!"

"But to pair with this grade of tuna—"

"Truly *divine* tuna."

Well, it wasn't like Pru could fault them. Even evil arms dealers needed vacations from time to time, and the tuna tartare had been pretty excellent.

As Pru finished her final plate—a miniature soufflé more decorative than edible—and stood to push her chair in, one of the other guests careened straight into its legs. The sandy-haired man grunted, splattering them both with his half-empty champagne flute.

"Shit," said Pru, hands reaching for the man's elbows to steady him. "Shit, shit, I'm sorry. I didn't . . ." She trailed off when he raised his eyes toward hers.

"Pretty, pretty Prudence!" slurred Dick Masterson, pupils blown over the rims of his red-tinted spectacles. "Fancy seeing you here, huh?"

The weight of unspoken barbs clung to Pru's tongue. *Found a new comic collection dealer to betray yet?* she wanted to ask, or *Better than last we met, asswipe*, or even just, *Fuck you. Fuck you, you sold me out, you almost ruined my life and now—*

"Masterson." Anabel slid between them, so silent and smooth, Pru hadn't even noticed the other girl's hand taking Masterson's elbow until Anabel was already there, smiling her society girl smile. "You've had a bit to drink, now haven't you?"

"Not *drinks*, babe," Masterson drawled, dragging out the word. He didn't look right. His eyes, unfocused, rolled wildly. His bicep flexed beneath Anabel's deceptively casual fingers. "Come on, pretty pretties, you two were always smarter than that, eh? You two were always . . ." He shook his head, as if to clear the fog in his gaze, and managed to still his eyes, for just a moment. "You should run while you can," he said to Pru. "Shoulda given you the chance, last we met, with those Incorporated enforcers, eh? Bunch of bitchy, fun-ruining, book-burning bastards, those UCC police brigades, am I right? UCC's full of bitches." He pointed a waving finger toward her. "Well, I'm giving you the chance now, huh? Poor little Barricader girl better run. Better run before . . . before . . ." Helplessly, he began to giggle.

"All right," said Anabel, still utterly placid. "Clearly, someone's been having more than No-Man's-Land-issued champagne. Guess even Incorporated types need to let loose every once in a while. Come on, let's go find your keeper."

She glanced at Pru, just once, past Masterson's lolling head, and nodded a subtle little Anabel Park "I got this" nod. Then, still gripping Masterson's elbow like he was some common party drunk—and not at all, say, the sniveling Incorporated book-smuggling customer who'd gotten them into this mess in the first place—she hauled him off to some corner of the party. Like magic, she deflected the inevitable stares from other guests with self-deprecating laughter and little smiles, as if to say, "Ah, look, someone's had a few too many uppers mixed into his drinks; isn't that a shame? You know how it is, of course you do."

Cat watched them for a beat, narrow eyed, and without a word, followed after, looking for all the world like Anabel's menacingly elegant, half-cyborg bodyguard, which, if you thought about it, was actually pretty on-brand for them both.

That left Alex to walk Pru back to the rental cabin, cautiously quiet in the wake of Pru's thin-mouthed reticence, until they reached the lift. "That was fun," said Alex. "Are you going to tell me who that guy was?"

Pru snorted. "What, you don't recognize him from the news reels your uncle blackmailed me with? He's the guy I used to sell black market comics to, up until he blew the whistle on me to those UCC enforcers. The rest, as they say, is history."

"Was he high?"

"On uppers? A lot of them, probably. And drunk, to boot." The beachside breeze had effectively blown dry the splatter of overpriced champagne on Pru's frock, but not the discomfort lingering beneath her skin. Trying to change the subject from Masterson's intoxicated pawing, she cleared her throat. "So. Dinner. Overhear any good leads from our friendly Incorporated neighbors at table seventeen?"

"Unless tuna tartare is code for a new breed of war mech, no. I also had no idea they thought I was such a shut-in."

"You are kind of a shut-in. I literally didn't even know you lived on campus until you stole my library study. Wait, were you just groping my leg under the dinner table because your manly virility felt insulted?"

"Me? I was merely following the orders of our uncrowned queen and future Head Representative Anabel Park." His voice was pure innocence. "Besides, you started it with your impromptu neck massage. I only escalated."

"I bet you say that to all the girls." Pru's heart drummed a steady staccato in her throat. "Typical pretty boy behavior, blaming us for your floozy ways."

She caught the rise of Alex's inky brows beneath the moonlight as he bent down to say, "You think I'm pretty?" He was taller than her. She forgot that sometimes, flying around above him on dragon wings, or talking hundreds of feet away over an earpiece, but she couldn't escape it now, the breadth of his shoulders, the play of tendons beneath the delicate skin of his neck, as he gave the lacy strings of her frock a little tug.

Pru's tongue, suddenly dry, cleaved to the roof of her mouth. Her pulse grew louder, insistent, drowning out any remotely witty comeback she could have formulated.

His hands drifted lower. The mech-sparring-hardened instinct in Pru's head had just enough time to register the span of his palms along her waist, before her back slammed into a cabin stilt, Alex's face inches from hers. "Bold move," he whispered, "to go straight for the neck. Now that's what I call audacity."

"Look who's talking!" Pru bucked against his grip in protest. "I'm not the ace mech pilot who sprang a surprise sparring match on an incompetent rookie as a *training exercise*." Her fingernails dug into his hips. She wondered if she was hurting him. She wondered if he cared. "You're sweet to pretend my prospects of passing the combat assessment aren't borderline hopeless."

Alex sighed quietly into the bare crook of her shoulder. "Why do you always assume the worst about yourself?"

"It's called realism. You should try it some time."

"It's *cruel*," said Alex. "I don't understand how someone so . . . you deserve kindness, Pru. I wish you'd be kinder to yourself. It's frustrating, that you're not."

Pru swallowed a sudden, embarrassingly hot lump in her throat. What was she supposed to say to that? Anabel hadn't given them a script for this. "Alex. I—"

"You're probably the most frustrating person I know," he continued. His lips ghosted along the dip of her clavicle, hesitation palpable, breath warm on her skin.

"You have a really weird definition of 'frustrating,' dude." Briefly, dizzyingly, Pru wondered what he'd do if she took matters into her own hands, closed the scant space between their mouths, and just—

He ducked his head and stepped back, detangling their bodies in one smooth motion. Pru stared up at him, heart thudding. Alex stared back, eyes a little wild. For a moment, he looked ready to catch her face between his hands and finish what he'd started.

Instead, his hands landed on the collar of her frock, straightening it with perfunctory haste. "I'm going to go find Anabel and Cat," Alex said as he worked. "Make sure they're okay, after that run-in at dinner."

"'Okay'?" Pru's hands closed over his, trapping them at her collar. "I'll bet you half my book smuggling savings that they've forgotten all about Masterson, and are canoodling in a sand dune somewhere."

Unlike us.

"Only one way to find out." He laughed softly, slipping from her grasp. "Go up and get some rest before the demo. And drink some water."

"Drink some *water*?" Pru echoed, incredulous.

Alex didn't answer, already ambling away across the sand. If she listened closely, she could hear him whistling the tune to an old Partition Wars ditty.

"Goddamn," Pru mumbled. She could still smell the clean notes of shampoo and cologne where he'd pressed himself into her skin and, guiltily, took a second to breathe it in. Then she collected herself and shouted after his cowardly, retreating tease of an ass, "You are the worst fake beach date ever!"

Alex just kept walking and whistling, the melody high and bright.

Pulse still humming hot under her skin, Pru checked an awful impulse to chase after him. *Nuh-uh, Pru. Remember the fake part of fake dating. Spies don't have time to chase boys. Not right before a monumentally dangerous weapons demo.*

Suddenly, getting a drink of water sounded like a great idea.

Hopping on the lift, shoreside breeze kissing the sweat-sticky back of her neck, Pru slumped against the railing to stare up at the moon rising over the sea. At least she'd get first dibs on the shower. A cold one.

◆

Metafeed Politics
"Inside Harold Jellicoe's Secretive Salesmanship: Is an Aging Father of Wyverns Making a Postwar Comeback?"
by Angelo O'Connor

Veteran weapons manufacturer Harold Jellicoe has long been a lynchpin of United Continental Confederacy Inc.'s arms dealing empire, but in an era of peace treaties and cross-continental co-operation efforts, the relevance of a man once dubbed the "father of wyverns" has grown questionable. Yet even as younger, flashier competitors declare his groundbreaking, bloodletting work obsolete, Jellicoe somehow continues to thrive, basking in the favor of his Executive General.

The UCC doesn't need open warfare to continue thriving—the cold war profits of an increasingly tech-driven arms race have lined the mega-corporation's pockets nicely—but the mega-corporation's appetite for expansion even in peacetime is an ill-kept secret. With a new Jellicoe-branded line of war machines rumored to debut this year, the biggest question on everyone's lips is: are these simply souped-up new war mechs, designed to intimidate non-Incorporated governments like the Barricade Coalition and democratic allies abroad—or something stranger and more sinister? And do they have anything to do with the wyvern-esque shadows spotted near the walls of New Columbia last month?

♦

AT FIRST, PRU THOUGHT she was dreaming about an earth-
quake. The soft-cushioned cot she'd staked out and collapsed into
after her shower shook beneath her every time she turned over,
which meant that either this weird treehouse-cabin-thing was
much more poorly built than Anabel and Alex's money should
have allowed—or the beach itself had decided to rebel against
their pretensions.

Something boomed faintly in the distance. Then the floor rocked
so hard, Pru nearly fell off the cot's edge. Swearing in a sleep-ragged
voice, Pru sat up, casting about blindly for her phone. "Guys," she
hissed into the dark. "Guys, did you feel that?"

The darkness-blurred edges of the cabin did not reply. Pru fumbled
her phone on, which displayed the time in bright neon numbers: 8:30
P.M. People were probably starting to gather on the beach for the
demo.

Fully awake now, Pru swung her legs over the side of her cot,
heart beginning to hammer. When her feet hit the floor, a second
boom nearly jarred her knees out from under her. "Holy shit," she
hissed, clinging to the cot's edge. Then, very gingerly, she jogged
over to the closest window. At first, she thought a storm was rolling in—a cloud, at any rate, huge and dark, blotting out the moon.
But no, it couldn't be a cloud, not with those shifting edges, scattering like—

Wings. Pru's fingers spasmed along the windowsill. Tens, maybe
dozens, of shiny metallic wings batted up against the ocean's horizon,
preparing to descend on the beach. Like Rebelwing's, but smaller,
jerkier in their flight patterns. The back of her brain screamed. She'd

seen this before, but back then, it had been confined to footage of wartime propaganda in the safety of a history classroom.

Wyverns.

So here was Jellicoe's fireworks display. Pru's friends would be waiting for her on the demo. The thought of them thudded into the pit of her stomach, along with her heart. She was supposed to go meet them. This was what they'd come to see. The enemy they'd come to scope.

So why couldn't she make herself move?

The cloud of wyverns shifted, just slightly. "Wait," Pru said aloud, her voice hoarse. She knew that formation from documentary footage, but this was all wrong. This was supposed to be a product demonstration. A thrilling display for potential buyers, nothing more. Pru's pulse thrummed through her ears, hairs prickling on the back of her neck. The cloud shifted once more.

"Wait," Pru whispered again, nonsensically, voice thick in her throat, "stop, you can't—"

A blast of pale blue exploded across her field of vision. Plasma fire, Pru registered distantly, ears ringing. The wyverns were loosing plasma fire. As it hit the edge of the sea, the ground shook beneath Pru's buckling knees again. Someone screamed in the distance.

♦

HAROLD JELLICOE'S FIREWORKS DISPLAY wasn't a product demo at all. It was an ambush.

Her friends. Pru had to get to her friends.

Shutting her eyes, Pru breathed out slow, the way Jay had taught her weeks ago, cradled in Rebelwing's cockpit.

She had no plan, no idea what to do about anything, but she'd been a book smuggler since she was fourteen. *Come on, Pru-Wu*, she imagined Anabel saying. *You've winged worse drops than this.*

That was a filthy lie, but Pru didn't really have a choice except to believe it. Her brain would just have to tough it out.

With one last exhale, she unstuck her fear-stuck feet, and ran for the lift.

THE MIDNIGHT AMBUSH ——————— 11

Running through sand on a normal day at the beach sucked. Running through sand that kept shifting and shaking with every crack of plasma fire along the shoreline was a new and exciting level of terrible that Pru really could have done without. Her legs were screaming by the time she hit the scant cover of the cabins at the beach's edge. These had no stilts or plexiglass elevators, but their wide verandas still lent her a better view than she would have gotten being trampled into the sand. Tiptoes straining at the edge of the deck, she scanned the panicked swarm of party guests for a familiar flash of dark hair and sharp bones, or a telltale wink of a cybernetic eye.

The edge of a neighboring cabin roof blasted off in an explosion of blue-white flame. A cool metal hand clenched around her elbow, yanking her away from scattering debris. "What took you so long?" demanded Cat.

"Me!?" Pru windmilled out of Cat's grip, rounding on the other girl. "I was looking for you! Plasma fire started raining from the sky, and I had no idea where any of you were. You scared the shit out of me!"

"We're handling things."

The situation did not look handled. Pru scanned the chaos on the beach for the familiar banner of Anabel's ebony hair. None of the people fleeing the beach had one. "Where's Anabel?"

Cat's jaw set. "Never mind that. Find cover!"

Pru hoped her answering scoff sounded as incredulous as she felt. "Right, and leave my best friend's lady love to fend for herself out here?"

"I can handle myself."

"Oh, for—" Pru bit back a snarl that was half frustration, half desperate terror. "That doesn't mean you can't use help! Weren't you the one who asked Alex to help you build Rebelwing?"

"You're not Alexandre."

Pru rolled the sting of that observation off with a curl of her shoulders. "Yeah, believe it or not, I've kind of noticed as much, after playing everyone's second choice for going on a month and a half. You dealt with my lack of Alex-ness then. You can deal with it now. So one more time." Pru grabbed Cat's shoulder to steady them both against the shake of more rumbles in the distance. The wyverns were gaining. "Where are Anabel and Alex?"

Cat stilled, her entire body taut beneath Pru's grip, then bit out, "Alexandre went to pitch a distress signal to Coalition forces."

"And Anabel?"

That muscle in Cat's jaw jumped again. "Come on." Seizing Pru's elbow, she dragged her the rest of the way inside the rattling cabin. Two figures sat hunched together at the very back of the room. It took Pru a beat to place Anabel's long hair, currently pinned back at her nape, her hands braced on the second figure's bicep. It took Pru a couple beats more to place the man trembling with giggling sobs beneath Anabel's grip.

Pru rounded on Cat. "What the hell are you guys doing with Dick Fucking Masterson?"

"Trying to keep him from joining his flock and killing us all," said Cat, with perfunctory sensibility.

"What—"

A throat-scraping shriek from Masterson derailed the rest of their conversation. "You gotta give me up, Annie," Masterson rasped at Anabel through chattering teeth. "It's happening whether you like it or not."

"Well, I don't, so long as you're soliciting my opinion on the matter," said Anabel in severe tones. "Fight it, Dick. You're a goddamn pain in the ass, and a traitorous little coward, but you've never done anything against your own interests. Don't you dare start now."

Masterson's reply was cut off by another strangled cry. Metal nubs spiked bloody from the back of his shirt. Pru's hands jumped to her mouth. "Shit," she hissed, "shit, shit, what the shit."

"I told you," said Cat to Anabel. "He's turning. You can't stop what's clearly already in motion. This is what Jellicoe does."

"Can't stop *what?*" yelled Pru, staring sick at the bloodstained bits of metal growing inch by inch from a whimpering Masterson's shoulder blades.

Cat spun her around by the elbow. "Isn't it obvious?" she hissed. "Jellicoe could never figure out how to perfect that first generation of wyvern mechs. He could never capture true sentience. So their engineers took a different tack with the second generation of wyverns. Congratulations, Wu. You're witnessing the up close and personal creation of the world's first organically grown and modded cyborg."

The metal spanning from Masterson's back was beginning to take a familiar shape. Wings, she realized. Batlike, metal wings. "You're say-ing they're turning *actual human people* into their own Robo Reptiles?"

"Not if I have anything to say about it," snarled Anabel, still hang-ing on to a chalk-faced Masterson. "Fight it, you slimy little bastard. Your stupid pervert mind is all yours, yeah? Don't give that up to Incorporation too."

"You don't get it, do you?" Masterson shook with the force of laughter ripped from his body. "That was never my choice, and nei-ther is this. You think anyone gets a choice under Incorporation? If the Executive General and his sycophants aren't going to let people choose what words they hear or read or speak, they sure as shit aren't going to give people a *choice* over who's implanted with a wyvern cell and who's not." As he spoke, metal scales flickered to life along pink flesh, razoring through the skin. "Incorporated tech has been inside me for longer than you've known me, Annie. I was bought and sold to Jellicoe from the moment I stuck my money in the wrong place at the wrong time—ah!" Another wave of scales bloomed, crimson edged. "They make it . . . so . . . easy." Masterson grimaced, but now that Anabel had gotten him talking, he couldn't seem to stop. "So easy to sell them everything, mind and body and soul, and just . . . stop . . . thinking."

"The comics you bought off us," Anabel began.

"Stupid indulgence," hissed Masterson. His voice was changing, like sloppy auto-tuning, robotic and full of fuzz. "There's the rub, isn't it? Thinking . . . questioning . . . worrying about things, it's all . . . such a . . . headache. Easier to just . . . sign it over. But that's the . . . human thing . . . I guess. Testing the . . . cage . . . you've bought. Always . . . testing . . . your choices." He giggled, once, nails scraping down metal. "*Choice.* Can you . . . imagine? So damn double-edged."

Anabel leaned in. "You've still got one."

Another brittle giggle. "You can't save me."

"No," agreed Anabel, with a resolute sort of chill. "No one can. But that doesn't mean you can't screw over the people you sold yourself to. I do know you love screwing over business partners."

"I can't—"

"You can. By answering me this." Anabel ticked off questions, one-handed. "One, how many wyverns are there? Two, who are they? And three . . . three, how do you take them out?"

Silence stretched between them. The scales were razoring in faster and faster, but Anabel didn't even seem fazed, waiting Masterson out, like they were on another UCC-controlled street corner, waiting for a mid-risk drop.

"Twenty-seven," Masterson choked out at last. "Twenty-seven, last I counted, with more in beta. They're . . . people who broke the rules of . . . Incorporation. With book smuggling . . . or protesting . . . or wearing the wrong-colored socks, I don't fucking know."

"Yes, you do." That came from Cat, who strode over to grip her own metal fingers against the still-human flesh at Masterson's chin. "Organically grown cyborgs that work in flocks like yours, they're just another kind of animal, like their flesh-and-blood cousins. I've studied this. Your flock has an alpha." Cat's eyes glinted under the slivering moonlight, the boom of plasma fire in the distance. "Take out the alpha, and you take out the flock. Who is it?"

"Not a . . . who," gasped Masterson. "A . . . what. I never . . ." The remainder of his words died inside a mechanical throat, as metal scales erupted over the last pieces of human skin. Cat jumped backward. Anabel swore.

A wink of blue-white plasma fire flickered to life inside Masterson's ruined mouth. Pru shouted, springing forward, but Anabel got there first, a revolver materializing in her hands out of nowhere. She fired once, a silent shot of plasma. Masterson—the thing that had been Masterson—went down.

It could be a film poster, or a video game ad, thought Pru, scrabbling backward from the bloody tableau Anabel and Masterson formed. Brigadier General Park's youngest, cleverest granddaughter straightened her spine over the wreck of metal and man crumpled at her feet, revolver still trained on the crimson ruin of his head. If any of the red had splattered onto her navy silk cocktail dress, the darkness of the cloth hid the color. The cloth billowed around her knees like a robe on some stylized goddess of death.

Pru couldn't stop staring at the blood she *could* see. Masterson had been a douchey but reliable black market customer. Masterson had betrayed them. Masterson had been bought and sold and used for parts by Incorporated arms dealers. Masterson had, by the will of whoever was pulling his mechanical strings, tried to kill them all in a spray of plasma fire right here in this No Man's Land cabin. And now, Masterson was dead.

Another tremble of the ground, followed by more shouts from outside, shook them all back to life. "We've got to find Alex," Pru croaked at last, dragging her eyes away from the corpse. "We've got to find him, and get the hell out of here."

"Can't," said Anabel grimly. She stepped around the body, looking faintly gray beneath her beach tan, but spoke steady voiced. "Routes in and out of No Man's Land are all blocked off right now, thanks to the attack. Our only chance is if Alex gets a signal out to the Coalition."

"Well, where is he? How long will that take?"

"I don't know."

"That's not good enough," said Pru. Blood hammered in her head, and pooled on the floor beside her. "We need to find him."

Anabel's fingers snagged on her shoulder. "If you think you're heading out to the beach, with wyverns dive-bombing the shit out of anyone stupid enough to be caught running across open shore-line right now—"

"I'm not!" Pru shrugged her hand off. The barest traces of a plan, riding on the edge of adrenaline, were falling together inside her head. *Come on, brain, don't fail me now.* "At least, not alone."

"Cat and I—"

"Are staying right here," said Pru. A grim sort of foolhardy determination had filled her up inside, making a heady cocktail of the amplified anxiety in her gut. "I've got another friend to call on."

Anabel sucked in a sharp breath, as Pru's meaning caught on. "You can't mean *Rebelwing*."

Pru ignored the extra terrified leap of her heart at hearing her terrible plan put into audible words, and said, coolly as she could, "Hopefully, it'll help me hold off the worst of more wyvern attacks until the actual Coalition military gets its ass over here."

"That . . . is so many shades of awful idea, I'm not sure I actually know where to begin."

Pru shrugged, trying to mimic her usual habit of shrugging off nerves before a book smuggling drop. "Not sure I've got many other options." Just like she was talking about firewall hacking versus physical drop-offs in an Incorporated zone. Options laid out easy, risky but familiar. Manageable.

"Do you know how far out No Man's Land is from New Columbia?" demanded Anabel. "Can your imprint even catch a signal from out here?"

"Depends." Pru turned to Cat. "Alex said you brought . . . toys. Anything useful?"

Cat gave a slow nod. "A neural amplifier. I had one disguised as a holo-drive. Amplifies the imprint as far as sixty kilometers. We're within range, barely."

Anabel bit her lip. Girls of Anabel's stock didn't stand down easy, but they were also canny enough to know when they'd been checked. "You really think this will work?"

"It will," said Cat, with the sort of finality that only the dragon's own engineer could really sell. Stepping up beside Anabel, she slipped a little chrome cylinder into Pru's hand. "I didn't think you deserved the dragon," she said bluntly. "I'd like, for once, to be proven wrong."

"Thanks." Pru looked down at the cylinder, so like the one she'd passed to Masterson almost two months ago, the one that had sealed her present circumstances. Plasma fire outside. Wyverns in the sky. No Man's Land stretched out untouchable around them, routes out back to the Barricade cities all blockaded.

Circumstances, though, could be rewritten. Stepping out to the very edge of the cabin's entrance, Pru squeezed her eyes shut. Jamming her thumb against the cylinder's top button, she screamed inside her brain, as loud as she could, *Robo Reptile, get your scaly ass out here and protect the things you were intended to.*

Time stretched out before them. Minutes ticked by, grew longer. The shriek of plasma fire kept streaking across Pru's eardrums, and still, she held the thought. She needed the dragon. She needed it to find her.

Then she saw it, the now-familiar flicker of a reptilian camera's gaze from behind her eyelids: a sprawl of shoreline, lit up in panoramic high definition, the dots of wyverns in the sky, the people scattering and fleeing below like ants. So distant, so far, but growing, growing, growing until—

The dragon's metallic roar drowned out the plasma fire, as a new pair of wings, broader and smoother than any wyvern's, beat up to the beach's edge. Pru's eyes fluttered open in time to meet that silver-blue gaze. She opened her mouth, half relief, half desperation, to call aloud to it.

Someone else was running across the beach, between Pru and the dragon, dark-headed, human skin exposed to the glimmer of plasma fire as he pelted toward them.

Alex. Alex, alive and caught in the open.

Pru recognized him in the same instant that one of the wyverns, adrift in its corner of the sky, sighted him.

And then, like something caught in slow motion on camera, the wyvern dove.

◆

Barricader's Daily
BREAKING NEWS ALERT

Shots of plasma fire have been dropped on a joint UCC-Coalition cooperation gala on a beach in No Man's Land, according to senior security staffers for the event. Official spokespeople from UCC Inc. deny any involvement by the Executive General or his associates. Sources close to the UCC Office of the Propagandist have alleged that the attack may be tied to a scheduled product demonstration by Incorporated arms dealer Harold Jellicoe. At least eleven reported injured thus far, and three casualties confirmed. Story is developing.

◆

PRU'S FEET ROOTED TO the cabin floor, shackled there by a wave of panic. Her brain had gone useless and disconnected from the rest of her again. A distant part of her wondered if she'd ever grow out of this horrible, cowardly sensation of being fear-stuck. Time slowed, temporarily rendered artificial. Oxygen compressed inside her lungs, as she stared at the tableau unfolding before her like a visual novel wound into exaggeratedly broken-down motion: the wyverns spotting the midnight sky over the ocean's horizon. Alex, shirt unbuttoned at the throat, unprotected on the bare and moon-pale beach beneath them. The flash of moonlight glinting off razor-edged wyvern scales onto vulnerable, human skin.

In Pru's mind, the dragon, roaring, wove unseen beneath the sprawl of wyverns, streaking toward Pru. She remembered Etienne railing against wyverns in the video camera of Rebelwing's memory. She remembered Quixote falling through the sky.

The first wyvern dove toward Alex, plasma fire blooming in a pale flash against the night.

Pru didn't think. She didn't speak. But something buried deep inside herself erupted to life at the sight of the metal monster making for Alex. And like a gear turning in the back of her brain, the dragon stopped, turned, and swooped.

Plasma fire exploded over Alex, who ducked his head, throwing himself uselessly into the sand and—

"Alex!" screamed someone behind Pru. Anabel, clutching at Pru's arm. The other girl's nails dug into Pru's bicep. "Alex!" She might have been crying.

But no, Alex was rising, untouched. Except it wasn't Alex at all. Silver scales glimmered in and out of focus around him, covering up the delicate human skin of the boy inside. Still, Pru knew precisely where he was. She knew, because she—no, the dragon, of course, the dragon—had put him there.

"Where," Anabel began faintly, and stopped. She swallowed, apparently gathering herself to say more. She sounded so young. Probably because she *was* young. As young as Pru, really, for whatever that mattered, their birthdays within months of each other. Youngest and cleverest of the Park brood, wasn't that what everyone in New Columbia always said?

Anabel had killed a man tonight. Anabel had killed a man Pru knew. Anabel had saved them all. Pru could still see smears of blood in the peripheries of her sight line.

Uncertain of control over her own muscles, Pru reached behind herself, fingers flailing to grip her friend's cold, gun-callused hand. "The cockpit," Pru heard herself say. "I put Alex in the cockpit of the dragon. He's all right, Anabel. He's safe."

The wyverns circled ahead on the beach, around the spot where the dragon—with Alex inside—hovered, still barely visible beneath its cloaking mechanisms. *Can you hear me?* she whispered desperately into the shell of her mind, fumbling for the imprint. *Can you do this? Can you fly?*

And then, louder and clearer than she'd ever heard through an earpiece, Alex's voice rippled back across Pru's mind: *We can.*

12 —— WE SHALL FIGHT ON THE BEACHES

Alexandre Santiago Lamarque was a spectacular combat mech pilot. Pru had known that, on a detached, "well, he works with the Coalition's military division, so duh" kind of level, and also a "this obsolete old combat mech named Quixote nearly strangled me and my sentient dragon out of the sky" level. Witnessing him in the dragon's cockpit, though, was a whole new plane of understanding just how good Alex was at what he did.

Witnessing was maybe the wrong word. Alex kept the cloaking mechanism activated for most of the fight, so all you could really catch via naked eye was a telltale blur of light between plasma fire blasts, weaving between the wyverns like some vengeful spirit. Every once in a while, though, he'd tweak the cloaking just a little, allow a sliver of silver scales to flash against plasma and moonlight. It worked like a laser pointer on cats, thought Pru, watching the wyverns jerk back, furious and disoriented by those unpredictable streaks of light on dragon wings: there, then gone again.

"I didn't know he could fly like that," said Pru.

"Fly like what?" asked Anabel. "I can hardly see shit out there."

Pru frowned. "But don't you—oh."

It didn't matter to Pru what could or couldn't be seen through human eyes. The piece of her mind that belonged to the dragon's imprint knew exactly where Alex was for every fraction of a movement, every evasion and release of plasma fire, every swooping dive and coasting sweep over the battleground.

"She's tracking Alexandre's movements," observed Cat. "That's how she can tell how he's piloting." To Pru, she added, rather stiffly, "I suppose that imprint has done you some good after all, if it's letting you fly Alexandre through this firefight."

"I thought only imprinted pilots could sit in the dragon's cockpit," said Anabel, turning to Cat. "But, I mean . . . Pru's right here, on the ground, with us, and Alex is the one out there, playing fighter pilot, which shouldn't be physically or mechanically *possible*."

"It appears that your friend has managed well enough."

"For the last time, Cat, her name's Pru. Did you know this kind of piloting could be done?"

"If I had," drawled Cat, "I would have been less worried about someone other than Alexandre having that imprint."

Pru didn't bother interrupting their conversation. Anabel was right, sort of. Some piece of Pru, tied up inside her human body, stood at the cabin door with Cat and Anabel. But Anabel didn't account for the bigger piece of Pru, which could see the beach like the battlefield the wyverns had made it. The bigger piece of Pru was up there in the sky, one with the dragon, and the boy inside. The bigger piece of Pru wove and dove and dodged, her reptilian eyes narrowed on points of black in the sky. Enemies.

Alex's voice, twining with the dragon's imprint, rippled through Pru's mind again.

I—we have the shot, he said.

Pru hesitated. *Do we take it?*

His weariness, linked up to her like this, felt palpable. *If we don't shoot them down, they're going to kill more people, if that's what you're asking.*

How close are the Coalition?

Not close enough. We're lucky Rebelwing's stabled as close to the walls as she is, otherwise . . .

Pru, who remembered the dance of plasma glow across Alex's bare skin, didn't want to think about otherwise. She thought of Masterson, a bloody pile of parts crumpled at Anabel's feet, not quite man, not quite machine. She thought of the pallor of Anabel's cold, grim-set face over navy silk, and the way she'd screamed Alex's name when that blaze of plasma fire nearly swallowed him whole. She thought of Cat, pressing the holo-drive-shaped amplifier between Pru's palms and saying, "Prove me wrong."

Pru closed her eyes, and opened the dragon's. Black points in the sky, sighted just as Alex had promised. *Take the shot.*

He took the shot.

Several things happened in rapid succession. Pru, watching them unfold through dragon's eyes, found herself breaking them down for catalogue. One, the roar of her own plasma fire streaking out across the sky in six quick arcs, taking out the six closest wyverns. Screaming, they hurtled toward the black sea below, light winking out into the swelling dark. Two, the collective focus of the remaining flock, as they zeroed in on their greatest source of danger. Three, the air cutting sharp around them, as Alex and the dragon spun toward the ocean to avoid a volley of return fire. Four, the flock diving after them, faster and faster, tailing the dragon like birds after prey.

There are too many, Pru's mind pressed against the imprint, like her spine curling into the corner of the fateful, falling lift that had first birthed this bond. *There are too many, Alex, you won't be able to take them all.*

We won't have to.

Are you insane?

My sanity's irrelevant to this fight. Look up.

Pru looked. The twist of her neck jarred her back into her human self on the beach. Her knees scraped wood when she hit the cabin floor.

"Pru!" Anabel's hands and, amusingly enough, Cat's—oh look, Anabel's right, her girlfriend really *does* care—braced along Pru's arms. Together, her friends pulled her back to her feet. "Shit, Pru-Wu. Are you okay? Hey!"

But Pru wasn't looking at Anabel, or at Cat. She was looking up, toward the night sky, above the wyverns, above the dragon, above Alex.

"Look," she whispered. "Anabel. Cat. Look."

Their sharp, synced-up inhales told Pru they had.

Flashing across the sky was a fleet of combat mechs painted over with the crest of the Barricade Coalition.

"Guess the cavalry's finally here," Pru croaked. "Took them long enough."

♦

New Columbia Preparatory Academy Student Message Boards

Saturday, 12:30 A.M.

SOUR16: have you guys seen all these breaking news alerts??

VIKTORIAN: dude, why are you even still awake.

SANSMERCI: f that, why are y'all still on our SCHOOL MESSAGE BOARDS. it's freaking midnight on a saturday.

SOUR16: kettle, black.

SANSMERCI: ha, touché.

SOUR16: seriously, did those alerts wake no one up? I thought it was a fire alarm, & it wound up being my effing phone.

VIKTORIAN: yeah, but I think most sane ppl turned it off & went back to sleep.

SANSMERCI: well, we're Barricader prep schoolers. we're over-achievers. continent's best damn hope for the future.

SOUR16: are you drunk?

SANSMERCI: on sleep deprivation, maybe. I've been watching the news on the shit going down at No Man's Land. some of the gossip blogs say New Columbia Prep students were at the scene.

VIKTORIAN: they're just gossip blogs.

SANSMERCI: still. do you think it's true? do you think they're ok?

SOUR16: well, not all the ppl the Barricader's Daily alerts just confirmed dead or wounded.

VIKTORIAN: fucking terrorism, man.

SANSMERCI: you don't know it's terrorism. maybe something went haywire with that product demo that all the tech gossip rags were teasing.

VIKTORIAN: haywire enough to drop plasma fire on a fucking beach party?

SANSMERCI: I don't know. I dunno what to think. you guys see-ing these reports? this shit is horrifying.

SOUR16: who do you think is dead?
SANSMERCI: hopefully no one we know.

◆

THE REST OF THE FIGHTING was brutish and short. Pru remembered her history lessons: during the Partition Wars, the Barricade Coalition military had needed three mechs to take on a single Incorporated war wyvern. This Coalition fleet had spared no chances, outnumbering the wyverns six to one. Even scattered and damaged by Rebelwing, the straggling wyverns put up a nasty defense, a flurry of vicious, close-quarters attacks, quicker and meaner than anything Pru had ever seen on a war reel. For several heart-hammering moments, Pru wondered if these strange new monsters might still win the day on cruel ingenuity alone.

Still, in the end, the Coalition's sheer numbers prevailed. Their hover mechs, all sharp-nosed precision, cut through the remaining flock with grim, brute force. Plasma fire bloomed bright over the sea. And then there was only the dead to see to.

The battle's aftermath was patchwork to Pru. She remembered the thud at the back of her brain, when Alex and the dragon landed somewhere opposite the cabin. Cut forward a bit in her memory, and she'd hit the sight of Coalition personnel ushering survivors to safety, or speaking in authoritative voices with the gape-jawed No Man's Land security personnel. Some bodies on the beach, still breathing, were loaded onto med evacuation craft. Other bodies, like Masterson's, found shrouds. Body bags lined up on the black-scorched, red-stained beach. Not as many as Pru had feared. But body bags, all the same.

Someone dropped a blanket over her shoulders. "Prudence."

Pru's gaze jerked upward, unfocused, toward the blanket's source. Her own body felt far too heavy, stuck in gravity's embrace, too close to that scorched and stained stand. Gradually, Jay Park's features fell into focus. How nice. "Are the others okay?" croaked Pru.

Jay didn't have to ask which others she meant. "Your three conniving friends are miraculously uninjured, alive, and accounted for." More wryly, he added, "Though whether you'll all remain that way depends on how black of a mood Hakeem's in, once he's properly briefed on the extent of your activities. A party full of rich Incorporated douchebags, at No Man's Land, no less? Really?"

"Blame your cousin." Pru pulled the blanket tighter around her shoulders. "She thought it would be a good chance to get some Incorporated war profiteers drunk and learn a thing or two about their latest military tech."

Jay sucked a breath in between his teeth. "Well, you certainly accomplished that much."

"I think she was also trying to get laid," said Pru.

Anabel's cousin mugged a slightly scandalized expression. "Thanks, but I really don't need your briefing on that part."

"Talking about me?" Anabel materialized, Cat at her elbow. Both were pale, sporting deep shadows beneath the eyes, but their gaits held steady.

Jay rounded on his cousin. "This isn't actually surprising, coming from you. You *would* waltz into one of the most controversial society parties of the season. What surprises me is how you convinced not one but *three* of your friends to go along with you."

"I'm charismatic," rasped Anabel. She coughed. "Doing Grandfather's legacy proud. My reputation precedes me."

"Also, one of us is already a juvenile delinquent anyway," Cat put in helpfully.

"Thanks," said Pru.

"I only speak the truth."

Jay groaned, rubbing his temples. "I would blame the folly of youth, but I don't think even I was this foolhardy at your age, and I'm *related* to you."

"Please," said Anabel, "you're, like, five seconds older than I am."

"I'm eleven years older than you are, thanks. What were you thinking? You could have *died*."

"I was thinking that a terror attack on both Barricaders and UCC Inc. personnel was definitely not what the party itinerary meant by 'fireworks display sponsored by Harold Jellicoe,' so you can quit laying the blame for tonight on me." Anabel's voice was almost flawlessly cool, except for the crack on the last word. In a smaller voice, she said, "My job is information gathering. I just took what I heard at face value. Naive of me, really. I should have expected him to do this. It's *Jellicoe*." Her hands, empty of plasma guns or microphones, looked delicate and very small when she twisted them together.

Jay covered them with his own. "Your job is being a high school student. And a teenager. I just wish you'd *told* me."

"Would you have stopped us?" asked Cat, eyebrows arched. She looked genuinely curious.

"Oh, he would have tried, but I would have overruled him. I believe in allowing precocious children long leashes." Emerging from the crowd of Coalition personnel just outside the cabin entrance, Hakeem Bishop strode toward them, a vision right out of the war reels with an old Barricaders' military jacket draped over his shoulders. It was the jacket, as much as the look on his face and heavy step of his gait, that reminded Pru of exactly what tonight's events would mean to a man with Bishop's history. A veteran who'd survived the wyverns of one Partition War in time to see a new flock return to the continent. Pru swallowed hard.

Beside Bishop, bearing the same under-eye shadows and pallid features as Anabel and Cat, was Alex, slightly shaky limbed. His eyes, dark and wide, locked on Pru's. Outside the dragon's cockpit, his voice no longer echoed inside her skull. The space between them, silence across two minds, felt oddly lonely.

Without really thinking about it, Pru closed the distance, and wrapped her fingers around his. To her surprise, he squeezed back, so hard she swore she felt her bones creak. Neither of them moved to let go.

Jay, meanwhile, had gone wry mouthed, but his face remained impressively free of any other indicator of surprise. "Hakeem. I didn't expect to see you out here in person. It's the middle of the night."

"My sixth sense for troublesome youths tingled," drawled the Chief of Staff. Bishop's gaze raked back toward Alex, and zoomed in. "Young Monsieur Lamarque. For the record, if you think I don't pay off snitches on both sides of the Barricades to keep an eye on your whereabouts, boy do you have another think coming."

"Interesting," mused Jay. "So you didn't predict that Jellicoe's demo would turn into an ambush either. Or you'd never have let Alex get within fifty miles of No Man's Land."

"No, I did not," Bishop admitted. "An error in judgment, on my part. But not one I can regret. You saved lives tonight "

"Not their job!" snapped Jay, head jerking up. His eyes, usually lidded half-mast, had gone wide and angry. Those eyes locked on the Chief of Staff's. An unspoken something shifted between the two men, some battle of wills neither seemed keen on copping to.

"Hakeem," said Alex. It was the first time Pru had heard him refer to the Chief of Staff by first name, but it held the lilt of the famil-iar. Gently detangling his fingers from Pru's, Alex turned toward Bishop, imploring, no longer the ace mech pilot, but a boy seeking counsel. "What do you know about the wyverns?"

Bishop's eyes softened on him. He sighed. "I know you won't get anywhere shooting them down one by one like we did tonight. You need to go after the—"

"Alpha, yes, we know," interrupted Cat, cybernetic eye glittering in the dark. "Take the alpha out, and you kill the wyvern nest for good. The problem is, we don't know who or what or where the alpha is. Any help, there?"

"For starters, the alpha isn't one piece on the board," said Bishop. "It's two."

Cat blinked. "Excuse me?"

"There's the wyvern alpha, the one that controls the nest, yes," Bishop went on. "But surely you don't imagine Jellicoe would allow the alpha any greater autonomy than the other wyverns. After all, what is the alpha at the end of the day but another sad, sorry person implanted with a cell of Incorporated tech? Destroy the alpha, and they can always implant the cell in a new one. No, you need to destroy the cell *itself.*"

Alex strode forward to stand with Cat. "And what do you know about this alpha cell?"

"Nothing your uncle isn't already aware of," put in Jay Park, before the Chief of Staff could respond. Anabel's cousin spoke in a dangerously light voice. He still hadn't broken eye contact with Bishop. "Isn't that so, Hakeem?"

"Meaning none of our business," translated Anabel. Scorn bloomed in her voice.

Her cousin turned his glare on her. "You may be as much Cornelius Park's grandchild as I am, but that doesn't mean you get to know every single piece of information the Head Representative of the Barricade Coalition is privy to." His gaze traveled over the rest of them, lingering on each face in turn, stopping longest on Pru's. "Any of you, regardless of surname, or any of the privileges you think they accord." He inclined his head once, toward Alex. "My apologies, young monsieur."

"None needed," said Alex. "So far as trading on surnames goes, I use my mother's for good reason. If my uncle doesn't want me to know his secrets, I'm sure Hakeem will keep them."

The Chief of Staff snorted, a muscle in his jaw working. "Keep double-edging your observations that way, and you'll make a fine politician yourself someday."

"Doesn't sound like a compliment."

"Doesn't make it an insult," Bishop shot back, but the words carried little heat. Moonlight glimmered over the silvering remnants of his hair, shading in the craggy hollows of a face that had seen better years. The weight of war's history, mapped across the body of a man.

"Ask your uncle," he added, "if you really think you need to know about those wyverns. The decision ultimately belongs to Gabriel." A bitter ghost of his own smile passed over the Chief of Staff's lips. "It always has."

WITH NO PLACE LEFT TO CALL HOME——— 13

At the end of it all, Pru went home. Not back to the Academy dorms, but properly home, to Mama's apartment above its little bodega. It took an exceedingly awkward transport mech route from No Man's Land back across the walls of New Columbia. Pru, Alex, Anabel, and Cat huddled together on one end of the compartment, while Coalition staffers crammed themselves at the other end, fiddling with uniform jackets and avoiding eye contact. Still, when they passed the Barricade checkpoint, Alex hopped off at Pru's stop without prompting.

She blinked at him. "You don't have to walk me home," she told him, shifting stiffly from one foot to the other. "No one's obliged to play the gentleman after such an epically and traumatically terrible date." Pru tried to keep her voice light, but her hands shook when they hefted her overnight bag across one shoulder.

Alex's hands, larger and longer fingered, covered her whitening knuckles, holding the bag's strap in place. "I could use the air. Besides, it's on the way."

"Suit yourself," she said, but was absurdly grateful when he followed along down the block, warm and quiet at her back. "So, are we going to talk about it?"

"Talk about what?"

Pru rolled her eyes at a passing lamp post. "Come on. Robo Reptile mind meld much?"

Alex's steps faltered. Their elbows knocked together. "I never thanked you."

"For sticking you inside a sentient mobile suit and flinging you into a flock of flying cyborgs?"

Lamplight spanned over the smile crinkling the corners of his eyes. "For protecting me."

"Oh," said Pru, unsure what to do about the inconvenient drop in her belly.

"The rest of it, the way the imprint reacted . . ." He shook his head. "Cat and I, we spent years and years building Rebelwing, but the fact that she has a literal mind of her own means there's probably always going to be things we don't know, about how she works, or what her true capabilities are. There's always going to be crap we never planned on."

Like me, Pru didn't say. *You never planned on me.* "So, what," she said instead, "does this mean Rebelwing's extended her imprint to include you too?"

His mouth worked. "I'm not sure. But I don't think so. Rebelwing only came for me because you wanted it. Didn't you?"

Pinned beneath those eyes again, Pru swallowed. "Yeah."

"Then it's still you that put me in the air," he said softly. "I think maybe, because you wanted me in that cockpit, Rebelwing allowed it. You're still her imprinted pilot. That link between us, that's your imprint too. It exists because your mech chose to cleave herself to your desires, for better or worse, and your desire was, well . . ."

A chuckle escaped him. "You wanted me to fly. So a dragon took me to the sky."

They climbed the spindly spiral stairs up to Mama's apartment. A pair of voices floated down from Mama's open living room window. One was recognizably Mama's, but the other was lower, male, but still, faintly familiar. Pru breathed through her teeth. "Holy crap."

Alex's eyebrows had gone up. "Is that—"

Pru cut him off with a sharp gesture, and pointed to the door. He nodded. Together, they leaned up to the window, taking in the sight of her mother and his uncle in the living room, facing one another over a bottle of red and a pair of wine glasses on the coffee table. The looked like opponents at a chess match, the cabernet casting a faint red glow over their faces in the dimly lit apartment.

"Your stories might have changed the world," Gabriel Lamarque was saying.

Mama poured them each a glass, then handed one to Lamarque, snagging the other with her free hand. "But they didn't. They were never going to."

"You don't think the Incorporated leaders employed gifted storytellers? The Office of the Propagandist is one of the Executive General's most well-funded departments. How else exactly do you suppose they convinced an entire continent to Incorporate?"

"And how many great storytellers have come and gone over the course of human history? You think I'm a greater wordsmith than Morrison, or Orwell, or Shakespeare? If books could save us all, surely they'd have managed it by now." Mama waved a hand. The freshly poured wine glass between her fingers cast ruby shadows across the faded couch. "But here we are."

"So why do it at all?"

"Kids used to write me letters, you know," said Mama. "About how they figured out how to mend broken relationships by listening to my wireless dramas. Or how one line from a novel made an impossible obstacle feel surmountable, an intolerable life worth living. Kids, some of them younger than Prudence. That's—it's not going to bring the UCC to its knees. It never was." She drank from the glass, one long swallow of red. "But for me, it was enough. One life, one bright moment in the dark, will always be enough."

The silence in the air felt heavy. Lamarque had turned his back toward Pru, obscuring his face. For pregnant seconds, the expression on Mama's, holo-smooth and unreadable, didn't shift so much as a millimeter.

Then the side of Mama's mouth curled. "Also, I think writing poetically raunchy missives to Prudence's father over the wireless helped get him into bed with me. Hello, Pru." She hit a buzzer on the table.

The door slid aside, perfunctorily traitorous. Pru practically tumbled over the threshold. Alex's hand snagged out to grab her arm.

"And . . . ah, Alexandre, is it?" Mama's eyes were dark and merry. "Pru's told me *so much* about you."

Pru clapped a hand over an undignified shriek. "I have not!"

"Sure," replied Mama, with a completely mortifying wink at Alex.

Cheeks burning, Pru's gaze darted between her mother and the Head Representative, who was drinking Mama's wine without comment. "What are you both doing up here, anyway?"

"Waiting up for you two," said Lamarque, setting the glass aside. "It's good to see you both alive, by the way."

"You've been watching the news reels," said Alex.

"We've been getting status updates from Hakeem Bishop and Jay Park," corrected his uncle. "Mostly concerning how utterly foolhardy you've both been."

Alex's jaw set, the sharp line of it cast in hard relief against the apartment's low lights. "I don't regret following Anabel's lead, if that's what you're getting at. We knew Jellicoe was cooking up something in his weapons factories. We had to find out what. You can't fight a boogeyman, Uncle."

"And you didn't think to ask anyone before waltzing off to an event full of intoxicated Incorporated who's-who types?"

"You've never had a problem with my social life before," said Alex.

His uncle's eyebrows climbed into an expression reminiscent of some in Alex's more lighthearted arsenal. "What social life?"

Mama made a sound suspiciously like a laugh. "Face it, Prometheus. You're about to lose any and all Cool Uncle points."

Pru turned toward her mother. "What, like you're not mad too?"

"Oh, I'm furious," said Mama, stretched out languidly on the couch, stirring the wine glass. "The only reason no one's gotten punched yet is because I've been receiving to-the-minute updates on your whereabouts from that paranoid Chief of Staff fellow who works for Prometheus, and hence have had the assurance for the past three hours that my only child has not been shot full of plasma fire." The glass trembled briefly, almost spilling, but her voice was smooth when she added, "Also, because this particular stunt isn't actually Prometheus's fault for once."

"Thanks," said Lamarque.

Alex strode toward his uncle. "Punish me however you like. But what are you going to do about the wyverns? They're different from the ones my parents went after when I was a kid. These are bona fide, human-grown cyborgs. The only reason we won at all tonight was because Rebelwing held them off until the Coalition fleet showed up in bigger numbers. What happens in a fight where the Executive General matches wyverns against fleet mechs one-to-one? It'll be a massacre. One-on-one, they'll make any war mech that's not Rebelwing look like something out of a bargain bin at a toy shop—"

"Yes, I'm aware, thank you," said the Head Representative, in startlingly icy tones. "As it is my actual job to know these things, Alexandre, not yours."

"I work for the Coalition too."

"On *work-study*. That doesn't make you any less a kid."

Alex's chin went up. "You can't have it both ways, Uncle. You can't give me and Cat the go-ahead on engineering the latest in war mech technology, sign Pru up to test-pilot, and then just shut us out of the loop like this."

"I gave you all the go-ahead on those things in controlled environments," snapped the Head Representative. "I wouldn't have allowed you to do any of it if I hadn't been assured of your safety."

"None of us are safe!" Alex's voice rose. "Not now that Jellicoe's new wyverns have gone live! If you'd seen the kind of violence we saw on No Man's Land tonight—"

"I have!" thundered Lamarque. Alex's mouth hinged shut, as his uncle continued, deadly quiet, "Do you think I've forgotten the Partition Wars, or our family's part in it? Do you think I've forgotten Etienne? Or Julia? I haven't. I can't. I relive every moment spent with them every time I walk into the Head Representative's office. Don't you dare imply that I don't know the price we paid for the existence of that office."

"I'm not implying—"

"But you are," said his uncle, grim toned. Lamarque set aside the wine glass. He ran a hand through his hair, pinching the bridge of his nose with the other. "Alexandre. Alex. I want you to grow up strong. I want you to grow up kind. I want you to grow up aware of your ability to change the world. But I don't want you to sacrifice your childhood to have those things."

"And how much of my *childhood* will be left once Jellicoe sells his new and improved wyverns to the Executive General? How much when the UCC reignites the Partition Wars?"

His uncle's mouth set. "I'll handle it."

"How?"

"Alexandre—"

"I'll tell you how," said Alex. "Let me take Pru's place in Rebelwing's cockpit."

Pru's head jerked toward him. Alex had gone still, hands folded in front of him, utterly calm and as coldly distant as a statue in a museum of someone long dead.

"It's the most obvious solution to the wyvern problem," he continued, each word carefully measured out, bargaining chips for the taking. He sounded so reasonable. "You need to take out the wyvern alpha, and for that, you need Rebelwing. You know you do, Uncle. That was the entire *point* of Rebelwing."

"That doesn't mean you should pilot her."

"And why not?" demanded Alex. "I worked with Cat on its design, and I've been training with combat mechs since I was thirteen years old.

I know that mech better than anyone, and I can pilot as well as anybody. I think we proved that tonight. If we transfer the imprint over to me—"

"The imprint is with Miss Wu," snapped Lamarque. "And with her, it will remain."

"Fine, then why not let us do what we did tonight?" hissed Alex. "Hakeem could tell you. We held off the wyverns, just me and Pru, until the Coalition fleet showed up. Let Pru keep the imprint and take point while I pilot from the cockpit."

"That was an incredible risk. Sharing the imprint that way, nothing in preliminary mech tests indicated that it would be safe, or even possible, much less functional. Doing what you two did shouldn't have worked—"

"Maybe it shouldn't have worked, but guess what, Uncle? It did. Pru and I, we did well."

"Alex—"

"We could do well again."

"Alexandre!" thundered the Head Representative, and he really was in Head Representative mode now, shoulders drawn back, chin lifted, eyes narrowed at his nephew. Pru rocked back on her heels, replete with the sort of self-preservative instinct that generally disinclined you from wanting to piss off the most powerful man in your home city. "If and when the Coalition addresses the wyvern issue, it will not involve putting you in that cockpit. That is my decision. It is not an invitation for a discussion. Are we clear?"

Alex flinched, as if physically slapped. Pru watched as he inhaled on the ensuing silence, Adam's apple bobbing, and held on to the pause, using scant seconds to pave over his hurt. "Yes," he said at last, crisp and cold. "Perfectly clear, Uncle."

The wind seemed to go out of the Head Representative's sails. His features smoothed back into something tired and worried, just this side of regretful. "Alex, listen. I don't mean—"

"No, Uncle, it's like you said," continued Alex, still speaking in that crisply brittle tone. "You've already made a decision. No need to waste time discussing it."

He slipped out the apartment door, pulling it carefully closed behind him.

Pru cast one baleful look at both adults in the room: Gabriel Lamarque, eyes drifting shut in resignation, Mama pursing her mouth beside him. Then, without another word, she followed Alex out the door.

He hadn't gone far, as it turned out. Pru found him leaning up against the rickety staircase railing, a lean and sharp-angled silhouette against the moonlit bruise of the predawn sky. She tucked herself awkwardly into the space beside him, shoulder to shoulder, and said, in as blasé a voice she could manage, "Wow, Alex, you want to be careful up here. Haven't you heard there are sentient robot lizards flying about, looking to carry off innocent schoolchildren like us?"

"Why do you do it?" His words came out angry and sharp edged, broken bottle pieces cleaving into the scant space between their bodies. "You're like your mum, aren't you? What she said in there, about how she never really believed we could bring down the UCC. You never wanted to take on the UCC either, so why do you keep flying Rebelwing? You could have given up three weeks into training when everyone was yelling at you, and said that the imprint was too much for you to handle. My uncle would have understood, at that point. He wouldn't force you to do something you really couldn't. After all"—his voice scraped over a bitter laugh—"we're just kids."

Pru, silent, didn't move. To her surprise, neither did he. She leaned on the rusty railing beside him, body heat layered between the thin cotton of their clothes, and let all the jagged pieces of his anger and hurt wash over them both. "Alex," she said at last, very quietly, "you know the actual reason why your uncle won't let you fly Rebelwing, right?"

His head jerked toward her, his parted mouth close enough to kiss.

Pru remembered what Mama had first said about Gabriel Lamarque: how he always meant what he said, how he'd ask you to give life and limb to his cause, and mourn the broken shell of your sacrifice afterward. Like any good leader, he'd carry your loss inside himself, then ask for another, believing too much in the world he envisioned to quit sending people to break themselves for the ugly and glorious triumph of those battles. That had been wartime, but what was the building of a dragon but continuation of a Partition War by other means?

"He can't bear to make you expendable," said Pru.

She cut him off even as Alex began to voice a retort. "I think you know that, in your heart of hearts. You're the last of your family. It would break his heart to lose you."

His mouth twisted. "Because it would be the end of the Lamarque legacy?"

"Because it would be the end of you, you dick," said Pru. "Nothing you said in there was wrong. You're hands down the best equipped pilot for Rebelwing. But you're also the guy who sings resistance songs in three languages, and actually believes in all the words. You don't just think *you* can change the world; you actually think the rest of us can too. You're never going to be expendable, Alex. Not to your uncle." She swallowed, and added more quietly, "Not to any of us."

Pru had been so absorbed in finding the right words to say what she felt that she hadn't actually noticed how close they'd drifted until she felt the puff of his exhale against her mouth. He'd been this close a few hours ago, before the wyvern attack, before blood on the beach, before his voice ringing across Rebelwing's imprint in her head. She'd thought about kissing him, then. She'd wanted, more than anything in that moment, to stop thinking and just take what she wanted, take and take and never stop.

She ducked her forehead, bumping it against his chin. "Thanks for not dying tonight," she said, and pushed gently back on his chest, disentangling them. "Your uncle will want to take you home. I'll go tell him you're ready to head off."

She kept her eyes low when she rounded back toward the door, buzzing it open and putting solid chrome between the rattling thump of her heart and whatever expression she'd left on Alex's face.

♦

Barricading Beat: Your Number One Source for Citizen Journalism!
Posted by XNation007

Anonymous sources confirm that "father of wyverns" Harold Jellicoe's sudden and deliberate attack on attendees at his own product demo at No Man's Land have taken out his closest rivals in the Incorporated arms dealing machine. How will the Executive General respond to this latest escalation in inter–UCC Inc. backstabbing? All eyes are on the big man in charge!

◆

IN LATER DAYS, PRU would more easily remember the aftermath of the wyvern attack in news reels and scrolling fragments of status updates to social media networks, punctuated by the frantic exchanges of message board posts. The chorus of New Columbia's people, old and young, called out for a culprit for the terror on the beach, the victims shell-shocked and weeping in blurry photos splashed across phone feeds.

Harold Jellicoe's name trended at the top of every social media network on the wireless. He'd reportedly disappeared halfway through the seafood course at the party, and the only sign of him since had been the wyverns raining plasma fire on the beach. Pru hadn't known any of the Barricaders who'd died, but Masterson aside, she recognized two faces among the Incorporated casualties: the elderly couple who'd watched her argue with Alex over dinner. Their bios on the news reels identified them as Zachary and Paulina Aberdeen, major executives in the Incorporated power structure: lifelong, trusted confidantes of the Executive General himself.

They'd also owned the only war mech manufacturing subsidiary in UCC Inc.'s sprawling empire that came close to rivaling Harold Jellicoe's.

UCC Inc. law boasted a wide margin of allowance for competition between arms dealers, but even the Incorporated drew the line at murder, at least when it came to their own. The Executive General himself, furious at the deaths of his closest lieutenants, had vowed to have Jellicoe "handled." Everyone knew what "handled" meant, on an official statement from the Executive General's office. UCC Inc. had no concept of trials or due process. Once found, Harold Jellicoe would disappear down a dark hole somewhere, and if he wasn't dead, he'd very quickly wish he was.

Something about the whole thing felt off to Pru. She didn't doubt that a man like Jellicoe—both clever and cold-blooded enough to climb so close to the top of the Incorporated ladder—would slaughter his enemies without blinking twice. Etienne and Julia had learned that the hard way. But why would he do it so publicly? The Aberdeens' relationship with the Executive General should have made them untouchable, even to Jellicoe. After all, what was the point of killing your enemies at the cost of your own life?

The tiny part of Pru that wasn't replete with bone-deep exhaustion wondered, with a brief pang, what Alex thought of such an anticlimactic fate for his parents' murderer.

The rest of Pru, however, had hunched her shoulders, tucked herself into her childhood bed, and swiped the news aside for e-mails about homework and deadlines. Jay Park had written a formal note indefinitely postponing her combat assessment "in light of the present situation," and reassuring Pru that "grading for this internship will instead hinge on conduct exhibited thus far in extraordinary circumstances," which seemed to be government-ese for "you get an A for kinda sorta piloting Rebelwing in the midst of a surprise terrorist attack, and not immediately getting you or any of your friends blown up."

Jay Park's opinions on Pru's valor under fire, however, did not apparently excuse her from calculus p-sets, bio readings, or an upcoming European History exam. Mama, who'd decided the whole near-fatal espionage thing more than called for Pru's long overdue grounding, demanded permission for her to take school assignments remotely for the week. School acquiesced with a nudge from its staff of therapists.

Which left Pru wrapped in an old quilt, screening messages from her friends, and staring at her ceiling, as she tried to wrap her brain around some European historians' arguments on the causes of the French Revolution. One of the revolutions, at any rate. Pru had lost track. Their stupid, war-loving continent had that much in common with their European cousins across the sea.

On the fourth day of Mama-mandated house arrest, Mama herself appeared at Pru's bedroom door and announced in conversational tones, "Okay, tell me if I'm wrong, but I think my attempt to discipline you for foolhardy beach partying in politically dangerous locales has backfired on me. The way you mope about under that blanket, I'd think you actually want to isolate yourself from your friends. Even the foolhardy beach-partying variety. Maybe especially the foolhardy beach-partying variety," Mama added, looking thoughtful. "Now, there's a wrench in my responsible parenting scheme. Figuring out the most effective ways to be tough yet fair on a teenager is its own battlefield. Remarkably, no one bothers to warn you about that when you're a seventeen-year-old dragged into a massive continental war."

"We're not at war," Pru informed the ceiling.

"Not yet, obviously. And I was referring to myself, you self-centered little ingrate." Mama's weight dipped the mattress. "I think we ought to talk."

"Why?" A thin crack ran from the age-stained linoleum ceiling tiles down toward the flickering white glow of her fairy-shaped bedside lamp. Pru had grown up in this apartment, but she'd never counted on feeling as if she'd grown out of it. "You've never wanted to talk about wars before."

"The Partition Wars?" Mama sighed. "No, I suppose I haven't."

"We always talked about other stuff," Pru continued, staring at that crack. "The stories you write. The special sales at the bodega downstairs. Your opinions about continental languages. The things Grandma and Grandpa told you about their life back in Old Shanghai, before they made the arguably terrible life choice of moving across the ocean to a mismanaged chunk of land, doomed to lose all its countries and governments within a century. Great call on their part."

"Yes, how tremendously short-sighted of my parents not to be psychic fortunetellers," said Mama dryly. "New Columbia was once the seat of democracy for the most powerful country in the world. It seemed a promising prospect, back in the day."

"And now it's the seat of democracy for a ragtag pack of rebel cities left over from three countries whose governments were handily bulldozed by a megacorporation with a chip on its shoulder."

"No one saw the Partition Wars coming, kiddo. Not the true scope and scale of them."

"Maybe someone should have."

"'Should have' is a very easy state of being when hindsight's twenty-twenty, wouldn't you say? Besides, who knows if it would have helped at all, or only made things worse. Maybe we'd all have been Cassandra, waiting for the fall of Troy, knowing what would become of our home, and helpless to prevent it."

"Is that what Gabriel Lamarque thinks?"

Her mother's pause was a tangible thing, lingering heavy in the air. "Who's to say?"

"Why were you arguing with him when Alex and I came home?" Pru blurted out.

"Because I take comfort in hobbies, and that one is an old favorite. You and your Lamarque boy took your sweet time finding your way from No Man's Land back to New Columbia. Forgive your elders for finding their own means to pass the time, not to mention the utter heart-numbing fear." Mama's voice went high on that last word, cracking into nothing. She inhaled once, gathering herself, and said, "I have never known a moment I wasn't afraid, from the end of the Partition Wars to the first time I saw you toddle on your own two ridiculous little feet. That, kiddo, is why I don't like talking about wartime."

"You don't like talking about Gabriel Lamarque either."

For a moment, Pru thought her mother might snap at her. Then Mama exhaled, and said, "The two might as well be synonymous, for me. If you don't understand anything else about those years, Pru, understand this much: for me, the war was Gabriel, and Gabriel was the war. I was an artist long before I was Gabriel's soldier, but he always thought that art had to exist in service of some grand battle. It was, quite frankly, exhausting."

"Okay, but art really was a battleground when fighting against the Incorporated, wasn't it?" Pru found herself arguing. "I mean, they imposed literal censorship zones."

"Ah, but why do you imagine censorship zones were created in the first place?" Mama wagged a finger in Pru's face. "Art is not always a weapon or a political statement, my girl. Sometimes, art is simply love with no place left to call home."

"The Head Representative disagrees?"

"Please. The Head Representative doesn't have enough hours in the day to think about anything that isn't a weapon or a political statement." Mama offered Pru a sideways little smile. "You remember asking me about why I started calling him Prometheus?"

"Because he brought fire to the people."

"Yes, and got himself chained to a rock for his troubles, and all the good it wound up doing anybody. What have we done with fire since? Equipped some giant robots with it, and threatened one another with deadly force while Gabriel Lamarque sits shackled to that ridiculous office. Nothing's changed, and nothing ever will. You know why I don't talk about the war? Because it never truly ended. We just hid behind our walls, and told ourselves it did."

Pru sat up and looked at her mother. The streaks of silver through her hair glinted in the light of Pru's bedside lamp. "Did you mean what you said to Lamarque?"

Mama made a derisive sound. "About what, the failure of books to magically save humanity from itself? I'll stand by that one. Really, I never understood why the Incorporated kicked up such a fuss about them."

"No. About the value of saving one person. The kids who wrote you letters," Pru clarified. She curled her fingers into the old patchwork quilt Mama had gifted her with when she was ten. "Maybe you didn't change the world, and maybe the Head Representative couldn't fix all the things you both wanted to, but if what you said is true, then, like . . . look, Mama." Pru pinched the bridge of her nose, and said in a voice that sounded horrifyingly like Alex's, "Because you guys fought for the Barricade Coalition, a handful of kids on this continent can read stories that they'd never have touched under Incorporated rule. Kids who cared enough to write to you, who said you changed their lives, if not the world. One kid's life. One person's life. Does that matter?"

Mama held Pru's gaze for a long moment. "You're being very philosophical for someone doing"—she spared a cursory glance toward the readings on Pru's phone—"what appears to be the dullest history homework known to man. Why?"

What to say? Curled on the tip of Pru's tongue were half a million stupid, juvenile reasons, some almost true, but none of them what she wanted to say. In her mind's eye, dragon wings spread across the night sky. In the back of her brain, nestled beside the imprint, were memories of Mama's earliest stories. Impossible fairytales. Simple stories. Stories for children.

But those stories had always been about dragons.

"Rebelwing saved me," said Pru slowly. "When I was . . . that day, when my customer sold me out to the UCC police brigades. And then, at the beach, I—the dragon and I—we saved Alex. And I know people died anyway, and that should never have happened, but some people *didn't*. Some people lived. Because the dragon was there, and Alex was inside to pilot it."

"And you," her mother added quietly. "You were there too, don't forget. With this imprint of yours everyone keeps telling me about."

Pru rubbed her temples. "Pretty hard to forget something that lives inside my head twenty-four seven."

"Were you glad for it, on the beach? The imprint."

"I wasn't itching to have a battle of the beasts with those wyverns, if that's what you're asking. I needed the dragon, so it came. That's how it works, you know? You have to want something. Believe in something. And I just wanted to save . . ."

"Alexandre Lamarque?"

"One person," said Pru softly. "I wanted to save just one person, if I could. It was so stupid, Mama. I know it was stupid. Pitting one experimentally built dragon against an entire flock of war wyverns. We were never going to win, not without the Coalition fleet. But I thought that maybe, if I could save one or two or three people from the wyverns first, then maybe . . . maybe the imprint wouldn't have been wasted on me."

Mama went silent for a long moment. "That dragon's imprint was never wasted on you."

"Thanks," said Pru. "Good pep talk."

"I mean it," Mama said, and released a long breath, pinching the bridge of her nose. "I think that maybe, underneath it all, you have more faith than I do. Than I ever did."

"Faith in what?'

Mama's mouth pulled sideways. "People." From one of her dress pockets, she slipped Pru a cylinder. "I believe this is yours."

Pru felt her eyebrows climb. "Last time I got caught smuggling books in an Incorporated zone, you promised to ground me all summer long. Guess we've wound up going a little preemptive with that, but—"

"Read what's on the drive, Pru," interrupted her mother, carefully expressionless.

"Why?"

A smile flickered across her mother's painted mouth, briefly lighting sad, tired hollows beneath Mama's eyes, as she rose. She winced, turning her hips from side to side to crack her back. "The cylinder, you might be interested to know, came to me from a pair of cheekbones more trouble than they're worth. Seems you haven't been answering your text messages. Or possibly reading them at all, for that matter."

Pru's heartbeat, to her chagrin, picked up. "Not like I could answer more disastrous beach getaway invites. I'm on house arrest."

"And so you are." Mama bent and closed Pru's fingers around the drive, the cylinder's metal casing cool inside the cradle of their hands. Almost airily, she added, "By the way, I have a meeting with a publisher in a few hours. Should run quite late. But I trust you'll be kept plenty busy right here with all these very interesting history readings, and shouldn't have the faintest notion of doing anything untoward in my absence."

Pru stared, cylinder digging into her joints. "Mama. Did you read it first? What did Alex say?"

But Mama had already dropped her hands, turning to go. "How on earth should I know? I am ancient and decrepit, well past the proper age for understanding the sweet nothings of young love—"

"Mama."

Mama looked over her shoulder, gaze cutting toward Pru. It was one of those moments she would later struggle to catalogue, Pru thought, her brain cobbling together all the little pieces of her mother, balanced on the precipice of that moment. The white of her knuckles on the doorjamb of Pru's childhood bedroom. The teeth sinking into the side of her red-painted lip, caught on a pause between unspoken words. But mostly, what stuck with Pru was the look in Mama's wide brown eyes, bright with an unnamable sort of fervor. Fear, or hope, or love, or perhaps all three, warring for dominance in the heart of a woman who'd been dubbed Scheherazade in wartime. A woman who told stories in the face of all things, because stories were how she survived.

"Yes," said Mama, before she left. "To answer your question from before. In a shithole of a world that refuses to change, one life can still matter. One life can be everything."

14   THE BLOODLINE TRAP

HJ is alive.

For several minutes, Pru stared in dumbfounded silence at the message blinking tersely at her from the holo-drive's 3-D display. Then she tossed it aside, grabbed her phone, and hit the first name beside the grinning dragon emoticon on her contact list.

"What the hell, Alex?" she yelled into the speaker.

"Hello to you too, Pru," replied the innocuous voice on the other end of the line. "How lovely that your phone works after all. Your mum's really gracious, incidentally. I wasn't sure she'd want us talking after the attack, but she said something about how good communication is crucial to love and war. Reminds me of Anabel when—"

"Would you shut up about my mom!" shouted Pru. "What the hell do you mean, Jellicoe's alive? How do you know that? More importantly, why hasn't the Executive General had him drawn and quartered or buried alive?"

"Because the Executive General has no intention of doing either of those things," said Alex. "Far from it."

Pru, head still full of news reels, huffed a disbelieving laugh. "Are you on uppers?"

"No. And we shouldn't keep talking about this on the phone. I'm meeting Hakeem Bishop at the Rose Room of Café Dupont at seven thirty sharp. I'll explain everything to you there."

"What—"

"Please," said Alex quietly. "I need you."

Those last words sat on her mind's edge for slowly ticking seconds as her pulse beat a rhythm inside her head. *I need you.*

She wanted to scoff. What role did she play in the life of Alexandre Lamarque? When they'd first laid eyes on each other, she'd been little more than an annoyance, an annoyance that had evolved into a potential threat after his dragon had decided to imprint on her. Nowadays, she was at best an inconvenient thorn in his side who'd usurped his rightful place in his uncle's cold war, and at worst, some mousy schoolgirl who refused to bend the knee and kiss his toes like everyone else in the Barricade Coalition. Needed her, indeed.

Then again, she'd also saved his life back on the beach. That probably counted for something, so far as needfulness went.

"All right," Pru said at last. "Seven thirty."

When she arrived at their designated meeting space—right at seven thirty on the dot, so ha, *take that, Alex*—she found Hakeem Bishop alone, facing the rear windows of the Rose Room, silhouetted by the city lights through frosted glass. The sharp-pointed shoulders of his suit rested like dragon wings poised over the hands clenched loosely behind his back. Pru hovered awkwardly at the doorway's edge, suddenly unsure of her welcome.

"Um," she said by way of announcement, shifting her weight from one foot to the other. "I'm on time."

Bishop did not look over one of those sharply tailored shoulders, but they did relax slightly. "And so you are. Good. You'll need punctuality, if that fool Lamarque boy is going to entangle you in his schemes."

"I'm guessing you don't mean the Head Representative."

The Chief of Staff did turn around then. The pull of his mouth was more grimace than grin. "No. I do not."

"Does he know we're here?"

"What do you think?"

Footsteps approached down the café's winding corridor. "Notifying my uncle about this meeting would kind of defeat the purpose of procuring this nice private room, don't you think?" Alex pointed out. He strode past Pru into the Rose Room. "We're not hiding anything," he added, taking a seat on the edge of one of the well-polished café tables.

"Oh, no?" challenged Pru, unable to stop herself.

"No," said Alex, refusing to rise to the bait. His dark eyes glittered when they rose toward her. "We're just taking certain matters into our own hands."

"Certain matters like the father of wyverns," said Pru.

"Among other things," said Hakeem Bishop. He produced a cylinder from one of his suit pockets, a fancier model than the ones Pru and her mother used—the kind that boasted extra features like instant video play and high-definition, three-dimensional hologram footage—and clicked the projection button. Two men in suits emerged, ghostlike in their translucency, to pace the room.

"There must be a catch," said one of them. His face was thin and angular, almost avian with its sharp-bladed nose and narrow gray eyes, the same color as the chrome-gray suit pulled tight over his shoulders, his chrome-pale hair slicked back over his paper-white scalp. He looked like an old-fashioned black-and-white film character, retooled for the modern age. "My new wyvern flock's a beauty, all right, but they're not worth what you're offering."

Pru rounded on Bishop, jerking her head toward the hologram. "I'm guessing the one in gray is Jellicoe." Her attention turned to second man, whose smile unfurled in increments that shot the dread of recognition through Pru's spine, straight into her belly. "But his buddy here, that's . . ."

"Roman Theodore Finlay III," said the Chief of Staff. "Currently styled Executive General of the United Continental Confederacy Incorporated."

The UCC didn't circulate much visual footage of their leader, but the few bits Pru had seen—from old wartime propaganda posters and videos of political speeches—were hard to forget. The Executive General looked the same in every one of them: a cold gem of a man with spun-gold hair as bright as Etienne Lamarque's, and eyes the color of blue-tinted crystal. He might have been handsome, if not for the odd drag to his facial expressions. His smiles, stretched too thin to be quite natural, constantly mismatched the deadened look in those eerily pale eyes, like a glitch in a holo-image.

"That's because I'm not just buying your wyverns, Harold," said the Executive General. "I'm buying a very specific kind of assassination." He spoke without inflection, laying the facts out, costs and benefits, profit and loss margin. "No Man's Land," he clarified. "Your flock will take out Zachary and Paulina, and a few others besides. I want this to look like true terrorism, not a targeted attack on a couple Incorporated executives, or the Barricaders won't care."

"The Aberdeens." Jellicoe whistled. "I'm surprised. Always thought they were favorites of yours."

"Why, because I bought their war mechs over yours from time to time? Because I expensed scotch and steaks and yacht trips for them?" That strange smile spasmed across the Executive General's face again. "That's not friendship, Harold. That's a business relationship. You of all people should know the difference. And when business relationships go sour in my company, someone's liable to get hurt."

"Ah." Cool understanding dawned over Jellicoe's features. "So it's true. They're gunning for your office."

"The Aberdeens want my seat in the company, and the Barricaders have been baying for your blood for years. The money I'm offering you will buy both, when your wyverns lay waste to No Man's Land in a nice, convenient public atrocity that I can decry for the deaths of my dear friends, the Aberdeens."

"Generous, Roman. But I can't spend your money if I'm dead."

"Relax," drawled the Executive General. "You'll only die on company record. Your assets, wyverns most importantly, will be ceded to me. But you, physically, will be sunning yourself on a nice little island, with a very fine money launderer at your service, far from the politics of this tiresome continent."

"You're shitting me."

The Executive General shrugged. "You're the one who wanted to retire soon. And this is a far better retirement than most executives of your age achieve." The crystalline eyes stared unblinking at Jellicoe. "Take the deal, Harold. You know it's for the best."

The clip ended.

"A very fine cyberintelligence officer—one of Jay and Anabel's cousins, in fact—remotely rewired one of the security feeds in Harold Jellicoe's main offices," said Bishop. "There are at least three other clips on that cylinder, plus documentation of some very large amounts of money being moved about, and a one-way travel itinerary for a dummy alias. It's confirmed: the Executive General will be acquiring Harold Jellicoe's new wyverns, and with them, the means to Incorporate the Barricade Coalition. Starting with its crown jewel: New Columbia."

Pru stared bleakly at Hakeem. Her heart thudded inside the empty cavern of her ribcage, the Executive General's empty, stretched smile playing across her mind's eye. "This is war. You have a recording of grounds for war."

"Not quite," said Bishop. "Jellicoe agreed to sell those wyverns and do the Executive General's dirty work like the coward he's always been, but he's got one last ace up his sleeve." He tapped the cylinder again.

A bright, blue-tinted hologram burst to life at the center of the room, between the three of them. Pru flinched back from it. "That's a wyvern."

"Not just a wyvern," said Bishop. "Take a closer look, both of you. This one's an alpha."

Pru looked, despite the prickle of gooseflesh rising on the backs of her limbs. She'd never be able to see another one of those things, even within the confines of a hologram, without reliving that night in No Man's Land all over again. Every wyvern she saw would always be Dick Masterson, razor-edged scales blooming to bloody life from his flesh, giggling and struggling to spit his own words out, minutes before plasma fire rolled across his tongue, minutes before Anabel's gun splattered his skull against the beach cabin floor.

This wyvern, though, once Pru took it in properly, was different from the flock at the beach. It was slightly larger, closer in size to the dragon mech than the other wyverns, its metal scales more smoothly tucked against the reptilian cyborg skin that hid the human inside. And its eyes, blinking out at Pru from the hologram—its eyes went right through you, dark blue and piercing. Not at all like the dragon's pupil-less silver-blue lenses, hiding tiny cameras behind the chrome. These eyes were not reptilian, not machine-like, not anything that could be read as alien. They had too much vicious and familiar expression behind them for that.

The wyvern alpha's eyes wanted to convince you they were still human.

Alex's eyes narrowed on the alpha's blue irises. "Who's hosting the alpha cell? You know. You must have known for some time now, or else Jay Park wouldn't have tried to keep you quiet."

He'd cut to the core of the matter, by invoking the alpha's identity. Pru could see it all over Bishop's face, the complicated, painful thing the older man's features did, an echo of the bitter expression he'd worn that night at No Man's Land. "We haven't known for as long as you think. Our operatives only got a hold of the footage of the alpha when . . . a week or two before that dragon mech of yours first made Miss Wu's acquaintance." The Chief of Staff chose his words slowly, syllables clipped with hard-edged care. Something shifted in his manner when he clicked the cylinder again, eyes squeezing shut for a moment. "For what it's worth, Alexandre, I am sorry you had to find out this way."

The hologram shifted. The wyvern, lifting its serpentine head, closed those uncanny eyes and began to transform itself. Metal scales retracted into human skin. A fall of fair hair emerged from the reptilian crown. The face beneath shortened and twisted, snout sliding backward into a human nose, while a pair of full, human lips closed over what had been the wyvern's jaws. The eyes blinked open, the same deep shade of blue as the wyvern's, but fully human now, wide and fair lashed.

The arrangement of the hologram's features struck a terrible chord in Pru's memory. Beside her, Alex drew an inhale like a knife to the lung, and buckled against the table. One of Pru's hands, helpless and shaking, found his shoulder, trying and failing to steady him. Silent save Alex's ragged breathing, they stared at the face of Etienne Lamarque.

"There's been a mistake." Alex's voice scraped sharp through his throat. "My mum said he died. It's . . . she said so, before she . . . before she . . ."

"Died," said Bishop softly. "Before she died, Alexandre. They were trapped in an Incorporated labor camp that had just exploded into a warzone. Julia was badly hurt, and terrified—brave, loving, determined to the very end—but no less terrified, and no less doomed. Your mother wouldn't have lied deliberately to you, but you can't trust her information under those circumstances either."

"Don't condescend to me," snarled Alex, shrugging out of Pru's grasp. He covered the length of the room in a few short strides and fisted his hands around Bishop's suit lapels. "I know what I heard."

"You're thinking with your heart, Alexandre. A useful quality, at times. But right now, I need you to think with your head." Bishop's fingers rested over the tops of Alex's hands, but made no move to shove the boy away. "Let go of me."

Alex's grip tightened.

Pru's legs finally jerked into motion. "Let go of him, Alex. Alex!" Her hands closed over his shoulder again, far less gently than before.

"Don't." Alex tried to shrug her off again.

With Anabel Park–taught military precision, Pru bent her knees, found her leverage, and twisted. Alex, caught by surprise, stumbled and slammed sideways into a stray chair. He barely had time to reorient himself before Pru had him shoved up against the frosted-glass window. "Get a hold of yourself!"

He struggled against her. He'd probably have won on superior height and strength alone, if he'd really been trying, but she had her entire body weight pinning him in place, and the determination to keep him there. "I'm sorry," she said. The words felt stupid and useless and small. Just like Pru. "I'm so sorry."

At some point, he'd stopped fighting her, and slumped forward, his forehead caught against her shoulder. For a moment, they stayed like that, stuck in this exhausted, grief-bent parody of an embrace, her cheek buried against his hair. "I'm sorry," she repeated, like a robot. Like all the sorry in the world could make anything better when your own father had been made into the thing you hated most in all the world.

"Why didn't you tell me sooner?" Alex asked at last. The question, half-whispered into Pru's neck, was directed at Hakeem Bishop. Pru could see the blurred shape of his reflection in the window, a lonely shadow of a figure standing to the side, hands tucked in his pockets. She thought he might have been concealing fists.

"I'm not your blood, nor your legal guardian. That's your uncle. The truth was never mine to disclose."

"But it was mine to know." Alex's weight vanished from Pru's arms, sudden and sharp as everything Alex did. He'd rounded on Bishop again, but he no longer looked poised for a fight. He looked lost. Gone was the young man lashing out at the world with blind violence, and here in his stead was a boy left hunting for answers, soft-eyed as the night Pru first saw him on an auditorium stage, singing love songs in his mother's language. "So why would Uncle go out of his way to hide it? I get pain. I get secrets. But I was a child who thought my father was dead, and now you're telling me that you've known for . . . what, months now, that we've had it wrong all along? Uncle Gabriel could have—"

"What," Hakeem wanted to know. The flickering blue light of the hologram cast the faint wrinkles of his skin into sharp relief. "Could he have comforted you with this alternative? Don't pretend that would have been better. You thought your father was dead, and for all intents and purposes, he was, from the moment the UCC took him. Don't make me repeat to you what happens to political prisoners in Incorporated jails. Death is the kindest of fates for the lesser offenders, and your father was not a lesser offender. This . . . thing he is now, that's not Etienne. Harold Jellicoe has been working on a new generation of wyverns since the end of the Partition Wars. Anabel Park told me all about the transformation of that UCC man on the beach, from human to wyvern, how he had nothing left of himself by the end. How long did Jellicoe have to exact horrors on that prisoner's brain and body: a few weeks? A month, perhaps? He had Etienne for nearly a decade. The man you called Papa is no longer your father."

Alex leaned across the space between them. "Then why, I'll ask again, did Uncle keep that from me?"

Bishop ran a hand over the close-cropped gray of his hair. He turned away from Alex. "Because the alpha's identity wasn't the only secret we had to keep from you. It's also how Jellicoe programmed the alpha cell." His mouth twisted. "Before their deaths, the Aberdeens were an abundant well of information for our intelligence operatives, at the right price."

Pru frowned. "That night on the beach," she said slowly, "you told us it wouldn't be enough to destroy the alpha. You said we'd also have to destroy the cell itself, for good."

"That's right," said Bishop. He dug the heels of his hands against his eyes. Sagging against the table, he mused, "Let me tell you both about the inherent problem with grooming a beloved hero's offspring as living insurance against the rise of your enemies. It all seems very good at first, of course. He's got the right name to rally behind, and what's more, he's passionate about precisely the right things. Genuinely so. If you're lucky, he's an ace pilot, an inventive dreamer who works closely with brilliant engineers to build bigger and better mechs to defend those passions he guards so righteously. He is, in any case, primed to take down whatever new mechanical monstrosities the other side throws at you. There is no one better for the task, the last, best hope of a flagging coalition of rebel cities. Brilliant. Goddamn great."

Bishop shut off the holo-drive, the mocking image of Etienne Lamarque, the wyvern lurking beneath his bones. "I'm not blaming you, Alex. You . . . truly are the best of your family." He closed his eyes with a hard swallow. "Where we went wrong was hubris. We were fools not to realize that the Incorporated had banked on our investment in you from the start. Which brings us back to the cell.

Fascinating, the different ways you can program a cyborg cell. How it can be built to map on to particular types of hosts, down to the most arbitrary specifications. Chromosomes. Blood type." Bishop's eyes opened, points of darkness over the silver. "Genetic makeup."

It took Pru several seconds to absorb the full implications of what the Chief of Staff had just disclosed. When her brain clicked, she sank into a chair, an expletive formed low in her throat. "That means—"

"Yes." Bishop's gaze was on Alex, standing a few feet apart from her. Pru couldn't see his expression, but she saw the moment the realization struck him too, the sudden clench of his fists. "We wondered for the longest time, why go to such trouble to keep Etienne Lamarque prisoner, specifically to serve as the alpha? He could make a fine enough figurehead, sure, the Lamarque turned Incorporated beast—but what would be the point, when no one would recognize the man's face behind a wyvern's scales?" His fingers spun the cylinder faster and faster. "Funniest little things, cyber-implants. I must hand it to Jellicoe. His engineers may not be as clever as our Cat, but he's cornered the market on ruthlessness. A cell—the alpha cell—won't suffer a dead host for long. It'll move on to the next best living thing it's coded to implant in, or go dormant until its engineer reprograms the code. But so long as another Lamarque lives, this alpha cell will always have a host."

"Alex," said Pru softly. "They bet on Alex. Just like we did."

"I become the new wyvern alpha when my father dies." Alex spoke without inflection. "They're building themselves up by breaking down our legacy."

"I won't accept that." Pru stood, propelled by an abrupt fury. "The

Executive General doesn't get to do this. *Jellicoe* doesn't get to do this." Her eyes narrowed on the Chief of Staff. "And you wouldn't have told us about all this, if you didn't know a way to destroy the alpha cell for good."

"We do," said Bishop. "Rebelwing." He palmed over the hologram projector. A glinting, metallic exoskeleton appeared, equipped with tiny, scuttling legs and a wicked pair of incisors that resembled nothing so much as repurposed, razor-edged wyvern scales. Pru shivered. "This is a closeup of the alpha cell. It's a nanotech parasite, almost naked to the human eye and near indestructible—except by dragon-grade plasma fire."

Alex turned halfway, body language opening up toward Pru. His mouth angled a humorless smile at her. "In other words," he said, "we have you."

"Like hell you do." It was easier to affect indignant airs than to acknowledge the cold seeping into her veins at Alex's expression. "I've been in the cockpit for less than two months. I can hardly pilot my way through Jay Park's stupid circus of an obstacle course, and now you're suggesting that I, what, fly Rebelwing over Barricade walls to single-handedly infiltrate Jellicoe's evil fort and take down his biggest secret weapon since the Partition Wars?"

"Well." Alex pursed his lips. "Not single-handedly."

Her heart beat once, twice, and then she was back in the chair. "You're joking."

"I am not. I haven't even said anything yet." Alex stuck his hands in his pockets. Leaning against the window glass, backlit by the city, he could have graced a hundred propaganda posters. No wonder Jellicoe had banked on him playing the Barricaders' hero. Jellicoe had probably taken one look at the boy who'd pulled Cat from the labor camps, seen all that stubbornly kind, hell-bent optimism, and thought to himself, *Ah, yes, this one shall be our key to fucking over the last living hope of democracy.* "But what you're thinking right now, you have to admit it makes a certain sort of sense."

"Don't presume to know what I'm thinking right now, buddy."

The corner of his mouth lifted. "Please. We've shared the same neural imprint. Forgotten already?"

"Right now, believe me, I wish I could." Pru buried her face against her palms. Her elbows dug into the tops of her thighs. "If we try to pull off what we did at the beach—me channeling the dragon's imprint, you flying in the cockpit—you're directly exposed to the alpha cell. Anything short of a perfect, fatal shot of plasma fire, and you become the Executive General's latest, greatest weapon against the Barricade Coalition."

"I know." Alex's thin smile went thinner. "Which is another reason I need you. Jay's taught you how to use Rebelwing's plasma fire cartridges, right?"

"What does that have to do with—"

"Did he teach you how to fire a killing shot?"

"No." Pru was back on her feet in an instant.

"No? Well, it's easy enough. If you remember what Anabel taught you about ordinary plasma guns, and apply it to—"

"Not 'no' as in I don't know how! 'No' as in I won't do it!"

"You might have to. One life, in the grand scheme of things—"

"Oh, shut your stupid would-be martyr mouth, already!" Pru rounded on Bishop. "You. You're his uncle's Chief of Staff. Are you seriously going to condone the suicide-murder of your boss's only nephew?"

"That's not at all what I'm condoning," snapped Bishop. "What Alex describes is merely a last resort, and, god willing, an unlikely one. The two of you, pursuing this objective as a pair, have a far greater chance of success than either of you going it alone. When confronted with invasive enemy technology, pairs of soldiers frequently mount a successful resistance more often than single operatives, and ordinary soldiers lack the advantage of having successfully shared Rebewing's imprint. You have overcome more remarkable odds than you realize."

"But I might have to kill him." Pru's eyes burned. She refused to look at Alex. "To destroy the wyverns before Jellicoe delivers them to the Executive General, I might have to kill Alex."

"Yes." Bishop's gnarled hands emerged from his pockets and folded together. "I won't condescend to either of you by lying. You deserve more than that. So instead, I'll suggest that you both become, if not comfortable, at least accustomed to that possibility."

Comfortable. "Great." Pru dashed a hand across wet eyes, wishing she could dash it across someone's face. She needed to hit something. Mama probably wouldn't bother restraining herself.

"Understood," said Alex, ignoring the rage simmering under Pru's voice. He straightened himself up, every inch the good Barricaders' soldier, the promised hero. His face, for everything that had broken him down minutes earlier, now gave nothing away. "You have my service to the mission."

Bishop cast his attention toward Pru. "Miss Wu? This doesn't work without your cooperation. I know you weren't raised to . . . throw life and limb behind power struggles against the Incorporated. I can't force you to do this." He followed her gaze—which flicked, damnably automatic, toward Alex—and added, in pointed tones, "Neither of us can."

Alex's jaw tightened, but he nodded. "I won't hold your decision against you. Whatever it is."

"You can't force me," Pru mimicked. "You won't hold my decision against me." Her shoulders slumped. "What a joke. You forced me from the minute Mama signed those waivers that enrolled me in your godforsaken internship. You *knew* what Jellicoe had in his back pocket, Mr. Bishop. You knew all along, and it wouldn't have mattered if he activated his flock two days or two years after Rebelwing imprinted on me. The six-week deadline, the so-called 'combat assessment,' all those stupid obstacle courses—none of it really mattered. It was all about this. The alpha." She gave a mocking bow, blinking away the burn behind her eyes. "So yes, you have my service to your ridiculous, incredibly illegal gambit. Congratulations. Is that all?"

The Chief of Staff released a gust of a breath. She didn't know what cut her more deeply: that he'd really doubted her that much, or the sense of being so expendable. Maybe it shouldn't have surprised her. She'd only become this important because, as everyone was so fond of reminding her, she was technically a felon. "One more thing."

Pru's jaw clenched. "What?"

"Hit him—it—between the eyes."

"I don't—"

"Et—the alpha," clarified Bishop. His dark gaze was a fixed point in a haggard face. "That's where the alpha cell implants in a wyvern. Between the eyes. Don't miss. Do you understand?"

Pru opened her mouth. Nearly choked. "Yes," she said at last, in a small voice that made her feel smaller still. She couldn't bear to look Alex's way. "Yeah. Got it."

"Good." He cleared his throat, and looked away, rubbing a palm over his forehead. "We'll be in touch regarding details of the mission, as this is highly irregular—"

Pru was already halfway out of the Rose Room, head tucked. With one hand, she swiped the tears from her cheeks. She waved the other over her shoulder, affecting what carelessness she could. "Yeah, yeah, handle further highly illicit activity with care. I hope you know that Gabriel Lamarque will fire your ass once he finds out, and possibly lock you in prison for the next million years, but hey, you'll go down for a good cause. One for the history books. Don't worry, Bishop. I promise not to flake on our super-secret mission to prevent cross-continental civil war."

"Pru."

Pru's feet stopped at the Rose Room's exit. Alex's voice, as ever, arrested her. She could hear the break in her name, the echo of all the things probably breaking inside him in the space of this evening. She almost turned around.

Her fingers gripped the doorjamb. "I'm sorry about your dad, Alex. I . . . call me, or text, if you need to. I'll pick up this time."

She fled before either Bishop or Alex could say anything more. Hand over mouth, she pelted down the quickest exit she could find from Café Dupont, back onto a train platform. The metro ride toward Mama's apartment blurred into faceless, nameless strangers milling through the underground, jostling Pru on the train, laughing without a care in the world. And why shouldn't they? People who didn't imprint on dragon mechs didn't get whammed with bloody family secrets that held the security of the Barricade cities in balance. Good for them, really.

Pru slammed into Mama's apartment with a crash of the sliding door that sent Mama herself swearing out into the hall. "Good god, Prudence, what—" She stopped when she got a look at Pru's face. "Oh, *bao bei*. Kiddo."

The sob Pru had been holding back all night bent her double, a great heaving gasp. Without quite noticing what her feet were doing, Pru pitched herself across the length of the hall, into Mama's waiting arms. "Mommy," she wailed against her mother's cotton shoulder. "Mama, I don't, I can't—"

Her mother's arms closed around her. She smelled like the pork buns she used to make when Pru was little, which, ridiculously, made Pru cry even harder. "I know, *bao bei*. I know."

Pru wasn't sure how long they stood there in the hall, clinging to one another and rocking back and forth. Her temples throbbed when she finally lifted her face from her mother's now thoroughly snot-stained nightshirt. "I'm sorry."

Her mother snorted. "Kiddo, I've been a single mother since I was in my twenties. I've had worse than your snot on my clothes, thanks. Now, what's that Lamarque boy done, and who do I need to punch?"

Pru laughed wetly. "Nothing, actually. It's what I've agreed to do."

A pause bloomed between them. Mama cleared her throat with exaggerated awkwardness, and said, "Now, Pru, I know he's a handsome boy, but we've had the talk about certain intimacies—"

"Not that!" shouted Pru, face aflame. How weird, that under threat of war and wyverns and Alex's secret undead dad, Mama could still embarrass her in the most juvenile way imaginable. "It's nothing like that. But I don't know if I can talk about it. Just . . . Mama."

"Kiddo."

Pru bit the inside of her cheek. "If I told you that I'd promised to do something scary and dangerous to save some arbitrary handful of people—not because I wanted to be a hero, or impress a boy, or get into a good university—but because I'm literally the only person equipped to do it. Would you be mad?"

Her mother's arms tightened over her shoulders for half a minute that felt like half an hour. Then, a little hoarsely, "I'd say you're the girl I wanted to be, at your age. You watch yourself, *bao bei*."

Pru hugged back, eyes screwed shut. "I'll try, Mama."

Later, after Mama had gone to sleep, Pru lay awake in her childhood bed. For agonizing minutes, she stared up at that crack in the ceiling. Surrounded by the warmth and smallness of the room, the ache of her failure to fit throbbed harder than ever beneath her bones. Would she ever be able to face this room again, after this mission with Alex? If they saved the Barricade cities? If she shot him dead?

Finally, frustrated by her own insomnia, she tugged her phone out from beneath her pillow. The messages she'd screened from her friends and schoolmates glowed back at her. In a display of either great kindness or great passive-aggression, one of her bio lab partners had sent her bullet points from the two lectures she'd missed since No Man's Land. Another had invited her to a pre-curfew dorm party. One of the kids in her History class was still puzzling over the actual causes of the first French Revolution, and wanted to know if Pru had an opinion, or at least some notes he could borrow that would be less boring than the assigned texts.

At the top of the chatter, however, read a single name from her contacts list: ANABEL PARK.

The all-caps font blinked accusingly at Pru. "Oh, all right," she told the screen. "Just quit guilt-tripping me. I've had enough of a night, thank you."

What she was about to do would probably make Hakeem Bishop's blood pressure skyrocket. Well, turnabout's fair play, she thought, a bit pettily. Besides, the last time Pru had ventured into Incorporated territory alone, she'd gotten kidnapped by a dragon for her troubles. Alexandre Lamarque was all very well, but imprint sharing or no, Alex wasn't the one who'd been wingmanning her gambits in UCC zones for the past two years. Better not to chance things, given the foundations of liberty at stake.

Pru scrolled to a blank messaging screen on the phone, and flipped the security switch in the sidebar to its highest setting. Carefully, she began typing out a reply to one of Anabel's texts.

♦

HONESTY-NET
Your Virtual One-Stop Shop for Missed Connections & Anonymous Confessions

7:24 P.M. To my jerk of a chem teacher: I can't believe you confiscated the footage I had of the No Man's Land attack! Those winged mechs were SICK, man.

8:00 P.M. To Head Representative Lamarque: that terrorist attack on No Man's Land is exactly what happens when you're soft on the Incorporated. Grow a pair.

8:03 P.M. To the user posting above me: sure, blame UCC-sponsored terrorism on the guy who's pretty much the only reason your ungrateful ass hasn't been forcibly Incorporated yet, good job.

9:17 P.M. To my maybe-girlfriend: hey, why aren't you answering my texts? I thought we were done playing games.

11:40 P.M. To the boy I kissed at No Man's Land: I didn't know your name, or even whether you were Barricader or Incorporated, but I cried when they carried your body off the beach. Your mouth tasted like champagne the last time I saw you alive.

1:45 A.M. To my uncle: I love you. I'm lying to you. I'm sorry.

◆

"YOU'RE NOT SUPPOSED TO be here."

Anabel Park blinked a pair of unimpressed eyes at Alexandre Lamarque. The boredom in her expression, by some sorcery, only served to highlight the perfectly winged tips of her eyeliner. "Really? I had no idea."

Alex glared past Anabel's shoulder toward Pru. "You spilled the beans, didn't you?"

"Only to Anabel!" Pru raised her hands in surrender. "Your message in a bottle—or cylinder, whatever—said Bishop's information was for your ears, and mine. You didn't say I couldn't bring a backup pair of ears to the wyvern heist party. Besides, you can't talk, Cat is right there!"

"I am Rebelwing's primary engineer," said Cat, without looking up from her phone. When she'd arrived at Café Dupont in tow with Alex, she'd commandeered a corner of the Rose Room with hardly a word, and hadn't stopped scrolling through mech design notes since. "Of course I was clued in on Alexandre's ridiculous scheme."

"It wasn't my scheme," protested Alex.

"Yet here you are, running headlong into an absurd amount of danger with nary a word of protest." Cat wrinkled her nose at an unlikely mech add-on, tapping the corner of her screen to delete the offending part. "Again."

"If you keep pacing the room like that, Café Dupont is going to bill you for wearing a hole in their nice overpriced carpet," Pru observed.

They all looked up when the white gilded doors reopened to admit a fifth guest. "Then they can add it to my tab," said Hakeem Bishop. The Chief of Staff shrugged off his suit jacket. His eyebrows wedged themselves into a peculiar shape when he took note of the Rose Room's occupants. "It seems the number of ears I have invited to these little meetings has managed to double in my absence."

"I needed Rebelwing's engineer for consulting purposes," said Alex.

"And I needed her girlfriend for emotional support purposes," said Pru. "Ow! Anabel, that hurt!"

"Spare me, it was a love tap." Anabel shook the fingers out of the fist she'd rapped against the back of Pru's skull. To Bishop, she said, "Pru and Alex needed backup. Someone discreet who can handle a weapon, understands basic escape and evasion tactics, and"—here, her tone went dry—"is used to working with both of them, and their squabbling."

"I see." Bishop took his usual spot by the frosted-glass windows, backlit by the city. "Was there anything else, Miss Park?"

"Yes, in fact," said Cat. The engineer had finally set aside her phone. That bright, asymmetrical gaze of hers panned across the Rose Room with its cold, camera-eyed awareness. Her mouth, painted azure today, was a thin line of color across her bone-pale face. "They needed someone with the stomach to put Alexandre down like a dog."

Neither noise-cancellers nor schoolmarm glares could have dictated a deeper silence than the one that followed. Anabel's gaze locked on her girlfriend's. Or maybe former girlfriend's, the way Cat was looking at her now. Anabel, for her part, gave nothing away. "It shouldn't come to that," she said.

Alex made to cross the room toward Anabel, then hesitated, angling himself toward Pru instead. "I thought that was your job." His voice rasped beneath the forced lightness he'd infused in his tone.

"I delegated," said Pru. Her hands twisted together, bones straining. "But like Anabel says. It shouldn't come to that. And don't you dare do anything stupid enough to mess with those odds."

"There shouldn't be odds at all," hissed Cat. "This shouldn't be happening." She rounded on Bishop. "This is on you. You should have told us what really happened to Etienne as soon as you had the intel. If we'd known earlier, we could have—"

"Could have what? What would you have done, little cat?" Bishop's hands turned toward her, palms out, body language open. "Do you imagine all your engineering skill, all Alexandre's piloting prowess, would have changed what has already been done to a dead man?"

Cat's head jerked toward Alex, her cybernetic eye a small, searing beacon of fury. "We deserved the truth. *Alexandre* deserved the truth."

Alex laughed, sudden and soft. "Why? Hakeem is right. Knowing the alpha cell was going to target me eventually wouldn't have kept me from the fight. We were always going to fight. Wasn't that the entire point of Rebelwing?"

"The point," Cat began, outraged.

"Was to defend the Barricade cities." Alex's jaw set into that stupid, noble expression he got whenever he talked about something he believed in. "From Jellicoe's wyvern flock, to be specific. This is what I look like fulfilling that promise."

"No, *this is what you look like joining the wyvern flock*," shouted Cat. Pru dropped her hands. She'd never heard Cat raise her voice like that, not in person, not even in that awful camera recording from Jellicoe's camp. "Do you think I haven't studied how genetic mapping codes work on implant cells? If the alpha doesn't manage to destroy you first, its cyber-implant will. The alpha cell will track you, latch on to you unseen, and burrow into your blood like the parasite it is. It'll do worse than kill you, Alexandre, it'll turn you into a monster."

"Not if we destroy its host with dragon-grade plasma fire," said Alex, very softly. "It's a risk worth taking, Cat. You knew my father before he became . . . what they made him. You know he'd do the same." He flashed a humorless smile at her. "Besides, so long as the alpha cell survives, I'm a goner either way. The walls of the Barricade Coalition were designed to protect us from war mechs, not the terrors of genetic engineering and nanotech. I could hide behind New Columbia's gates. Or spend my days on the lam, trying to outrun a pre-programmed fate." The smile grew warm, as he leaned toward her, confessional. "But between you and me, *mi gato*, I'd rather go down fighting."

Cat's face crumpled, cybernetic eye glittering. For a moment, Pru thought the engineer might slap Alex clean across the face. Or fling herself into his embrace. Even odds. He held himself open toward her, arms splayed and chin lifted, as if he'd welcome either touch.

Cat angled away from him to round on Pru instead. "Wasn't this the entire point of you?" she spat. "Rebelwing was never meant to imprint on you, but she did. You should have been good enough by now. You should have been ready to pilot her alone, but instead you cling to Alexandre like a coward. If he dies fighting, it'll be your fault."

"Don't you dare take this out on her!" Anabel strode between them, the very picture of the ice queen. "When you don't let your assholery get the better of you, you have one of the best analytic minds behind the Barricades. Pru's been a combat mech pilot for all of six weeks. If you stuck her in the dragon's cockpit alone and tried to ferry her behind enemy lines on a real mission right now, she'd die before she got anywhere close to the alpha."

"I can't actually tell if you're insulting me or defending me right now," Pru informed Anabel. She'd started twisting her hands together again.

Anabel, bearing down on Cat, continued as if Pru hadn't spoken. "You saw what happened on the beach. Alex is still one of the best pilots we've got, and the only one who knows the inner workings of the dragon as well as you do. Pru can map her imprint onto him, which means they can share the cockpit. Her bond, his piloting skills. Meanwhile, I follow in a transport mech, with a plasma rifle at the ready.

"If something goes wrong, if they hit Et—if they hit the alpha, but miss the alpha cell, and it survives long enough to turn Alex into . . . what you say, I'll be on standby. A plasma rifle won't be strong enough to destroy the cell for good, but it'll be enough to . . . to kill the new host." Anabel swallowed a visible knot. "The alpha cell would remain a threat, but losing two hosts in rapid succession should buy us more time to shut it down. I hope we won't need it. But we should plan for it. It's the best strategy for a bad situation."

Cat pressed her mouth together. "Yes. I did see what happened on the beach. And I remember what happened in the cabin, to that man who turned into a wyvern." Her regard was a spotlight, Anabel enveloped in its glare. "I understand why you're here. If Alexandre might require an executioner, better to choose a tried and true killer."

Cat pivoted away from Anabel, body language dismissive, but when she spoke, her voice had returned to frosty rationality. She might have been delivering a schoolroom lecture. "I have finished uploading the specs Alexandre requested on Rebelwing's current capabilities. There's no further purpose for my presence here."

"Cat," said Anabel. A question, an order, a plea.

Cat walked out of the room. The door clicked neatly into place behind her.

Anabel's manicured fingers clenched, and unclenched. Pru waited for Anabel to go after Cat, to follow and explain and make things somehow all right again. But Anabel didn't move.

Heart stuttering, Pru made an aborted move toward Anabel. "This was wrong. I shouldn't have dragged you into my mess. You don't have to—"

"Yes, I do." Slowly, Anabel's gaze lifted from the closed doors toward the corner where Alex stood, watching his friends quarrel over the right to kill him. "I really do." Her voice broke. "Don't I, Alex?"

Alex closed his eyes, and the distance between them, with two long, shaky strides. His hands landed on either side of Anabel's shoulders. As a pair, their figures cut jagged shadows against the city lights filtering through frosted glass. Never had Pru seen two people stand so close together and look so lonely at the same time. "Yeah," said Alex. "Yeah, you do. I'm sorry. And grateful." Over Anabel's shoulder, that ineffably dark-eyed gaze snagged on Pru. "To both of you."

Like Pru and Anabel had agreed to help him move into a new dorm room or something. Pru's gut lurched again, threatening to expel its contents.

But already, Alex's attention was shifting away from them. "We need to discuss strategy."

Hakeem Bishop, still standing in the shower of light through the window, offered them all a grim smile. "Let's get started."

DIFFERENT KINDS OF BREAKING ——— 15

Jellicoe's wyverns would be delivered to the Executive General on a Saturday. The date coincided with Jellicoe's own departure from the continent. "We hit Jellicoe's compound in the morning," said Anabel, who'd either bribed or blackmailed—at this point, Pru was afraid to ask which—one of her cousins in the intelligence services for the logistics. "His resources and most of his staff save a couple goons have already been stripped and distributed among the other UCC execs, which leaves him vulnerable, and his labs unguarded. That gives me the perfect opportunity to sneak in and destroy the main blueprints for the wyvern flock—and the alpha cell—so some other bastard doesn't get the bright idea to try rebuilding these beasts."

"What about electronic backups?" asked Pru.

Anabel's mouth thinned. "I was going to ask Cat to take care of them, originally. Obviously, that's not currently viable, so Cousin Jinwoo from the cyber security department will just have to do his worst. Meanwhile, you and Alex fly Rebelwing down to the delivery compound to take on the alpha. The wyverns are packaged for delivery; that means they'll be in sleep mode." She offered her audience a grim smile. "Which leaves the alpha without the support of its flock. The one thing left to figure out here is our cover for getting past the Barricade checkpoints unauthorized."

"Excellent point, Miss Park," said Bishop, as he pulled up a hologram from his phone. The corner of his mouth tilted upward. The expression was not reassuring. "Certain cross-territory deliveries go out on Saturday mornings, as it so happens. The off-the-books kind. Since you've had a hand in implementing the program, Miss Park, I believe you're aware of which ones I mean."

Anabel made a slightly strangled sound.

Pru took a long, doleful look at the contents of Bishop's hologram. "Wow. Not really pulling the social propriety punches on this one, are you?"

"In the defense of democracy," Bishop countered, utterly unrepentant, "we all must sacrifice. Clutch all the pearls you like, but you did sign up for whatever this plan called for."

Which was how, at ass o'clock on a Saturday morning, Pru got stuck buttoned up to the neck in a heavy military jacket, riding shotgun to Anabel while the latter piloted a squat little transport mech up to the city walls.

"Halt!" The Barricade intercom crackled over the mech's loudspeakers. "Identify yourselves."

"Jeez, ain't you heard?" Pru called back. She channeled all the early morning grouchiness she could muster into her voice. "Transport shuttle number oh-five-two-six-one, reporting for duty. Some asshat at your command calling for another hush-hush special delivery."

"Ah," said the voice over the intercom, in a slightly different tone. The sentry's awkwardness was palpable. "Right, and so you are."

A few minutes later, several crates had been loaded into the mech's back end compartment. "You have a good day now," said one of the sentries. He hopped off the mech's spindly legs as soon as the final crate was dropped, as if he thought it might bite him.

The gate opened to let them pass. Pru glanced sidelong at Anabel, who kept her eyes resolutely focused on the path ahead. Their mech scuttled on its long metal legs toward Hakeem Bishop's prescribed route, climbing around cars and pedestrians, spiderlike. "So."

Anabel's eyebrows twitched. "So?"

They'd chosen a relatively sparse piece of Incorporated territory, the route trickling along toward one of the abandoned districts. Over-rapid tech development had left the skeletons of half-finished construction projects hollowed out over vehicular lanes like a depressing, haunted forest of chrome and concrete.

"Lovely view, isn't it?" said Anabel.

"Weak dodge, Park." Pru jerked her head toward the back of the mech. "Want to explain what's in those crates?"

Anabel actually blushed. "When I pitched a Coalition-sanctioned book smuggling program," she said carefully, "I had to delegate some of the work. I had little say in, um, curating some of the actual material—"

"I believe it is popularly called erotica," interrupted a no-nonsense voice in the back.

Anabel swore, and nearly swerved one of the mech's legs into oncoming traffic. Righting herself, she twisted her head toward the voice's source. "What the hell are you doing here?"

Slowly, Cat's bright head of hair emerged from the stacked up wall of crates. Her face rippled into view, as her thumb flicked aside the lever on the rotund cloaking device at her wrist, a miniature of the same sort the dragon used. In her other hand was—judging from the cover—unmistakably an erotic novel. Old-fashioned and paperbound, Pru observed faintly. How romantic.

"Isn't it obvious?" Cat's voice was, beneath its default monotone, faintly petulant. "I am here to help you. If you're depending on that half-wit Jinwoo Park to wipe Jellicoe's blueprint backups from the wireless, you are, in a word, fucked."

"My cousin's not a half-wit, he's just not you!" snapped Anabel. "Besides, I thought you were angry with me."

"That was a week ago."

"And now?"

It was Cat's turn to falter. "It doesn't matter," the engineer settled on at last. "There are more pressing matters at hand than . . . us." Her eyes flicked up toward Anabel's face, softening briefly, before narrowing again. "Besides, Alexandre explained your plan to me. You will need me."

"He could have warned us," said Pru.

Alex's response rippled across the imprint at the back of her mind. He was soaring somewhere overhead, white clouds flashing over Rebelwing's sight line. *But what would be the fun in that?*

Pru shivered, scowling. She wasn't sure what was weirder: hearing his voice in her head, or hearing that voice crack the same terrible jokes it usually made aloud. "Great. Any other fun surprises?"

The underground library sits on a network of tunnels for ease of access, one of which, unknown to Jellicoe, leads directly to his compound. Anabel will head that way with the shipment, as planned. Cat will go with her to cloak them, and to direct their passage toward Jellicoe's. A second transport mech should be waiting for them.

Pru felt her mouth twitch. Silently, she asked, *Is this a life-threatening heist on Jellicoe military tech, or is this a matchmaking scheme?*

Cat's spent more time on Incorporated land. She knows the tunnel network better than Anabel does.

Uh-huh, thought Pru, very dry. Aloud, she announced, "Our fearless leader declares that the plan proceeds as discussed, except that Cat will be lending cover and navigation aid to Miss Directionally Impaired here—"

"Honestly," huffed Anabel, "I turn us down the wrong street on one drop-off, and you never let me live it down."

"You're a strategic communications guru with perfect hair and perfect aim," retorted Pru. "If you had a sense of direction on top of it all, I'd have thrown myself off a building by now." In her peripheral sight line through the window, Pru kept an instinctive lookout for the glimmering hint of the dragon's wings, but Alex had piloted himself high out of sight. "Meanwhile, I go with Alex."

From the other end of Pru's sight line, some of the mirth fled Anabel's features. "You sure?"

"It's what we agreed on with Bishop."

"I still don't like the risk."

"I know." Pru lifted her shoulders, wishing she could shrug off the growing anxiety in her gut the same way she shrugged off Anabel's worrywarting. She tried a grin on for size, thin and wry. "Trust that I know what I'm about, at least when it comes to petty crime."

"Because that went so well last time."

"Hey, I got a dragon out of it, didn't I?" Mentally, she tapped at the imprint. "All clear up there, Alex?"

Clear.

They pulled up at a decrepit wreck of a building. "You sure this is it?" asked Pru.

"Positive," said Anabel and Cat as one. They looked at each other, grinned, then remembered they weren't doing that anymore, and quickly glanced toward opposite ends of the transport mech, color high on both their faces. Pru rolled her eyes so hard, they could have popped from her skull.

"Right then," said Anabel, braking the mech. "One illicit underground library shipment, here we go." She opened the latch on the bottom of the mech, and hopped out of the cockpit. Cat and Pru trailed after. Sure enough, a circular little hovercraft was waiting just outside, already half-stacked with book crates, ready to be transported underground.

"You know," said Pru, grabbing a crate, "when you said you pitched book smuggling as a means of resistance from within Incorporated territory, I really thought you meant, like, some George Orwell or Ray Bradbury or something. Not . . ." She glanced at one of the covers topping the crate. Upon it, an improbably muscular man—who'd apparently misplaced his shirt—dipped another man, similarly disrobed, in a sultry lovers' embrace. ". . . um, explicit gay porn."

"Romance novels are traditionally undervalued and overly scrutinized, and queer romances more so than most!" said Anabel, who had apparently recovered from her earlier bout of pearl clutching. "Also, this title was definitely Jay's pick. The library was, as you might imagine, overjoyed."

Pru bet it was. The UCC zones just outside New Columbia didn't boast many underground libraries. That close to the jewel of the

Barricade cities, it was harder to keep unlicensed book distributors properly hidden, secret tunnels or no. Still, given how many of Pru's customers sold to them, she wasn't all that surprised to find an underground library still standing, even one as shabby as this. Camouflage on Incorporated land wasn't usually pretty. If police brigades turned up their noses at raiding buildings that looked like haunted halfway houses, so much the better for the libraries. And if ritzy Incorporated patrons who liked easy access to the odd black market romance had quietly funded the labyrinth of underground tunnels that linked up those libraries, well. So much the better for sneaking undetected into private company compounds.

"You know the plan?" Pru asked Anabel.

"Do I ever not know the plan, Pru-Wu?" She softened at Pru's expression. "Relax. Right now, my only real job is to head toward Jellicoe's labs to destroy the alpha cell blueprints. Precious little point in risking your life and Alex's just for the Executive General to hire some other half-rate Incorporated engineer to build his monsters all over again. The . . . other thing. The plasma rifle thing. It probably won't be necessary."

"Right." Pru's knuckles whitened on the final crate she passed to Anabel. In the distance, the dragon's—and Alex's—presence beat softly against the back of her mind. "I guess this is where we say goodbye."

The crate shook slightly. "For the moment," said Anabel, with forced lightness.

"For the moment," Pru agreed. She let the crate sink into her friend's arms. "Don't you dare get my favorite partner in crime trapped forever in some dank-ass tunnel, Cat. I don't care how mad you are."

Cat sniffed. "Keep Alexandre alive."

Pru bit her lip on the reply she wished she could make. She knew better than to give voice to breakable promises.

Come on, said Alex softly across the imprint.

The dragon landed opposite the library, rippling unseen beneath its cloaking mechanisms, in the shade of what looked like an enormous factory building that had been abandoned, like so many of its ilk, halfway through its construction. Now, it lent cover to their operation. Pru jogged beneath the canopy of the factory's tilted rooftop, heart pounding. She eyed the spot where Rebelwing had dropped, squinting. "You sure this will work?"

It worked during the dry run.

Back at those training fields, Pru thought at him. It had been easier than Jay Park's circus of an obstacle course, on a technical level, but scaling Mount Everest might have been comparable to Jay Park's obstacle course.

A mental shrug answered her. *The training fields are a perfectly useful metric for what does and doesn't work for a combat mech.*

Yeah, but training fields are also a controlled environment. Who knows if what's true there will hold true in an Incorporated zone?

His awareness, pressing against hers, felt wry, for lack of a better way to put it. *That what you told yourself before all your other book smuggling drops?*

Pru shot one last look over her shoulder at the transport mech Anabel had driven them in on. Most of the crates had been unloaded, passed along from Anabel and Cat on to their second mech, its golden plating winking in the sunlight, a perfect match for Cat's lipstick. Anabel and Cat climbed side by side into the cockpit, every inch the good Coalition delivery grunts. Caught from Pru's view across the street, they could have been grumbling about their early morning weekend shift, just a pair of government types from the bottom half of their chain of command, stuck overseeing what they no doubt judged to be a completely frivolous waste of taxpayer dollars.

The mech sealed itself up, stretching out a pair of long golden legs that shot the spherical little cockpit into the air, as the mobile suit climbed to its feet. With spindly arms, it twisted itself down into one of the tunnels, and was gone.

The corner of Pru's mouth curled. *My book smuggling drops were different. I only had me and Anabel to think of.*

Somewhere in the cockpit, Alex was chuckling. *I'll try to play a good Anabel Park understudy.*

Don't even; I don't think you can pull off eyeliner like she can.

We'll just have to find out when we get back to the other side of the Barricades, then.

When, she thought. Hope fluttered its foolish, precious wings inside her chest. When, not if. For the first time since she'd agreed to this whole terrible heist, she felt warm.

Alex's response floated gently across the wake of that thought: *I do want to live, Pru.*

Pru didn't have anything clever or meaningful to say to that, so she refocused her mind on the task at hand. Taking care to keep cover beneath the slope of the factory roof, she followed the hum of the imprint in her head toward Rebelwing's cockpit. Just like that first moment in the broken-down lift—like the moment outside Cat's coffeehouse, like a hundred million moments after—Pru felt the cool chrome of a snout against her forehead. Her eyelids dropped shut. Her hands flew up to clasp the sides of the dragon's head. "Do it," she whispered against the mech's metallic skin. Her voice was hoarse. "Fly us up and away."

Beneath her touch, across the expanse of its presence in her head, the dragon shuddered to life. Wings snapped outward. A roar rumbled deep inside its throat. And then dragon skin was unfolding and stretching around her. Cybernetic scales encased her limbs in their cool embrace. Slowly, surely, the dragon pulled her into its depths, wrapping itself around her like a shield—no, a suit, the living mobile suit that had chosen her, chosen this.

When she opened her eyes, the first thing she saw was Alex's chin, barely an inch from her nose. They were crammed into the cockpit, shoulder to shoulder in what could have been a parody of an embrace, but probably looked more like one of the New Columbia metro trains at rush hour. His skin was warm on hers, their clothes wrinkled between them. When Pru wiggled her head from side to side, it nearly collided with Alex's nose.

"Well," she said aloud.

His chest shuddered with what might have been a laugh. Or possibly a sob of despair; that would have been valid too. "Well," he answered.

Detangling them to the extent possible, Alex settled into the pilot's chair. Pru wiggled into the nook at the side of the seat, flush against the cockpit's interior. She blinked at the window of the dragon's eyes. The world, magnified, blinked back at her. It wasn't a comfortable fit, but fit they did, the two of them curled together in the dragon's heart, hardly able to tell where her limbs ended and his began, where human skin met silver scales. Pru remembered those first early days in the training yards. How she'd wondered at the walls of the cockpit, how those living metal scales had fluctuated around her. One moment, tight as a second scaly skin; the next, expansive enough to leave her lonely in the belly of the beast.

Mostly, though, she remembered how badly she'd wished for a copilot. It was kind of nice, even under these circumstances, to be validated.

Pru didn't ask Alex if he was ready. She already knew in the moment she dug her fingers into the walls of the cockpit, imprint humming inside and around them. They both did.

"Fly," they whispered as one. The earth fell away from them.

◆

Barricading Beat: Your Number One Source for Citizen Journalism!
Posted by DeepState461

Spotted at 3 A.M. this Friday evening — or is it Saturday morning? — lights still on in the Head Representative's Mansion, where someone's favorite war hero is apparently still burning the midnight oil. Rumors have emerged of a disagreement between Head Representative Lamarque and longtime aide and Chief of Staff Hakeem Bishop, who was seen entering the offices earlier in the night, and hasn't yet left. Sources close to the Coalition government claim that Bishop had an urgent briefing for the Head Representative. Could this have to do with the mystery terror attack launched at the No Man's Land beach party? Let's stay tuned to find out!!

◆

"THIS IS TOO EASY," said Pru.

Alex stirred against her. "I appreciate the confidence."

The whole endeavor was a bit like one of those half-waking dreams you had after too many hours of running on caffeine, your heart still palpitating as you lay in bed, trying to drag your exhausted brain into unconsciousness. On one hand, this: Pru's limbs entangled with Alex's, stuck against the cockpit walls, one foot falling asleep while a cramp built along her thigh. On the other hand, this too: the world through the dragon's eyes, through Alex's eyes, filtered into the imprint like light through glass. It was too vast to feel quite real, yet too real to be denied. Her entire brain practically lit up with the sprawl of Incorporated land below and the whisper of clouds around their translucent wings.

"No, really," said Pru, more urgently now. "It's too easy. Something's wrong."

They'd been airborne for just seven minutes, cradled by unmarked enemy sky, still unseen, thanks to the cloaking mechanisms. Beneath them, just coming into view through the zoom of the dragon's eyes, were the walls of the Jellicoe company compound. Their visuals gave no warning of wyverns or hovercraft coming to intercept them.

"It shouldn't be this easy," she pressed. "Should it?"

Alex's hesitation twined with her own. He'd been here before. He knew how to handle Jellicoe's security, could probably break things as well or better than Pru could. But back then, he'd been escaping. Finding an exit, rather than an entrance. It was a different sort of breaking.

Pru knew about this kind of breaking, the sort where you wedged yourself into a place you didn't belong. She knew how to lie to Barricader sentries and smile boringly at UCC enforcers. She knew how to run, she knew how to hide, and she knew how it felt to throw yourself down a route no one else wanted to take, crashing through the dark like a falling lift.

Through the imprint, she narrowed her gaze at the unmarked blue of the horizon over the Jellicoe compound. The thing about putting yourself someplace you didn't belong was that, inevitably, you met resistance. You could deal with resistance any number of ways, when you were a book smuggler, depending on what form that resistance took. You could trick a security guard, or hide from the police, or run from an unsavory customer.

Just as long as you did the unexpected. Become predictable, and the job was kaput.

They were directly over the compound now.

Some reflex in Pru's lizard hindbrain twitched. Her fingers closed around Alex's wrist. "Drop," she croaked at him. "Fall from the sky."

"What—"

"Do it. If there's anyone who can nosedive a mobile suit without killing us both, it's you. Do it now."

He must have sensed the same thing in the back of her mind. The blue disappeared abruptly from Pru's field of vision. Her stomach dropped, and the sky fell. Just in time. Above them, the rapidly departing sky exploded in a spray of silver-edged plasma fire, impossibly bright through the dragon's eyes.

"Worst fireworks display ever!" Pru yelled at no one in particular.

Of course, that wasn't the whole of the problem.

Beside her, Alex was a plane of muscle, tension pulling him stark beneath his skin as he fought the dragon's descent toward the compound. "We're coming in too hot."

Caught between a rock and a hard place, Pru thought grimly— or rather, caught between an explosion and gravity's pull. Fat lot of good it did them to evade Jellicoe's plasma fire booby trap, if it just meant crash-landing to their deaths on unforgiving concrete. The fear of it caught Pru by the throat. She croaked out, "Can you—"

"I'm slowing the drop as best I can." And he was. The surety of Alex's mind blazed against the dragon's imprint, all precisely implemented willpower. For a few harrowing seconds, Pru thought it might work. After all, they'd fallen together before, and lived. The ground was terribly close now.

Then the dragon *screamed*.

The force of its cry cleaved through Pru's eardrums, vibrating through every bone beneath her skin. Something slipped away from her. No, not something. Everything. The rippling layers of silver scales that had previously kept her secured inside the cockpit retracted. Pru's body jerked forward, momentum rattling her bones as she tried to brace herself against Rebelwing's rippling walls. The chrome kept retracting, splitting apart until the cockpit itself opened beneath Pru's legs. Blue sky, sunlit, flooded through the cracks between rapidly disappearing chrome. Air shrieked past her, as her body tumbled downward, limbs flailing for purchase, damnably human without the dragon's scales to shield her.

Beside her, Alex gave a shout. He'd managed to anchor himself against the remaining dragon scales, one arm straining with the effort. The other reached for Pru. For one harrowing second, her fingers scrabbled against his. With all her strength, she clung to him, as if the sheer desperation of sweat-greased human palms might hold her place inside the dragon.

All her strength wasn't enough. Pru fell.

Wind, impossibly cold, shrieked past her ears, biting into her skin. Sky and earth fell away from her in a disjointed jumble, the sun blinding her too-human eyes, as Pru tumbled unprotected through the air's freezing embrace.

No scales, no suit, no dragon. She was falling alone, like that moment in the lift all those months ago.

She screamed. It might have been for the dragon. Or Alex. Or her mother. Anyone.

Her body slammed against something soft. Air crackled around her like lightning. The world stopped dropping away.

"For Christ's sake," said an auto-tuned voice very close to her ear. "Quit making such a racket. It's not like anyone's died. Yet."

Pru's throat was raw. Her world was upside down, still silver and blue at the edges, blindingly white when she blinked. When she blinked a second time, the force field—the force field that someone had used to break her fall—was gone. Her cheek dug into hard-edged concrete. That would leave a bruise, she thought, nonsensically. She was on a concrete platform of some kind, at least fifteen feet off the ground, the sky yawning above her. Beneath her, silver stilts like the legs of a mech rooted the structure to the earth. It reminded her a little of the training arena where she'd first flown Rebelwing, but bigger, taller, and definitely likelier to get her killed.

Someone yanked her roughly to her feet. "What the hell is the meaning of this?" Another voice, also auto-tuned, deeper than the first.

Auto-tune Number One chuckled. The grip holding Pru upright tightened. The scattered fragments of Pru's brain tried to piece it all together: like a rag doll, she was being dragged across concrete by someone covered from head to toe in a slick, chrome-plated suit of body armor. The latest in UCC Inc. arms dealer designs, all white-washed shine, topped with a black-painted helmet that obscured its wearer's features. Auto-tune Number One, the voice that had told Pru to stop screaming, came from the helmet. It had a voice box, so the wearer could talk through their symbolically democracy-destroying regalia. How hip.

Auto-tune Number Two wore similar garb, standing at attention a few feet away, accompanied by a lankier companion in matching uniform. The first man stood at least a head higher than Pru's captor, broader across both shoulders and waist. All three wore the same badge pinned to their lapels, the winking silver emblem of the United Continental Confederacy Incorporated.

Like something out of a memory, Auto-tune Number Two lifted the great black helmet from his head. Pru's shoulders rose in knots beneath Auto-tune Number One's grip. There he was in the flesh: the monochromatic, gray-suited man from Bishop's recordings, eyes like chips of flint in his paper-pale face.

"Mr. Jellicoe, I presume," she croaked.

"Well, well. So the brave little Barricaders figured Roman's gambit out after all." His voice, without the auto-tuning modulator to bleach out its venom, rasped low and vicious. He stepped forward. Jerking Pru's chin upward between gloved fingers, Jellicoe turned her face this way and that, as if seeking out physical evidence of Barricader treachery. "Didn't expect my surprise, did you?"

"What, that little cache of skyborne plasma bombs?" Pru shrugged. Or tried to, beneath that iron grip. "I think I did pretty well for myself, all things considered." She just had to keep talking past the anxiety, her mouth on autopilot, like she was dealing with a drop-off gone bad. If she didn't think about how completely screwed she was, maybe she could keep her head intact. From the corner of her eye, she tried to take stock of how far the platform stretched. A kilometer or two, give or take, with neighboring, identical platforms of roughly the same size, hovering a few meters away. Far enough to run, and jump, if she could get free. The drop down, if she fell, would be a problem—they had to be at least twenty meters up in the air—but that was a problem for future Pru.

"We must have very different ideas of what doing well for yourself means," said the other UCC flunky. Their grip dug into Pru's shoulder, a bird of prey's talons gloved in UCC whites. "Mr. Jellicoe's, so far as I believe, does not include breaking and entering on Incorporated property. It certainly doesn't include being violently ejected from your . . . vehicle by force field traps, and being caught quite so handily."

Mr. Jellicoe dropped Pru's chin. "Ah yes, the vehicle. Curious device, something that can duck a grid of plasma bombs with not even a minute's warning, and keep its cloaking mechanisms operational. Not many engineers—or pilots—can manage the trick of it."

"Yeah." Pru stretched her grin as shit-eating as it would go. She thought she might vomit all over this nice dreary concrete right here and now. "Curious, that's it."

"Doesn't seem the sort of trick a schoolgirl should be able to pull."

"I go to prep school," said Pru, with a wink. "We're all snot-nosed overachieving elitists behind the Barricades, didn't you know?"

Mr. Jellicoe's answering twitch of the lips was thin and alarmingly thoughtful. "No, not a schoolgirl trick," he repeated. "At least not one that a schoolgirl could pull off alone."

His words jabbed at the darker uncertainties in Pru's head. She'd fallen into the force field trap, crashed right into it like one of Jay's obstacles in training. She'd lost Rebelwing. She'd lost Alex. Instinctively, she reached out across the length of the dragon's imprint. A tendril of headache whipped back at her. She hissed, and tried again, eyes watering. Nothing. Her chest clenched. She was standing in the Head Representative's bunker all over again, after flying all night, useless, incapable of summoning Rebelwing, incapable of even knowing where the dragon was. Whether she had escaped. Whether Alex could still pilot her across Pru's malfunctioning imprint, or if he'd even survived dodging the bombs. Where were they, without Rebelwing? Without the means to destroy the alpha cell?

Useless, useless, useless.

"You're giving the girl far too much credit," objected the flunky. "Children don't simply fall from the sky. She's not one of our wyverns."

"Not yet," countered Jellicoe. The pale, runny eyes narrowed. "That can always change."

Cold seeped into Pru's veins.

Stop panicking, she ordered her brain. Her fingers flexed. The force field trap was no different from Jay's force field hoops. Jellicoe and his flunkies were no worse than overaggressive Incorporated customers trying to stiff her book smuggling pay.

"Rich talk," she managed. "For a wanted criminal on both sides of the Barricades." So far as the public knew, anyway. Pru forced herself to remember the business deal he'd made, the lives he'd bargained away to the Executive General, careless sacrifices on an Incorporated altar. Remember, so she'd stay angry instead of scared.

Jellicoe, for his part, only looked amused. "Spoken like a true Barricader. Do you think the laws of either your Coalition or the UCC matter to me now? I'm *retiring*, and retiring rich. This time tomorrow, the Executive General will own the most powerful weapons on the North American continent, and I'll be sunning myself in the tropics. How's that for a happy ending?"

The flunky laughed, a sound like breaking glass over the helmet's auto-tuning. "If you'll excuse my say-so, sir, you've been reading too many Barricader fairytales if you really believe in happy endings."

"Don't be absurd. I'm giving the girl the finest dose of reality money can buy." Jellicoe's gray eyes slitted toward the flunky. "Nothing could be further from that children's garbage."

"Then you've read them," continued the flunky, obstinate. "To know they're children's garbage. Look, I won't turn you in to the Executive General or anything. We all know we all do it."

"Your point?" demanded Jellicoe through grinding teeth.

"Oh, I haven't got one. And I suppose you wouldn't know much about storytelling at all, pleasantly kowtowing to the UCC as you do. I, on the other hand, take a rather personal interest in the art form." As her captor spoke, pressure eased up on Pru's shoulders. The flunky gave her a shove toward Jellicoe's silent companion, who seized her by her arm. With a pop, the flunky removed the black UCC-branded helmet.

Sophie Wu, the woman who'd once been called Scheherazade, cast a benign, red-painted smile over the top of her chrome-plated uniform. "We apologize for the deception," said Pru's mother. "But as representatives of a would-be government-in-exile, we weren't at all sure how else to get a meeting with some politically disgraced Incorporated arms dealers. It's all just too much shadiness to wrap our heads around."

We, thought Pru, staring openly at her mother. *Who's we?*

"Who the hell are you?" snarled Jellicoe.

"You don't know?" Mama mugged a wounded face. "Well, I suppose I should have known you weren't much of a reader. Some Incorporated types are, keeping book smugglers in business and all, but I was perhaps overly optimistic—"

Jellicoe turned to the flunky hanging on to Pru, face flaming with rage and confusion. "You! Get rid of this woman!"

Pru's new captor actually sighed. Pru stumbled forward, as he freed his grip, and removed the UCC helmet. "I'm afraid I don't take orders from you," said Gabriel Lamarque pleasantly. His hair fell in an unlikely layer of well-coiffed waves across his forehead, his cheeks slightly pink, as he grinned at Jellicoe with all his teeth. "That said, my associate and I did come here to negotiate in good faith. So far as we're able, at least, given the gambit to get ourselves into the same room as the famous Harold Jellicoe."

The flattery, at least, seemed to puff Jellicoe up a little. "What, so the great Head Representative of the Barricade Coalition"—he spat that bit out, curse-like—"would deign to ask favors of little old me?" He spread his arms, all false invitation and false smiles. "Or perhaps it's an assassination attempt. You're too hungry for the old battles of our youth, Lamarque, for playing the blood knight, the war hero. Perhaps you've come to finish me for a little taste of that old rush. Why else would you come alone, instead of sending some merc to do your dirty work?"

"Oh, he's not alone," Mama reminded Jellicoe, a deadly little caress of a whisper.

"I mean you no harm," Lamarque reiterated, all cajoling tones.

"No?" Jellicoe paced around the length of the concrete, and paused, right in front of Pru, just a few feet from Mama and the Head Representative. For one wild moment, Pru thought Jellicoe might seize the back of Pru's ponytail, toss her to the floor, put a plasma gun to her skull.

But Jellicoe only had eyes for Gabriel Lamarque. "Give me a reason not to call the Executive General right now."

"Exactly what I said." Lamarque bowed his head. "A negotiation."

"And what could you possibly want to negotiate for?"

Lamarque's blue eyes blinked once. Carefully, his expression schooled itself smooth, politician pleasant. "I'd think that would be obvious." He glanced once toward Pru. For one dizzying moment, she wondered if this really was a fairytale, if the hero of the Partition Wars had come here with her mother to fix her screw-up, to rescue her from this mess and take her home to New Columbia, where Alex and Anabel and Cat would be waiting, safe and sound. She wondered if he was here to save her. If the adults had arrived to make everything all right.

Then the Head Representative's gaze flicked back toward Jellicoe. "We're here for my brother," he said.

——————————————— **THE ART OF WAR**

Jellicoe's face was a creature unto itself. It twisted slowly from a sneer into self-satisfied disbelief, moving in pieces, from wide mouth to runny gray eyes to wrinkling nose. "What, and you think to storm my compound and take him, the two of you and this . . ." He barely spared a glance for Pru. "This insolent little freak?"

"A child," corrected Mama, all smiles. "Playing a prank, no doubt. We are sorry for not keeping a better eye out, the Head Representative and I." Like Pru had wandered into a neighbor's suburban flower garden and trampled on some roses.

"Sorry!" Jellicoe's wide mouth went wider still, disbelief painted in mottled red across his features. "That's one hell of a prank, breaking and entering on Incorporated territory, don't you think?"

"As the girl says," continued Mama, unperturbed, "Barricader children are precocious."

"Like your brother," said Jellicoe. His eyes flicked toward Lamarque. Predatory intent glittered behind the pale irises. "He was precocious too, wasn't he? The idealist who never quite grew up. You should have heard his old speeches here on our side of the Barricades, whenever he rallied attacks on my compound. Liberty and equality and justice for all. Such a firebrand! Perfect, really, for my . . . marketing purposes."

Pru's attention followed Jellicoe's gaze toward Alex's uncle. Gabriel had a face like marble, symmetrically carved and well shaped, but he'd won his following on warmth, the kind of heat that came with human approachability rather than the wild burn of his younger brother's flames. Now, though, he looked cold as any statue. "No doubt," he said. Cool voiced, the politician emerging slick and certain, angling for a deal. "You've had your way with him, but now I'd like him back, if you'll please."

"Like him back," Jellicoe echoed, mocking. "As if you can waltz in here and demand anything you'd like without making an offer in return."

Lamarque did smile then. "Only because you've been too preoccupied with marking your territory to allow me or my colleague here the chance. Believe me, it's not one you'll want to refuse lightly."

"Oh?" Jellicoe's lip curled. "And what's this marvelous deal of yours, Head Representative Lamarque?"

"Isn't it obvious?" Lamarque spread his hands. "I come to you in disguise, with only one aide in what should have been an entourage, and no security detail so far as the eye can see. I'm here against the express wishes of my government. Which can only mean one thing." He leaned forward, the way Pru sometimes saw on news networks, the same body language he used to create the impression of confiding great intimacy for the safekeeping of some interviewer or talking head. "I'm offering the best thing I have of value. I'm offering myself."

Jellicoe's wide mouth went thin. "This is a trick."

"Oh, but it's not," Mama tossed in casually. She mirrored the Head

Representative's motions, drawing close on Jellicoe's other side. Predator circling prey, or a seducer circling a mark. "The terms are quite simple, really. You get Gabriel. We get Etienne." Her wide brown eyes narrowed briefly on Pru. "And the schoolgirl. She's only a child. We'll handle her with our own kind of justice."

Jellicoe followed Mama's sight line toward Pru, and snorted. "You really expect me to believe you would trade your precious war hero, your leader of the free cities of the Barricade Coalition, for a snot-nosed teenager out past her curfew?"

"And my brother," said Lamarque.

The sneer was back. "What's left of your brother, you mean. You haven't even gotten a look at the goods you're bargaining for. Bad business, that. How will you know you like what you're getting? How do you know you're not leaving your precious Barricade cities leaderless for nothing at all?"

"They won't be leaderless." That even-toned quality had returned to Lamarque's words. "A man of your repute is, I'm sure, familiar with my advisors. I couldn't have governed forever anyhow, and the Coalition will remain in the quite capable hands of my Chief of Staff, and others like him. In time, the people will choose a new Head Representative. That's the beauty of democracy at work."

"Ah, yes, the venerable Hakeem Bishop. Your ruthless military man, the so-called 'power behind your throne.' What part did he play in this delectable little offer of yours, I wonder?"

"None." And you could believe it, looking at that marble politician's face of Lamarque's. "This was my call."

"What, to remain here at the compound as my hostage in exchange for a brother you haven't seen in more than a decade?"

Lamarque bowed his head. "I didn't know he was alive until now. If I had . . ." He trailed off. The blue eyes hardened. "For all the talk of my role in the Partition Wars, Etienne was always the idealist. My little brother wanted a better, brighter world. He could see possibilities I couldn't, and he and Julia Santiago traveled beyond the Barricades without my blessing. It's my fault, in a sense, what happened to them. I just want to make things right."

It was the answer Jellicoe had been waiting for. "Then you're a fool after all."

And maybe he was. None of this made any sense to Pru. Why sacrifice the leadership of the very thing the Lamarques had thrown their lives into building, all for the sake of one long-lost, broken life? Lamarque had known about Etienne's real fate, the wyvern alpha born of his skin. Bishop had as good as said so.

Then again, Lamarque hadn't been present at Bishop's meeting, and Pru only knew what Bishop had shared. The possibility of a deception flashed unbidden and wild through her head. Had the Head Representative's own Chief of Staff kept that from him, somehow? What if Alex's uncle really was a fool, throwing himself on Jellicoe's sword for nothing?

"I may be a fool," agreed Gabriel Lamarque, almost as if he'd overheard the cacophony in Pru's mind. "But I'll be a fool who sees his little brother one more time."

Jellicoe's teeth were very bright. He touched the earpiece at the side of his head. "Go on then," he said. "Come on out."

One of the panels in the concrete groaned. Beside the platform, a previously hidden lift rumbled to life, a low-walled narrow box of an elevator. Attached to it was a leash.

The sky darkened. Pru made the error of looking up. A silhouette blacked out an edge of the sun, sure enough, wings unfurled just like one of those terrible wyverns back on the beach. Too distant for her to puzzle out its features, too distant for her to see if its eyes were blue or brown, if its gaze still carried human-made hurricanes.

The leash, which Jellicoe snatched up with greedy fingers, was clearly one of those fancy high-tech models, the kind that came equipped with all sorts of levers and controls, all attached to a slick, metal-cased cord. For all the myriad buttons spanning the delicate handle between Jellicoe's fingers, Pru didn't take long to figure out what the cord itself was attached to.

A few feet away, Gabriel Lamarque stood with his face tilted toward the wings blotting out the sun. The Adam's apple in his throat worked.

"Etienne," whispered Mama. She sagged inside the stolen uniform. "So it's true."

"We knew that much," said the Head Representative. "We had to."

That couldn't be all, thought Pru hysterically. Mama and the Head Representative were both smarter than that. They had to have a plan. Pru refused to think of her mother or Alex's uncle as idiots. They wouldn't just throw themselves into a pit of Jellicoe-branded vipers. Not for a dead man, a memory who'd become a monster.

Jellicoe gave the leash a sudden tug. The winged figure at the end of its length streaked overhead. Wind cut across the top of Pru's head. Instinctively, she threw herself low over the concrete, just as the wyvern alpha swooped over them, sunlight winking white-hot off those cruel, curved metal scales.

"Brother," said Gabriel Lamarque.

The jagged wings paused. Slowly, the figure inside turned around. From her spot on the ground, Pru made out the long reptilian snout, narrower by several inches than the dragon's, snapping with metal-cased, razor-edged teeth. Teeth concealing plasma fire blasts, no doubt. The eyes, as ever, though, were what arrested her. Human eyes, blue as Gabriel Lamarque's, blue like a brewing storm. A hurricane.

The thing behind the metal, behind the monster, had been Alex's father once.

"You knew," said Jellicoe, sounding pleased. He wound the cabled leash lazily over one arm, walking around the landing platform. He could have been the father of one of Pru's classmates back at New Columbia Prep, showing some beloved purebred dog at a prize show. "My god, if you could see the face you're wearing. You look like a fool, Gabriel. What a complete, empty-headed, pretty boy idiot you've turned out to be." He chuckled. "A common effect of the Lamarque genes, it would seem. Do you know how easy it was, to lay that trap for your brother?"

Lamarque genes. Something stirred at the back of Pru's head. They'd come here to destroy the alpha cell planted deep inside Etienne Lamarque, the same cell that had a razor-scaled wyvern blinking cold reptilian eyes at the man who'd once been his brother. They'd come to destroy Jellicoe's means of making another alpha, another flock, another No Man's Land.

The thing in the back of Pru's head stirred again. A flash of silver winked on the edges of her mind's eye. She swallowed a gasp, afraid to hope, and desperate for it.

Let Rebelwing be alive, she begged silently. *Let* Alex *be alive.*

Time. She needed to buy time. With an effort, she stood and squared her shoulders. "So, you attacked the beach, huh?" Her voice emerged rusty, like overspent droid parts, but she forced herself to keep speaking. "At that fancy-ass No Man's Land party."

Her gaze darted between Jellicoe and Lamarque.

Schoolgirl, Pru thought. He said it himself. Jellicoe doesn't know what to make of you. At most, you're a clueless, impulsive teenager manipulated into following Gabriel Lamarque's lead. At worst, you're some dumb high schooler who committed grand theft auto on a Barricader war mech, just like Alex assumed all those months ago in that coffeehouse. Either way, play stupid and young. Just like any other smuggling gig. Lean into the stereotype, and make it work for you.

"What was the point, huh?" She let real fear make its way from the pit of her belly into her voice. "Did you just want to spark another war?"

"You ask a lot of questions for a girl who never seems to listen." Jellicoe's fingers jerked at the leash. Pru tried not to look at the creature at its end. "The Barricade Coalition does so love defending the naïveté of its children. Don't you get it? War, peace, win, lose, who gives a shit? Wars are nothing more than a means to sell a product. And I *sold.* That's the only real way to win."

Selling a product. Scales razoring through Dick Masterson's human flesh while plasma fire stole his speech. Explosions shaking the sea. Barricaders and Incorporated alike lying in red-stained pools on moon-pale sand. The price of Jellicoe's retirement. Selling a product indeed.

Pru turned toward her mother. "You guys can't be serious about this."

Mama didn't meet Pru's gaze. "If you're satisfied with this macabre little display," she called out to Jellicoe, striding forward, "we'll go about making our deal then. I'll handle the schoolgirl." As she passed Pru, she slipped something cool and round into Pru's hands.

A cylinder. Pru's fingers slid along the familiar grooves of the device. The same cylinder that had once carried Alex's invitation to the Rose Room.

"Restore Etienne to his proper form," continued Mama, still focused on Jellicoe, "and you'll have the Head Representative himself for a political prisoner to parade for ransom to the Executive General. How's that for *selling a product?*"

The ringing at the back of Pru's mind grew, almost drowning out the voices around her, but she heard what Jellicoe said next, loud and clear.

"You sweet, stupid woman," said Jellicoe, mouth twisting, "Don't you see? Etienne Lamarque no longer exists. There is only this."

The leash snapped off. The creature that had once been Etienne shot overhead, circled once. Dread clamped down on Pru's heart.

Come on, come on, whispered the silent mantra from Pru to the thing curling back to life inside her brain. The flash of something else in the dark, quicksilver bright, flush against her very being. *Come on.*

Once upon a time, Pru's mind would have been ablaze with frantic, terrified imaginings of every worst-case scenario. If Rebelwing arrived, would she still trust Pru to pilot her? What if the dragon arrived without Alex? Could Pru figure out how to fight without him?

Now, with teeth gritted, Pru forced back the wave of fear, letting her focus crystalize instead on the imprint fluttering to life inside her. Panic wouldn't rule Pru's heart. Not today. When Rebelwing arrived, Pru would have access to dragon-grade plasma fire. When

Rebelwing arrived, Pru would destroy the alpha. She'd find a way forward. Even when plans wandered astray, there was always a way forward.

"If there's no Etienne," said Mama, "then there's no deal."

"A pity," said Jellicoe. With a sigh, he stomped on one of the concrete tiles at his feet. Instantly, the same translucent force fields that had pulled Pru from the dragon sprang up in a protective bubble around him. He looked toward the creature darkening the sky, smiled, and stroked a thumb over one of the controls on the leash. "Attack," he said.

The circling wings paused. And then, with a great, inhuman scream, the wyvern alpha came streaking down toward the humans below.

Mama's weight hit Pru with the force of a train barreling through the underground. Pru's back struck concrete with a bone-rattling smack. Tears sprang to her eyes. Her ears rang. For a dizzying, horrible moment, Pru thought it must be plasma fire. The wyvern alpha must have struck home with a blast, caught Mama across the head or belly or ribs, knocking her body into Pru's, and now—

Mama's fingers clenched around Pru's wrist. Pru's fingers twitched in response, still sweat-sticky around that little metal cylinder.

"Read it," rasped Mama. "The cylinder. Read it, after all this." She was a shield over Pru, forcing them both flush against the platform. Pru tried in vain to look past her mother's armored shoulder for the alpha, but saw only a pale sliver of sky. Beneath her, the platform rumbled. Someone gave a shout. Mama swore violently, and forced them back against the concrete. Her shoulder dug into the side of Pru's face, as Mama tried to protect them both from whatever was happening. The gunmetal scent of the stolen flunky's armor filled Pru's nostrils.

"Mama," whispered Pru against her mother's side. "Mama, what the hell is happening?"

"No time," mumbled Mama. "I wish we had more time, goddammit, I wish—"

A wyvern shriek cut through the remainder of Sophie Wu's wishes.

"Get up and run," said Mama, barely audible over the clamor beyond them. "Do you hear me? You get the hell away from here, understand? Get off this platform. Jump if you have to. You have to put as much distance as you can, between you and—"

Another wyvern scream filled Pru's ears.

Her mother shoved her across the concrete. Plasma fire bloomed between them. Pru shrieked, scrambling backward on her palms, her legs still a tangle beneath her. "Come on," she snarled at herself, at the stupid, dormant imprint. What good did the dragon's choosing her do, if it wouldn't come when called? "Come on, come on, come—"

She swore and rolled to avoid another blast from the wyvern. Something landed with an echoing thud on the platform beside her. The momentum of Pru's somersault nearly sent her colliding with the hunk of metal. She caught herself over one aching shoulder, then stared. It was a mech, loosely humanoid, stomping its way across the platform. Pru had narrowly avoided taking out one of the legs it had used to leap onto the platform.

In the back of her brain, the imprint fluttered weak-willed wings, but it bore no connection to this mech. The mobile suit striding up the platform now was pretty standard issue, typical UCC design, wingless, built for ground-based combat training. The black metal casing bore the logo of UCC Inc., but Pru would never mistake the voice booming over the mobile suit's comms for anyone else's.

"Hello, Dad," said Alexandre Santiago Lamarque, nestled into the enemy mech he'd commandeered. He was all stage voice now. You could probably hear him from the opposite end of the Jellicoe compound. "I think it's time we laid some family ghosts to rest."

The UCC mech spun sideways with the sort of grace you expected from a human ballerina, not a glorified giant robot, but that was Alex all over. Like the dragon coasting through the sky, like Quixote, the red-and-blue combat mech back in the Coalition training yard. Mobile suits came to elegant and deadly life when wrapped around the Lamarque boy's skin.

The wyvern alpha narrowed predatory blue eyes at its new prey, and dove again. Pru gave a shout, but no plasma fire emerged from its jaws. With one hand closed around the grooves of Mama's holodrive, she jogged the perimeter of the platform, trying to get her bearings. Blue sky above, silver stilts below, an expanse of concrete, and a monster in hot pursuit. Fantastic. Pru grabbed her phone. Her thumb swiped the number at the top of the screen.

"We have eyes on you." Anabel Park's voice crackled businesslike from the phone. "What the hell is going on down there, battle of the beasts?"

"Where are you?" howled Pru. She dodged a stream of plasma fire meant for Alex. His stolen suit skidded down the length of concrete. The wyvern followed, dipping just a hair too close.

"Look at your six o'clock," said Anabel.

"Little busy right now!" *Come on, come on, come on.* "Wait, did you destroy the blueprints?"

"Every last one of them. Wasn't exactly a walk in the park. Had to stun-shoot the whole security squad guarding that shit. Those assholes don't go down easy. I'll show you all the sexy battle scars, once you destroy the original. Preferably, like, now."

Pru cast her eyes sideways, and made out the golden transport mech, clinging spiderlike to one of the neighboring platforms. "Tough ask, without a dragon." Her stomach lurched at the thought of their backup plan. The one Alex wouldn't survive.

The muffled sound of metal parts clicking together emerged over the line. Pru, imagining the plasma rifle being assembled between Anabel's manicured hands, panicked. "Don't take the shot yet! The imprint's still live. Rebelwing might—"

"I know." Her best friend's voice was soft. "I won't shoot unless I have to. I promise."

Alex's mech pivoted and swung a giant metal fist toward the wyvern's head, catching the edge of its jaw before it could spit more plasma fire. The wyvern went crashing sideways. Pru swore and jumped, trying to give it as big a berth as she could without toppling right off the platform's edge. "Anabel, this was so incredibly not the plan."

"Tell me more!"

"Where in hell has Alex been until now anyway?"

"He says you were both thrown from the dragon by a force field trap. It was a close call—he clung to Rebelwing long enough to roll into a soft landing down below, then pinged me from the comms system on that hunk of junk metal he commandeered, if you can believe it. The ride he's hitched might hold off a wyvern for a little while, but a standard-issue UCC combat mech fighting a wyvern is like taking a knife to a gun fight. We need to fix this."

"Yeah, no shit." Pru squinted toward the sky, bracing for the next plasma fire blast. "Any bright ideas?"

"Rebelwing. Where is she?"

"Hell if I know!"

"Pru." Anabel's voice steadied out. "You need to figure it out. You're the only one who can."

"I've!" Concrete blasted apart not two feet from her. "Been!" Pru jumped over the hole. "Trying!" The tendrils of smoke and debris spiraling from the mech battle made it near impossible to place her mother, or the Head Representative, or even Jellicoe himself.

"Shame. What would our teachers say?"

Pru, windmilling backward from another hole in the concrete, gnashed her teeth. She knew exactly what the faculty of New Columbia Prep would expect of one of its students. Trying didn't matter, if you couldn't deliver results. It had always been so much easier for Pru to assume she'd fail.

Unbidden, Alex's furious, judgmental face flickered across her mind's eye. *Why do you always put yourself down?* he'd asked over that ill-fated dinner on the beach.

Because it was better to embrace mediocrity than to try, and try, and try, only to emerge with nothing at all to show for it. Pru had scraped by three years of prep school alongside overachievers of every stripe on that rule. She was a good book smuggler. That had been achievement aplenty, for Pru. It should have been enough. More than enough. And it was.

Until a cybernetic dragon had plucked her brain up for its own unfathomable, arbitrary use. What could you do about that?

Bullshit, whispered a voice in her mind that sounded suspiciously like her mother's. *As if you're some snoozing passenger in the train com-partment of your own life. Who ran headlong into that abandoned lift like an idiot? Who rooted through all that footage of Alex's childhood in some mad attempt to win his dragon's favor? Who called Rebelwing down to the fighting on the beaches during the attack on No Man's Land?*

That night, she'd wanted to put Alex behind armored scales. She'd wanted him skyward among the stars. So the dragon had complied.

And what do you want now, Pru-Wu?

The wyvern emerged through the debris, great blue eyes like points of ice narrowed on Pru. She heard Alex's shout over his sto-len mech's speakers, saw him racing toward her.

Pru looked unblinking into the eyes of the thing that had been Etienne Lamarque more than a decade ago. "Come on!" she screamed. Cold blue filled her sight line. "Come on, you great, big, stupid, ugly—"

The wyvern's jaws opened wide.

Silver scales unfurled around Pru. Like a reversal of that first aw-ful fall onto the platform. Scale by scale, chrome encased her once more, until her human skin was engulfed in the sleek, winged ar-mor of Rebelwing's cockpit. A creature of metal and fire, larger than life, and at its core, Pru. At its core, a living, breathing girl, nothing more, but nothing less. There was a strange sort of comfort in that realization.

People always went on about how your entire life flashed before your eyes before death. Pru thought it was stupid. Life was full of inconsequential crap. Right now, frozen on a precipice of some-thing unknowable, all Pru could see were the moments that mat-tered: the first stories her mother had told. The pleased, assessing look on Anabel's face after their first smuggling drop together. The scent of Alex and the warmth of his skin, hours before No Man's Land changed everything. The way the world looked from behind dragon eyes, writ large and sharp edged and lovely, colors cast painfully bright. The moment Pru had realized that those eyes were hers to see through.

It all happened in seconds.

Over the tinny speakers of Pru's phone, Anabel emitted a whoop of pure, mad delight, tapering off into relieved laughter.

Then Pru spread newfound metal dragon wings, and launched herself toward the jaws of the beast.

◆

Con-Tech-Nental News Roundup
The latest on developments, disasters, and designs emerging from across the continent!
Preview: "Are We Partying Like It's Ten Years Ago Again?"
by Jace Alexander

Reports of new mech technology spearheaded by the constituent companies of the United Continental Confederacy Incorporated have fueled rumors of a growing arms race between Incorporated forces and the Barricade Coalition. Sound like the stuff of a Partition War to you? Denizens of the wireless forums sure seem to think so. Reported sightings of everything from complex force field traps to enormous man-shaped mechs — big as giants! — have filled the unregulated corners of the interwebs. But in our modern world of information sharing, which rumors have substance to them, and which are, well, just rumors? For a limited-time offer, get *Con-Tech-Nental*'s inside scoop — subscribe today!

◆

THE SCALES OF THE dragon's cockpit cleaved skintight around Pru.

This wasn't a fight she was meant for. This had always been a fight for Alex. What she'd known in theory from the moment she'd first stepped into his uncle's training yards cemented itself into truth at No Man's Land, when she'd put him in the sky herself, the dragon wrapped around him and cutting through the wyvern flock, all beauty, all terror.

But Alex was locked away inside a ground-bound UCC suit, and right now, the sky was on Pru's side. As one, she and the dragon wheeled high above the wyvern's spurt of plasma fire. Sunlight slit its way through the dragon eye lenses, but still, Pru caught sight of the ground below. Alex, his mech's legs bent in a protective stance, waited for the wyvern's next attack. Jellicoe was nowhere to be seen. Presumably, he had already fled. Probably holed up in a safehouse, watching the wyvern alpha do its work from some distant flat-screen, deciding whether to send the rest of the flock to finish them off. Pru inhaled slowly, a decision forming around the knot in her belly. She fumbled for her phone. "Anabel. You still there?"

"Always, Pru-Wu."

"Can you get eyes on Jellicoe?"

A pause. "That wasn't the plan."

"Yeah, well, the plan's gone kind of haywire, if you haven't noticed! But I can't handle the current battlefield and worry about what he's up to at the same time!"

"I'd have to leave you," pointed out Anabel. "And Alex."

"I know." Pru swallowed. "Do you trust me?"

A long pause. Then Anabel laughed softly. "I always have, Pru. More than you trust yourself, I'm willing to bet, but my judgment rarely errs. I'll call you when we find the bastard." The line clicked off.

Praying to all the gods of risk aversion that sending her best wingwoman away wasn't a horrible mistake, Pru took stock of the scene below. Mama was huddled at the Head Representative's side, seeking cover from the battle between beasts. Side by side, the two of them moved around platform's perimeter, like soldiers on patrol. Mama clutched something tight in one fist.

Before Pru could figure out what it was, the wyvern streaked toward Alex's mech.

Instinct woke her body and brain alike. Pru hurtled after the wyvern. Rebelwing's mouth parted in a roar. Plasma fire skimmed the edge of one of the wyvern's wings, toppling it off course. Alex pressed the advantage, his mech bending its knees and leaping upward to meet the wyvern. Two powerful metal arms crashed around the wyvern's reptilian head, trying to crush the source of its plasma fire. The wyvern screamed. Its wings snapped to attention. The momentum broke Alex's grip.

The wyvern slid backward across the platform, trying to recover from Alex's clinch. Its wings emitted a flurry of sparks, as razor scales scraped along concrete. The beast shook its head. Its jaws snapped open and shut, trying to cough up more plasma fire. None emerged. Alex wasted no time. His mech crouched low, like a fighter preparing for a killing blow, and launched itself back toward the tottering beast.

Only to collide with one razor-edged wing. With a sound like a thousand nails scraping down an old-fashioned chalkboard, the wyvern's wing cleaved through the protective metal casing of Alex's suit. The mech crashed to the ground, torn in two.

"Alex!" screamed Pru.

The boy who emerged from the wreck couldn't hear her. Not from outside the dragon. Not without the imprint. Magnified through her dragon eyes, sweat gleamed on Alex's unarmored skin, as he stumbled from his mech's ruined cockpit. Without a suit, without a weapon, without anything at all to protect him, as the beast that had been his father clambered toward him, roaring.

Pru tried to turn the dragon around, but the wyvern was so much closer. Its broken jaws, cast in high definition, were full of metal-spiked teeth. Pru flew toward those jaws, one more time, trying to line up Rebelwing's sights on that spot between the cold blue eyes where the alpha cell rested. She had to make the shot. She had to keep the thing that used to be Etienne from slaughtering his son. *Come on, come on, come on, don't let it end this way, it can't end this way.*

The beast sprang with a terrible flap of its razor-edged wings. Alex flung up useless, human arms. A terrible, desperate sound knotted deep in Pru's chest forced itself from her throat. The crack of a plasma blast rang through the air. But not from Rebelwing's jaws.

The wyvern gave a strangled cry. Its wings pumped once. Slowly at first, then with growing speed, it plummeted to the ground below.

Pru pulled Rebelwing up sharp, searching for the source of the shot. Directly below her, Alex lay back on the concrete, chest rising and falling rapidly. Alive. A scant few feet away lay the carcass that had been the wyvern. A smoking, blackened hole lay between dead blue eyes.

Shielding Alex from the wyvern was Gabriel Lamarque, Head

Representative of the Barricade Coalition and long-ago hero of the Partition Wars. A plasma rifle was angled against his jaw, his feet spread in a soldier's stance, long hands still resting on the trigger. He'd shed the UCC flunky armor. Pieces of it were still strewn across the concrete platform. Between the chest plate and helmet lay an oblong pocket. A weapons compartment, where he must have concealed the rifle parts. Anabel Park wasn't, it seemed, the only Barricader who knew how to smuggle weapons into a UCC zone.

Caught through the eyes of the dragon, in that moment, Gabriel Lamarque looked like the young soldier he must have once been, spine straight, carriage proud and heroic.

A spark flashed across the wyvern's dead blue eyes. The cyborg's body twitched, crumpling in on itself. Razor-edged scales retracted into pink, human flesh. Slowly, the ruined human body of Etienne Lamarque emerged, blood-spattered but still golden-headed. The eyes, still blue, but horribly human, blinked once at Gabriel through the blood dripping across Etienne's lashes, and caught on Alex, still sprawled a few feet away.

Etienne's mouth parted. The dying throat worked, Adam's apple bobbing once, and was still.

A speck of something dustlike moved between the brothers, too quick and sudden for Pru to follow. She thought she caught a scuttle of spidery legs, the flash of a chrome exoskeleton, disappearing between the Head Representative's sweat-plastered curls. Her belly turned cold with recognition.

Gabriel went to his knees. At first, Pru thought it was grief. Then she caught the twitch of his shoulders. The proud, straight spine curved. A wink of razor-edged metal emerged along the length of the Head Representative's neck.

Alex was struggling to rise, to help his uncle, but nothing could stop this. Not hurricane boys or metal dragons. Gabriel's rifle had taken out the alpha's host, but without dragon-grade plasma fire he couldn't destroy the thing implanted deep inside. The alpha cell had created a new wyvern.

Pru flew downward. The imprint flared white-hot inside her head, but she ignored the pain. The dragon's wings spanned over Alex. Metal scales parted, and Pru leaned low into the cradle of the cockpit to undo the escape hatch. She reached for the broken boy below.

"Come on," she whispered.

Crushed up against the cockpit floor, she couldn't see his face, but she felt his arms twine themselves roughly over hers. "Pru," he murmured. Dazed, as if he wasn't quite sure it was her. One of his legs dangled at an awkward angle beneath them. With care, they managed to pull him inside the dragon. The hatch closed. Together, they curled around his injured leg, pressed up against the cool metal scales of the cockpit.

"You're hurt," said Pru, stupidly.

He only shook his head. "Sorry."

"Don't be."

"No," he said, still in that strange, dazed voice. "Not me. I'm not the one who said it. I—" He cut himself off with a hiss, flinching around his bad leg, as the cockpit shook. Pru scrambled back into the seat, trying to get eyes on the ground below.

Beneath them, Gabriel Lamarque's body heaved and gasped. Metal sprouted from his skin, leaving streaks of blood down the remaining flesh. On the other end of the platform stood Mama. Sunlight bared the tear tracks on her cheeks, but her expression held no surprise. She had one fist raised to the sky. Pru saw what she held now.

It was one of Rebelwing's spare plasma fire cartridges. Dragon-grade. Mama had rigged it into a makeshift detonator.

They'd planned for this. The realization sank stone-deep into Pru's gut. The two of them, Mama and Gabriel Lamarque, sneaking into the compound ahead of Pru and Alex, wearing UCC uniforms. Then later, how they'd huddled together along the platform's perimeter, scoping its dimensions. They'd been preparing. *Put as much distance as you can between you and the platform*, Mama had ordered. Her brown eyes wide and desperate. *Run, Pru, run. Get out of here.*

Pru tried to move the dragon toward her mother, but the mech only clung to the air, frozen in place, wide metal wings useless. Her mind crashed against the imprint, over and over again, but still, the dragon refused to move. Rebelwing, her carefully programmed sentience so much more efficient than any human being's, had already accepted what Pru's mind refused to.

The remnants of Gabriel Lamarque's human face turned toward Mama. "Scheherazade," he said. His voice, at least, was still his own. Mama's nickname hung between them, spoken warm with the weight of years lost since that smiling, blue-eyed soldier boy had taken the Barricade cities for their Coalition. Years lost since they'd last stood together on a battlefield. "Come to tell one last tale?"

"Something like that, Prometheus," rasped Mama. She stumbled toward what remained of the Head Representative, detonator held high. She managed a shaky smile. "I was always more artist than soldier. Forgive me. I'm without other weapons."

The blue eyes closed. "But never without what's needed." Gabriel Lamarque bowed his head once, as wyvern scales razored their way through his final smile. "Never without a home for love."

Mama's free hand found Gabriel's, clutched tight over the human skin. She ignored the blood that seeped through her grip when wyvern scales bit through her palm. Instead, she slanted her face toward the dragon above. Something like relief colored her features, as she drank in the sight of Rebelwing, the great protective wings of the creature holding Pru and Alex at her core.

"Fly," Mama told them, hoarse with desperation. Then her thumb hit the detonator.

The world erupted into flame. And Pru flew.

The sky streaked around Pru, a haze of incongruously sunlit blue. *Get out of here, get out of here, get out of here,* the refrain pitter-pattered inside her skull. Mama's words. Her final warning, punctuated with plasma fire and crumbling concrete.

"We have to go back," she croaked, as the blue narrowed bright around them. She wouldn't look down. Couldn't.

"Don't," whispered Alex, almost a snarl. He stirred against her, hissing with each jostle of his leg. She wondered how bad it was. She couldn't look at him either. Couldn't look at anything but the blank, beautiful tilt of the sky.

When Alex spoke again, the voice that emerged was cold and soldierly. "They're dead."

"No."

"Pru. It's gone. The entire platform. They're all—"

"I shouldn't have run." Pru's fingers dug mindlessly into the cockpit walls. They were too small again, cleaving close like the mech had been expecting one pilot instead of two. Great, stupid, lumbering metal beast. "How the hell do we turn this thing around?"

"Pru."

"She didn't mean it," mumbled Pru. The sky was very blue. The world a dizzy whirl around the dragon's flight path. "Mama's always been overprotective. We need to go back, the alpha might still—"

"Pru, you have to listen." Strong, long-fingered hands closed over Pru's cheeks. Alex knelt on his one good leg, pressed almost violently into the crook of her arm, as he tried to make her look at him, nails digging into her hair. His bad leg must have been in agony. "The alpha is gone and done. He—it's dead."

Pru's gaze twitched stubbornly toward the dragon eye lenses, the blue beyond. "The implant cell—"

"Is destroyed. Exploded, with the rest of . . ." His chest shuddered once, twice against her. "It's done. We need to find Anabel and Cat, and go home."

"Not without Mama. She and your uncle—"

"Pru." His fingers twisted into her hair. "It's over."

"How can you say that?" She jerked free of his grip. Fury pounded inside her veins. "It's not over until we turn around. Maybe they survived. Maybe they—"

Pru's phone buzzed in her pocket, blaring to abrupt life. In the same moment, something rocked against the dragon's outer shell. The mech gave a horrible roar, and suddenly blue spun into a dark, ugly gray. Downward, they went. Azure skies vanished from view, giving way instead to the wreck Pru had left behind. Charred, smoking remains of the platform rushed past her sight line as she fought instinctively for control of the dragon.

"The alpha," gasped Pru over the phone's insistent rings. "The wyvern's not—"

"That's no wyvern," said Alex. His dark eyes were flinty. Gripping the sides of the cockpit for balance, Pru followed his gaze toward the attack's source.

The head came into view first, cleaving through the smoky sky. Pru thought it was another platform at first, rising through the air. Painted black as pitch and flat-topped, the metal skull's only humanoid features were a pair of makeshift eyes, glowing like lamplight cast through windows in a noseless, mouthless face. The mech—the biggest mech Pru had ever laid eyes on—lumbered toward them on powerful metal legs. A mountain in the shape of a mechanical man. A giant, stolen from the same fairytales that had birthed wyverns and dragons.

A voice crackled loud across the dragon's sound system. "Schoolgirl," breathed the giant's pilot, spiteful and familiar. "The Executive General won't be pleased with how you've damaged his bill of goods."

Of course. They'd come ready to fight wyverns. They hadn't thought about other mechs Jellicoe might be selling in his final package to the Executive General.

"There aren't any grown-ups left to clean up your mess now, little girl. And the Executive General will want his compensation for what I sold him." The giant's great metal fists flexed. Jellicoe breathed hard against the speaker, like he was genuinely eager to fling a couple of broken-down teenagers from the sky. But then, he'd been doing exactly that since girls like Cat were children in an Incorporated camp. It was how men like Jellicoe made themselves feel bigger than they were. "Didn't your mother teach you any manners?"

A tight, hot knot of something unnameable came undone inside Pru. Crooking her fingers through the dragon's scales, she jammed the wireless on, jacking the volume as high as it would go. "Please." A hysterical note bubbled into her voice, magnified over the mech's speakers. "What kind of question is that? Mama raised me polite as anything."

Plasma fire struck one of the giant's eyes, then the other. The giant flinched backward, roaring.

"There's your goddamn manners," hissed Pru.

"Pru," said Alex.

Pru jerked her fingers from the wireless. "I don't need a lecture right now." The dragon wheeled high over the stumbling giant. Narrowly, Pru ducked a flailing metal fist. Swearing, she wheeled in the opposite direction, trying to muster up the same wordless rage that had conjured the plasma fire, but the giant was too quick. With a low hum, its other fist lengthened into a long, sickle-shaped blade.

"Shit!" Pru dropped the dragon with barely enough time to avoid getting her head taken off.

Alex's fingers clamped down on her wrist. "Pru."

She shook him off. "I said not now!"

The blade arced through the air before she could fully recover. She dodged again, but felt the blade crunch through the tip of one wing. The dragon fought to recover itself, but its flight arc was messier than before, wheeling jagged through the sky.

Pru. Listen to me. The strange, familiar meld of Alex's mental voice against the inside of her mind pulled her up short. Outside, the dragon tossed itself back and forth like scrap metal caught on the edge of a hurricane, but the hurricane inside Pru's head was, at least, familiar territory.

That same hurricane shattered the tight, hot knot inside her. She slumped over in her seat, hands raking across her temples. Air shuddered out of her. Her eyes cut through the space between her fingers, toward the rattling view screen of the dragon's eyes. How long would she have to brace for the giant's next blow? "I can't keep this up."

"Not this way, no," agreed Alex, speaking aloud now. He'd pulled himself close, half draped over the cockpit seat. He watched the sharp-edged world blooming across the dragon's gaze, his own dark eyes intent on the screen. "You don't win mech fights without changing up your tactics to adapt to your opponent's assumptions."

"I can't—"

"Can't you?" he countered, annoyed now. "I remember lots of 'I can't do this, I can't do that' back in the training yards, but you still fought Quixote to a draw."

Quixote. Mechanical red-and-blue limbs flashed through Pru's mind, a product of memory, or imprint, or the piece of Alex in her head. Spindly, flexible, but flightless. The dragon had taken the upper hand when Pru had flown skyward, Quixote's long arms rattling around its neck as he struggled to hang on to Rebelwing.

The scythe arced toward them again, shrieked against a wall of metal scales with a spray of sparks. Pru swore through rattling teeth. "The giant's too heavy for us to lift far off the ground," she yelled over the noise. "Way bigger than Quixote."

Alex snorted. "Bigger's not always better. Any advantage in excess is also a weakness. Last time, you didn't just win the upper hand by flight alone. You won it by forcing Quixote out of his natural element. Quixote wasn't made to be airborne. Wrong environment."

His words clicked on some half-formed thought in the back of her mind, and hung there. Bit by bit, like the solution to a difficult problem set, a plan flickered to life. "Maybe the giant's not the one whose natural element needs disrupting," said Pru. "Maybe it's mine." She hesitated. "Ours."

The imprint warmed the scant space between them. Alex's presence tickled along the edges of her mind. She could feel him pushing gently at the idea, wandering the periphery of the bond the dragon's cockpit walls had forged across two minds. *You think it might work?* she asked without speaking.

Alex smiled, then, one of those devastating, hard-edged smiles, the smile of a hurricane in the shape of a boy. "Only one way to find out."

She found herself reaching for his hand. His palm covered hers. And together, girl and boy and dragon, they dove toward the ruins below. The scythe followed, then the giant behind it, movements sluggish, as Jellicoe tried to readjust his mech toward a direction he hadn't anticipated. The dragon, airborne, should have flown skyward, should have tempted the scythe higher and higher. Instead, it shrieked a rapid arc toward the earth, until its belly practically skimmed the concrete-covered ground. Pru waited until she sighted a pair of mechanical feet. Each was big enough that the giant probably could have left a trail of craters in a walk across soft ground. It was a clever visual effect. Jellicoe's engineers had wanted to build something that would flood an opponent's veins with fear. The humanoid largeness of the giant, its dumb ironclad strength, was made to frighten, just like its fairytale counterparts.

But its design had neglected the question of practicality. The great tree trunk legs carried an impressive girth, but moved slowly. Too slowly.

Pru switched on the comms system, and jacked the volume up as high as it would go, so Jellicoe could hear her loud and clear. "You should have invested in wheels," Pru said, and rammed the dragon against one metallic ankle. The giant, already unbalanced from bending toward the diving mech, buckled. One enormous hand groaned toward the dragon, but Rebelwing was too nimble. Again and again, she and Alex wove their mech out of reach.

The giant began to fall. Slowly, at first, then faster, as gravity did its work.

Pru felt Alex counting seconds in the back of her head.

Teeth clenched, Pru shouldered the dragon upward. With a mechanical hiss, its wings folded downward. A pause.

Alex finished their count. *Now, Pru!*

The mech rocketed high, past the giant's grasping fingers, past Jellicoe's roar of fury. The afternoon-kissed sun blinked at Pru through the dragon's eye lenses, a spatter of light across the view screen. They would make it. For a crazy, rabbit-hearted moment, Pru really thought they would make it.

Then a shadow crossed the sun. No, not one shadow. Five. Fingers. The giant, reaching still, canting up from the ground.

Alex shouted. Pru tried to brake. The dragon's wings gave a jerk. A headache snarled through Pru's head. Too little, too late.

She heard a horrible shriek, a mechanical scream specific to metal being torn in two. A roar from the dragon. The entire cockpit spasmed.

They plummeted as one. Pru and Alex and the dragon, wheeling helplessly through the air. A single wing beat uselessly against the sky. Someone screamed. Maybe Pru. Maybe all of them. Through the blurring dragon's eye lenses, a final image seared itself onto Pru's mind: the dragon's other wing, ripped from its body, dangling dead between the giant's fingers.

Earth and sky tilted around them.

Mama's voice echoed giddily across some broken vault in Pru's memory. Maybe that was what happened when you died. You heard the voices of other dead people.

In a shithole of a world that refuses to change, one life can still matter. One life can be everything.

How stupid and fitting and infuriating, thought Pru, to spend more of her life falling to her death than not, and only realize, just now, how terribly badly she wanted to live.

Alex's fingers clenched through hers. He knew what she intended.

Pru shut her eyes and dreamed of flames.

Plasma fire bloomed from the dragon's open mouth, white and blue light licking across the sky, filling the view screen, blotting everything out. The last of their ammunition reserves. The last a crippled dragon had to give.

Jellicoe didn't even have a chance to scream.

The dragon, plasma fire spent, kept falling. The view screen flickered out. The warmth of other minds pressed up against Pru's went cold. She gasped with the force of the loss. She hadn't realized how lonely it would feel, to be by herself inside her head again, until she was.

Time slowed. And so too, it seemed, did the world.

The dragon, gone dark inside, stopped falling. Beside her, Alex hissed. The world without plasma fire was dark, and far too cold. How dumb was that? Pru hadn't thought she'd complain about a world without death-dealing, explosive mech ammunitions. But it was dark, and cold, and unsettlingly still, and all Pru felt was alone.

Light buzzed from Pru's phone.

Pru lifted her head. It might have been an illusion. She might have lost her mind. A stupid illusion to have, on the brink of death, the cracked screen of your cheap-ass phone lighting up some forgotten corner of your broken-down cockpit. If you were going to die, you might as well go out with a bang, not some telemarketer's vacation scam.

"You gonna get that?" Alex's voice sounded like a pipe rusting in a mech mechanic's failed experiment, but Pru sagged against him all the same. Relief drained the strength from her limbs. Alive or dead, neither of them were completely alone. With bone-cracking effort, she untangled their fingers, and dropped from her seat. On her elbows, Pru crawled across the cockpit, until her hand, numb from clutching Alex's, clamped around the phone. She swiped the screen.

"Hey," croaked Pru. "I don't care how good your deal to Timbuktu is, you're not getting my life savings." She considered those words, then added, "I'm not sure I'm even alive. So there."

"Good thing the only place I'm taking you is back across the Barricades to New Columbia, then. You can board our new ride once we find a good landing spot."

Pru froze. That was no telemarketer. A shaky pause filled the other end. Then, like a waking dream, Anabel Park added, voice thick, "About damn time you picked up, Pru-Wu. I could kill you myself for screening my calls on the brink of a life-and-death mech fight."

Stumbling to her feet in the narrowed space of the cockpit, Pru flashed her phone's glow over one of the darkened eye lenses. The faint blue of a force field cradled the mech's broken body. And bare meters away from it, still sitting on its concrete perch, was the force field's source: a familiar spherical transport mech.

"While Anabel was busy knocking out Jellicoe's goons to get to the alpha blueprints, I took the liberty of hacking the codes to his forcefield traps," announced Cat's clipped, no-nonsense voice. She was farther from the speaker than Anabel, her voice warped and tinny, but unmistakably hers. "You'd think that in the course of a decade, that man would have learned not to keep all his security algorithms in the same place. In any case, these fields do much more nicely as a portable crash bubble, wouldn't you say?"

"Absolutely," said Pru faintly. "Anabel, please never break up with your engineer girlfriend ever again."

Anabel made a strange, small sound. "When you asked me to come along on this ghastly little misadventure, it was because you knew I could take a life without flinching." That hitch in her breath echoed across the phone's speaker in the small, dank space. Someone shuffled in the background. Cat, probably. Cat, moving to stand beside Anabel, where she belonged. "I'm glad I got to save one instead. Much better for the university applications, you know?"

Pru's eyes squeezed shut. Her knees went out from under her. Absurdly, she found herself leaning into Alex's shoulder. His arm went around her. The day had been so brutally long. She'd spent far too much of it plummeting through the sky, or staring down plasma fire. She didn't think anyone could fault her for the tears leaking down her cheeks. So Pru cried, ugly and hard and unrelenting. She must have seemed ridiculous, cradled in a broken dragon's cold and darkened cockpit, sobbing snot all over the last living Lamarque, listening to her best friend's voice. She didn't give a damn. When you almost died as many times as she had, Pru was pretty sure you got a pass on what was and wasn't worth giving a damn about.

One life could still matter. One life could be everything.

Even if that life was no more and no less than your own.

Pru opened her eyes against Alex's soft, tear-soaked shirt. Breathed in the scent of sweat and grease and blood. Breathed in the scent of life. "All right," she told Anabel. "Let's go home."

◆

Dear Kiddo,

You brave, foolish, reckless child. Could I ever find the words to tell you how proud you make me? I never did find words for things that really mattered.

What I've left for you on this cylinder isn't much, but it's what I have to give. Forgive your silly mother. Foolishness is all she has ever offered the world, but it is foolishness made precious by you.

I love you, *bao bei*.
Always,
Your Mama

◆

HAKEEM BISHOP SUMMONED PRU to his offices a scant three days after the funerals. Pru couldn't really find it in herself to be surprised, or even all that offended. She hated funerals. To be honest, she wasn't sure there was any actual reason to like funerals, and state funerals centered around the loss of a leader as beloved as Gabriel La-marque had to take the cake. Pru had clenched her teeth together and fiddled at the hem of her repressive black dress through the droning ceremony. For hours after, she'd tried without success to kill the scent of funeral flowers lingering on her skin.

At least she didn't have as many condolence offerers crowd-ing her space as Alex did. Small blessing, when the death of your mother, minor entertainer, ranked an afterthought in the face of greater losses. When Pru checked the usual bevy of netizens' fo-rums, some enterprising conspiracy theorists had already started at least three threads speculating on the truth behind the chemical plant accident that had claimed the lives of an Incorporated arms dealer, the Head Representative of the Barricade Coalition, and a teller of fairytales.

Keep on keeping on, kiddos, thought Pru with studied dispassion, and turned her phone off for twenty-four hours. When she'd turned it back on, the first message to appear was from a dead government leader's Chief of Staff. Pru wondered what it said about her life, that her only response was to groan, toss the phone aside, and bury her head in her pillow for another three hours.

Sleep fixed a lot of things. But sleep couldn't fix the ringing cold of the new emptiness at the back of Pru's head, or the citizens in mourning black projected across every public flat-screen and 3-D display in the city, or the strange, cottony blankness that filled Pru every time she sat alone in Mama's flat above the bodega, and no one darkened the door of her childhood bedroom.

Three days ago, Pru had been a girl with armored wings, a dragon's eyes, a mother who loved her. Now the shattered dragon wings had been donated to some engineer's scrap heap, Rebelwing's watchful eyes dimmed. Pru's mother had been reduced to barren corners of a dust-gathering apartment, unfinished paperwork piled high on an empty desk in an unused kitchen. Three days, to make three ghosts: Rebelwing, Mama, and the girl that Pru had been before the silence of their absence.

You had to wake up to the end of your world, eventually. You couldn't sleep away the scent of funeral flowers, which wouldn't quit cloying at your nostrils no matter how hard you wished them into oblivion. So Pru quit screening Hakeem Bishop's calls, shrugged out of her pajamas, and took a ride share to the Head Representative's offices to see the Chief of Staff. If that was even his title anymore. Could you still be Chief of Staff to a dead man? Pru wasn't sure of the protocol here. She had never paid as much attention to the gov classes in school as she probably should have.

Music—a single guitar, strumming a darksome, complex little melody—floated down the hallways of the mansion, growing louder as Pru approached Gabriel Lamarque's onetime offices.

She was the last in an obvious list of invitees to arrive. Hakeem Bishop stood a ways from the Head Representative's old oak desk. He had his usual spot by one of the windows, his back to the room. Sunlight dappled his gray hair a snowy shade of white. Opposite the Chief of Staff sat Anabel, shadow-eyed, hair a severe chignon at the nape of her neck that made her look years older. Beside her, rigid backed, was Cat, one mechanical hand fisted loosely between them.

Alex Lamarque, meanwhile, had taken a seat atop his dead uncle's desk. In his lap was a guitar, the source of the melody haunting the mansion's hallways. One brace-bound leg thumped against the oak in time to the melody. His hair, untrimmed since their return from the smoking remains of the Jellicoe compound, curled in loose tufts around his ears. It fell away from his eyes when he lifted his head at her approach, but the gaze she caught wasn't interested in holding hers. His lids drifted shut as he played.

"So," said Alex, over the strumming, eyes still closed, "you told my uncle about your plan."

It took Pru two heartbeats to realize he was addressing Bishop, not her.

Hakeem turned. Pru inhaled sharply. The Chief of Staff's expression was stony as ever, but his eyes were red, and tear tracks streaked the creases of his cheeks. "Yes."

Alex's fingers never faltered on the strings. "And here we all thought you were putting us to use behind his back."

"When I first called you to the Rose Room? When you brought Miss Wu here on board? When I deployed the dragon?" Bishop produced a handkerchief. He scrubbed the tears away with sharp, economic motions. "Yes, yes, and yes. But the secret was never going to stay under wraps forever. All that was left to me to control was when and how Gabriel would discover the truth."

"My cousin thought you should have been criminally prosecuted," said Anabel. She spoke offhandedly, but her fingers fidgeted at the hem of her uniform skirt. She'd just come from some study group or another. Ridiculous, that study groups still existed, in a world that had lost so much else, seemingly overnight. "Undermining the Head Representative's authority, reckless endangerment of minors, et cetera and so forth."

Bishop snorted into the handkerchief. "Jay would. He always had a soft touch for kids. When's he lobbying to drag me to court?"

"Thought," reiterated Anabel. Her eyes snapped up, narrowing. "Past tense. I convinced him to spare the courtroom dramas."

Something like surprise crossed Bishop's features. "And why would you do a thing like that?"

Anabel shrugged. Even that motion looked tired. "Yours was the only way to put an end to Jellicoe and his wyverns, wasn't it?"

Pru's tongue found her voice. "How do you figure that?" Her words scraped against the back of her throat, sandpaper-rough with disuse. It occurred to her that she hadn't spoken aloud to anyone since the funerals. "Gabriel Lamarque is dead. My mother—" Her voice failed. Listlessly, her fists clenched and unclenched.

"Someone was always going to die," observed Cat.

Pulse jumping with bitter anger, Pru rounded on the engineer. She paused at the downward cast of the other girl's mismatched eyes. "It is what Jellicoe does," continued Cat. "Even when he loses, he's still bleeding you out. It is what he has always done. It's the only way anyone survives UCC Inc."

Cat would know, Pru supposed. The girl who'd been born Incorporated, just like Mama. The girl who'd escaped. The girl who'd dreamed of dragons with Alexandre Lamarque.

The engineer's head canted toward Anabel. "Jellicoe was the one I should have been angry with, before." Her mechanical fist loosened between them. Hesitantly, Anabel's human fingers slipped up alongside the cool metal digits. "You were always going to save more lives than you took."

Anabel blinked rapidly, wordless, but her fingers tightened on Cat's metal hand.

"Sweet pillow talk there," said Pru.

Cat's gaze slid back toward hers. "I am sorry about your mother."

And what did you say to that? Pru swallowed a distasteful knot in her throat. "Yeah." She looked down at the carpet, kicking one shoe along the Head Representative's seal. "That makes two of us." Then, because that felt indecent, she added, "I'm sorry about Rebelwing." The thought of those torn and useless wings still twisted up a hurt inside her, twining with Mama's absence from the apartment. All part and parcel with too much silence in her head.

Cat made a derisive sound. "Just because I built it doesn't make it mine, not like you're thinking. I thought you knew that. I'm not a pilot. And a sentient mech chooses its own."

"Oh," said Pru.

"I can always build another," continued Cat, with the studied indifference she always affected, but Pru caught the twitch of her shoulder, the way Cat's grip tightened on Anabel's hand. Another dragon wouldn't be the same. Pru just wasn't a big enough asshole to say it aloud. Pilot and engineer, they both knew about truths better tucked into silence.

Anabel spoke to Bishop, saving Pru the indignity of saying anything further. "You must have told Head Representative Lamarque what you did with his nephew after it was too late to stop us. After we'd already been deployed into Incorporated territory. Otherwise we'd never have gotten past the Barricade sentinels."

Bishop regarded her with swollen eyes almost as weary as her own. "Gabriel was never going to let his nephew risk himself in the presence of the alpha cell. I knew he'd go after Alexandre."

Pru's glance wavered toward the figure bent over the guitar. "So, bourgeois boy here was bait. What about my mother?"

"That Gabriel brought Sophie Wu along on his mission was—not explicitly my intention, but it wasn't surprising either. Old war habits die hard. And he needed . . . someone."

Pru wanted to laugh, or hit someone. Brought her along. Needed her. As if Mama was some biddable piece of luggage who would have gone anywhere but exactly the destination she intended. Her death, as it turned out.

Anabel slumped back in her seat. "You wanted to force the Head Representative's hand. Force him to confront Jellicoe himself."

"What," Pru cut in, "so he could die in Alex's stead, and you could conveniently seize the Head Representative's job for yourself?"

Bishop's entire body went rigid, like someone struck, and surprised by the hit. Slowly, that red-rimmed gaze refocused on Pru. "Is that what you truly think this has been about? My own ambition? Me?"

Uncertainty prickled beneath Pru's skin, alongside guilt, but the flash of hot violence running through her veins overwhelmed both emotions. "What else?" she bit out. "Why else would you put us through this whole hush-hush song and dance, only to wind up with the Coalition's leader blown to smithereens?"

She'd braced herself for him to shout at her, or slam the desk where Alex was seated. She hadn't braced herself for the strange, broken quality to Bishop's voice, when he said, haggard but sure, "To preserve the Barricade Coalition, you little fool. To ensure that no matter what else we lost, its future would remain safe. I never wanted Ga—the Head Representative to die. But no one gets to have everything they want, and only idiots refuse to plan for a worst-case scenario."

Like a crowded platform with no clean shot. Like Rebelwing arriving too late, too slow, too far from the action. Like the exact moment they'd all seen Etienne Lamarque prepare to kill his son, and Gabriel Lamarque make a choice.

"You wanted Alex alive," said Anabel. Soft, barely audible over the lilting guitar strings. "You knew you'd have to risk a Lamarque, to face down Etienne. But you decided, at some point, that if the chips were down, and you had to lose one of them, better Gabriel than his nephew."

Bishop pocketed the handkerchief. "Interesting theory."

"Interesting because it's true," said Anabel, steelier now. "Alex wasn't the one who MacGyvered a spare plasma fire cartridge from Rebelwing's inventory into a detonator that would spell certain death for the user, not to mention anyone stuck within twenty feet of the explosion. Hell of an insurance policy."

No, that had been Mama's work. She'd been a soldier, once. She'd known the price of the weapon she carried, and paid it anyway, without a beat of hesitation. Pru bit the inside of her cheek until she tasted blood.

Hakeem Bishop's gaze fixed on Anabel. "Every conflict necessitates risk, Miss Park. Cornelius—your grandfather—would have taught you that. But did you really think that I wouldn't do everything in my power to protect the children who will grow up to shape the future of this Coalition? Almost two decades ago, Gabriel fought and won a war. Cornelius and I, we spent Gabriel's entire goddamn youth on that war. Two decades. That's older than most of you are now. I wasn't going to spend a boy's life to snuff out the father's, and neither was Gabriel."

Bishop's head bowed over the desk, his fingers steepling on its surface. For a moment, he looked nothing more and nothing less than what he was: a survivor, weighed down by life's weariness. "There's precious little point in preserving a legacy when no one's left to inherit it."

"So now we're, what, exactly?" Pru strode forward, until she stood opposite the desk. Blood salted the back of her teeth. Before her on the left sat Alex and his guitar, seemingly lost in his music still; on the right, this ancient-eyed man who moved people about like chess pieces in some unending battle. Her feet splayed over the center of the Head Representative's seal. "Kids playing dress-up in our dead parents' clothes?"

"Kids who have to grow up, just like your parents did, not so long ago," said Bishop. He snapped his fingers under her nose. "Wake up, Miss Wu. Men like me built this world, but you're the ones who are gonna have to live in it, once we're all bones rotting beneath the dirt. Best figure out what kind of world it's gonna be."

"So that's why you wanted to talk to us three days after the funerals," said Anabel. "To plan for what happens now."

"The world doesn't stop spinning just because people die, Miss Park. Jellicoe may be dead, but he wasn't the only arms dealer servicing Incorporated interests, and the Executive General's not exactly pleased to have had the most powerful weapons in the UCC arsenal mysteriously destroyed on the very day they were to be delivered."

"Can't we expose him?" Pru demanded. She thought of the slow, eerie drag of the Executive General's smile, his tonelessly delivered ultimatums. "He's the one behind this whole shitshow, isn't he? He ordered the attack on No Man's Land. He bought the wyverns. He was going to arrange for Jellicoe's goddamn retirement in paradise!"

Even before she finished speaking, Hakeem Bishop was already shaking his head. "If we expose the Executive General, we also expose our own espionage networks, and our own violations of the peace treaty. We'll return to war. Gabriel Lamarque's legacy will have been for nothing."

"Fuck legacy!" yelled Pru. "If the Incorporated want a war so bad, let's give them a war. They've earned it."

"Right now?" Anabel spoke quietly. "We can't afford it. We're still recovering from the first Partition Wars, and Project Rebelwing's in traction. Even without wyverns in the Incorporated arsenal, we couldn't face down the entire UCC army. We'd lose. Badly."

Bishop nodded. "To say nothing of emergency elections, and reshuffling the Coalition's leadership, and—Alexandre, would you quit plucking at that damn instrument!"

Alex's fingers stilled, aborting the music so suddenly that the melody's absence felt violent. His lips twitched upward. Pru tempered a flinch. She'd witnessed an entire catalog of Alex Lamarque's smiles, from the bright-toothed stage grins of the hurricane boy, to the small, private curves of his mouth. She'd never seen his lips carve his face into something calculated to mock. To cut, not for the sake of some greater cause, but for the sake of cutting. He hopped off his uncle's desk, guitar in hand. It was shaking, very slightly.

"Very well," he said placidly. "If you're going to continue this wonderfully amusing exercise in political theater, my damn instrument and my plucking fingers and I will all take our leave." He cut a jerky parody of a bow to a gape-mouthed Chief of Staff, and limped through the office doors without so much as a backward glance.

"Where are you going?" Bishop thundered. "Alex—Miss Wu!"

But Pru was already following hot on Alex's heels. She caught sight of him rounding the corner from the foyer, past the couch where Pru had once lounged, crimson-faced, listening to Mama fight with the Head Representative. Both ghosts now.

Alex was heading outside. Wordlessly, Pru slipped through the wobbly French doors, and dogged him down the long, winding staircase toward the mansion gardens. The limp should have slowed his movements, but instead he seemed determined to spite the injury, pace lengthening. His doctors were going to kill him. Jogging around one last turn of the stairs, Pru lost sight of him.

She swore. "Alex!" She jogged through rows of neatly clipped rose bushes. "Alex, wait—"

A strain of guitar music cut her off. Pru followed it, and found Alex sprawled on a bench beneath a cherry blossom tree, guitar balanced between belly and knee as he strummed, eyes half lidded. He looked like a boy on a book cover. If the injury beneath the leg brace bothered him, he refused to give any indication. "What do you want?"

A million responses bubbled to the tip of Pru's tongue. Pru bit back every last one. His music, oblivious, mocked her. That, more than anything else, was maybe what wrought real words out of her.

"I want the world to stop turning."

Alex's fingers paused on the guitar strings.

The hot, thick anger of the words didn't abate. "I didn't think Mama believed in anything for the longest time, you know that? She was tired of wars, and tired of causes, and tired of Lamarques. But she died for it all anyway, and what does the world care?" She sank down beside the bench, chuckling around the familiar pressure in her chest that meant she'd start crying if she didn't keep laughing. "So, yeah. I want the world to stop turning. Give me a week. Give me a day. Give me five damn minutes. Wouldn't that be enough?"

"No." The guitar strings made an ugly sound. "It's never going to be enough, not even goddamn close." He jerked upright, hands curling white-knuckled over the guitar. For one blood-hammering moment, Pru thought he'd fling the instrument aside, smash it apart like dragon wings being pulled to pieces by Jellicoe's giant. She thought of guitar strings yanked asunder, the scream of her own living mech, and her heart twisted inside her chest, like an ankle folding under a bad fall.

He seemed to sense her thoughts, pausing. The observation made Pru flinch. Wishful thinking, believing he still knew her mind. A stupid notion, without the dragon's imprint to bond them. Still, he set the guitar aside in the grass, rose from the bench, walked around it with a jerky, limping stride. He was favoring the bad leg worse than before. Probably from all that idiot speed walking down the stairs.

"It's not," he snarled. "Ever. *Enough*." With tranquil, thunderous force, he shoved the bench down the side of the garden slope, where it crashed hard against a tree trunk. Cherry blossoms shuddered from their branches, weeping into the wreck of wood.

"Don't!" Pru grabbed him by the elbow before he could hurt himself worse. Fury seemed to have bled off her, into Alex. Now, guilt tempered the edges of her own anger, turning it to something else. She hadn't known Gabriel Lamarque well. A warm presence, charismatic and effusive, but more icon than man, even after meeting him in person. He hadn't been her uncle. He hadn't been her parent.

"It's never going to be enough," Alex panted, one more time. His chest heaved, shuddered, stilled. He trembled beneath her grip, eyes squeezing shut. "You're always going to want more time."

Pru didn't move. She hadn't taken her eyes off him, not once. She hadn't dared. Very quietly, she said, "You'd know."

He turned. The rage in his face died, giving way to an emotion she couldn't identify. Her heart crumpled and crumpled, along with the look in his eyes. Hoarsely, half empathy, half mockery, he whispered, "I think you do too."

She dropped his elbow like a brand. Felt her mouth curl into something almost as ugly as the look on his face. She hadn't known how much a heart could crumple, not until this afternoon, wondered if she'd have anything left of it. "Yeah. Guess I do."

"Sorry," said Alex.

She made a sound, part gasp, part laugh, wondered if that could cover the terrible metal-shrieking creak inside her chest cavity. "For what?"

Alex laughed. It boasted the same sandpaper texture Pru's did, the sort that suggested it was a sound that wanted to be something else, grimacing and ugly. "No, that's what my dad said, back in the Jellicoe compound, right before he died. The wyvern alpha." His lips pulled back from his teeth. "I thought we were all finished, and he looked at me, and said, 'Sorry.' That was all."

"Was it?" whispered Pru.

Alex's shoulders lifted, gathering strength. Then he dragged himself into the grass, remaining limbs slumping in around the bad leg, like a doll with his strings cut. One hand rested on the edge of his abandoned guitar. The other curled atop his good knee. "I'd be sorry too."

Pru walked carefully around the guitar to sit beside him. Grass tickled her thighs beneath her skirt pleats. She closed her eyes. Behind them played images of Alex's father, Etienne, the wyvern alpha, whose cell had infected his uncle. The cruel, peculiar genetic trap Jellicoe had built into the Lamarque legacy. All blown apart, in the end, by Pru's mama.

"God," managed Pru. She chuckled again, sandpaper laughter scraping against Alex's. "Kids playing dress-up in our parents' clothes," she repeated. "That's what they left behind."

Her shoulder bumped against his good knee. For one bizarre instant, they were back in the dragon's cockpit, stuck skin-to-skin before the giant clipped their wings. Seconds before free fall. Seconds before a save. Tears on Alex's shirt, and Anabel's voice in Pru's ears. The broken pieces of the mech had gone to some Coalition repair shop, but no one knew if the dragon returned to them would ever again be the same dragon Alex and Cat had dreamed up as children.

"This is the part where you're supposed to give a bittersweet yet inspiring speech, you know," said Pru. "That's what the old Alex would have done. You have a guitar and everything. You could turn it into a rock song." She swallowed the lump in her throat. "We don't even have a stray Robo Reptile to distract the masses from, this time around."

"Robo Reptile or no, the old Pru would have poked my speech full of holes," drawled Alex. A hint of his old self colored the words, despite the hoarseness of his throat. "All in the name of your beloved realism."

"Oh, I could be persuaded to put realism aside. Depends on how prettily you say your argument. Or sing it. Something about bravery, and sacrifice, I'm sure all those stodgy old funeral orators would love to have gotten their hands on a good song about—"

"Pru."

"What, too soon?"

Instead of answering, he lifted the guitar. Hesitantly, then with stubborn determination, his fingers began to strum. Up-tempo, frenetic and thoughtful. "Listen. You remember what you told me, about why Uncle Gabriel didn't want me in the cockpit?"

Like Pru could forget. "He didn't want to risk you. You weren't— you aren't expendable."

The Lamarque legacy, preserved.

"That's the thing." Alex's fingers danced over the strings. "Neither are you. That's—that's what the old Alex always wanted to tell you, in all our arguments, you know. You're not expendable either." His voice dropped. The music paused again. "You'll never be expendable. I just thought you ought to know."

Heat pricked at Pru's eyes. When she twisted her head away from him to stare with sudden interest at the rose bushes, she was obscenely grateful that he didn't comment. "And what does the new Alex want to tell me?"

Silence, for a moment. Then he played a chord. "We can't make the world stop turning," said Alex. "But I don't think our lives always have to revolve around saving it. I think maybe we're allowed to carve out our own space in it too."

"Oh yeah?" Pru snorted. "And what could possibly occupy the noble mind of Alexandre Santiago Lamarque, besides his quest to save the world from itself? What would he do in a space of his own?"

"Isn't it obvious?" Slowly, carefully, the song bloomed again under Alex's hands. At last, she heard a smile wavering in his voice. "He'd play music."

◆

PRU ALMOST FORGOT ABOUT Mama's cylinder. It wasn't until after the funerals, after Bishop's speech, after the end and beginning of the world rewritten strange and new, that Pru finally remembered the little scrap of metal Mama had pushed between her hands. Even then, she let it sit for days, idling away on the edge of a desk in her dorm room at the Academy. Sometimes, she dreamed of what it might contain: a living hologram like a modern-day ghost, a long-forgotten secret manuscript, left unpublished, or perhaps nothing at all.

The first time she finally gathered the courage to turn the holo-drive on, she barely got past Mama's covering note before she had to put it away again, crying too hard to continue.

The second time, though, she persisted. It wasn't a hologram, and it wasn't a manuscript of any particular importance. But Pru sat with her mother's words for a long, long moment, preserved between her hands, a flicker of warmth to fill the empty space inside her mind. She cried, for a little while. Then she read it again.

Alex had been right. They'd always want more time. But here, within a small stretch of story, time could run eternal, for a little while.

◆

The first revolutionary I ever met in the flesh wore a low-slung hat and a blood-red scarf. I mistook him instantly for a ghost. Wartime curfew is a bitch and a half, and all I wanted was to make it home from the bodega without running afoul of any crossfire. Instead, I walked straight into this great looming shadow of a guy, and dropped all my grocery rations into the December snow.

"Help me," he rasped, a wraith of a man, all dark-swathed against glittering white snowbanks.

"Aaaaah!" I screamed. In my defense, I grew up on my mother's ghost stories, and Asian ghost stories are the most terrifying ghost stories there are.

"Please stop that," begged the wraith.

"Aaaaah!" I fished a stray apple from the snow, and pelted it at my would-be assailant. "Aaaaah!"

The apple, bouncing off his head, knocked his hat slightly askew. "Ouch!" cried the ghost.

Probably not really a ghost, then. Probably just a common mugger. I picked up a banana and threw that too. "Aaaah!" In films, heroines are always so witty when confronted with menacing strangers. Evidently, I was not cut out to be a film heroine.

The ghost-slash-mugger ducked my fruit barrage, though not without stumbling. That was when I saw the gleam of blood under his scarf, seeping lazily through the half-gloved fingers he'd clutched against his chest. "Please," he whispered.

I stopped lobbing produce at him. "What are you?" I demanded instead. I still had one hand curved on a second apple, in case he tried any funny business.

He huffed a laugh. "I'm a soldier. Or trying to be," he amended. "Right now, I'm just in trouble."

I understood at once. "You're fighting against the Incorporated!" Turning the half-frozen apple over between my hands, I considered what that implied. "Wow are you terrible at picking the good side of a war." Insofar as a good side existed.

The second laugh that bubbled out of him, louder than the first, made his hand spasm against the chest wound. Sympathy pangs twinged under my own chest. "I'm terrible at picking the winning side of a war," said the soldier, who really made a sorry sack of a revolutionary, tattered and bleeding as he was. "That doesn't make mine a bad side." He lowered his head, as if confiding a great secret. Above the red wool of his scarf, I thought I saw him wink. "It's not always bad, for people to have their differences. Life would be awfully dull, otherwise."

Before he could say much else, a familiar whistle pierced the night, straight through my eardrums. The revolutionary and I flinched as one. I saw the line of his shoulders tense, and grabbed his forearm. Before I could think better of it, I pressed my apple between his palms, and blurted out, "There's a bodega two blocks down. The owners sell bandages cheap, and hide rebel soldiers in the basement if you ask nicely." I closed his fingers around the apple. "Go. And for god's sake, eat something."

I let go, and gave him a little shove. He stumbled, blinking at me in the dark, over the muted red of the apple. Its color matched his scarf. I wondered what his face must look like, beneath all that wool.

Then came the second whistle, closer than the first. "Thank you," he whispered, tucking my apple into his coat, and ran.

The Incorporated troops showed up a couple minutes later. This far from a city proper, you could see starlight winking off their epaulets. The leader, lithe and blond as a propaganda picture, spotted me, and strode forward. I looked down at my grocery rations, half-buried in snow at my feet, and swallowed the lump in my throat. So much for avoiding crossfire.

"You, girl," he snapped. "It's almost past curfew for civilians."

I looked up at him. He was young, probably not much older than

I was, but held himself like he had years aplenty under that fancy uniform belt of his. "I know. I was waylaid by a rebel."

Blaming trouble on the rebels, you see, was an excellent excuse for ordinary civilians to get out of trouble back in the days of the war. We always looked so well-behaved in comparison.

"A rebel!" The young Incorporated officer's pale eyes widened. "In a red scarf, by any chance?"

"The very same," I confirmed, trying to look suitably traumatized. "He looked like a wraith!"

The officer snorted. "I'm sure."

"He practically flew toward me, he ran so fast," I invented wildly. Surely, the revolutionary had reached the bodega by now, but it didn't hurt to buy a little more time. "Terrifying, in that great black coat and hat of his. I've never seen a man move so quickly."

Skepticism crossed the officer's face. "The man we're looking for is injured."

"Oh, this one was bloody, all right," I confirmed cheerfully. "But he shrugged off the flesh wound like he was superhuman!"

"Superhuman," repeated the officer dully.

"Did you fight him?" I asked, trying to sound both fearful and bloodthirsty. "I'm amazed you survived the encounter. He seemed so strong! And dangerous."

"Of course we survived!" snapped the officer. "He's one stupid in-surgent, and we are men of the Incorporated!"

"Gosh," I said, opening my eyes very wide. "Incorporated soldiers are terribly brave."

The officer rolled his eyes at this display of girlish hero worship. "And which way did your superhuman wraith . . . fly?"

I pointed over their heads. "Round about that way, doubled back the way you came. I bet he meant to sneak attack you! Oh, do be careful, sir." I twisted my hands together, looking anxious. "The Incorporated do so much for the common folk who support you."

"We will," muttered the officer. Now he just sounded embarrassed, like I might infect him with my dumb commoner girl cooties. "Now, if you'll please, your contact coordinates, in case we need to pass your testimony on."

I gave them to him, giggling and worrying the whole time. The officer continued rolling his eyes, but he made a couple of his men help me regather my grocery rations. "You be careful now, girl," he said, rounding off into the night, the troops at his back. "Don't break more rules!"

"Oh, don't you worry, sir." I clutched an armful of fruit against my chest. With the other arm, I waved the soldiers off with back-straining enthusiasm. "I'll be good!"

I watched in satisfaction as they disappeared into the dark, marching in the opposite direction from the bodega. I thought that would put an end to my involvement in wartime business, and for a little while, it did.

Until, three days later, I received a summons to the Office of the Propagandist.

Everyone in the Propagandist's office calls me Scheherazade. Maybe nicknames stick, around here. Or maybe they refuse my real name because the Propagandist's men know my employment here hinges more on bribery and sufferance than true, hand-to-heart love for the Incorporated. No one likes a sellout, not even the people we sell to.

But you need a storyteller, to win a war like this one. The Executive

General figured that out, early on: a body in wartime can be conquered by bloodshed, but how to conquer a mind? Why, through culture, of course. The words you speak, the languages you're allowed, the ideas bouncing about thump-thump-thump inside your skull. Which is why the first conquest the Propagandist made on behalf of the Incorporated was media—art, entertainment, even newsreels—for what's media, really, except the uncontrolled expression of free thought?

Regulate people's ideas, thought the Executive General, and you could make them want anything. Including their own subjugation. Which was how, I suppose, the very first Propagandist got his job.

In my first week, the Propagandist asks me to invent an insurgent, properly frightening, and sensationally unmasked. I understand. I make the first revolutionary I met into a boogeyman. Now the monster in the closet needs an origin story. Lucky for him, I imagine several to choose from.

In one version, my insurgent has ivory skin and sea-blue eyes and a nose as thin-bladed as an Incorporated officer's. He's born to a sunlit house with a vast veranda, and grows up in starched, expensive shirts. Cruelty should come easy to boys like him, but he enjoys the company of people too much to fall for such a petty pastime. He listens more than he speaks, and that, perhaps, is what makes him see the world through such funny lenses.

In the wake of a war for the continent's soul, he figures out quick that being rich and pretty makes him less likely to get shot at by Incorporated soldiers than some of his friends. This makes him useful. This also makes him frightening. Boys born into his world—princely and self-assured—have a remarkable capacity to weaponize their power. Their near-invulnerability.

Boys like him are born to be aimed at people. The only difference between an Incorporated officer and an insurgent, when both are fair and fine-boned, is what target they decide to fire themselves at. My insurgent has spent a lifetime listening. He doesn't hesitate when he chooses.

"It's a good story," says the Propagandist, brow furrowing, "but it'll never do, for our purposes. An insurgent must be frightening, yes, but he must be frightening for the right reasons, you understand? He can't seem too familiar. We must fear him, but we mustn't imagine being him. Tell another tale, Scheherazade."

The next version of my insurgent is as pretty as the first — the public does love pretty — but he's born in a poorer neighborhood, the sort rich folks call "bad" and "dangerous," which equips him with canny, self-protective edges the first never sharpened. Like me, he's got no interest in the war effort. Keep your head down, his mama advises. The less easily seen you are, the harder it is for folks to shove you low. His mama's a clever woman, so he keeps his head down like she says, and that helps a little.

It's not enough, though, when war comes. People in wartime, determined to prove their own mettle, go looking for excuses to shove others lower and lower, until some lie six feet underground. When folks take on a warlike mood, poor boys are found wanting, every time. So he buys himself a tacky, low-slung hat, a great wool scarf, and hides himself from sight.

The Incorporated call this deception insurgency, but in the insurgent's eyes, he's only saving his own life.

"No, no, no," interrupts the Propagandist. "Really, I applaud your imagination, but such an insurgent is far too timid to frighten anyone. People are more likely to feel sorry for him than not. Tell another."

My third insurgent isn't a he at all. After all, I never got a good look under the hat, and revolutionaries can be anybody, really. So this insurgent's born a she, who, wrinkling her nose, tries on "he" in his adolescence, before finally settling on "they." They like that one, a single pronoun for one person somehow implying the many.

This one, at least, harbors simple motives for all their troublesome, frightening, revolutionary tendencies. They enter the war as an insurgent because they never had the option to choose otherwise.

"How dreary," interrupts the Propagandist, wrinkling his nose. He doesn't seem to like any of my stories, yet he won't stop asking for more. "I've never liked a foregone conclusion, and neither will the public. You disappoint me, Scheherazade. Why can't you conceive of anything tastefully frightening? A clever girl should know how to spark the public to action!"

His patience with his Scheherazade wears thinner, day by day. I'm careful to bide the time. At night, when my work shift ends, I buy produce from the bodega. I don't ask the owners about the revolutionary in the low-slung hat, and they don't volunteer any stories. When I return to my apartment—always well before curfew nowadays, thank you very much—I lie back in the creaky wooden bed, and toss an apple overhead, over and over again. It bounces gently against the ceiling, then back into my palm. I watch the red of its skin flicker through the shadows of my room. I think of a scarf-masked face. I think of blood on snow. I remember half-gloved fingers cold beneath mine, the skin of cheap fruit between us.

I imagine my insurgent—pale and princely, dark-skinned and subtle, one person who lived a life of many — and feel terribly young. In films, revolutionaries always burn so bright and die so fast. No wonder I mistook the first one I ever met for a ghost.

"You ought to grow old," I tell the shadows. They never answer me.

Here's the part I don't share with the Propagandist: I tell him stories, but he's not my only listener.

The Office of the Propagandist boasts countless wireless channels. The Incorporated spared no expense on their greatest asset. An employee of the Propagandist can upload 3-D holograms, or vocal recordings, or even old-fashioned, plain-typed text. Do it right, and the whole continent can access your transmission, all part and parcel with the wonders of wartime broadcasting. When you work the office shifts long enough, no one pays you much attention when you fiddle with the wireless. Everyone here is very busy and important, you see, and no one has time to do anything so banal as sorting through the thousands of wireless uploads we process each week.

I drop my stories sparingly, secretly, one at a time, like crumbs charting the path from a monster's house in the woods. I space my insurgent's adventures out painstakingly between weeks, then months. Any girl worthy of a nickname like Scheherazade gets good at biding time. Things happen slowly, at the very beginning, in small and quiet ways. A mention in a digital magazine read by twelve people. A title drop in an obscure talk show. A scathing review on a late-night holovid network.

People begin to talk. They tell each other about rich boys turned righteous, and insurgents' low-slung hats hiding frightened children beneath. They whisper of a boy — or is it a girl, or both, or neither at all? — like a wraith, infinite and untouchable and deathless. Slowly, very slowly, in small ways, and then larger ones, the public stirs, waking drowsy after a long, long slumber. It's not that these made-up tales of rebels are really so extraordinary. But people have only been allowed to hear one story for so long that they are starved for literally any other. They lap mine up with greedy, wagging tongues.

People begin to ask questions. What does it mean to be Incorporated? Is this what I want? Is this what you want? Some answer yes. Some answer no. Some simply hum, thoughtful, and ask more questions still.

It's an unmitigated disaster for the Office of the Propagandist.

If I fancied myself a folk hero, I'd sign everything Scheherazade, but I wish to be shot by Incorporated soldiers even less than I wish to be a folk hero, which seems like a troublesome business to begin with. Even so, the Propagandist doesn't take long to catch on. One day, the bodega owners tell me not to go to work. I launder my week's paycheck through a dummy side hustle, then transfer the whole thing into their account. They prepare a cot for me in the basement.

When I hear booted footsteps hurtling down the cellar stairs, I shut my eyes. I imagine the shine of Incorporated epaulets. I hope against the worst, but that doesn't mean I don't prepare for it. I wonder if the bodega owners are safe. I hope so. I hope they escaped, and grow fat, and old, and happy, and spend every coin in my paycheck.

But when I open my eyes, I see no epaulets. Only a wraith in a low-slung hat and a blood-red scarf, leaning on the bannister. "You've made me into quite the legend," says the insurgent.

I'm on the cot, still, and pull my knees into my chest, self-protective. "I thought you were dead," I inform him.

"Curiously not," he says cheerfully. "The way illicit media goes on, you'd think there were a hundred of me, collectively immortal."

"Rebels do a shit job of recruiting, if you only have a hundred men."

"Some of us are women too."

I curl my arms around my knees. "Why are you here?"

The revolutionary shrugs. "Why did you make up all those stories about me?"

"The Propagandist told me to. He wanted everyone to be afraid of you, so they'd understand why people need the Incorporated. I don't think I did a very good job." I try to make out his expression through the scarf. "The stories were never really about you, anyway. Like I said, I thought you were dead."

"You leaked them, though," he presses. "Those stories the Propagandist asked for, the ones he didn't like. That's why you're in trouble now, right? You must have known the risk. Why did you do it?"

Because I'm sick of ultimatums. Because I'm tired. Because I got lonely, and wondered if perhaps I shouted into the dark, someone else — anyone else — might shout back.

"Even if you're made-up, or doomed, or dead," I say at last; I'm thinking of princes and paupers, children frightened and soldiers defiant, questions whispered from ear to ear to ear, "you could exist. I figure people ought to know you're possible."

The insurgent doesn't speak for a while. In weeks and months and years that follow, different versions of what happens next will emerge. In one story, he will thank me and depart, a ghost once more, never to be seen again. In another, Incorporated soldiers will storm the bodega basement and finish us both in one great spray of gunfire. We'll die bloody, my revolutionary and I, fingers entwined, just like a film scene.

But in my story, the one unfolding right now, the one that's true, *he offers a hand, half-gloved, human skin peeking out from dark wool, and just says, "Come on, then. People ought to know you're possible too."*

We emerge from the basement, to a war still raging. But as we climb out the bodega door through sleet-covered streets, that great wool scarf whips like a crimson banner between us, blending our shadows dark against the fresh-fallen snow. We run with winter nipping at our skin, and for just a moment, defiant of death, fear, and gravity itself, we fly.

ACKNOWLEDGMENTS

I knew, from the first inkling of *Rebelwing* that entered my head, that this would be a story whose emotional through line centered on family, a generational saga, and the things we choose to carry from those who came before us. So, thank you, first of all, to all three of the parents who have raised me. To my first mama, such an endless reservoir of love and artistic creativity, who instilled such deep adoration of storytelling in me before she passed. To my second mama, who steered and supported me through my own turbulent adolescence, and who remains one of my greatest role models to this day. To my wonderful father, whose unwavering support, guidance, and friendship have been such a blessing throughout my formative years whether I was struggling to draft a novel or struggling to power through my junior-year problem sets. No, Dad, I still don't know how to engineer a sentient AI-fueled metal dragon in real life, and if I did, I'd have both a much more impressive LinkedIn profile and much less appalling high school physics grades, but I love that you love me anyway.

To my remarkable agent, Thao Le, who has been such a stalwart champion for myself and for this book through thick and thin, and to everyone at Sandra Dijkstra Literary Agency: thank you for all your incredible advocacy and support. The literary miracles you collectively work continue to floor me, and I truly could not ask for better partners with whom to ferry my work out into the world!

To my brilliant editor Julie Rosenberg, whose tremendous creative vision and guidance whittled my many frantic, rambling manuscript drafts into the best book they could be, and to the all-star publication team at Penguin: Alex Sanchez, Casey McIntyre, Kim Ryan, and Jessica Jenkins—collectively, you've taught me that the old adage about publishing being a team sport is absolutely true in the best way. Special thanks also to Mike Heath for his beautiful illustration work, and to Kyle V. Hiller, whose insight and empathetic wisdom proved invaluable to taking this novel to the next level.

To the friends who have handheld me through this roller-coaster journey, among them Catherine Redfield, Tara Ohrtman, Nan Wang, Emily Tafaro, Elizabeth Chen, and Alix Bruce—I really, truly couldn't have done this without you, and I feel lucky every single day for your companionship. Thank you for believing in me even when I didn't always know how to believe in myself. To my fabulous and formidable JAMME gang: Mallory Yu, Esther Kim, Jade Feng, and Margaret Huey—your mutual support and genuine passion for diverse representation of the Asian diaspora in the arts has been such a source of inspiration and joy to me.

To fellow writers Grace Li, Kelly Powell, Francesca Flores, Nicki Pau Preto, Cassandra Farrin, Morgan Al-Moor, Becca Mix, Katie Zhao, Amélie Wen Zhao, Suzie Samin Sainwood, Elaine Cuyegkeng, Victoria Lee, Molly Chang, May Myers, June Tan, Alice Fanchiang, Kellan Szpara, Chelsea Beam, Lyla Lee, Marina Liu, Hannah Whitten, Rebecca Kuang, the brilliant members of #TeamThao and #AMM, everyone in the Razorbill 2020 chat group, and so many other marvelous wordsmiths I've met over the past year: thank you for sharing your words, your creative wisdom, and most importantly, your friendship. Penning fiction so often feels like a lonely calling, and you have all reminded me time and again that it doesn't have to be.

And finally, I owe a debt of gratitude to so many creators who came before me. *Rebelwing* is, in many ways, my love letter to storytelling itself: equal parts pastiche and homage to everything from the giant robots of mecha anime to every dragon who's ever flown through the pages of a high-fantasy epic to classic literary novels and popular musicals and video games. Thank you to the authors on my high school summer reading lists, to the screenwriters behind summer blockbusters and soap operas, to fanfiction writers, to romance novelists, to comic artists, to the countless creators who have shaped my love of story, without whom this fledgling novel would never have existed. *Rebelwing* is for you.